Hellbound

A former journalist for the *Parisien*, Eric Giacometti spent several years uncovering some of France's biggest medical scandals. He also spent the end of the 1990s investigating freemasonry, a subject he then explored in fiction with his writing partner, Jacques Ravenne. Together, they form a highly successful author duo, and have written more than fifteen books together, including the several million-copy bestselling Antoine Marcas series.

GIACOMETTI
RAVENNE

Hellbound

Translated from the French
by Maren Baudet-Lackner

HODDER

First publi | *Cycle du*

First p | hton

The right of Eric Giacometti and Jacques Ravenne to be identified as the Authors of the Work has been asserted by them in accordance with the Copyright, Designs and Patents Act 1988.

Maren Baudet-Lackner asserts her moral right to be identified as the Translator of the Work.

A CIP catalogue record for this title is available from the British Library

Paperback ISBN 9781529300338
eBook ISBN 9781529300345
Audiobook ISBN 9781529305357

Typeset in Plantin Light by Palimpsest Book Production Ltd, Falkirk, Stirlingshire

Printed and bound in Great Britain by Clays Ltd, Elcograf S.p.A.

Hodder & Stoughton policy is to use papers that are natural, renewable and recyclable products and made from wood grown in sustainable forests. The logging and manufacturing processes are expected to conform to the environmental regulations of the country of origin.

Hodder & Stoughton Ltd
Carmelite House
50 Victoria Embankment
London EC4Y 0DZ

www.hodder.co.uk

"There is both creative and destructive energy in every animate and inanimate entity on earth. In everything. Light and darkness coexist side by side. The four relics are made up of this union of energies, whose power is so all-consuming and terrible that Christ himself averts his gaze in its presence."

Excerpt from the *Thule Borealis Kulten*

21 June 1942

From: SOE headquarters, Echelon E
To: The Prime Minister's Cabinet War Rooms
Classification: Top Secret, Level 5

Place found:
Yarlung Valley, Tibet: 29°21′26.7″N, 90°58′23.3″E
Montségur Castle, France: 42°52′32.1″, 1°49′57.5″E
Heiligenkreuz Abbey, Austria: 48°03′23.2″N,
16°07′50.5″E

Last known location:
Wewelsburg Castle, Germany: 51°36′25.6″N, 8°39′04.9″E
MIT, United States: 42°21′36.6″N, 71°05′39.1″W
Venice, Italy: 45°24′17.9″N, 12°22′14.2″E

Prologue

Ipatiev House, Yekaterinburg, Russia
July 17, 1918

It was a warm July night. An enchanted hiatus as rare as a bumper year here, at the foot of the Ural Mountains, the border between Europe and Asia, where summer lasts but the blink of an eye before the land is petrified in solid ice again.

A perfect night for drinking and laughing far from the log cabins and for falling asleep under the stars without the risk of catching pneumonia. And yet, in this July night, not a single soul was enjoying the balmy air in the streets of Yekaterinburg. Since the Revolution, they had all been living in permanent winter—huddled away behind locked doors. Out of fear. Fear of the communists who held the city, first and foremost. The region was nicknamed *Krasnyi Ural*—the red Urals—because of the local council's zeal when it came to mass extermination of the enemies of the people: the bourgeois, kulaks, and reactionaries of all stripes. Fear of the Whites, too. Of the heterogeneous army made up of imperial regiments loyal to the deposed tsar and hordes of Cossacks under the thumb of cruel and intrepid warlords. The Whites were emerging from the plains of Siberia in droves, getting ever closer to their goal. In a matter of days, they would reach the city.

Two rabid bears were ripping Russia to pieces. Red against White. A blind and ferocious fight that only one of them would survive.

"Comrade Evgueni, do you think they'll spare us if we fall into their hands?"

"The Cossacks will give no quarter. Pity is not one of the rare qualities displayed by Ataman Krasnov's white dogs. They'll cut you into such little pieces your own father won't recognize you. And all while you still breathe, of course."

Evgueni Berin, who had just spoken, wasn't yet thirty but spoke slowly, like an older man. His eyes were dull, faded by the horrors he had seen. The young soldier by his side seemed to be barely more than a boy. He was drowning in his oversized coat, which had been mended in several places.

Sitting in the sentry box of the watchtower, the two men were sharing a half-spent cigarette with their feet up on the Maxim machine-gun's ammunition reserve. The weapon was trained on the shutters of Ipatiev House. The Ural council had transformed the opulent two-storey house nestled into a hillside on Voznessenski Street into a makeshift fortress. A tall wooden fence with two watchtowers surrounded the property. The windows had even been painted white to keep anyone from seeing inside. A Red Army detachment was assigned to guard the house full time, and, as if that were not enough, a team of Cheka agents had arrived as reinforcements a week ago. The reason for this display of force was no secret. All of Yekaterinburg knew the identity of the family that had been sequestered at Ipatiev House since the end of April.

"To lull me to sleep, my mother used to tell me that whenever one of us dies, a new star is born," whispered the young man. "According to her, the Milky Way is a pearly fabric in which each star represents a soul."

"Tolia Kabanov, your mother is surely a good woman, but she's also a fool!" exclaimed Evgueni Berin as he slapped the other soldier on the back. "The people mustn't believe in such nonsense anymore. Souls, God, heaven . . . All invented to keep peasants and workers from rebelling. The only heaven there is, is the one we build here on earth." *If we manage to do so*, he thought to himself.

The Revolution was less than a year old and had so many enemies that not a single communist would have bet on its triumph any time soon. Broad swathes of territory were under the control of the White Army, quietly aided by the English and French, who were unhappy about the peace treaty signed between the Bolsheviks and the Germans.

Evgueni stubbed out the cigarette on the floor of the sentry box and checked his watch. It was time. He had been waiting for this moment for too long. An eternity. Thirteen years to be precise. Said to be one of the most feared Cheka officers, Evgueni Berin was proud to be an early convert to the Revolution—a soldier activist forged from the purest ideals of Bolshevism. Comrade Lenin had chosen him personally to relay what would happen here tonight within the walls of Ipatiev House. Evgueni had travelled nearly 2,000 kilometers east from Moscow, on the Trans-Siberian Railway. It had been a long and difficult journey dotted with a seemingly endless number of stops between Nizhny Novgorod and Yekaterinburg.

Light escaped through the front door to the house as it opened slightly. Comrade Pavel Damov appeared with a wave. Evgueni despised the man. Damov was an unscrupulous brute. Unfortunately for Evgueni, he was also remarkably intelligent. Having successfully climbed the ranks during the Revolution, he had joined its most feared branch—the Cheka. It was there that he had earned the nickname Lord of Lead, during a crackdown on a monastery in Kostroma, on the banks of the Volga. On a whim, Damov had forced the monks to swallow molten lead before finishing them off with an axe. The exploit had earned him a promotion within the Cheka: in less than six months he had become the official assassin of the regime's most vocal enemies. People whispered that he was corrupt to the core, but no one had ever proved it.

Evgueni stuck his fingers in his mouth to whistle at the lorry driver parked in the street. The old ZIS's engine coughed three times before roaring into life.

"I don't understand, comrade," said the young soldier, Kabanov. "This is the third night in a row you've asked Grigori to start up that heap and waste petrol idling there for fifteen minutes. You can hear it from the other end of the street. The neighbours complained yesterday."

"I'm delighted to hear it," replied Evgueni. "Stay at your post."

"Are you sure you don't want me to come with you?" the boy asked hopefully.

Evgueni studied him. How old was he—sixteen, seventeen, maybe? He may not live to see his next birthday. The latest reports of Red Army casualties were gruesome. No, Kabanov didn't need to see what was about to happen. "You better stay here and watch the stars," Evgueni replied firmly.

He climbed down from the watchtower and strode up to the heavy front door, which had been left wide open. A waft of sweat and tepid wine welcomed him. A seven-cartridge Mauser in hand, Lord of Lead stood flanked by a dozen men with *Nagant* revolvers. Half of them were Latvians—non-Russian allies to the Bolsheviks. Yakov Yurovsky, the commander sent by the Ural council, was also present.

"You're just in time, comrade," said Yurovsky with a tap on Evgueni's shoulder. "They're all gathered upstairs."

"We told them we were going to take their photograph in the cellar, to show the world they're still alive," chuckled Damov.

One of the Latvians raised his hand in annoyance. "It's the boy. He can't walk because of his illness."

"Have his father carry him," laughed Damov. "And don't bother me with such details again, do you hear?"

Evgueni followed Lord of Lead and Yurovsky down to the cellar. Their boots clicked on the stone steps. Twenty-three. There were twenty-three steps. Evgueni knew the number by heart, having run through the scene several times. He was no amateur.

Damov reached the cellar first. He was pleased to see his instructions had been followed to the letter. Wooden boards covered the back wall of the room, which was large enough to house a neighbourhood party committee. An out-of-place chandelier with teardrop beads shed a frigid light on the room.

"Even in their cellars, the bourgeois have to boast," he spat.

Evgueni had withdrawn into a dark corner for the best view of the room and its occupants. He watched as the council's representative stood in the middle of the cellar and took a crumpled piece of paper from his jacket. In a solemn voice, he read out the terse text that authorized their presence in the house on this night. No one had dared sign the official document.

The clicking of heels and clogs echoed in the stairwell. Evgueni stepped even further back into the darkness.

The servants came first. A valet, a chambermaid, a cook, and the family doctor. Their eyes darted fearfully around the room. Evgueni thought one was missing, but wasn't sure. Not that it mattered—the staff were not important.

The Chekists ushered them towards the far end of the cellar. "Stand against the wall. Slaves behind the masters, for the photograph," one of them ordered.

Then came softer steps. And whispering. Five women appeared in the dim glare. With weary faces and wild hair, they advanced in their thick grey dresses as if they were sleepwalking. The eldest, the mother, moved slowly, followed by her four distraught daughters. The ghostly figures seemed to be tied to one another by an invisible chain. A man appeared at the rear gazing affectionately at the child he carried in his arms. A bushy moustache and full beard covered his hollow cheeks, and his oversized shirt only highlighted his thin frame.

"May we have chairs for my wife and son, please?" he asked hesitantly.

Lord of Lead grabbed him by the collar. "Do you really still think you're the master, Kolya?" he barked.

Commander Yurovsky intervened. "Let him have his chairs, comrade. We're not monsters . . ." He signalled to one of the Latvians, who pulled up two rickety chairs.

The mother sat down without a word as the father settled the boy. "Sit up straight, Aliocha," he said. "They're going to take our photograph. Look dignified." Then he turned to his daughters: "You too, remember who you are."

The group was finally ready. Masters and servants were perfectly lined up, awaiting the photographer.

An eerie silence filled the cellar.

From his spot near the stairs, Evgueni Berin studied every detail of the scene before his eyes. A long-forgotten feeling arose in him: pity. Just like him, these men and women were flesh and blood.

Steadied by her older sister, one of the girls was desperately trying to stifle her sobs. The mother didn't seem to realize what was about to happen. Evgueni knew their names by heart. The four daughters were Olga, Tatiana, Maria, and Anastasia, and the mother Alexandra. As for the youngest, weakling son, his name was Alexei.

Evgueni felt his determination falter but knew he could not lose track of his goal. He had waited for this moment for too long. His hand closed around his little sister's silver necklace in his pocket. She had never taken it off in her lifetime.

At once, his courage returned. This was not a family like any other: the five women, the boy, and the man were the Romanovs. The imperial family that was part of a dynasty that had ruled the country with an iron fist for the past three centuries. The thin patriarch, who was trying to adopt a flattering pose in front of an imaginary camera, was Nicholas II, former Tsar of All Russia. But today, this man, who he hated more than anything else in the world, seemed about as fearsome as a famished old dog. Evgueni struggled to chase the image of the brave father from his mind. This was Nicholas the Bloody!

On a freezing night in 1905, at the Winter Palace in Saint Petersburg, this man's frail hands had ordered his troops to fire into a crowd of hundreds of poor, defenceless people.

Evgueni tightened his grip on the necklace. Natalia had just turned thirteen. In the early morning, he had found her dead body on the frozen square, her face appallingly disfigured by a sword.

Comrade Lenin was right. There must be no pity for the oppressors.

Damov's voice broke the silence. "Comrade Yurovsky, it's time to end this."

The commander walked over to the tsar and puffed up his chest. There were rules to be followed. "By ruling of the Court of Justice and the unanimous vote of the Ural council, you, Nikolai

Romanov, your wife, and all your children, have been condemned to death. The sentence is to be carried out immediately."

The sound of the Nagant revolvers being cocked echoed through the room. There were panicked cries.

The tsar stood his ground and kept his head high. "This is not justice—this is murder," he said. "The murder of women and a child. You are evil incarnate. God and men will judge you for your crimes."

Evgueni came out into the light and walked over to the deposed emperor. Their faces were nearly touching. "You know a thing or two about murder, don't you, Nikolai?"

The former tsar shook his head. "I don't understand," he said.

"This is a waste of time," interrupted Yurovsky, coming over to join them, gun in hand.

Evgueni raised his hand and shot him an imperious look. He was Lenin's right hand and his authority was the law for everyone in the room. The commander retreated.

"Let me finish," ordered Evgueni. "Then you can do your duty." He turned back to Nicholas II. "My father and my sister were protesting beneath the windows of your palace on the 9th of January 1905."

Nikolai went pale.

Evgueni continued, his voice tense. "Do you remember? All they wanted was a little bread and a few freedoms. My sister loved you. She said you were a good and generous ruler. There were many women and children among them. Hundreds. Children the age of your own. And what did you do that night? You sent out your dogs. Your soldiers charged them, swords drawn. People say they even laughed. When I reached the square in the early morning, I found my sister's dead body. My father had been disembowelled, bled like a pig for an Easter feast." Anger coursed through Evgueni's veins. "They say that the very same night, in the same palace, your wife and daughters were trying on fine gowns embroidered with pearls and emeralds that had arrived straight from Paris. And that you sat smoking a cigar as the carnage raged below."

"My God, no! I love my people far too much for that," said the tsar as he shook his head. "I never ordered that massacre. The general made the decision on his own. I ask God for forgiveness every single day."

"Well, that's lucky. You're about to be able to address him directly," replied Evgueni with a sign to Yurovsky.

"No, wait!" begged Nikolai. "Spare my wife and children. In exchange, I'll tell you an invaluable secret. A secret that will make you powerful men, more powerful even than Lenin and Trotsky."

Evgueni studied the former emperor. He was used to being lied to; it came with his job. But this man seemed sincere. "I'm listening," he said.

"Our dynasty has passed it on from generation to generation for centuries. It bestows wealth and power on us. At the beginning of the Revolution, I foolishly sent it away for safekeeping. I'll tell you where it is if you free my family."

Evgueni took out his pistol and glued it to Nicholas II's temple. "You are in no position to give orders, Nikolai. Tell me your secret."

"It's a relic. A sacred relic from the depths of time. It's—"

A gunshot rang out. The last tsar of Russia was unable to finish his sentence. He staggered as a red stain spread across his chest. Then he collapsed as his family and servants looked on in horror and began to scream again.

"A relic! What utter nonsense," exclaimed Lord of Lead over the top of his smoking gun. "Lenin says superstition muzzles—"

"I give the orders here!" shouted Evgueni.

"You came to watch. I came to execute them. Would you like me to report your counter-revolutionary attitude?" scolded Damov. "Stand back before you get shot too."

Evgueni glanced discreetly at the commander and other executioners, who were staring at him. He knew those looks. The slightest hesitation on his part would be relayed to the authorities. He stepped towards the firing squad.

"All right, but spare the girls and the boy. They don't—"

"No room for bourgeois sentimentalism here!" shouted Lord of Lead as he brandished his Mauser. "Comrades, aim for the heart, like I taught you. Whatever you do, don't shoot them in the head—it's too messy."

The rifles and revolvers fired one after the other amid screams from the imperial family and their servants. One of the executioners ran out of bullets and resorted to his bayonet, which he plunged into the throat of the tsarevich as he crawled across the floor. The crown prince died with his head on his father's boots.

"You idiot!" shouted Yurovsky. "He'll bleed all over the place!"

The empress and one of her daughters seemed to still be alive. Damov leaned over the tsarina, who was writhing like an exposed earthworm. Red and green shimmers of light escaped from the bloody bodice of her dress. "Look at this! The bullets bounced off these gemstones sewn into their dresses." The Chekist grabbed two emeralds and a ruby from Alexandra's chest, then nonchalantly shot the nearest daughter, who was grasping for her mother, in the eye.

Evgueni was beginning to feel nauseous. The execution had turned into a bloodbath.

"Finish them off!" shouted Yurovsky. "And take the bodies upstairs to the lorry."

"And then what?" asked Evgueni.

"We'll take them to Four Brothers Forest, about thirty kilometers from here. We'll burn them and dump them in a well. Make sure to state in your report that everything went to plan. The comrades fulfilled their revolutionary duties without hesitation."

The killers knelt over the bloody corpses to collect their jewels. Now all Evgueni wanted to do was murder *them*. They were just like the soldiers who had killed his father and sister.

"I will be sure to underscore your courage when faced with these women and the boy," he replied disdainfully. "And, Damov, you'll need to hand over all the jewels your men are so eagerly collecting. They are the property of the Revolution."

With that, Evgueni turned to leave. He was about to be sick. The revenge he had waited so long to claim had turned into an indescribable horror. The floor and wall were covered in a viscous mixture of flesh, blood, and urine. A foul smell wafted through the cellar, tormenting his feverish mind. This would be his final memory of the Romanovs.

When he stepped outside Ipatiev House, he took a deep breath of clean air and contemplated the night sky, where he was certain he could see new stars twinkling.

PART ONE

"Success is not final; failure is not fatal. It is the courage to continue that counts."

Winston Churchill

I

Pomerania, Germany
July, 1942

The car glided slowly down a gravel road that looked like it hadn't been travelled for years. A grey, impenetrable wood stretched as far as the eye could see on either side. Tristan Marcas wondered if the region was truly inhabited; there was an occasional path breaking away from the road and disappearing into the trees, but he hadn't caught sight of any village rooftops or even a squat, isolated farm. When he looked carefully, Tristan could indeed see a few traces of human activity—bundles of branches tied together with brambles and a tree cut down with an axe and already covered in moss—but the place seemed abandoned.

Since they had left Königsberg, the road had wound deeper and deeper into this opaque forest that blanketed the land right up to the sea. Every now and again, Tristan had seen the uniformed chauffeur glance feverishly at the maps spread across the passenger seat as though he too had the dizzying and absurd impression that they were lost in an endless land.

"Are we far from the castle?" asked Tristan.

The driver took his time before answering. In the SS, it was always best to think long and hard before speaking. "I think it will take half an hour to reach the coast, then another solid hour before we arrive at the von Essling estate," he responded.

Tristan rolled down the window and stuck his head outside. High up over the road, the heavy branches formed a vault of leaves so thick he couldn't see the colour of the sky. But he could smell the salt in the sea breeze. The Baltic Sea was near. Given the dwindling distance to his destination, he decided to collect his thoughts.

He'd left on direct orders from Himmler himself. During the brief meeting the Reichsführer had granted Tristan, he'd made it clear that, with the United States now in the war and the intense fighting on the eastern front, the Ahnenerbe would need to take on new responsibilities. And Himmler wanted to know if Erika von Essling was fit to lead the institution, despite her injuries.

"Look," said the chauffeur.

The once-dense forest was growing sparser. Through the trees, Tristan could see light reflected off an immense grey surface. Twisted pines groaned in the wind. They were almost free. Suddenly, as they rounded a bend, the sea appeared. The endless grey expanse seemed to touch the heavy white clouds on the horizon.

The car came to a halt, and Tristan stepped out into the wind. In an hour, he would see Erika and meet his fate.

Liebendorf, The von Essling estate

Erika von Essling had not been in her childhood room for years. When she had returned to the castle to recover, her family had chosen to place her in a different bedroom, to avoid confusing her. The doctors said she had amnesia, and that they mustn't strain her memory. What idiots! She remembered everything, from the first tooth she had lost and slipped under her pillow to her last torrid night with Tristan. The one thing she couldn't recall was what had really happened in Venice, the night of the meeting between Hitler and Mussolini. She had woken up at the hospital, her right temple mangled by a stray bullet. They told her she had been hit during a firefight between German soldiers and the English commando who had tried to assassinate the Führer, but she couldn't remember any of it. She had been trying in vain to piece things together ever since.

Erika opened the door and stepped in. The shutters were closed, but she didn't bother opening them. Ever since she had injured herself, bright light had been provoking dizzy spells, so she preferred to remain shrouded in darkness. And besides, she knew the view behind them by heart: a long hedge-lined drive that wound through the estate to the main gate. The gate Tristan would arrive at.

She lay down on the bed. It felt softer than it used to. Several blankets must have been layered on top to protect the mattress from damp. The walls were bare, except for one, which featured two photographs in glass frames. The first one, in sepia, depicted a woman wearing a sparkling gold diadem and countless necklaces. It was Sophia Schliemann, the wife of the archaeologist who had discovered the legendary ruins of Troy and Mycenae. Adorned like an idol, Sophia was wearing ancient jewellery her husband had unearthed. She had always fascinated Erika and had impacted her decision to become an archaeologist in a decisive way. The second picture was of a tanned, jovial man in his thirties. He stood in front of an ancient wall holding a pick. Hans had been her archaeology professor at university—and her first love. Full of nostalgia, she reached out to stroke the frame. What would he say if he knew she was running the Ahnenerbe? Erika still wondered how she had ended up leading it. She had gone from being a promising young archaeologist to a leading Reich scientist. How had she—a young woman from a good family—ended up scouring the globe for sacred swastikas, from Montségur in Spain, to Crete, and then Venice? The first time around she had been following the Reichsführer's orders, but what prevented her from quitting after that?

The answer had a name: Tristan.

He was the reason she had continued with the quest. She got up from the bed and steadied herself against the wall. Once again, she felt dizzy. Where had he been when that bullet had nearly killed her in Venice? What had he been doing? Why hadn't he protected her? The memory of that night kept escaping her grasp. A memory she knew involved the man she loved.

The Baltic Sea

The road ran alongside a dune covered in wild grass. Tristan was leaning against the parked car. He closed his eyes to keep out the sand that was being blown about by the wind. Summer was an alien concept here. He pulled away from the car and ran towards the narrow path that led through the dune to the beach. The sand was littered with grey flotsam and empty shells. It was like crossing a crowded marine cemetery. He felt better once he reached the narrow strip of darker sand right by the water. As his feet sank into the wet ground, he finally felt like himself again. Deep down, he had always hated the ocean. The endless horizon was too much for mankind: its limitless space kindled the desire to go beyond what was possible. He was certain mad conquerors and insatiable dictators were once men who had spent too much time contemplating the sea. As for Tristan, he needed to feel his feet on the ground to think—now more than ever.

As the telephone didn't work well, the Frenchman had been writing to Erika since she had retreated to her family estate, but the young woman's replies had been terse and trivial and full of contradictions. Was her amnesia getting worse, or was she suspicious? Had she been more seriously injured than everyone had thought, or was she preparing her triumphant return, or even revenge? Tristan had grown wary. He was constantly looking over his shoulder, watching his back. He did his best to be discreet. He hadn't sent a single message to London since Venice. He was playing dead.

He turned around and headed back through the dune. In just an hour, he would come face to face with Erika and know where they stood. Either she remembered nothing, or she knew exactly who had tried to sink a bullet between her eyes.

In which case, he would be left with no choice.

Liebendorf, The von Essling estate

Broad steps led up to the castle, whose central building, framed by two smaller wings, looked out over the park. The forest reigned all around. The former hunting residence had belonged to the von Esslings for centuries. Erika's parents had renovated and added to the estate to make it a more comfortable summer residence for the family. But even so, despite the French doors and the colourful roof tiles, the castle remained austere.

Tristan couldn't help but frown as he got out of the car. The castle looked like a tomb waiting for winter to bury it in the snow.

Then Erika stepped out. Her hair, which she had neither cut nor plaited, hung down to her waist. She had lost a lot of weight. As he strode up the drive, Tristan wondered if he should kiss her. Over the course of their long separation, they had never mentioned their relationship. As she drew nearer, he noticed her face had grown nearly transparent. Only her eyes still seemed to belong to the world of the living. She was wearing a pair of old boots over riding trousers that were too big for her. Her bust was invisible beneath a woollen shawl.

"Are you cold?" asked Tristan, reaching for her shoulder.

"It's always cold here, even in summer," replied Erika, quickly taking a step back.

She led him through some French doors straight into a vast sitting room with views over the drive. Out of the windows, Tristan could see smooth grey ponds reflecting the crowns of the surrounding trees.

Without so much as glancing at the view, Erika settled in an armchair near the fireplace. She held out her hands to warm them. "I'm still recuperating, but I want to get back to my post as soon as possible. What news do you have from the Ahnenerbe?"

Tristan noticed her tone grow more serious with every word. "Wolfram Sievers, a prehistorian, has been named interim director. He's managing daily affairs. Given the intensification of the war effort, most of the research programmes have been suspended," he explained.

"What about the quest for the swastika? There's only one left now."

Tristan walked towards the fire. He wasn't cold, but the glow of the flames in this huge, gloomy house felt reassuring. "As you know, we got all our information on the swastikas from the *Thule Borealis*," he said. "It led the Ahnenerbe to Tibet, Montségur, and then Crete. But there's nothing whatsoever about the location of the last relic."

"But the manuscript is perfectly clear about the fact that four swastikas were hidden," insisted Erika.

"Yes, but the book is incomplete. Either a part of it was cut out, or the author of the *Thule Borealis* didn't have time to finish it," explained Tristan.

Erika's face lit up; it was as though she suddenly had a new lease of life. "We must determine which of these hypotheses is correct. When you get back to Berlin, put together an interdisciplinary team including a philologist, to see if there are any linguistic clues that would indicate that the book is unfinished, as well as a paper specialist. They should be able to determine if one or more pages were removed by studying the manuscript closely."

"That's true," said Tristan with a nod. "But it would be even more useful to follow the *Thule*'s trail to the present day. We know it was written in an abbey in the Middle Ages, but where did it travel after that?"

The Frenchman stood up to study a display case at the far end of the room. Its shelves were filled with bronze torcs and fibulas, funerary urns, and a ceramic statue of an enigmatic character brandishing a mallet. Had these relics encouraged Erika to read archaeology?

"Weistort is the one who first found the *Thule Borealis*," explained Erika.

Tristan turned around abruptly. *Weistort, the former head of the Ahnenerbe, whose methods were often rather summary?* "Why have you never told me that before?" he asked.

Erika shrugged. "I only found out myself right before we left for Venice, through some of Weistort's unclassified documents. He got the manuscript from a Jewish bookseller in Berlin in 1938."

"I doubt he purchased it . . ."

"That doesn't matter. But we need to find that bookseller."

"Do you really think Weistort let him live?" exclaimed Tristan.

"His family then. Maybe they know something," concluded Erika.

Tristan's eyes widened. "You want me to find a Jewish family in Nazi Germany in 1942? Where should I look first: the camps or the cemeteries?" he asked ironically.

"Why don't you tell me why you're really here instead," she replied dryly.

"Himmler has plans to restructure the Ahnenerbe and wants to know if you're well enough to return."

"And he's asked you to assess my condition?"

Tristan kept quiet.

"With the exception of occasional dizzy spells, I'm well. But I would be even better if I knew what happened in Venice," said the archaeologist sharply.

"You really don't remember anything?" Tristan asked, incredulous.

This time Erika didn't reply.

"You were hit by a stray bullet. A commando unit tried to—"

"I don't want the official story," she interrupted. "I've heard it a thousand times. I want your version. Where were you when I was shot?"

"Right next to you on the terrace at the Cinema Palace. That's where they evacuated the German delegation. Across from the beach," Tristan lied.

"And you didn't see anything?"

"I saw you fall. I hurried over to find your face covered in blood. Help arrived quickly."

"That's it?"

"Why would you imagine anything else?" asked Tristan, who was growing more agitated by the second. "Everyone tells the same story. There were dozens of witnesses."

"Well what if *I* remember something different?" asked Erika.

Tristan studied her face. Either she was bluffing, or a part of her memory had suddenly returned. But be that as it may, she clearly didn't trust him anymore. The risk had become too great. "Sometimes with amnesia," he explained, "false memories come in to fill the void."

"I didn't know you were a neurologist, too," she said with a smirk. "I can see you've done your research. Why?" she insisted.

Tristan looked through the French windows to the drive. He hadn't seen anyone on his way in. Not a single gardener or maid. Who lived in this castle with Erika?

"No answer? Do you think I'm crazy? Is that what you're going to tell Himmler?"

Through the open door, Tristan glanced at the oak staircase that led from the hallway to the second floor. The smell of turpentine wafted through the air: it had just been polished. Erika stood up and had to grab the armchair to steady herself.

"Why don't you go and lie down," Tristan suggested. "You're not feeling well. You need to rest. I'll go with you. Is your room upstairs?"

Just as he placed his hand on Erika's shoulder, the sound of an engine came from the courtyard. Tristan looked out of the window to see two SS officers heading up the steps to the main entrance. A door slammed shut and the squeaking of boots could be heard in the hallway.

"Herr Marcas?" The officers stepped into the living room.

Tristan nodded.

"Come with us."

2

The old man was clad in a long white tunic that fell to his ankles. Despite his advanced age—he was clearly over eighty—the man stood tall like an oak, the sacred tree he had worshipped since childhood. His meticulously groomed goatee gave him the air of a respectable 19th-century aristocrat. His grip was closed around a stick as knotted as his tendons and of wood as dark as the pupils of his time-worn eyes.

The high priest of the United Ancient Order of Druids of England, Scotland and Wales looked kindly upon the other ten officiants, all robed in the same white tunic. Then he struck the age-old stone under his feet three times. His ancestors had trodden the very same stone when invoking the ancient gods.

"Free men and women: welcome, and thank you for travelling so far to attend this extraordinary coven here at Stonehenge, our most sacred site."

Hovering directly overhead, as if pinned to the black fabric of the night sky, the silver disc of the moon glowed above them, as if to protect the coven, shedding its wan light on the heath as far as the eye could see.

"Our lands are once again under threat of invasion, not by soldiers from the Great North or Rome, but from forces that have escaped the black forests of Germania. These ferocious warriors massacre their adversaries and take women and children as slaves, following a ruthless leader who wants to rule over us all. Free men and women of Britain, Wales and Scotland, our armies need our support because they are fighting two battles—one is tangible, the other out of this world."

The high priest closed his eyes and stretched out his arms as if to embrace the sky. Murmurs spread through the gathering.

"Ag nan Gorath, ulban neflet," muttered the Druid, pronouncing the first words of the ritual in an ancient tongue. The old man could feel the life force flowing through him again, rising from the earth, travelling through his body, and shooting up towards the cosmos.

"Ag beran Noad!" replied the congregation in unison.

From her position at the entrance to the megalithic circle, Laure watched the impressive ceremony through a pair of binoculars. She scanned the surroundings and caught sight of an army lorry parked behind the ranger station.

Operation Witchfall was under way and could not be delayed. All the roads leading to Stonehenge had been closed by military roadblocks, and a detachment of thirty soldiers had cordoned off the area around the monument. These stones had seen many a Druidic ceremony, but this was definitely the first to be surrounded by armed guards. While they were under strict orders not to take any photographs, an army film crew was allowed to record the event.

The young SOE agent checked her watch. The most important part of the ceremony was about to begin, provided the Druid kept to the schedule. She listened in intently.

"Free men and women, reveal the face of our mortal enemy," bellowed the high priest.

The beam of a spotlight shone up from the ground towards a vertical stone covered by a sheet of white fabric with ragged edges that reminded Laure of a spent parachute. Two Druids tugged on the attached ropes until the surface of the rock was unveiled.

A huge, three-by-two-meter face of the Führer appeared in the light, focusing his wild, hypnotic gaze on the gathering.

"This is our enemy: Adolf Hitler! May his evil spirit burn forever in the fires of hell. May his bones rot, his blood dry up, and his flesh fail. I invoke our divinities, Lugh, Elargrl, and Meldor, to curse him and his loved ones and all their descendants."

One of the Druids lit a torch and walked solemnly towards the portrait of the German dictator.

"May this purifying fire consume your body and soul for eternity!"

At once, the flames of the torch were devouring the face, beginning at the chin, then climbing up the cheeks and across his moustache. Before long, the dictator's face had crumpled into a disgusting, red-hot grimace.

Laure picked up her walkie-talkie and whispered, "Go!"

Seconds later, three columns of light appeared. Laure watched in awe as the anti-aircraft searchlights shot incandescent pillars towards the sky as if attempting to reach the moon above.

"Now our enemies know that our fires are lit and that we will hunt them down, no matter how dark the war gets," continued the high priest.

Laure sighed. A question had been bothering her since the beginning of the ritual: how could anyone in their right mind believe in such rubbish? Yet she knew that this very minute, in three other sacred places, similarly strange ceremonies were under way. On the Isle of Man, Wiccan witches were lighting bonfires to burn effigies of Himmler, the head of the SS. In Edinburgh, the Order of the Golden Dawn was hanging a mannequin dressed up like Göring from a sacred oak tree. And in the New Forest, cherished by pagans for millennia, the followers of Pan were sacrificing a goat bearing a photograph of Goebbels on its haunches. Soldiers protected the officiants of each ceremony from curious onlookers, while a film crew immortalized the rituals.

Suddenly, the columns of light disappeared, leaving only the moon to bathe the sacred stone and Druids in its silvery light. Laure tucked away her binoculars and made her way towards the ranger station. She was starving and dying to learn more about Witchfall, the new operation mounted by her boss at the SOE.

"Commander, do please tell me why you've organized this circus?" asked Laure as the door slammed shut behind her, blowing a damp draught across the cabin.

"You're right on time. The eggs are ready," replied the head of Department S, who was stooped over a camp stove.

The delicious smell of fried eggs and bacon filled the small ranger station. Towards the far end, a second man sat at a roughly hewn wooden table. His clothes were bursting at the seams as he wolfed down an egg sandwich. "Malorley is right," said Aleister Crowley. "A hearty breakfast will do you some good. You seem troubled."

"You think *I'm* troubled? You must be joking," snapped Laure as she tossed her gloves onto the table. "What about the raving madmen outside? Which asylum did you find them in?"

Crowley let out a heavy sigh. "You misunderstand, my dear. The learned assemblies gathered by Commander Malorley and myself at the country's four most sacred sites are the cream of the crop, the elite from the worlds of magic, sorcery, and Druidism. It was I who came up with the name Operation Witchfall. The last time such a concerted effort took place was over a century ago, and the portraits were of Napoleon and his marshals."

"Give your rubbish a rest, Aleister," groaned Laure as she removed her coat.

Malorley set two plates of bacon and eggs on the table. "But it's true," he said. "I found a report detailing a nearly identical ceremony in 1803. The country's Druids and sorcerers gathered to cast a spell on your emperor, who wanted to invade England with an army of a hundred thousand soldiers waiting to embark from Boulogne."

"And it worked!" added Crowley. "They say that Bonaparte had convulsions in his bed that night. And when he woke up in the morning, he decided to give up on his vile plan."

"Right," replied Laure dubiously as she sat down. "Your common sense also seems to be suffering from convulsions, if you ask me. Just like those conmen in Druid gowns and the witches on the Isle of Man with their broomsticks."

"Don't be so condescending," scolded Crowley as he gulped down a mouthful of runny yolk. "They're rebels in their own way, light bearers, revolutionaries!"

"Is that so?" asked the young woman, eyebrows raised. She tucked into a piece of bacon before continuing. "Strange that my history teachers never mentioned Robespierre or Lenin sacrificing any virgins or hosting black masses, then."

"For those two particular characters they would have been red masses, given the number of cemeteries they filled," replied Crowley sharply. He got up surprisingly quickly for a man of his size. His eyes were frenzied as he leaned towards Laure. "You really don't understand at all, my dear. Magic and ancient religions are subversive, no doubt. But true mages, Druids, and witches are rebels. They have been fighting the tyranny of Christ and his watchdogs for centuries. In the Middle Ages, sorcery was brewed in the evil cauldron tended by the Church and the aristocracy. Since Jesus and the Virgin Mary condone oppression of the people by popes, kings, and priests, we should spit in their noble faces. Let us kiss the ass of Satan or Pan and topple the statue of the greatest dictator the world has ever known—God!"

"Aleister seems to have come down with a case of acute Marxism," Laure retorted coolly, throwing an ironic glance in Malorley's direction.

"As a woman, you should understand all this better than most," continued the occultist.

Laure remained focused on her plate. "I don't see what you're getting at. I have no interest in Lucifer's backside."

"Are you even listening?" raged Crowley. "Women were the ones who harnessed magic in the Middle Ages. People called them witches, but they were above all healers and seers. They restored hope to the oppressed—yet, they were burned and tortured by the Church and king after king. And don't get me started on the power of desire . . ."

"Ah, at last," said Laure with a laugh. "We've reached your favourite topic: sex. Clearly, you believe the surest way to supreme power is a roll in the hay. I've read your SOE file about your teachings on the subject. A very practical way to fulfil your various deviances with women—or men."

Malorley watched in amusement as his agents sparred. Now that he was all worked up, Crowley couldn't hold back.

"I worship both Isis and Osiris! So what? I'm not ashamed. Deviance, you say? Really! I defy the morality that castrates us and keeps us from living as free men and women. I defy the Vatican, walled up in its fortress, which lets the German antichrist bleed the people of Europe like livestock. I defy a world ruled by booted men who steer us straight to the apocalypse. Indeed, I defy this world—supposedly guided by reason and morality—which has been sending its children to the abattoir for centuries. To the melodies of 'Te Deum', 'The Internationale', 'La Marseillaise', and the anthem of the Nazi party. Sex is not deviant, war is!"

"You certainly have a point there," she conceded. "But my, are you twisted. Clever, but twisted to the core."

"A compliment at last. Thank you," said Crowley as he sat back down.

Laure turned to Malorley. "In all seriousness, Commander, it makes sense for your esoteric friend to believe in this nonsense, but you? Isn't it a bit much to mobilize a civil defence battalion to protect these gatherings, and organize anti-aircraft searchlights and army film crews on top of that? You haven't *really* convinced Churchill to curse Hitler, have you?"

Malorley had lit his pipe and was savouring it as he let himself be entertained. "Best to stack the deck in our favour. Misinformation and magic make for a delicious cocktail."

"The problem with you, Commander," said Laure, "is that I can't decide whether humour is your weapon of choice or a way of eluding my question."

"Probably both," he replied.

Crowley's attention had turned to a rasher of bacon. "Pork is so very scrumptious. Pigs are among the only animals that can't be sacrificed in magical rituals. Lambs, cows, bulls, cats, roosters, sure. But no pigs. Too impure for both God and Satan."

Laure gave Crowley a scornful look and pulled a wrinkled newspaper from the pocket of her coat. "Speaking of sacrifices," she said, "have you read today's papers?"

"We haven't had time. We've been preparing for the coven for the past two days. Why?" asked Crowley.

The young SOE agent spread a tabloid out on the table. The catchy headline stood out above a photograph of a body bag: *Swastika Killer Strikes Again!*

"They've found a woman's body on a gravestone at West Brompton cemetery," Laure explained in a tense voice. "She had a swastika carved into her forehead. Exactly like Moira O'Connor's victim. You know, the poor girl she slaughtered and dumped at Tower Hamlets cemetery last year. The crime she's been using to blackmail our friend the satyr here."

Crowley spat a large piece of fat onto his plate with an impassive glance at Laure.

"Let Scotland Yard handle it," replied Malorley. "It's probably just a copycat."

"Maybe, but maybe not. We should give the police a hand."

"Absolutely not! Need I remind you that Moira O'Connor is an Abwehr agent, whom we're secretly manipulating? Aleister still feeds her whatever information I please every month. She has become an important pawn in our game of chess with the German intelligence services."

"But what if she keeps killing? We can't let her run wild like Jack the Ripper," said Laure indignantly.

Malorley stood up and glared at his agents. "The war is our priority. The war and the hunt for the swastikas. As for the rest, let the police do their job."

"But she's right," insisted Crowley. "It might be useful to know if the Scarlet Fairy has unsheathed her sacrificial daggers again."

"I'm surprised to see you two agree," balked Malorley.

"Moira has compromising pictures of me with her first victim. It's quite enough to be accused of one murder."

The commander nodded. The argument was valid. "Does the paper specify the date of the second girl's death?" he asked.

"What does it matter?" replied Laure. "The markings on the bodies are identical, and both were left in a cemetery."

Malorley picked up the newspaper and skimmed the article.

His features brightened. "According to this, the murder took place less than three days ago, which means our witch is innocent."

"How can you be so sure?" ventured the young woman. "Have you run into her recently at her sadomasochist brothel?"

Crowley noticed the SOE leader had taken offence and intervened. "Malorley's right. Moira is participating in the ceremony on the Isle of Man. She arrived there last week. Her alibi is as solid as Churchill's bunker."

"I don't understand. Why would you use her for Witchfall?"

"For starters she played an active role in its organization, but also, Aleister here will be slipping her copies of the footage to share with Berlin," explained Malorley.

"You're not making any sense."

"We have to keep the department busy while our quest for the swastika is on hold. Our psychological propaganda operation targets the leaders of the Reich with a penchant for the occult, and Himmler in particular. The thought of having been cursed may impact their behaviour and lead them astray. The idea came to me after meeting with that madman, Rudolf Hess. He explained that the head of the SS believes in reincarnation and sorcery and makes many decisions based on recommendations from his astrologers." Malorley checked his watch. "Time for me to get back to London and rest up. I have a meeting tomorrow afternoon with our friends at MI6 who still haven't come to terms with the failed assassination attempt on Hitler and Mussolini in Venice."

"What about us? How will we get back to the capital?" asked Crowley. "I have a big gallery opening to attend tomorrow."

"I'll leave you a van to get back to the city, but make sure our friends the revolutionary Druids get back on their buses first."

"Still no news from Tristan?" asked Laure.

Malorley remained silent.

3

Pomerania, Germany
July 1942

It had been an hour since they had left Erika's estate when the car stopped in front of a gate defended by SS soldiers in combat gear. Beyond them, behind a line of trees dotted with watchtowers, Tristan could make out a clearing. He hadn't asked his armed escort a single question during the drive. He had sat next to the window to observe the route, but the car had quickly left the main roads and the forest had become too dense. It occurred to Tristan that if they wanted to execute him, this would be an excellent spot. Discreet. No traces left behind. But why wait? The SS soldiers would also have interrogated him first—after all, this was their speciality, their twisted pleasure. No, there had to be another reason for this journey.

They were still waiting outside the gate. The guards were circling the car like wild dogs hunting their prey. One of them opened the bonnet, while another inspected the wheel arches. *They're looking for a bomb,* thought Tristan, surprised by the stringent controls. Suddenly, the gate began to open. The guards returned to their stations and the car started up again. Soon, they were no longer on a bumpy dirt path, but on a perfectly smooth asphalt road. The wood slowly grew sparser. Tristan could make out buildings shaped like long tubes protected by anti-aircraft defence units. As they reached a fork in the road, a patrol flanked by dogs appeared and signalled for the driver to stop.

"Random inspection," explained the warrant officer. "Cut the engine, but don't get out of the vehicle for any reason."

The dogs had already surrounded them. One of them jumped onto the bonnet and sniffed around the windscreen with a growl. Several others clung to the windows with their claws, their lips curled.

"Charming welcome committee," joked Tristan. "Will there be canapés later?"

The barking dogs provided the only reply. The abrupt trill of a whistle brought them to heel and the patrol stepped aside and disappeared into the brush near the road. The car began inching forwards again, then turned left. Tristan was utterly surprised to lay eyes on a landing strip, which vanished into the fog. A light atop a concrete tower blinked weakly. The chauffeur parked on the embankment and gestured to the Frenchman to get out.

"If I'm to attend a fancy party, I must warn you: I don't have my tuxedo," said Tristan in a second attempt at humour.

The car moved off, leaving Tristan alone on the tarmac. The landing strip had just been cleaned, and tidy piles of pine needles dotted its surface every ten meters. He felt around his pockets but found only his lighter. He'd left his cigarettes at Erika's. The brief visit had been a fiasco. He still had no idea whether his lover remembered what had happened and had therefore been threatening him, or whether she had been threatening him to find out what had happened. Whatever the case, he had gotten carried away. His first impulse was always to handle a problem immediately; often without even thinking about the consequences. This most recent event proved that he was under so much stress he was unable to think clearly and take all variables—first and foremost his own safety—into consideration. Luckily, the SS goons had turned up to fetch him. Tristan thought back to his travel companions. They were just following orders. He had done well to go along and keep quiet. When dealing with Nazis, and particularly the SS, it was best never to behave like a potential suspect. It was the first rule of survival in a totalitarian regime. Unfortunately, he hadn't had the same reflex with Erika. He needed to know why.

A sudden roar jolted the Frenchman from his thoughts. A door had just opened at the entrance to one of the tunnel-shaped build-ings. Tristan recognized the characteristic hum of propeller blades, and his intuition was confirmed when the nose of a plane and two long black wings emerged. The aircraft moved away from the hangar and took up position on the runway. A door opened in the middle of the fuselage, then a metal staircase unfolded. An SS officer in dress uniform strode across the asphalt and came to a brusque halt in front of Tristan.

"*Heil Hitler*," he barked. Before Tristan could lift his arm in mechanical reply, the man continued. "The Reichsführer wants to see you."

The Reichsführer's staff was hard at work. The inside of the plane, a Focke-Wulf 200, had been specially outfitted for him. Indeed, maps of military positions, police reports, industrial statistics—all of the SS's activities were managed from inside this aircraft. Himmler could stay perfectly informed as to the state of his empire while flying over Germany. He had considerably expanded the influence and power of his organization; so much so that the SS had become an octopus whose tentacles controlled every inch of the Reich. It had hundreds of thousands of loyal soldiers on the Eastern Front, managed the forces of law and order through the Gestapo, and supervised countless prisoners and camp residents in its munition factories. A proper state within the state, the SS had become the beating heart of Nazi Germany.

As Tristan advanced amid the busy hive, the engines began to thrum in earnest. The plane was taking off. The officer who had guided him in turned around. "I'll check if he's ready for you," he said solemnly.

A partition separated the rest of the plane from the meeting room. Tristan concluded Himmler's lair would be behind it. The officer knocked, stepped in, then quickly came back out.

"You'll have to wait another moment," he explained.

The room Himmler occupied was in stark contrast with the rest of the plane. There was no bustle and most noticeably no noise.

Even the purring of the engines seemed to be far away, as though the world stopped on the threshold of the SS leader's den. While his staff scurried to and fro, Himmler preferred to focus in quiet isolation.

Sitting at his desk next to a window, Himmler was studying a confidential file. It was a report from Heydrich's secret archives. Since the death of his faithful right hand, Himmler asked for his personal files to be sent directly to him at all times. No one else was to see them, not even the Führer. Himmler had recognized Heydrich's hand at once. The report covered a book collection the Reichsführer was anxious to reassemble. Comprising no fewer than thirteen thousand volumes from all over Europe, it was the largest collection of antique books on witches in the world. The poor women's tragic fate had kindled as many imaginations as stakes at the dawn of the Renaissance. Ever since Göring had heard the news, he'd teased Himmler for his passionate interest in these madwomen who thought they could fly on broomsticks. But Himmler had let it go. His obese colleague was always two steps behind and probably thought Himmler was looking for a magical empowerment potion for the SS, or an elixir of immortality for Hitler.

Himmler smiled.

He had different intentions.

Since the invasion of Russia, the extermination of Jews had become an industrial process, which had also led to leaks. A few neutral governments, like those of Switzerland and Sweden, had already started to spread these rumours. Himmler had been one of the first to learn of the massacres and—more importantly—he had realized at once how dire the consequences would be if the Nazis lost the war.

He'd planned a pre-emptive counter-attack right away, to show that the Reich was simply doling out payback for the first genocide in history. Tens of thousands of German women had been accused of witchcraft and burned at the stake by blood-thirsty priests and murderous pastors, who were nothing but homicidal Christian descendants of Jews. In his report, Heydrich asserted that the argument was unconvincing and therefore likely to attract more attention rather than deflecting it favourably. Himmler was disappointed. How could the life of a German woman burned alive be worth less than that of a Jew? The Führer was right. The Semites were the cause of all their problems. The world would never be at peace until they were rid of them.

He decided, albeit regretfully, that he'd have to let the idea go.

Tristan was ushered in. Surprised, he came to a stop in front of a book on display.

"*Mein Kampf*, the edition signed for me by the Führer," explained Himmler. "It never leaves my side."

"A real talisman," replied Tristan.

"More than you imagine. Some books are meant to survive the ages. Their words are the blood of their authors, who are destined to live on for centuries."

Caught off guard by Himmler's unexpected love of Hitler's ambiguous sermons, the Frenchman nearly proffered an ironic "amen". He knew the former chicken-farmer had his own logic when it came to his favourite topics, like history and esotericism. Many of the other Nazi dignitaries, including Göring and Goebbels, used to openly mock Himmler, convinced that he was away with the fairies. They'd stopped laughing when the Reichsführer had sent them hefty files on their turpitudes for their birthdays. They clearly hadn't realized he was in the know. The full catalogue of his mistresses sent Goebbels into deep depression for days. As for Göring, he would shut himself up in Carinhall whenever he received an updated list of his morphine suppliers. The Reichsführer was not one to be trifled with.

"So, you saw Erika von Essling? Is she ready to return to work?" asked Himmler in a nasal voice.

"With the exception of her amnesia regarding certain events in Venice, she's in perfect health," replied Tristan.

He had used the journey time to think about the account he should give of Erika's condition. It would be best for him if she returned to her job at the head of the Ahnenerbe. Should her paranoia grow out of control, Himmler himself would notice and put a stop to it. According to the official story, Hitler had escaped an assassination attempt thanks to the valiant efforts of the SS. A competing version of the attack in Venice would be an embarrassment for the Reichsführer.

"The Ahnenerbe's missions are about to change," retorted Himmler. "From now on, Germany's best scientists need to help materialize the Reich's bright future. We must provide the Führer with the means to successfully implement his crusade to renew the human race."

It was like listening to a speech on the radio. Tristan wished he could turn down the volume.

"Our troops are on the offensive in the Caucasus," continued Himmler. "If all goes to plan, we will have control of the Black Sea in just a few weeks. We have big plans for the region: most importantly, we want to help the people there rise up against communism. But first, we must sort the population."

"I don't understand, Reichsführer," Tristan interrupted.

"The peoples of Crimea and the Caucasus have been corrupted by Jewish blood. We have to flush it out to purify the region. And to do that, the Ahnenerbe must provide me with specialists who can identify the Jews we need to exterminate. This will be von Essling's priority."

"But she's an archaeologist, not a—" objected the Frenchman.

Himmler picked up his notebook. "And you were an art smuggler when we picked you up in Spain in 1939. That's why you're here. So tell me, where do we stand in the quest for the fourth swastika?"

"As you know, Reichsführer, all of the information we used to find the sacred swastikas came from the *Thule Borealis Kulten*. Unfortunately, the manuscript says nothing about the last relic."

Unlike Hitler, who lost his temper whenever he encountered

an obstacle, Himmler always kept his cool when he received bad news.

"Do you have any leads?" he asked.

"We know that Colonel Weistort got the *Thule Borealis* from a Jewish bookseller in Berlin in 1938. I need to talk to him about it."

"The colonel is still in a coma following his injuries at Montségur—I visit him regularly. I'll ask him about it myself when he comes round."

"We could also gather insights from having the *Thule Borealis* analysed by specialists. We may have missed an important detail," pursued Tristan.

"I'll give the order, but any examination will have to take place at Wewelsburg. The manuscript can't be allowed to leave the castle."

"As you wish, sir."

There was a discreet knock at the door. Himmler gestured for Tristan to open the door. An officer appeared and clicked his heels.

"We'll be landing in Frankfurt in less than three hours," he declared, then turned and left.

Himmler invited Tristan to sit back down. "You studied art history in France before developing your business. Could you tell me what exactly that business was?" he asked.

"I exploited a niche: art collectors are insatiable, and works of art are their drug of choice. They need a constant supply of new objects to fuel their desire. My job was to provide it."

"How?"

"A client either had a particular work in his sights and I would find a way to obtain it, or I would track down a rare piece and explain why he needed it."

The Reichsführer opened his notebook to a page held by a silver skull bookmark.

"And what exactly were you doing in Spain in 1939?"

"Because of the civil war, I was valuing collections, gathering the best pieces and finding ways to keep them safe. Most often by shipping them abroad."

Himmler seemed preoccupied. He hadn't summoned Tristan just to talk about Erika's future and the fourth swastika. They could have got through all that at the foot of the plane steps.

"I've mentioned the new direction the Ahnenerbe needs to take, but the institute mustn't lose sight of its primary mission: finding and protecting everything ever created by German culture. When the war is over, we will Germanize every European site touched by German genius."

Tristan was afraid he understood only too well what Himmler was saying.

"All of Europe, Reichsführer?"

"All, and beyond!" exclaimed Himmler. "We now know that the Aryan race predates all other races, and that the degeneration of peoples in Europe is due to them mixing with inferior races. Any work of art must therefore be of Germanic origin, because only Aryan artists can create masterpieces. And that's why I've asked for you to be brought here today."

As he leaned towards the window, Tristan noticed that the wings of the Focke-Wulf were not adorned with the large black swastikas that typically decorated the Reich's official aircraft. The leader of the SS was travelling incognito. Was he afraid of marauding English planes, or were this trip and its purpose a secret?

"Have you heard of Dr. Alfred Rosenberg?" asked the Reichsführer.

Tristan ran through the main Nazi dignitaries. Rosenberg was neither a member of the government nor part of Hitler's inner circle. The only thing the name brought to mind was a round face with vague features he'd flicked past in the newspaper. As for the Doctor title, it needn't mean anything. The Nazis were terribly generous with their honorifics and handed them out to anyone who had set foot in a university.

"I haven't, Reichsführer."

"Alfred Rosenberg is one of the Reich's foremost thinkers. His ideas on the evolution of the races are pure genius. And even more importantly, he has the Führer's ear."

Tristan had learned to be wary when Himmler heaped praise on someone. His compliments were always followed by biting criticism.

"Unfortunately," continued the German, "Rosenberg is also a theorist, not a man of action. Since Germany has been at war, his usefulness has dwindled."

And his sidelining has clearly been a boon to you, Tristan thought.

"But, as everyone knows, the Führer never abandons his friends, which is why he tasked Rosenberg with retrieving books and archives from the Reich's most reviled enemies throughout Europe: the Jews and the Freemasons."

Tristan remained impassive.

"Yet it seems that, in addition to books and manuscripts, Rosenberg has also been borrowing paintings, sculptures, and any other art he has deemed worthy, whenever he has found it in the hands of enemies."

"And presumably, his definition of the Reich's enemies has become rather vast?" ventured Tristan.

Himmler's lips curled into a smile. "Yes, to the point it's begun to infringe on our prerogatives. I have already had to deal with Göring's insatiable appetite for whatever he could find in even the tiniest museum. In short, I've decided to put an end to Rosenberg's mission. He'll soon be assigned a new position, but I'm afraid he won't give up pillaging. He seems to have developed quite a taste for it!"

Like others have developed a taste for blood, thought Tristan.

"Here's where you come in. You will be joining Rosenberg's team as an observer from the Ahnenerbe and report to me personally regarding his plans with his men. I want to know where they intend to intervene and why. I also want a detailed inventory of all the works they confiscate, based on which I will determine what belongs to us."

"With all due respect, Reichsführer, I doubt Rosenberg and his men will willingly give up their treasures," said Tristan.

Himmler returned to his notebook. "In January 1939, you spent an evening at Montserrat Monastery in Catalonia. It seems that the holy place has been unable to locate several of its most cherished pieces ever since."

"Am I to understand that I'm being given carte blanche to get whatever you like, Reichsführer?"

"Not blanche, Marcas. Red. Blood red."

4

Elephant and Castle, London

Rosemary Benton opened the oven to marvel at the miracle—a juicy chicken, which had been roasting for over an hour. The Bentons' oven hadn't welcomed such a plump bird in three months. Her two girls, safely tucked away at their grandmother's house in Sussex, would have jumped for joy upon seeing it.

The skin was a nice golden brown, so Rosemary wagered it would be done in half an hour. She happily removed her apron and headed for the lounge. A suave, colourful voice emanated from a walnut Marconi 401 radio—the most elegant model around, and a birthday gift from her husband. It was always loyally tuned to the BBC.

> *We'll meet again*
> *Don't know where*
> *Don't know when*
> *But I know we'll meet again, some sunny day*

Like millions of other Englishwomen, Rosemary cherished the young singer, Vera Lynn, who had been voted Forces' Sweetheart by the men on the front. She turned up the volume and lit a cigarette as she cast a glance into the mirror. She wasn't quite as pretty as Vera Lynn, but she wasn't displeased with what she saw.

> *Keep smiling through*
> *Just like you always do*

An insistent ringing sounded at the door, blocking out much of the singer's second couplet. Rosemary glanced at the clock. It was only a quarter past six; her husband was never home before seven. And he wouldn't ring the bell.

She peered through the front window. A young couple stood at the door, both in Salvation Army uniforms. Rosemary put out her cigarette and flapped her arms around in a futile effort to dissipate the smoke, then opened the door.

"Can I help you?" she asked.

"Hello, Madam. We're collecting donations for war orphans," said the handsome young man, whose curly hair was so blond even his eyebrows were golden.

The woman by his side seemed to be older, just under thirty. She sported a light-brown bob, was of rather athletic build, and her fair cheeks were dotted with freckles.

"I'm sorry, I'm afraid my husband isn't home. I don't have any money on me," lied Rosemary.

"No need to apologize," said the boy. "No one seems inclined to donate today. I'm sure we'll do better tomorrow."

"I doubt you'll find many families around here," Rosemary offered. "We're the last ones still in our home. Half of the neighbourhood was destroyed in the bombing last year."

"Something inside smells fantastic!" the young man exclaimed, changing the subject. He turned to his companion. "Come on, let's go. There's a pub nearby. I'm thirsty and I'll have to head back to the front the day after tomorrow."

Rosemary felt a wave of guilt wash over her.

"You're returning to combat?" she asked.

"I am! Second Guards Brigade, shipping out to Cairo. But I wanted to help out the Salvation Army for two days before leaving."

"How generous of you!" cried Rosemary. "All right, come in then. I have beer, or tea if you like."

"A warm cuppa would be lovely," replied the young woman.

"I won't say no to a pint!" the blond angel said enthusiastically. "Might I use your toilet as well?"

"Of course, my dear. Come on in."

She ushered them through the door and directed the young man to the bathroom at the end of the corridor, before inviting the woman to sit down in the lounge. A few minutes later, she brought in a tray with a beer and a bright-pink teapot full of hot tea.

As the volunteer studied the busy décor, a framed picture of Churchill gnawing on a cigar caught her eye. "You have wonderful taste," she said. "Very British. But if I may say so, the photograph of the Prime Minister doesn't really fit with the rest."

Rosemary poured some tea into a cup. "You're right . . ." she replied. "I'm sorry, what's your name?"

"Susan. And you?"

"Rosemary. The picture of Winston in the lounge was my husband's idea. I would have put it in the kitchen. Anyway, thank you so much for volunteering. It breaks my heart to think of all these poor British children who have lost their parents in the war."

"We're actually collecting for German war orphans," replied Susan as she sipped her tea. "Delicious, thank you. The RAF isn't especially precise when bombing Berlin and Hamburg."

Rosemary let out an awkward laugh. "Very funny. You have the same sense of humour as my husband."

"I'm not joking," replied the young woman. "To be perfectly frank, the orphans are cared for by the Hitler Youth, which does a fantastic job, but they need more funds. I admit it's been difficult raising awareness of this sad situation among my countrymen."

"I don't understand. You're . . . you're English, aren't you?"

"Through and through! I was born and raised in the rolling Yorkshire dales. Before the war, I joined a wonderful nationalist movement. Maybe you've heard of it? Sir Oswald Mosley's Blackshirts. You can't get more patriotic than that!"

Rosemary frowned. "Mosley . . . I don't know much about politics, but I seem to remember he was friendly with the Nazis. Isn't he in prison now?"

"He is indeed—and so is his delightful wife Diana. Such a shame. Sir Oswald loved both England and Germany and was devastated by this war that has been instigated by these bloody

Jews. It felt to him like he was being asked to choose between his mother and father. In the end, he chose his country, but it was too late: they convicted him without proof. A plot orchestrated by Churchill and the Freemasons. But I digress, what matters now is helping the children."

The sound of the toilet flushing reached the lounge. Rosemary wiped her hands on her green polka-dotted tea towel. She didn't like what she'd just heard. How could anyone believe such nonsense!

"But we're at war," she countered. "You can't collect donations to help the enemy."

"So you think these children are our enemies just because they're German? How heartless."

Rosemary tensed further. "Miss, I don't know why the Salvation Army is collecting funds for the Germans, but I don't like it one bit. Please finish your tea and leave with your friend. At least *he* is doing his duty."

The young man had returned and was leaning against the china cabinet in the entryway. "I'm sorry to disappoint you," he said, "but nothing could be further from the truth. I'd rather not fight for your king, thank you."

"*Your* king?"

"I might have told a fib earlier. I'm not one of His Majesty's subjects after all," he replied. "Speaking of which . . . let's change radio stations." Without waiting for a reply from his host, he leaned over the radio and turned the dial through a series of frequencies. "The BBC is so terribly boring. I've got something better."

Vera Lynn made way for static, brief interludes of classical music and then jazz. Finally, a nasal voice filled the room.

"Ah, the best station in the world!" exclaimed the young man. "Radio Berlin! We're in luck—it's time for their English-language programme."

"*My dear English friends, if only you could spend a few days on holiday here in the Great Reich. Ah, my comrades . . . Life in Berlin is just splendid. The streets are clean, the people never go hungry. Criminals and parasites are re-educated in camps run*

*by the SS, which doles out just the right doses of firmness and
instruction. The Führer recently confided to me that he is sick at
heart about this absurd war between our two countries. He loves
England—an Aryan nation—even though it has been contaminated by the virus of democracy. He knows that many of you
are favourable to the National Socialist ideal but remain loyal
to your king. He never wanted . . ."*

Rosemary jumped up, her face flushed. "Please turn it back to the
BBC and leave my house immediately. We do not listen to that
traitor Lord Haw-Haw in this house!"

"Calm down, Rosemary," urged the man. "We're just trying to
open your mind, but it seems Churchill's propaganda has you
brainwashed. The Führer is—"

"I don't want to hear it. Hitler is a monster. Get out!"

"That's oversimplifying things a bit, don't you think?" he
continued. "The good Allies on one side and the evil Nazis on the
other. Germany never went looking for war. We just want what's
best for mankind."

"Be precise, Conrad," added the woman. "You mean what's
best for Aryans."

Rosemary pointed forcefully towards the door. "Get out or I'll
call the police!" she shouted.

"Let's not get carried away," said Susan. "Conrad, could you
please put the BBC back on to help Mrs. Benton relax?"

Rosemary went cold and her hands began to shake. "How . . .
How do you know my surname?"

The intruders exchanged a knowing glance as Susan took a
Browning from her pocket and glued it to their host's temple.
There was something grotesque about seeing a gun in the hands
of a Salvation Army volunteer. Like seeing a ballerina brandish a
chainsaw.

"Because we chose you, Rosemary," explained Susan.

"If it's money you want, I—"

"We're not thieves. Now, come along. You're going to come on
a little walk with us."

"I will not."

The rich, sweet sound of a clarinet filled the room.

"Glenn Miller, 'Moonlight Serenade'. I bet Rosemary loves this song," Conrad said ironically.

"It's jazz, Conrad! Negro music! I can't believe you'd—"

Before Susan could finish her sentence, Rosemary had smashed the teapot down onto the hand holding the gun. It fired but missed, sending the bullet right into Churchill's forehead. Rosemary pushed past Conrad, trying to escape through the front door, but he caught her by the ankle. Her forehead hit the corner of the wall as she fell hard and face-down onto the floor, toppling the exquisite imitation Ming vase she'd received as a wedding gift. An excruciating pain ripped through her skull.

Having managed to turn over onto her back, she could make out the man's handsome face through a veil of blood. He stood bent over her, stroking her cheek.

"You're not making this easy, Rosemary," he scolded.

"Help! Help!" she shouted, or rather tried to. Was there any sound coming out of her mouth?

Her forehead was being wiped with a cloth.

"Well isn't that great," said Susan. "You've given yourself a nasty gash. This won't do. I hope there's enough skin left for us to give you a proper tattoo."

"Don't worry," replied her companion. "We can probably work it into the swastika."

Rosemary didn't understand a word. Her head was throbbing.

"Please, I beg you," she mumbled.

Susan checked her watch. "It's getting late. We need to get going. Strangle her so we can get her into the van."

The last two things Rosemary took in before she died were the final bars of "Moonlight Serenade" and a smell. The delicious smell of a perfectly roasted chicken.

5

On the road from Frankfurt airport to the city, Tristan was once again astonished by the exceptional security measures that had been taken. The Reichsführer's escort seemed to be travelling through a deserted city whose only inhabitants were police roadblocks and SS patrols.

Riding in the car reserved for Himmler's close collaborators, Tristan turned to his neighbour, a captain in a perfectly tailored uniform, and asked, "Where is everyone?"

"For safety reasons, the population has been asked to stay at home," he explained.

"I didn't know the Reichsführer could empty a city single-handedly."

The captain ran his hand through his carefully groomed moustache. "There's a rumour going around."

Tristan looked out of the window to feign disinterest. It was the best way to get more information.

"They say the Führer is in Frankfurt," continued the SS man.

"But he's not greeting the people?" asked Tristan, surprised. He still remembered the pre-war propaganda images of Hitler strolling through adoring crowds.

"It's a private visit."

Another explanation occurred to Tristan. Since German troops had been forced to retreat from Moscow, the Führer's popularity had suffered, and he wouldn't risk organizing a tour unless he was certain the people would hold up their end of the bargain.

Since the Frenchman kept quiet, the captain continued in an intimate tone. "The Führer is here to visit Rosenberg's new institute. You must know that Dr. Rosenberg is one of Hitler's oldest advisors and the party's official ideologist. It's a shame that every time he's given any sort of responsibility, he makes a terrible mess of it."

Tristan felt like he was listening to Himmler again. "Yet it's a great honour to have the Führer visit his—what was it again?—oh yes, his institute."

The captain shrugged with the self-assurance of a well-informed man. "You're way off the mark! This is more of a state funeral. The Führer has come to inaugurate Rosenberg's future tomb. He's no longer a member of his inner circle."

"Like Rudolf Hess?"

This made the captain jump. "Never say that name again. A mad traitor!"

Tristan let it go. One by one, Hitler's long-time companions were disappearing: Hess was a prisoner in London, having thought he could negotiate a separate peace with Britain, and Rosenberg was locked away in a golden cupboard—a provincial institute. Only Göring, Goebbels, and Himmler remained. Who would be next?

"Do you know much about Dr. Rosenberg's career?" asked Tristan.

"Do I ever! I wrote a biographical report on him at the Reichsführer's request."

The Frenchman knew vanity when he saw it. He knew he mustn't be stingy with his admiration if he wanted to learn more. "Might I take advantage of your extensive knowledge, then? You must know Rosenberg like the back of your hand."

"I know him better than he knows himself!" exclaimed the captain, before launching into his story with a deep breath worthy of an opera singer about to begin an aria. "First, you must know that Rosenberg is from the Baltics. And the Balts claim to be German when Germany is winning, but turn into Russians whenever Russia is ahead."

"Turncoats?" said Tristan, humouring the SS man.

"Precisely. Until 1918, Russia had the advantage, so Rosenberg chose to study architecture in Moscow. He says he fled Russia during the Revolution, but I can't help but notice that it took him over a year to leave the birthplace of communism. And he had some very questionable friends."

"Bolsheviks?"

"Worse. Groups of fanatics who think communism is the Christian Kingdom described in the Book of Revelations. As you probably know, the tsar's entourage was rife with prophets and messiahs."

"Were they influential groups?" asked Tristan, surprised.

"Hard to tell today. Stalin disbanded them all. But Rosenberg was left with a strange fascination for esoteric theories. And when he turned up in Munich, he'd become a member of the Thule Society."

Tristan kept quiet, but he knew that the Thule Society, with which both Hess and Hitler had dealings, had likely fomented the rise of National Socialism.

"The Reichsführer was very interested in that," the captain continued. "In any case, while in Munich, Rosenberg used his knowledge of the Russian Revolution to style himself as a specialist in the fight against communism. He gave quite a few talks on the topic."

"He can't have been the only one," countered Tristan. "At the time, anti-communism was *the* national pastime in Germany."

The captain ran his fingers through his beard. "Yes, but he stood out from the rest. And it was then that he came up with a very particular theory about the origins of the red plague, which Hitler found intriguing."

The Frenchman noticed the convoy was now driving along a road lined with vast wooded estates. Occasionally, a mansion's shiny roof emerged from among the leaves.

The captain leaned in and lowered his voice. "You see, for Dr. Rosenberg, communism is more than a theory fashioned by the twisted minds of Marx and Engels. He considers it a deadly, insidious drug carefully designed and deployed by a specific group of people."

Tristan had heard many theories about the birth of bolshevism, but this one was new. "A drug?"

"It's not a spontaneous movement born of animosity between the classes or the exploitation of the proletariat. No, communism is the latest poison invented by the Jews—the snakes of humanity— to destroy western civilization."

The Frenchman was unable to mask his surprise.

The captain's tone became more instructive. "In short, Rosenberg considers communism to have been thought up, developed, and rolled out by the Jews."

Tristan was speechless.

"But what's most interesting are the consequences of his theory."

The lead car had just stopped in front of an ornate gate guarded by SS officers in dress uniform.

"It means," continued the captain, "that no matter how hard we fight against communism, no matter how great our military triumphs, and even if we hang Stalin from the top of the Kremlin, communism will persevere as long as even one Jew survives. You see?"

Tristan was relieved to get out of the car. Another minute with the SS man and his crazy ideas and he would have lost his temper. And this was no time to risk giving himself away. Himmler stepped through the massive gate, followed by his staff. The Frenchman fell in line. At the far end of the drive, he could make out the façade of an aristocratic manor house. The moustached captain had disappeared into the cluster of men—most likely to get as close as possible to his commander and make a good impression. In any case, the portrait he'd sketched of Rosenberg was enlightening. The moon-faced man was much more dangerous than Tristan had suspected, and the broad influence of his deadly ideas was particularly troubling.

The Reichsführer came to a stop, and dozens of pairs of heels suddenly clicked in unison. Adolf Hitler had just stepped out onto the porch in front of them. Alfred Rosenberg stood at his side, wearing a dark suit that contrasted with his pale complexion. Large circles under his eyes made him look like a decadent Roman emperor, both cruel and secretive.

The Führer offered a perfunctory gesture in response to the sea of arms raised in salute. Despite the heat, he kept his hat on, low on his forehead, hiding most of his face. Only his moustache—which looked greyer than usual—was visible. Tristan wondered if it was really him. Rumours circulated throughout Germany, suggesting a doppelgänger had taken Hitler's place at public events. People said there were several of them and even suggested that each of the Reich's dignitaries had his own man waiting to step in for the Führer, should he ever be unable to govern. Tristan imagined Goebbels teaching his imposter to shout speeches and Göring showing his to march in step. He couldn't help but smile.

"*Mein Führer,*" announced Rosenberg. "Now that we're all here, please let me give you a tour of the Institute."

The first room, which featured a glass dome, was a large rotunda. Its walls were entirely covered in books. Employees stood in front of tables at regular intervals, notebooks in hand. Tristan felt like a guest in a grand hotel, surrounded by an army of bellboys and concierges ready to satisfy his every request.

"You'll find every book ever written on the Jewish question in this room, my friends," explained Rosenberg. "Philosophers, theologists, doctors, ethnologists, anthropologists—every brand of scientist and thinker who ever devoted pages to Judaism or the Jewish people. It's the only such collection in the world."

Hitler remained silent. Rosenberg's showmanship seemed to fall short of his expectations.

"Who has a question? Reichsführer, I'm sure you have one at the ready!" urged Rosenberg.

Himmler tensed. He hated being pushed into things. "My dear Dr. Rosenberg, I'm sure your library is exceptional, but the best specialists work at the Ahnenerbe, and I've always found men more reliable than books. At least I know I can count on their loyalty. Moreover, I imagine many of your authors are Jews themselves . . . Do you have any idea what percentage they represent?"

The naturally pale Rosenberg went scarlet. "To truly know your enemy, you have to—"

"Collect hundreds of copies of the Torah? Of course. And let's not forget the Masonic archives you've confiscated all over Europe. Jews and Freemasons—the two viruses that plague European civilization. If I weren't wearing an SS uniform, I'd worry about being contaminated . . ."

The Reichsführer's jibe was met with generalized laughter. He had gained the upper hand in his battle with Rosenberg.

"I'd like to see the paintings," said Hitler in a hoarse voice, restoring order to the room.

"Of course, *mein Führer*!" obeyed Rosenberg as he hurried over.

Tristan noticed the doctor wasn't wearing any socks. The man was terribly unkempt—a characteristic the Frenchman had noticed among several Nazi officials. Their positions seemed to be unsuited to their adventurous natures. The Reichsführer did not share this weakness. He had worn uniform after uniform with style and outgrown them one by one. The former chicken-farmer had been almost bankrupt when he'd met Hitler—still he had blossomed like a dark and poisonous rose in the stinking manure of Nazism.

"This room is home to the most beautiful pieces we retrieved from Jewish collections," explained Rosenberg. "Here, for instance, we have an incredible Rubens."

Hitler got so close to the painting he could've touched it but he remained impassive. He moved on to two smaller works that had piqued his interest. A flick of his chin made it clear he wanted more information.

"Those are some of Géricault's preparatory studies for *The Raft of the Medusa*," Rosenberg hastened to explain.

Everyone was trying to get closer now, to see what had captivated the Führer. When he finally caught a glimpse of the paintings, Tristan had to fight the urge to recoil. Dismembered arms stood out against a grey background. They had been dissected to reveal muscles, turned purple from lack of blood flow, and tangles of tendons.

"To ensure he did justice to the corpses in *The Medusa*, Géricault painted pieces of cadavers in anatomy classrooms. They say he even asked to keep a few limbs so that he could study the changes in colour during the various stages of decomposition," Rosenberg pursued enthusiastically, eyes glued to the Reichsführer.

It was common knowledge that Himmler had an unfortunate tendency to faint at the sight of blood. If he passed out, the ideologist would have his revenge.

Hitler broke away from the painting. "Rosenberg, you must redouble your efforts! I'll open the largest museum in the world in my hometown of Linz, to set a shining example of German ingenuity."

The crowd applauded. The power of the Führer's convictions and visionary genius remained untouched. He simply had the astounding ability to hoist any topic to new heights.

"*Mein Führer*, be assured that paintings and sculptures will arrive by the truckload from all over Europe, from the Atlantic to the Ural Mountains, to fill your brilliant museum and make it the eighth wonder of the world!"

"*Heil Hitler!*" shouted the attendees in a fit of enthusiasm. Rosenberg was bursting with pride. Hitler took his hand and shook it firmly.

"My dear Rosenberg, I'm certain that you are the man Germany needs for this project, just as you have been for many others," affirmed the Führer.

Before another round of salutes could begin, Hitler raised his hand. "But now, please continue the visit without me. I need to speak to the Reichsführer."

6

"An utter failure!" raged Lieutenant Colonel Sir Stewart Menzies as he paced his office staring at the floor in irritation. The portrait of Admiral Nelson hanging on the wall seemed to watch the scene impassively. "I've read Captain Fleming's bloody report. The operation in Venice was a total disaster."

Comfortably seated in a Chesterfield armchair and puffing on his pipe, Malorley observed the scene in silence. He'd been invited, or rather summoned, by the new head of MI6, to "go over" an operation from the previous year—Menzies' way of marking his territory, no doubt.

Malorley had made his way to MI6 headquarters—a perfectly unremarkable building on Broadway just behind St. James's Park—knowing full well that the meeting would be tempestuous. But his superiors at the SOE had instructed him to do his utmost to stay on good terms with MI6. This wasn't the first run-in between the two entities, and Churchill himself had ordered them to stop quarrelling.

Three secret intelligence services had helped organize the operation in Venice last year: naval intelligence, responsible for Mediterranean operations; MI6, which managed all foreign operations and had given the green light for the assassination of Hitler and Mussolini; and the SOE, whose goals and scope were less respectable. A copy of Fleming's report had been sent to all three commanders in chief.

"You not only blew the assassination attempts, you also

jeopardized our network in Venice. And we've lost contact with your agent 007!" continued Menzies.

"I'd rather you call him Marcas," replied Malorley. "He's more than a number. And as far as I know, the official goal of my operation was not to take out two dictators. That was tacked on as an afterthought, when I asked for approval to send my agents to Venice."

"That's right: the famous 'strategic object' you wanted to get off Hitler, as Fleming put it. I'd certainly love to hear more about that!"

"I'm afraid that information is classified. Only the Prime Minister has access to it, and that's all I can say."

"Everything that goes on in your bloody Department S is classified! I've heard about your little circus at Stonehenge with all those nutters. Unbelievable. Everyone knows the SOE is basically an asylum, but your department really takes the cake."

"It was part of a psychological propaganda operation," Malorley countered and left it at that. Menzies's scepticism came as no surprise, and telling him his department had been created to find magical swastikas destined to save the free world would be like explaining the benefits of chastity to a pimp. Hopefully the meeting wouldn't go on forever.

"Anything else?" he asked. "Or did you ask me here just to bury me in recriminations?"

Menzies settled into an armchair opposite Malorley.

"We're all in the same boat, so I'll be honest with you," he said in a more conciliatory tone. "I couldn't care less about your hunt for 'strategic objects'. But I am interested in your agent. Marcas."

"Ah, we're cutting to the chase at last."

"We don't have many agents in Germany—unlike the Russians, who control an established network of former communist sympathizers. And you are running the only man England ever managed to get close to Himmler, who happens to be the second most powerful man in Germany. Have you heard from him yet?"

"No, not a word since he left Venice. He may very well have been found out. You better believe me."

"Oh, knock it off, Commander. The word 'believe' is as useful to a secret agent as a pair of gloves to a double amputee. We are professional liars. We lie to our enemies, our families, and even our colleagues," said Menzies wearily.

Malorley slowly rose from his chair. It was time to conclude the meeting. "I really should be off now."

"I could get in touch with your superiors," threatened the MI6 man.

"Do as you please. The SOE is not beholden to you. We report directly to the Prime Minister."

"What if I had some vital information to share with you? Could *that* put you in a mood to share your agent?"

"Go on," said Malorley, intrigued.

Menzies opened a red file that was sitting on the corner of his desk. "This concerns you personally, Commander," he explained. "The Nazis plan to assassinate you."

Malorley scanned the document, which was printed on Government Code & Cypher School letterhead. He tried to appear calm when handing it back to Menzies. "Are you sure this information is authentic?"

"One hundred per cent. As you know, Bletchley Park intercepts and deciphers enemy communications. Your name appeared in this cable sent by Himmler's secretary to Ernst Kaltenbrunner, who is said to become the new head of the RSHA. He'll be replacing that butcher Heydrich who was assassinated in Prague last May. Apparently, the Reichsführer asked for further information about you."

"None of this implies they're looking to have me killed."

"Perhaps not, but they have correctly identified you as the head of Department S, the man in charge of the SOE's archaeological research."

"And it's Himmler himself who's taking an interest in me. What an honour. Thank you for the heads-up," said Malorley matter-of-factly.

"I'm not done yet," continued Menzies. "This message may mean that they've captured and tortured your agent. That would explain how they got your name."

Malorley thought for a second, then replied, "If that were the case, Marcas would have revealed everything, and Himmler wouldn't be asking his man for further information. I will be careful though."

"I'm sure you're right. But, if anything were ever to happen to you—a misfortune I would rather avoid, of course—who should I contact about your agent?"

"My superior at the SOE knows all about Marcas's activities. And I'll be sure to share your concerns."

"That would be very kind of you. Good day, Commander."

Malorley stepped outside the white stone building and made his way towards Laure, who was waiting on a bench. She had traded her military coat for a more flattering trench.

"Hello, Commander. Come across any fires in there?" she asked mischievously.

"I'm sorry?"

The young agent pointed at the MI6 building. "The sign at the door says *Minimax Fire Extinguisher Company*."

"British humour," conceded Malorley. "Let's just say I've tried to put out the fire with our friends at MI6, but I'm not sure I've succeeded."

"Are you all right? You've got a funny look on your face."

Malorley was staring up at the dark-grey sky. Laure had never seen him look so confused.

"You look like you've just seen a ghost," she continued. "Could it be Moira O'Connor's latest victim?"

"You never give up, do you?"

"I'm happy to go to war. To kill as many Nazi bastards as you like. But I can't be an accomplice to the murder of innocent people. How do you sleep at night?"

"I haven't had a good night's sleep in years. I have some good news for you, though. Before my meeting, I asked the head coroner, Sir Purchase, to examine the body and let me know about any similarities to the young woman Moira dumped in Tower Hamlets."

"I don't believe you," said Laure.

"Wrong answer. As punishment, you'll have to accompany me to the meeting."

"Is the prospect of visiting the mortuary what's got you looking so preoccupied?"

Malorley shook his head. "No. Menzies warned me that the Germans know who I am and most likely quite a bit about the rest of our department. I'm in their sights—and at the highest levels. Himmler himself is taking aim."

Laure paled. "Tristan must have been caught out!"

"I don't think so. I'm worried about something else entirely. I've been terribly foolish to think of myself as immortal. If something were to happen to me, no one would know how I became a part of this quest for the *Thule Borealis* and the swastikas," explained Malorley with a meaningful glance at Laure. He took a deep breath and continued. "Would you be willing to come to my place to discuss it? Certain secrets can't be kept forever."

"Well, that depends," said Laure with a smile. "You're not planning on showing me erotic prints, are you?"

"Don't worry. I'm too old for such nonsense."

"That's your first lie of the day. Men are never too old for that kind of nonsense."

Malorley gave her a stern look.

"I'm only joking," laughed Laure. "I trust you entirely. It's just that . . ."

"What is it?"

"You signed off on my leave, which is scheduled to begin later this evening. It's my first time off in three months."

"I'm too good to you," he replied mockingly.

Laure struggled to hide her lack of enthusiasm for her boss's invitation. "I need to relax and go out with my friends. It's my first night out in ages!"

"Is that worth missing the scoop on the true ties that bind me to Tristan?" Malorley asked, raising one eyebrow.

Half an hour later, they were sitting in the lounge of Malorley's flat, on the second floor of a Georgian townhouse in Kensington. Laure had never thought she would get a chance to study his home. It felt lonely. And very masculine. Clearly, no woman had set foot in it in a long time. The décor was minimalist and functional—the reflection of a life devoid of whimsy. The only painting on the walls depicted the Pyramid of Cheops. The only element that brought any life to the room was a large bookcase overflowing with books, which had been crammed in this way and that. Malorley came back from the kitchen with an uncorked bottle and two wine glasses.

"A Saint-Émilion 1933," marvelled Laure. "I didn't know you were a connoisseur."

"The best wine is to the French, just as common sense is to the English," he replied.

He made his way over to the painting and pushed it aside to reveal a small safe with three dials. The steel door opened with a click, and Malorley withdrew a green file tied shut with string. He leafed through a few pages and handed them to Laure.

"I reckon my uncomfortable meeting with Menzies has a silver lining now. If I die, the truth about the *Thule Borealis* will outlive me. And that story isn't in any SOE file. Please read these: they're from a friend's diary. A dear French friend who passed away long ago."

"Who?"

"Tristan's father. Paul Marcas."

Laure tried to remain impassive. "You knew his father?" she asked. "You really are full of surprises."

"We met over twenty years ago. During the Great War."

Laure settled on the sofa, her wine glass within reach, and began reading the first page of meticulous handwriting.

Journal of Lieutenant Paul Marcas
Chemin des Dames, May 1917

I've decided to start writing in this journal again, after ten days of silence. I'm still not certain I should conserve what I'm about to put on paper. Should it fall into the hands of my superiors, I could be accused of colluding with the enemy, as could my

English friend, Lieutenant Malorley. We would both end up in front of firing squads. All the military decorations in the world couldn't save me then. Fraternizing with the Germans is a crime punishable by death.

But what we've witnessed is so unbelievable that I feel compelled to keep a record of it for myself, provided God deems fit to save me from this abattoir. It all began nine days ago. My company had just attacked the tiny village of R, in the Aisne region, as part of the army's plan to sneak around enemy lines to the south and attack the Hindenburg Line. The villagers had long deserted their town, whose only claim to fame was having been bombed by the English, the French, and the Germans.

There was nothing but abandoned fallow fields as far as the eye could see. We ended up taking the village from the enemy in a battle that ended with close combat and bayonets. I can still see the piles of dead bodies. The thought makes me sick. They were everywhere. So many young men died to defend this miserable village they had never set foot in before—yet another mission designed by a high-ranking general sleeping soundly in his warm bed.

That day I was with Malorley, a lieutenant in the 8th Cavalry Brigade of the Royal Horse Guards, which had been helping us out for the past two months. We met in Nancy at a Franco-English Masonic lodge gathering. I suppose I should also keep quiet about our status as members of the brotherhood, since many in the army look unfavourably upon it.

It was a mild, sunny day. The enemy seemed to have vanished, as if by magic. Once our companies had regrouped, we were granted some time to rest. Malorley was terribly excited when he came to find me. One of his sergeants had just discovered an empty chateau nearby. He was convinced its cellar was full of fine bottles of wine and wanted to go and see for himself. Like many Englishmen, he worshipped only two saints: Saint-Émilion and Saint-Estèphe. I agreed to accompany him on his expedition once I'd given orders to set up camp.

Laure stopped reading for a moment to glance discreetly at her boss. She had a hard time imagining him drinking whenever the opportunity presented itself. She smiled and returned to the journal.

It took us over a quarter of an hour to reach the Château de R. The road had been battered by recent battles. Though there were no bodies in sight, a burnt-out German lorry sat mired in a rut. The thick, bitter smell of burnt tyres wafted through the air. The castle finally appeared as we cleared an eerie wood. It was an austere rectangular building with a central tower. As we drew closer, a strange feeling washed over me. An inexplicable uneasiness, particularly given all the terrible things I had seen in battle. As I write these lines, I have concluded it must have been due to my exhaustion, but at the time, I felt like something was haunting the place.

A hostile presence.

7

The Rosenberg Institute, Frankfurt
July 1942

Hitler and Himmler had been shown to a room that hadn't been readied for visits. Dozens of paintings sat against the walls, waiting to be hung up. The Reichsführer took hold of one and handed it to Hitler.

"A Cézanne from his final period," the Führer observed dryly. "Picasso looked to it for inspiration. This piece gave rise to the cubist aesthetic."

Himmler was always surprised by Hitler's breadth of artistic knowledge.

"Tell Rosenberg I don't want any of these modern paintings in my new museum. He can pass them on to Göring—he's not very discriminating."

Himmler nodded slowly in agreement, although he couldn't stop thinking about how much paintings like these would go for on the international market. Collectors—mostly Americans—would be willing to spend a fortune on them. As he placed the Cézanne back on the ground, an idea took hold. What if he managed to gather all these Impressionist paintings pillaged abroad and exchange them discreetly for foreign currencies in Switzerland? That would make him a tidy sum.

As he stirred the cup of tea he'd been brought, the Führer's features darkened. "How many works of art has Rosenberg retrieved in Europe so far?" he asked.

The Reichsführer whipped out his notebook. "According to my sources, nearly twenty thousand. In March alone, he requisitioned twenty-eight train cars to transport what he acquired in France."

"Private collections?"

"Yes. Most of them belonged to Jews who had fled the country. Rosenberg snatched them from under the nose of the Vichy government. Speaking of which, I regret to inform you that Marshal Göring has been skimming off the top. He has, of course, taken the best pieces."

Hitler wiggled his moustache. "Hermann should focus on the Luftwaffe! Three months ago, the English managed to bomb all our factories in the suburbs of Paris. Not a single German plane managed to stop them. Göring is only good for hunting, feasting, and stealing. He's incompetent—just like Rosenberg!"

Every time Hitler went on a tirade against one of the Reich's dignitaries, Himmler would defend them. He always played the devil's advocate to fuel the Führer's rage.

"Rosenberg is one of your oldest companions," countered the Reichsführer. "When you were jailed following the failed putsch in Munich in 1923 you asked him to run the party for you, remember?"

"One of my biggest mistakes. I never should have trusted that opportunist with anything in the first place. Rosenberg is Estonian. And as you know, you can't trust people from the Baltics."

"No doubt, *mein Führer*, but Rosenberg is privy to many secrets and—"

The head of the SS knew he had gone too far when Hitler's eyes darkened. "What secrets?" he asked. The Führer obviously feared Himmler might be alluding to his youthful indiscretions, to the time when he attended Thule Society meetings with Hess—a chapter that had been artfully omitted from his official biography. Since then, most of the members of the organization had found refuge in exile or in the grave.

"All I'm suggesting, *mein Führer*, is that we mustn't get ourselves into the same situation as with Hess."

Hitler's anger immediately vanished as the politician in him took over. Hess's capture by the English had been a national humiliation. He couldn't tolerate a new defection among his high-ranking officials. "What do you suggest we do?" he asked.

"Place a man we trust at his side. That way we'll know about every step Rosenberg takes."

"That's an excellent idea, Heinrich, as usual."

Hitler turned on his heels. The meeting was over.

While the rest of the visitors milled around, Tristan stayed in the rotunda. He'd taken a few dusty volumes from their shelves and examined them. According to their bookplates, most of them had come from collections in Germany, France, or Belgium. Quite a few private collections must have been pillaged to constitute such a large selection of works on Jewish culture and religion. Tristan wondered how Rosenberg's teams operated. Were they relying on a network of local informants, or did they resort to information amassed by the Reich's various intelligence services? Tristan knew he would find out soon enough, but wanted to confirm a hunch. He singled out one of the employees: a short man whose long, dark hair covered his forehead.

"Do you have a catalogue of the collections that make up the Institute's library?" he asked the man.

"Of course—they're organized by geographic origin. Are you interested in a particular country?"

"Germany, before 1940."

"We have three different lists for that period: one for institutional libraries like those of Masonic lodges or synagogues, another for private collections, and one for bookstores."

Tristan pursed his lips. "I'd like to see the collections taken from bookstores, please."

The man couldn't be older than thirty. He placed a long wooden box on the table and removed the lid with care—clearly, he was trying to make a good impression.

At his age, he should be holding a rifle somewhere near Kiev on the hunt for Russian resistance fighters, Tristan thought, and suddenly realized why he was so eager to please.

"The cards are organized by city. Which one interests you?"

"Berlin."

The young man sought out four cards—surprisingly few for the German capital. It was true that the bookselling profession had been quite dangerous for those who weren't peddling copies of *Mein Kampf* by the hundreds.

"Do you know when the books were taken?" asked the Frenchman.

"Of course. Everything's dated and recorded."

"Do you have anything from 1938?" That was the year Erika had mentioned.

"I have two collections taken from booksellers in Berlin that year. First Randolf Wolker on Potsdamer Strasse, who specialized in kabbalah. It seems he abandoned his shop with all of its stock still inside."

"Smart man," said Tristan.

"The other man specialized in rare books and manuscripts."

"Was he Jewish?"

"How did you know?" asked the surprised employee.

"A hunch."

"He was indeed Jewish. Otto Neumann was his name."

The sound of hurried footsteps made them both turn around. Himmler and his escort had just returned to the rotunda. The employee instinctively stood to attention.

"Do you have a copy of this card?" asked Tristan as a crowd of black uniforms invaded the room.

"No, why?"

"Because you're going to give it to me."

"But I can't. Dr. Rosenberg would be furious and—"

Tristan moved closer. "Something tells me Dr. Rosenberg won't be running this institute for much longer, and that the man standing behind me, all dressed in black with lovely round glasses, will soon be your new boss."

The employee stared past Tristan at Heinrich Himmler, a look of terror in his eyes. "Here's the card. Take it," he said hurriedly.

"Thank you. And this conversation never happened, of course. Did you know that the Reichsführer is fascinated by long hair like yours? I'm sure he'd love to see it float in the wind on the eastern front. What do you say?"

"Nothing. I won't ever say anything."

Tristan slipped the card into his jacket pocket. He had no intention of telling Himmler he had just found a new lead on the *Thule Borealis Kulten*.

8

The caramelized scent of tobacco wafted through Malorley's flat. The commander watched Laure with his pipe between his lips, back resting against the bookcase. Still sitting on the sofa, the young woman was devouring Paul Marcas's journal. It was as though she had jumped aboard H.G. Wells's time machine and joined the two young officers in their discovery of the mysterious castle.

> There was something uncanny about the castle, which had appeared as if out of thin air. Something unsettling. Malorley scarcely seemed to notice. The idea of getting his hands on a good bottle of wine had him so motivated he could have taken on an entire brigade of Germans to get to it. I didn't want to worry him. When we reached the front steps, I spotted a strange symbol carved into the stone lintel. It was a thick cross with perpendicular bars at the end of each branch. I knew I had seen it before, but couldn't remember where, or what it meant.
>
> Malorley came to my aid. "That's a swastika," he said, and added that he'd seen them during his time in India, in Madras and Delhi. According to him, it was the symbol of life. A good-luck charm often sold in open-air markets. But the cross I was looking at hardly seemed benevolent. On the contrary, it exuded something macabre, some indescribable hostility.
>
> The door to the castle was open and the smell of a wood fire filled the entrance hall—a reminder of its recent occupation by

the Germans. I went to inspect the upper floors while Malorley
made his way to the cellar. The bedrooms were bare. Not a single
piece of furniture, painting, tapestry, or decorative object. The
chateau had been thoroughly pillaged. As I walked back down
to the main hall, I heard Malorley calling me from the cellar. I
remember walking down the stairs, but I must have passed out
right after. When I awoke . . .

Laure looked up. The last page ended with this unfinished sentence.

The clock in Malorley's lounge chimed seven times.

"That's it? It just stops there in the cellar, when Tristan's father loses consciousness?" she asked disappointedly.

"The next part of the journal was irreparably damaged by the mud from the trenches. But let me fill you in—I was there, after all. Paul is right, I went down to the cellar first. I did indeed find a collection of fine vintages, but I also found a man. A man who immediately trained his Luger on me," explained Malorley.

"A German?" asked Laure.

"Yes, an officer hiding in the cellar. I lied and said my unit was stationed right outside the castle, leaving him no chance of escape. Then he heard Paul's voice and threatened to shoot me if I didn't ask him to come down. We stared stonily at the German, and he back at us. He was certain his unit was about to begin a counter-attack to take back the village. It was only a question of time. I told him our men would come looking for us before long. In the end, a cigarette case got us out of the impasse. And forever changed our fates."

Malorley paused to pour Laure another glass.

"The case bore an engraving on the inside of the lid. A compass and square, along with the name of Paul's Masonic lodge—La Chaîne d'Union in Paris. As he took a cigarette, the German smiled at us for the first time. He was also a brother, from the Die Drei Kronen lodge in Heidelberg. By the light of a makeshift torch made of a stick and some scraps of fabric, we exchanged the Masonic salute. After that, things got off on a much better foot."

"So, it's true what they say then? The ties of your brotherhood are stronger than national identities? Even at war? It's a bit like the communists, really," ventured Laure while running her hand through her hair.

"Certainly not! If Paul had heard you say such a thing, he'd have given you a proper thrashing. He would have given his life for France! I never said we were colluding with the enemy. It's much more complicated than that. Put it like this: when you capture a brother from the enemy camp, you afford him a minimum of courtesy. Anyhow, the German went on to properly introduce himself. Lieutenant Otto Neumann was, when not at war, a professor of comparative history at the University of Heidelberg. When we asked him why he was roaming the chateau's cellar, he explained that his unit had spent the past month building a secret munitions store beneath the castle. And he'd made a remarkable archaeological discovery. Once the French had taken back the village, he'd secretly returned to smuggle out the precious object."

Malorley pulled four more pages from the file and handed them to Laure. "This is the rest."

Just as the German officer began to relax, a huge explosion rang out above us. Stones began to tumble from the roof of the cellar. It seemed Neumann had been right about the German counter-attack. He gestured to us to follow him to an underground tunnel, whose entrance had been hidden behind a wooden panel. The explosions continued and the walls shuddered all around us. I feared we would be buried alive.

After what seemed like an endless walk, we got to a room that I will never forget. It looked like a chapel, with rows of pews on either side of a central aisle. False windows in the shape of ogival arches were carved into the walls and adorned with stained glass panes featuring the same swastika I had noticed at the entrance to the castle.

At the far end of the sanctuary stood a stone altar. By the light of the torch, I realized at once that no one came here to worship Christ. A tall, rectangular stone engraved with the swastika stood where one would have expected a crucifix. Neumann

called it alternately Hakenkreuz or gammadion and explained
that he had found the place quite by accident while digging
tunnels. He believed the chateau had been built in the Middle
Ages over an ancient temple, most likely by heretics given the
lack of Christian symbols.

I stepped closer to the altar and found an ancient book with
a cracked old cover sitting atop the stone. It bore the title Thule
Borealis Kulten.

While I felt an inexplicable aversion to the tome, Neumann's
eyes shone with excitement. I have no explanation for what
happened next. The temperature in the chapel dropped several
degrees and the darkness seemed to deepen. Even the glow of
the torch waned, as if covered by an invisible, frozen hand.
When I asked Malorley and the German if they shared these
sensations they said they did not. Malorley put them down to
sleep deprivation.

Neumann had begun reading parts of the Thule. It was
written in Latin and told the story of an ancient legend according
to which four sacred relics—four Hakenkreuze—had been
worshipped since before the dawn of time. They had preceded
Christ as well as the Roman Empire, and were said to have the
power to change the fate of mankind. Neumann wasn't sure since
his Latin was a bit rusty, but someone had decided to scatter
the relics to the four corners of the earth to keep them from
falling into the wrong hands. I don't remember everything, but
he also mentioned Templar Knights, kings with supernatural
powers, and secret brotherhoods.

While he spoke, we were all perfectly aware of how absurd
the situation was. Up above, the land had been tilled by steel
and irrigated with blood. Men were slaying each other as we
listened to an enemy officer, who almost killed us just hours ago,
tell fairy tales. The sounds of the battle picked up again and the
walls of the chapel began to shake in earnest. Neumann was hit
by a stone, and although the wound seemed superficial, he was
bleeding profusely. We had to get him outside. This is when I
came up with the idea of a pact—a pact sealed by our Masonic

brotherhood. No matter which side won the battle, we would make sure the others were taken care of if taken prisoner. Neumann was hardly in a position to negotiate and accepted. Malorley and I dragged him back the way we came. Just seconds after, the chapel vault collapsed in a cloud of dust.

But the Thule Borealis *had been rescued along with Neumann.*

Laure stopped reading. "A pact with a German in the middle of the war? That seems hard to believe. Were you trying to trick him?"

"Certainly not," replied Malorley. "A promise made between Freemasons is as strong as Toledo steel. At least among those who take their oath seriously."

Laure returned to the handwritten pages.

When we left the castle, the bombing still hadn't ceased. We were surrounded by nothing but ruins and devastation. All we could hear were explosions and the whistling of shells hurtling through the air. A gruesome symphony. The acrid smell stung our throats and eyes. My companions and I staggered towards the village, where we'd left our troops. But the path had disappeared and been replaced by smoking craters. It was as if earth and sky were doing their utmost to prevent us from escaping that cursed place, from taking the book.

Suddenly, shots rang out and a group of soldiers appeared ahead of us. The Germans were retreating in disorderly fashion. One of them caught sight of us and aimed his rifle in our direction.

Lieutenant Neumann drew his pistol and rammed it into my side. He ordered the soldier to put down his gun since we were his prisoners. The other German was young, maybe twenty-five years old, and pale faced. His uniform was much too big for him. The man explained that he was a courier and had come to relay a message from another unit. Three German companies had taken back the village, but a French counter-attack had sent them scrambling. "What's your name, Corporal?" asked

Neumann. The soldier mumbled terribly. I gathered his first name was Adolf, and his last name was something like Hidger or Higler. Strangely, I still remember the poor chap's dazed face as I write these lines. He's probably dead by now.

Laure looked up from the journal, gobsmacked. "Unbelievable. Was it really—"

"Yes. The young Adolf Hitler," Malorley replied dryly.

Shoreditch, London

With his back resting against a darkened brick wall, Constable Brian MacMurray eased a chunk of chocolate out of its wrapper, popped it into his mouth and let it melt slowly to enjoy it to the fullest. It was close to midnight, and his shift was almost over. He'd been wandering the streets of Shoreditch for the past four hours. The police officer glanced at his silver pocket-watch—a gift from his mother who'd been killed by a German bomb a year earlier. Nearly midnight. In just a quarter of an hour he could go back to the station, and then to bed.

As he was about to cross the street at the intersection of Montclare and Old Nichol, he heard a creaking noise about ten meters to his right. Like a rotten board about to give under a weight. He spun around to look but couldn't make out anything suspicious. Just darkness. Probably a stray cat or a couple of rats.

The taste of the chocolate lingered on his tongue, and he couldn't bring himself to go down the foul-smelling alleyway of wheelie bins overflowing with rubbish.

MacMurray sighed and continued in the direction of the Thames. If he was lucky, he might even finish this last round early by taking the shortcut past Dudley's. Just as he was about to cross to the other pavement, he heard something behind him. Shattered glass and stifled cries. Definitely not rats this time.

He whirled around and drew his night stick and torch. "Who's there?" he shouted.

He walked over to the wheelie bins. As he got close, his foot hit something soft. He trained his torch on the ground.

A body in a beige trench coat lay on its side amid the rubbish.

The officer assumed it was yet another drunkard—the city had been full of them since the beginning of the war. "Wake up, sir!" MacMurray said sternly.

He turned him over.

A woman's puffy face stared up at him. Her wide-open eyes were surrounded by dark circles, and her tongue hung from the corner of her mouth. A bloody swastika had been carved into her pale forehead, which was framed by a crown of blonde hair.

The constable stifled his urge to recoil and opened the coat. The body beneath was naked. Naked and covered in dried blood.

"Oh, bloody hell," mumbled MacMurray.

His heart seemed to beat right out of his chest and his hands no longer seemed to do his bidding as he fumbled to get his whistle. This wasn't the first time he'd found a body. He'd participated in more than his fair share of hunts for survivors amid the rubble after the Blitz. But this was different. This was a real . . . corpse. He couldn't think of any other word to describe it.

Suddenly, he heard wheels screeching. He had just enough time to jump aside before the huge wheelie bin next to him toppled over. MacMurray felt a sharp pain in his ribs and realized he'd just been kicked to the ground. Someone was swearing.

He dragged himself to his feet in time to see two silhouettes flee the scene. As they turned the corner and disappeared from view, MacMurray finally found his whistle. He blew it with all his might.

Standard procedure. He was to alert his colleagues before chasing after a criminal. If he could even manage it—the shock had left his heart reluctant and his blood seemed to have frozen in his veins. He tried to run, but he was already out of breath by the time he reached the corner. The two figures were nowhere to be seen. He bent over to recover, then blew his whistle again.

Overhead, someone opened their shutters. A woman wearing a head scarf leaned out of the window. "What's all this racket?"

"Police, madam. All is well," MacMurray replied confidently.

"Poppycock!" shouted the woman. "If all was well, you wouldn't have woken the whole bloody neighbourhood with your whistle."

As MacMurray turned back to the body, steps resounded at the entrance to the alleyway. He looked in their direction to find one of his colleagues running towards him.

"MacMurray, is that you? Are you all right?"

The young bobby recognized the gravelly voice of Sergeant Richard Nolan, who was patrolling the same sector that night. The tough, incorruptible Scotsman was always itching to teach the neighbourhood thugs a lesson.

"I'm fine, but I'm afraid this poor woman's not. It's just awful."

Nolan leaned over the mutilated woman.

"I'd bet my grandmother's pocketbook the Nazi killer's struck again. Bad luck for you. If you had caught him, you'd have earned a promotion to sergeant and a hefty bonus."

"I've never been particularly lucky," sighed MacMurray. "But this madman didn't act alone. There were two of them," he said as he let his torch wander across the body.

"That's a good lead," said Nolan as he went through the victim's pockets. "But I'm afraid Scotland Yard will have to do some legwork on this one. There's nothing to identify her."

It was then that MacMurray's torchlight fell across a few scattered cards. He gathered them up to find a ration card with the woman's photo. She was smiling mischievously, as though laughing at the lens.

"Not this time," corrected MacMurray. "This is . . . Mrs. Rosemary Benton."

PART TWO

9

The park that surrounded the Ahnenerbe headquarters was starting
to look like a summer camp. Thoughts of the war, which raged
on both fronts, seemed to be few and far between. Beneath the
warm blue sky, the young scientists who weren't away on research
trips enjoyed their lunch breaks on the grass, their laughter and
bouts of song echoing off the building's façade. On the second
floor, right above the main entrance, the director of the Ahnenerbe,
Wolfram Sievers, envied their mirth. Standing at the window that
looked out over the estate, he wished he could go back to that
happy time when he had devoted every waking moment to his
passion: prehistory. He missed his work even more given that he
was among the rare academic authorities to have achieved his
status without help from the establishment. Of course, this incredible feat was made possible, at least in part, by the Nazis' rise to
power. When Hitler became Chancellor in 1933, the regime quickly
purged the universities of potential dissidents. They forced shy
conservatives into early retirement, sacked progressives, and did
away with the few remaining Jews. This left many positions open,
and the Nazis hadn't been too picky about degrees when filling
them, as long as the candidates supported the Führer. As a result,
many intellectuals, seduced by the opportunity, had eagerly signed
a deal with the devil. As for Sievers, he had ended up at the head
of the Ahnenerbe. A dream of a position that had morphed into
a nightmare.

He turned his back on the window and returned to his desk.

Usually covered in books and articles, it was now bare except for two letters signed by the Reichsführer. The first named him director of the Military Scientific Research Institute, a newly created branch of the Ahnenerbe. It wasn't clear to Sievers what the real aim of this new entity would be, but he knew exactly what this nomination meant: Erika von Essling was about to return. The second, more straightforward letter ordered him to create a research group, so as to define the morphological and anatomical features of the Jewish race once and for all.

Sievers shook his head. He was a prehistorian, not a race specialist! Why were they asking him for results in fields he knew nothing about? And the whole Jewish question was starting to get out of hand. There were rumours, fuelled by stories soldiers told when they came back from the front. They said there were mass killings of Jews. The SS was exterminating entire populations in occupied territories. And now they were trying to saddle him with the terrible responsibility of determining who was Jewish. It would send him round the bend. But maybe there was a solution . . .

"Sir, your next appointment is here."

When Bruno Beger stepped inside, Sievers thought there must have been a casting mistake. The man was built like a Swedish lumberjack, with a Viking beard and eyes as bright as the Northern Lights. Beger belonged on SS recruitment posters. How had such a perfect Aryan specimen ended up hidden away at the Ahnenerbe instead of playing the hero in Goebbels' propaganda films?

"I hear you partook in the famous expedition to Tibet in 1939?" began Sievers.

"Yes, sir. In fact, that's where I developed a method that could be quite useful now."

The director of the Ahnenerbe was beginning to feel hopeful. Maybe this Beger, with his perfect German physique, would be able to help him satisfy Himmler.

"Tell me more about this method then," continued Sievers.

"I studied skull shape. I measured the skulls of many Tibetans. 367 to be precise. And I am certain that skull measurements directly correlate to race superiority and inferiority," explained Beger.

"Certain?"

"Absolutely. All of the Tibetans belonging to the subservient class had smaller skulls. We could easily apply this method to Jews."

Just as the director of the Ahnenerbe was about to ask another question, the door swung open and a familiar silhouette burst in.

"Frau von Essling," mumbled Sievers. "You're back then?"

"The Reichsführer asked me to return immediately to supervise the Ahnenerbe's new missions." She turned towards Beger, who had gone silent and stood stock still. "But I've interrupted you," she said matter-of-factly. "Please continue."

Sievers tried to regain control of the conversation. "We have an urgent mission to define the characteristics that will allow us to properly identify Jews."

Without a hint of surprise, Erika turned towards the anthropologist. "And what do you suggest?" she asked.

Despite his imposing frame, Beger felt his confidence fade. "Well, um, I thought we could measure . . . skulls."

Erika nearly burst into laughter at the ridiculous idea. "Where exactly do you plan to measure these skulls? In camps? Are you going to turn up at Dachau with your instruments, line up the prisoners and get to work?"

"Well, I actually haven't, um, worked on live subjects," mumbled Beger, trying to explain.

"I'm sorry, what was that?"

"I thought I might have access to a collection of skulls."

"A collection?" shouted von Essling, incredulous.

Sievers decided to attempt a final manoeuvre to de-escalate the situation. "Dr. Beger was simply offering an idea. The Ahnenerbe, which I represent, would never—"

"You no longer represent the Ahnenerbe," declared Erika. "I believe you have received word of your new position. Your transfer is effective immediately. As for you," she said, turning back to Beger, "get out of my office."

When the door shut behind the colossus, Erika noticed she was short of breath. She wasn't used to power play anymore. She sat down, turned the chair towards the window and gazed at the landscape. All she could see from her vantage point was treetops and blue sky—not a world where scientists stole skulls from the dead. The thought alone disgusted her. She imagined the head severed from the body, the skin being removed, the muscles hacked to pieces. Feeling sick, she closed her eyes and instinctively brought her hand to her temple, where the bullet had struck in Venice. She suddenly felt the burning sensation of the impact, the warm blood on her cheek. She heard the terrified screams around her, felt her legs give out. Her memory was coming back. She was sinking to the floor, and turned her head to look for help, but only saw figures running to and fro. She looked for Tristan, but he wasn't there.

IO

Laure was in such a state of disbelief that she had stopped reading. She was less preoccupied by the revelations regarding the discovery of the *Thule Borealis* and the ancient legend of the four sacred swastikas than by the identity of the young German corporal with whom Paul Marcas, Malorley, and Neumann had crossed paths.

Malorley pursed his thin lips and stared off into space. It was as if he too had gone back in time to the outskirts of the bombarded French village. He clenched his fist so tightly his knuckles went white, then pounded it into a bookshelf. "That's right, it was bloody Adolf Hitler! Within range of my pistol. If I had shot him, there never would have been a Führer or a Second World War. One bullet between the eyes and Nazism would have remained a small group of loud-mouthed fanatics. But who would have thought that the fearful, nondescript soldier we met that night would become the monster who now reigns over Europe?"

"The coincidence is unbelievable," mumbled Laure as she returned to the pages.

Neumann decided to make his way back to the German lines. As soon as the young corporal was gone, we hugged and promised to find each other after the war, regardless of which side won. Neumann took the book with him. I didn't dare say as much, but I was relieved to see him walk away with the sinister tome.

Laure flipped to the final page, and noticed that the handwriting was now completely different, with sloppy, halting letters, as if the author's hand had been trembling.

"I attached what was left of his journal," explained Malorley, his voice shaky. "Two months later, he was gassed in a trench at the Somme and was never the same again."

10 June

The doctors say there's no hope. I'm writing these last few lines before making my way to Heaven or the eternal Orient. I've never really been able to choose between the two options that offer themselves to Freemasons. I leave behind my beloved wife Emilie and a son. A ten-year-old son. Tristan.

16 June

I won't live to see the end of this blasted war, but it seems, thank God, that the Germans are struggling. Malorley has promised to watch over my family. I can move on to the next life with one less worry. I've been having strange dreams. Terrifying dreams.

18 June

Last night's dream was the worst so far: I saw the young German corporal with the crazy eyes we met in R. He was riding a dragon through a hurricane of flames. There were thousands of others like him, everywhere. The army of the apocalypse. I could see hills, no, mountains of skulls. Screaming skulls! Everywhere. Oh God, I'm losing my mind.

21 June

Nightmare. The chateau where we found the book . . . Thule. I saw swastikas spinning in the night. I . . . I'm afraid. Find Neumann. Destroy the relics. Before they kill us all . . .

The page ended with these disjointed sentences. Laure handed the journal back to Malorley.

"Paul died on the summer solstice. A cruel irony for a

Freemason: for us, it's Saint John's Day, when the sun reaches its zenith and begins its long descent towards the winter solstice, the day of its rebirth," explained the Englishman.

Laure looked up at Malorley. "So, you were best friends with Tristan's father. That makes sense. And you became his guardian after the war?"

"I wish. Things didn't quite go to plan. After Paul's funeral, I got in touch with his widow. Emilie Marcas was a strong and beautiful woman, but she made her decisions based on her own best interests. During the war, she had had an affair with a powerful politician. When I went to see them at their home in a leafy Parisian suburb, to give Emilie some of Paul's personal effects, she reluctantly invited me in—I was clearly not welcome. It wasn't until later that I reconnected with Tristan."

"What was Tristan like back then?" Laure asked eagerly.

"He was a carefree little boy. Rather shy. But impressed by my uniform. He asked me a slew of questions about his father. That was the first time we ever met."

"How did you end up hiring him as an agent?"

"I don't want to talk about that. At least not right now," scolded Malorley. "Focus on the story of the *Thule Borealis*. That's what's important."

"All right," conceded Laure, "just for the time being. But I won't forget. Tristan is even more intriguing now that I know all this. So, the *Thule* . . . "

"After the war, I had more important things to do than finding a German officer who was passionate about esotericism and a dusty old book. Many years went by, and the story of the magical swastikas took its place in my memory between *Alice in Wonderland* and Grimms' *Fairy Tales*. I joined military intelligence and spent several years traipsing around the Middle East, Syria and Egypt. Then, in September 1929, the *Thule Borealis* made its way back into my life. I—"

The lounge suddenly went dark, lit only by the streetlights below.

"Don't move, Laure!" Malorley whispered urgently.

Laure could hear the anxiety in his voice. He tiptoed over to the secretary desk, took out a Browning, and loaded it. He took cover next to the window, then opened the curtains to study the street outside. Moments later, the light came back on, as if by magic.

"Another damn fuse," he mumbled as he set the gun down on the table.

"Are you okay, Commander?" Laure asked worriedly.

Malorley shrugged. "I'm a little overworked, that's all. Let me finish my story. I had been sent to the Ruhr Valley to oversee the legislative elections to the Reichstag. The Foreign Office wanted detailed information on the mood among the population. The country had become a powder keg. The 1929 crash had left millions of Germans jobless, and the Reichsmark was worthless—a loaf of bread cost a million marks. The population resented the Allies, and the French in particular. The far-right nationalist parties were milking the sentiment. Especially a certain National Socialist German Workers' Party that was rapidly gaining traction. You can imagine my surprise when I attended one of their rallies in Cologne and caught sight of their leader."

"The short corporal from R."

"I couldn't believe it. A frail soldier had become the authoritarian leader of all these fanatics. And then there was the party's symbol! A swastika identical to the ones we had seen at the chateau. A *Hakenkreuz*. It was time to find Neumann. I remembered that he was a professor at the University of Heidelberg. From there, it wasn't too difficult to track him down. The secretary gave me his address."

"How did your reunion with the chivalrous German go, twelve years after the fact?" teased Laure.

"I knocked," continued Malorley, ignoring Laure's ironic tone. "His house was actually located on the university grounds. He didn't recognize me right away, so I offered him a Morland, holding out Paul's cigarette case with the Masonic seal. Neumann could hardly believe his eyes. We fell into each other's arms, and he invited me to stay for dinner with his family. Otto had been named the Chair of Comparative History thanks to his work on the High Middle Ages, which had been hailed as a reference in the field. I had a wonderful time that evening. To think that we might as easily have killed each other, just because we were from different countries!"

"How very touching," said Laure sarcastically. "Had he fallen for the leader of the Great Reich?"

"Not exactly. Otto was half Jewish—a *Mischling*, as the Germans say. And a Freemason to boot. Enough to disgust even the tamest Nazi. For him, Goethe, Novalis, and Rilke were the real lights of Germany. He was certain that Hitler was just a passing anomaly."

"Well, now we know for sure that your friend was no psychic. You got me *this* close to liking a German, Commander. Hats off!"

Malorley continued to ignore her digs. "At the end of the meal, we got to talking about the *Thule Borealis*. I showed him Paul's journal. I'll never forget the terror in his eyes when he looked up from the pages. He also remembered meeting Hitler during the war. I asked him if he'd managed to translate all of the book. 'The *Thule* opens the doors to heaven or hell,' he said solemnly. 'The problem is that one man's heaven is another man's hell.' He took me into his office and pulled the volume off its shelf, where it was nestled among his collection of atlases. 'No thief would ever steal an atlas!' he laughed. The bright-red leather cover was not as I remembered it. A bookbinder had given it a new lease of life."

The light in the lounge flickered again, along with those in the street. Malorley was about to reach for his pistol but thought better of it.

"Neumann proceeded to sum up what he had learned from the manuscript and other sources. In short, the *Thule* revealed the existence of an ancient civilization—older than Egypt or Sumer. A civilization that disappeared in a cataclysm thousands of years ago, but not without leaving traces like the swastikas throughout the globe. According to the book, its priests and engineers had harnessed a power, an unbelievable energy. An energy contained in the relics—the power of a thousand black suns capable of destroying humanity."

"Like Marie Curie's radioactivity?" asked Laure.

"Yes and no. Otto thought the text might also be referring to spiritual energy, to a force that could impact people's psyches. The manuscript gave hints as to the locations of the four relics, which had to be reunited to activate their unbridled power. When I asked him if he planned to try to find them or write a paper on the *Thule*, his features darkened. He felt the times were too uncertain and feared violent confrontations between nationalist extremists and communists. The Weimar Republic was too fragile for him to reveal the existence of the book. I argued that no political party would take the legend seriously. That's when he told me more about the real nature of Nazism."

"He was more lucid than most, then."

"Neumann considered the movement to be radically different from other parties. Many of its leaders believed in mysticism and considered the German race to be superior to others. I was stupefied to learn the party's irrational and destructive convictions. Neumann told me about a secret esoteric society named 'the Thule'—after the book—that had helped found the party and contributed to Hitler's rise to power. They saw him as their new messiah, and their doctrine left no doubt that they knew about the *Thule Borealis.*"

"What happened next?" asked Laure.

"He made me swear to keep quiet about the book, even though he could tell I wasn't entirely convinced it even mattered. I loved fairy tales as a child, but grew out of them in my early teens. I'm a man of reason. When I left, I invited him to come see me sometime soon in England. He accepted and asked me for a favour: if things grew too dire in Germany, he wanted me to take the book, to keep it safe."

"And that's what happened in 1938, when you went to him in the Kristallnacht," concluded Laure.

"Yes. When the Nazis came to power, Otto lost his professorship and the family moved to Berlin. He became a bookseller, with a shop devoted to rare volumes. But he knew his life was in danger. The SS was looking for the book. I managed to get his wife and daughter out of Germany, but I was too late to save my friend. Just a few hours too late. Colonel Weistort had murdered Neumann and stolen the *Thule Borealis*."

Suddenly, the phone rang. Malorley picked up, exchanged a few words with the person on the other end of the line, then hung up.

"We have to go," he said. "Get your things."

"But your story!" objected Laure. "You haven't finished about Tristan."

"Another day. I've told you quite a bit already. I know it's late, but they're expecting us at the mortuary."

I I

Dr. Rosenberg was discreet when it came to important business. Though the official offices of his organization were located near the Garnier opera house, the Nazi leader had also set up a more covert facility on the left bank of the Seine.

After a long stroll through the narrow streets surrounding the Pantheon, Tristan made his way there. The entrance to the courtyard was carefully hidden behind a row of trees. Inside, a gravel path led the Frenchman to a former orangery—probably the vestiges of a private mansion destroyed during the Revolution. The path wound between huge laurel bushes, then stopped at the steps to the building, where a man in a dark suit was smoking a cigarette. Tristan instantly recognized Alfred Rosenberg. Despite the bright sunshine, his complexion remained disturbingly pale.

"Herr Marcas, I see you've found our hideout. I suppose it wasn't too difficult given the time you spent in Paris during your studies. The Latin Quarter must have few secrets for you," said the Nazi dignitary.

Tristan nodded. Hitler's old friend had done his homework. "Lovely place you've got here," he replied.

"Thank you," said Rosenberg as he gestured to him to enter through the French doors that looked out over the garden. In the 18th century, the large windows had provided light and warmth for exotic plants in the winter months. A lost world.

"So, you've come to help us? Maybe I should send Himmler a piece to thank him," said the ideologue. "You must know what he likes. Does he prefer paintings or sculptures? Italian Renaissance or Spanish Golden Age?"

"I'm afraid I don't know the Reichsführer well enough to answer. Just don't send him a still life."

"Ah, that subtle French humour. But tell me, are you really as knowledgeable about art as they say? I'd like to give you a little test," announced Rosenberg, pointing at a nearby painting.

Tristan recognized a Corot. Two monks were contemplating a bucolic scene framed by tall cypresses. The red dome of a church emerged from a tangle of roofs, which shone brightly in the relentless summer sun.

"Jean-Baptiste-Camille Corot. His Italian period. A view of Florence from the Boboli Gardens," said Tristan matter-of-factly.

"I see why the Reichsführer hired you," Rosenberg said appreciatively.

"And I see why he sent me to you," replied the Frenchman.

"I'm afraid your humour escapes me this time, Herr Marcas," said the Nazi.

"The original of this painting is located in the United States. And since I doubt you pillaged the Metropolitan Museum of Art in New York, this must be a copy."

Rosenberg angrily stomped his feet on the white marble floor. "My men bought it from a French fence. He assured them he'd got it from a Jewish family fleeing Paris."

"If I were you, I'd change suppliers. Corot paintings are the most widely copied in the history of art. It's estimated that more than half of the works that bear his signature were not painted in his studio."

Rosenberg stared at the painting in horror, as if he'd just woken from a nightmare. What would have happened if they had discovered the mistake as they were hanging it in Hitler's museum? He didn't dare imagine. This Frenchman had just saved him from certain disaster.

"They say you're also a remarkable sleuth," said Rosenberg, changing the subject. "Apparently you worked wonders in Spain."

"It all depends on what I'm looking for," replied Tristan.

"I'd like you to find a discreet collector for me. A man who disappeared just before we searched his flat on Rue de Varenne, where we found nothing."

Tristan almost smiled. During the war in Spain, he'd met several people who were truly gifted at finding things. Men who could pinpoint the only remaining food in a ravaged farm or uncover hidden gems in a palace ransacked by hordes of drunk soldiers. He had watched and learned a lot.

"You must not have looked properly then," ventured the Frenchman.

"Do you really think you can do better?" asked Rosenberg, surprised by his certainty.

"That depends on several factors. Does your collector have any family? Children, for example?"

"He has a son hiding somewhere in Paris. We've yet to get our hands on him."

Tristan looked out at the garden. The sky he glimpsed between the trees was an even deeper blue now. He needed another walk through the city.

"In that case, you're in luck," said Tristan, abandoning his daydream.

"I don't understand," replied the Nazi as he lit another cigarette.

"Imagine you're an art collector on the run from the Nazis. You know that if you've hidden something somewhere, there's almost no chance you'll ever see it again. But you have a son. So you play the only card you have left and take a bet on the future. You leave him a sign. One that he alone will understand."

"But where? In the flat?"

"Yes, because that's where his son will go first. He'll expect his father to have left some sort of clue."

Rosenberg inhaled deeply. He was fascinated by logic, despite his tendency to defy it in his fanatical attacks on the Jews. But the suggestion alone, though convincing, wasn't enough. He had to be sure. "Let's go there now," he said. "I need a few minutes to issue some orders first, but I want to see you at work."

The Nazi made his way towards a spiral staircase and disappeared from sight. Tristan remained alone in the orangery. Though he wasn't Rosenberg's biggest fan, he felt safer here by his side than at Ahnenerbe headquarters in Berlin. If Erika's memory returned or the SS became overly interested in him, he would at least have a shot at escape here.

"Herr Marcas, a car is waiting for us."

Rosenberg had returned within minutes and Tristan had no more time to think about his future. They crossed the courtyard and climbed into the back seat of a vehicle, which got under way immediately. The Frenchman couldn't help but smile at his recklessness. What if he didn't find anything? All he could do was hope that this collector, about whom he knew next to nothing, really had felt a twinge of paternal guilt before vanishing into thin air.

Rue de Varenne, Paris

Tristan had never seen Paris so empty. At the intersection of Rue Soufflot and Boulevard Saint-Michel, where traffic was usually bustling, only a few cars hurried past on their way to unknown destinations. Tristan rolled down the window as they turned onto Rue de Vaugirard. The silence was startling. He could hear the birds chirping in the thickets at Luxembourg Gardens, but the pavements were deserted. The occasional passer-by hugged the walls, seemingly afraid of their own shadow. He couldn't believe his eyes—his city, his capital, was occupied, humiliated, and disfigured. At Place Saint-Sulpice, soldiers on leave were having their picture taken in front of the fountain. Paris was no more. A great, grey wave had eaten away at everything. As they passed Rue du Four, he noticed the signs erected by the occupants. Their gothic letters were proof that the City of Lights had become a city of darkness—the darkness Nazism was spreading across Europe.

"We're nearly there," announced Rosenberg. "I've alerted my men, so they'll be there as well."

"How did you recruit your team?" asked Tristan. "Are they archival researchers? University professors?"

The ideologue chuckled heartily. Tristan noticed that his teeth were so tiny they barely emerged from his gums.

"No," he said between laughs. "They're not exactly intellectuals. You'll see for yourself shortly."

The collector's building was located across the street from the entrance to the Rodin Museum. They crossed a run-down court-yard before climbing a flight of heavily worn stairs, and even the flat's welcome mat had been pummelled by so many German boots it was completely shapeless. The entire building was like a metaphor for France itself: beaten and broken. A man, whom Tristan imme-diately identified as a French collaborator, was standing on the landing.

"Herr Marcas, please let me introduce Marcel Pilorges, also known as 'The Paw'," said Rosenberg.

Tristan understood why when he shook the man's hand. His bones nearly crumbled in the vice-like grip.

"Our friend Marcel is a former boxer. A rather useful skill in discussions with the owners of fine art. As you know, they are . . . a fairly secretive lot."

"And I suppose that Marcel's presence tends to loosen their tongue?" asked Tristan with a smirk.

"Nothing gets by you, Herr Marcas. But let's focus on the flat."

They walked down a short corridor to a spacious lounge with floor-length windows that looked out over Rue de Varenne. Tristan immediately noticed an important detail. The walls, which were covered in burgundy fabric, were perfectly uniform, with no faded areas. When paintings had been hanging on the walls for years, they always left behind a square or rectangle of the brighter, ori-ginal colour of the wall, untouched by the light. Not a single painting had ever been hung on these walls. He made his way to the fireplace. The marble mantel was perfectly pristine, without a trace of a statuette that might have been placed there. Tristan realized he was being played.

"Since we're not looking for paintings or sculptures, why don't you tell me what it is you really want me to find for you?" he ventured smugly.

Rosenberg was stupefied. "How did you know?"

"You said it yourself. I'm a rather good sleuth. But if you want me to be of use, you'll need to answer my questions. Whose home is this?"

"Not a collector's, that much you've guessed," said Rosenberg as he invited Tristan to sit down on the sofa. "The apartment owner is named Vassili Gurdjieff. Until last week, he taught Russian at the private girls' school nearby. As you might imagine, he didn't have many students."

This time, Tristan was confused. Why would Rosenberg be interested in someone so insignificant?

"The building manager informed on him. She didn't understand how a teacher could afford a flat like this one. And she obviously thought he must be Jewish."

"Of course!"

"Except that the French authorities are overrun with real Jews, so they don't have time for fake ones. In short, his file ended up in our hands, and we asked ourselves the same question as the building manager: where did this nobody get the funds to pay for a big flat in one of the nicest neighbourhoods in Paris?"

Rosenberg handed a photograph to Tristan. It showed a man in a straw boater and white shoes helping a frail child in a sailor's outfit climb onto a bicycle. "This picture was taken in the summer of 1914," explained the Nazi. "The man is Vassili Gurdjieff."

"And the child?" asked Tristan, intrigued.

"Let me introduce you to Alexei Romanov, the heir to the Russian throne."

12

East Ham Mortuary, London
July 1942

The first body was lying on a metal table with a black plastic tarpaulin pulled up over the chest. Rosemary Benton's ivory face appeared above it. She looked ten years younger than when alive—even her undereye circles had gone white. On the neighbouring table lay another woman. She was older, around sixty, with brown hair. Her naked body was fully exposed. Besides their simultaneous presence in East Ham mortuary, the bodies had one thing in common: the swastikas carved into their foreheads.

Laure and Malorley remained at a respectful distance from the head coroner, who bent intently over Rosemary Benton. The doctor regularly scribbled notes on a pile of papers he had placed on the victim's stomach. He seemed troubled.

"To sum things up, Commander Malorley," he began, "I have examined both these bodies as you asked, and studied the file on the woman found in Tower Hamlets cemetery six months ago." Sir Bentley Purchase removed his thin-rimmed glasses, and forcefully blew his nose. The coroner was a portly man in his fifties with a face that would be jovial were it not for his faded eyes. "Catching a cold in a mortuary seems unfair, don't you think?" he continued wryly.

"And what have you concluded?" asked Malorley. "Were all three killed by the same person?"

"These two here definitely fell victim to the same murderer. As for the older case, I can't be certain. My colleague's report is too succinct, and the body has since been cremated."

"What do you think the chances are then?" pressed Malorley.

"They all feature the same symbol on their foreheads. The photograph taken of the body found at Tower Hamlets proves as much. But these two women could well have fallen victim to a copycat. Especially since the press published pictures at the time of the first murder. Between us, carving a swastika into a forehead isn't as complicated as eviscerating a prostitute à la Jack the Ripper." Proud of his joke, the coroner laughed heartily. When Laure and Malorley remained silent, Sir Purchase cleared his throat and grew serious again. "To answer your question, I'd say there's only a thirty per cent chance that the first woman was killed by the same person. The shape of the gashes on the forehead is different. That's what I told the detectives from Scotland Yard who were here yesterday."

He walked over to the sink, turned on the tap, and rubbed his hands with a large bar of brown soap. "I'm sorry I couldn't be more helpful," he said. "I'll take you back up."

Laure thanked God for answering her prayers. Another minute in the mortuary and she would have been sick. The smell—a combination of rotting flesh and pungent disinfectant—was unbearable. They left the main room and took a lift to the ground floor.

"It appears the young lady hasn't enjoyed my hospitality," said the coroner with a chuckle.

"Does anyone?" asked Malorley dubiously.

"You don't know how lucky you are. Imagine what it was like during the Blitz! There were bodies everywhere. Men, women, and children piled up in every room. Worse than rugby finals at Twickenham! We had to requisition cold rooms in abattoirs to store them all. Luckily, things have calmed down since," explained Sir Purchase.

The coroner escorted them to the exit, where he saw them off with a friendly wave. "My greetings to the Prime Minister. I used to know him quite well—we were members of the same cigar club at one point."

"I will," lied Malorley. He waited for Purchase to disappear, then turned to Laure. "See, he doesn't believe it was the same killer. Does that make you feel better?"

It started to drizzle, and the young agent turned her face up towards the dark-grey sky, letting the droplets of rain splash on her face, as if to rinse off the smell from the mortuary. She'd learned to appreciate rain here in London. "Hardly," she replied. "For all I know, you asked him to put on a little show for me."

"You're being paranoid," said Malorley.

"Maybe, but whose fault is that?" she asked, indignantly. "My SOE training taught me not to trust anyone."

"You're so stubborn. But no matter, we'll soon know for sure. Crowley is scheduled to visit Moira O'Connor to give her the footage from Operation Witchfall. He'll ask her about the murders, too."

"And you really think she'll open her mouth?"

"Our friend the mage can be persuasive. Even so, I'd like you to go with him, to make sure he gets out alive."

Laure shook her head. "Sir, I'm supposed to be meeting some friends in half an hour. I'm on leave. Can't you send someone else?"

"Crowley doesn't trust many people. He likes you. It'll only take a few hours tops. He said he'd attend an opening at a gallery near Leicester Square and then head over to the Hellfire."

"So?"

"Join him for his little outing and accompany him to the club—but don't go in. There's a phone booth on the corner that provides a perfect vantage point. Call me when you see him come out. You'll have plenty of time to meet up with your friends afterwards."

"Can I at least expense the cab ride?" asked the young agent hopefully.

"Certainly not," replied her boss.

"You really are no fun at all."

Battersea, London

The towering chimneys of Battersea Power Station spewed dark, poisonous smoke into the sky around the clock. Some days, the clouds were so full of noxious gasses that they hid the sun for miles in all directions. Locals cursed those responsible for the industrial monster's location on this portion of the riverbank.

Sitting nearby, behind the wheel of a greengrocer's lorry, Conrad couldn't help but marvel at it. "The biggest coal-based power plant in the world. What a magnificent creation!" he enthused.

"I think it's a blot on the landscape—a tangle of brick and metal that coughs poison into the air. You'll never convince me," his wife countered.

"Well, we can't always agree. Like the Führer, I believe Aryan civilization must push the limits of what is possible—in architecture, science, art, and war. The ultimate accomplishment of superior western society is superior technology. You, on the other hand, are more like Himmler. He appreciates progress but would rather Aryans returned to their roots as famers. To reconnect with the land of our ancestors, he'd have us learn how to live with the cycle of the seasons, far from polluted cities."

The young woman smoothed her hair in the rear-view mirror. "A wise man. I should have been born in Germany rather than in this corrupt and conservative country. I—"

She stopped short. She'd just caught sight of a man in his forties heading their way. Alone in the deserted street, he walked with his cap pulled down low over his face and a cigarette hanging from the corner of his lips. A leather satchel hung from his shoulder.

"What about him, Conrad?"

The German leaned his head out to get a better look. "I'd rather not have to kill him. He looks like a good Aryan. Plus, he's a worker, and I have the utmost respect for the proletariat. The same can't be said of bankers and businessmen . . ."

"English workers are idiots," Susan replied dryly. "Sir Mosley tried to get them involved with his Blackshirts, but the imbeciles voted overwhelmingly for the Labour party! And if you wanted a banker, we're really not in the right neighbourhood. They all work in the City, on the other side of the river."

"Your Mosley's a clown. He never had the charisma of the Führer or even Mussolini."

"That's enough, Conrad. We don't have time to bicker about

politics. We need a new body for tonight, and we've been hanging around this rotten place for hours now. Get ready."

Susan opened the door and looked around. Not a soul to be seen. She waved at the man. "Help! Please, help!"

The chap hurried over. "What's going on?" he asked, eyeing her décolletage.

"I don't know! It's my boyfriend. One moment he was driving and the next he passed out. I don't know what to do."

Conrad lay sprawled across the seat, groaning as if he'd been run over by a tank. The stranger climbed onto the running board to get a closer look. "I'm no doctor," he said, "but he doesn't look well. You'd better take him to hospital. I—"

He collapsed before he could finish his sentence. Susan stood over him, a club in hand. Conrad sat up quickly, pulled a syringe out of the glovebox and plunged it into the man's neck.

In under two minutes, they had heaved the worker's body over the top of the seats. The lorry took off with a squeal.

"It's a real shame. The bloke seems to have good genes," mumbled Conrad. "Dolichocephalic head, grey eyes . . . Such a waste."

"You must be joking! He reeked of alcohol! Probably a commie," argued Susan.

She sat back and placed her feet up on the dashboard. "Conrad, how long is this mission supposed to last?" she asked with a sigh. "I'm not sure I can keep doing this. I signed up for an ideal. Killing enemies of the Reich is one thing, but ordinary people? Where's the glory in that?"

"We're at war, Susan. You're a soldier and our victims are enemies fallen in battle."

"That's what you always say. But yesterday, with that Rosemary Benton, something about it all bothered me. She was a good Englishwoman. She reminded me of my aunt. You have a soft spot for proletarians; mine is for motherly figures . . ."

"You can't waver now. Our mission is above morality," said Conrad. "But it won't be much longer, my love."

She rested her head on his shoulder and caressed his forearm.

"Don't forget your promise," she exclaimed as she perked up. "Germany! A house in Munich with a big garden and a dog. I'm eager to make beautiful children with you and prepare delicious meals when you come home on leave."

"I'm sure you'll be a wonderful mother, *mein Liebling*. I'll make your dreams come true, I promise."

13

Rue de Varenne, Paris

Tristan studied the photograph in his hands, which had been taken against the backdrop of a Haussmannian courtyard. The dark-haired child on the bicycle looked about ten years old. His frailness was striking, but even more fascinating was the expression of terror on his face. The adult standing next to him offered attentive support as though afraid the child might collapse.

"Vassili Gurdjieff was the tsarevich's private tutor," explained Rosenberg.

"So the child ended up in France," observed Tristan.

"That's correct. Anyway—when the communists came to power, his father Nicholas II was detained along with his entire family and put under house arrest. The Soviet secret police watched them day and night. As you can see, Alexei was sickly. A haemophiliac. The slightest injury, any bleeding at all, could have been fatal. No one expected him to live past the age of twenty. That's why the communists let his tutor stay with him. They probably wanted to keep him alive to use as a bargaining piece, should the tide turn against them."

Tristan couldn't tear his gaze from the child, whose eyes appeared as dark as a bottomless well. His illness was a death sentence, and as if that wasn't enough, the poor boy had also become a pawn in a political power struggle. Being born to the throne had brought him nothing but misfortune.

"What happened to him?" asked Tristan.

"On the night of 17 July 1917, the authorities ordered the assassination of the imperial family. The communists—Lenin chief among them—feared the tsar would be rescued by the White army. Alexei was slaughtered with the rest of them," said Rosenberg.

"Given his condition, his death must have been swift at least," suggested the Frenchman. "He can't have suffered for long."

Rosenberg shook his head. "Quite to the contrary, I'm afraid. He survived the first round. One of the soldiers emptied his clip trying to kill him, but the boy was still breathing. It took another two bullets to the head to end it."

"And what about his tutor?"

"He wasn't among the eleven victims."

Tristan was starting to see why the Nazis were interested in this twenty-five-year-old drama. "He must have escaped before that night, then," he said. "The Bolsheviks wouldn't have wanted any witnesses."

Rosenberg nodded, then added, "There are two possibilities. Either Gurdjieff suspected the situation would end badly and fled to save his skin. The tsar's troops were only a few kilometers away. He could have reached them—"

"Or," Tristan interrupted, "he fled on the tsar's orders and took something with him. That's what you suspect. That's why you want me to find him."

Marcel had just entered the room. He walked over to the wall between the fireplace and the window, placed his ear flat against it and began moving slowly and systematically across the surface. To no avail—there was no secret cache behind it.

"Marcel is a former legionnaire," explained the Nazi. "He served in North Africa. He's successfully conducted a number of difficult searches, so this defeat has wounded his pride."

Tristan merely shrugged. Only Nazis said such things. Their need for superiority was so intense they couldn't stand the slightest failure. "The real question is: what are you looking for?" he asked.

Rosenberg didn't answer. Tristan wondered if he might be on the hunt for incriminating documents that would compromise the Soviets' budding relationship with the United States. A scandal might stem the flow of American aid and weapons to Russia. And Goebbels would ensure the story reached papers worldwide.

What if Himmler was better informed than he let on, and had sent him to Paris to get his hands on the documents first? Since Rosenberg still hadn't spoken, Tristan decided to go on the offensive.

"Whatever you're looking for, Gurdjieff must have already sold part of it to pay for this flat," Tristan said confidently.

The Nazi snapped his fingers. Marcel appeared carrying a leather folder embossed with an eagle whose talons were wrapped around a swastika. Rosenberg opened it. "We found this," he said. Tristan watched as he placed a tissue on the table. "Unfold it," he ordered.

Tristan unveiled a huge, extraordinarily bright, pink pearl set into a gold ring.

Rosenberg handed him a magnifying glass. "Read the inscription inside the band."

The Frenchman immediately recognized the Cyrillic characters.

"It's the engagement ring Nicholas II of Russia gave his future wife. It was the empress's favourite piece of jewellery. We found it in the back room of a high-end jeweller in Place Vendôme. Thanks to Marcel's powers of persuasion, the owner happily gave up Vassili's name. That's how we found this place."

"So you're convinced he fled Russia with the imperial family's jewels?" asked Tristan.

"If the empress was willing to give him her engagement ring, Vassili must have taken all of the Romanovs' treasures with him," said Rosenberg as he carefully wrapped the pearl back up. "They are worth a fortune. And the Reich requires funds." The Nazi leaned towards Tristan and lowered his voice. "An excellent opportunity for me to return to the Führer's good graces."

Unless I get my hands on it first, Tristan thought.

"And should you ever have any suicidal ideas of pushing me out to please Himmler," threatened Rosenberg, as though he had read the Frenchman's mind, "Marcel will be delighted to give you a demonstration of his skills."

Tristan couldn't help but smirk. "If he's as good with his fists as he is with his brain—"

"Your humour no longer amuses me, Herr Marcas," interrupted the Nazi. "You're here to find a clue, so find it."

The double agent stood up. "Do you know where the son's room is?"

"At the end of the second corridor."

Tristan opened the door to find a disaster area. The desk had been ripped to pieces, the drawers smashed to bits, the bed upended, and the mattress shredded.

"I gather this is Marcel's technique?" he ventured.

"Prove yours is better!" replied Rosenberg.

"Most children have a hiding place in their room. A place where they keep their favourite marbles and miniature soldiers. Their parents always know where it is and are careful to preserve its contents. If Vassili left a note for his son, that's where he will have hidden it."

The collaborator shrugged. "I've checked everywhere, every piece of furniture."

"Then the cache is still here somewhere, intact," said Tristan.

"I tapped the walls. There's nothing there!"

"Children don't hide their secrets behind plasterboard and wallpaper. Their hiding places have to be easy to access." Tristan got on all fours.

"What are you doing?" asked Rosenberg.

"Getting down to a child's level," he replied.

Marcel had already removed the stones around the bottom of the fireplace. Tristan checked the joints around the mantel. Bricks were simple enough to remove, and joints were easy to imitate with a combination of toothpaste and ashes. But none of them budged.

"There are only two places left," said Tristan. "The skirting boards or the floorboards."

"I'll check the skirting," said Marcel as he took out a knife and got to work.

Tristan took off his shoes and felt around the parquet with his bare feet. The boards were all the same size. Nothing seemed to stand out. As he moved, he studied the gaps between them as well.

If a board had been removed, there would be less dust in the spaces around it. Marcel continued to rip off the skirting boards one by one as Rosenberg looked on.

"You're wasting our time, Herr Marcas," said the Nazi. "There's nothing here. Nothing in the flat. It's empty."

"Where was the bed?" asked Tristan.

Marcel gestured vaguely towards a corner. The double agent made his way to the area and found marks from the feet of the bed on the floor. This was his last chance. He got down on his knees again and examined the parquet. The collaborator had nearly finished with the skirting when his blade caught on a bulge in the wood and sent it flying. Tristan quickly dodged it, causing his elbow to land hard on the floor, which collapsed in a cloud of dust.

"My God, Marcas, you've found it!" cried Rosenberg.

Marcel dove his hand into the hole and pulled out an object rolled up in a piece of blackened fabric. "Bloody hell, it weighs a tonne," he said.

A stone fell from the tissue onto the floor. Tristan turned it over. It was a chunk of rubble from a building. A series of letters and numbers was carved into the largest side.

^ C ^ G^ 1777

Rosenberg came closer. "If I follow your reasoning," he said, "which has been right so far, this inscription will lead us to Gurdjieff?"

"If it holds some sort of meaning for his son, it will for us as well," replied Tristan.

Marcel took the stone and wrapped it back up in the fabric.

"You have until tomorrow to figure it out," announced the Nazi.

"That's impossible. I'll need more time to conduct some research. Unless you'd rather I inform the Reichsführer. He loves a good mystery. Codes are his favourite—"

"That's enough. We're going back to the orangery. Marcel, stay here until I can send someone to replace you. We have to keep an eye on the flat in case Vassili or his son turn up."

Tristan took the stone. It was very heavy indeed. The person who had removed it from its wall had done so for a reason.

Upon leaving the room, Rosenberg turned abruptly. His usually expressionless eyes seemed to dance like those of a snake. "As for you, Marcas, you have twenty-four hours, like I said. But first, you're going to prove your loyalty. Remember the Corot I showed you?"

"The fake Corot, you mean?"

"Quite right. Before coming here, I asked my men to go and get the fence who sold it to me. He's waiting for you now."

"Why me?" asked Tristan.

"Because you're going to make him confess."

14

Leicester Square, London

A concierge in a dinner jacket stood at the entrance to Gallery 12. Laure gave him her name, as Crowley had instructed. The concierge opened the door for her with a charming smile. Her polka-dot sundress with its subtle décolletage seemed to enchant him. Satisfied, Laure smiled back. She hadn't chosen the dress for this gallery opening, where she wouldn't spend more than a few moments, but for the evening out with her friends.

She checked her watch. She had plenty of time to collect the mage and escort him to the Hellfire. Then she'd make her way across town to enjoy her leave. She needed to let her hair down. Malorley's worrying revelations about the discovery of the *Thule Borealis*, followed by the visit to the mortuary, had left her feeling anxious.

The gallery was full to the brim. She tried in vain to locate Crowley in the crowd. Two shows were going on in the same space: one on Patriotic British Art and another on Tarot and Esotericism. *Interesting combination,* thought Laure as she made her way through the first room and into the next, where a series of small, rectangular paintings the size of art books hung on scarlet walls. Tarot cards. There was black graffiti at the centre of the main wall. *THOT*, it read.

The guests had formed small, compact groups. Laure finally located the mage, who was strutting for a group of elegantly dressed women of a certain age. He met her gaze and gestured for her to wait. Laure gestured to let him know he had five minutes. As she waited, she studied the works on display.

She recognized the different cards immediately: the World, the Devil, the High Priestess, the Chariot and the Fool. Before the war, she'd enjoyed playing with a deck of Marseille tarot cards her father's friend had given her. These paintings were quite different from the original cards, but they were pleasing to the eye.

Laure walked over to a canvas depicting a languid woman whose long hair weaved its way between two vases. Behind her, in the centre, was a globe, and a bright star at the top. A pile of crystals lay by the woman's feet.

"The Star," said a voice next to Laure. "You couldn't have made a better choice, Miss. It's one of the most positive omens in tarot."

The man who had just spoken stepped closer to study the card. He must have been about sixty, with short light-brown hair, a perfect aquiline nose, and an elegant mouth.

"I'm afraid I don't believe in fortunes," Laure replied. "The painting is remarkable though."

"I wasn't trying to predict your future. I simply meant to allude to its symbolism. In traditional tarot, the Star symbolizes hope—a quest for happiness or knowledge. Things to which every human worthy of the name must aspire."

He stopped and turned towards Laure. From this angle, his face was warmer than she'd expected.

"How foolish of me," he said. "I haven't introduced myself. Lord Basil Corduran at your service. And you are?"

"Laure. Just Laure," she replied.

"Well, my dear Laure, would you like me to continue my analysis of the work?"

"Yes, please."

Corduran pointed at the top of the painting. "You'll notice there are three heptagrams, or seven-pointed stars, hidden in the image. Wiccan witches call this version the elven or fairy star. It offers protection from curses. You also see it in manuscripts on alchemy. Each point of the star corresponds to one of the seven astrological planets. As for the kabbalists, they'll tell you the heptagram represents the days of the week and the seven angels who guard God's throne. The Star infuses the female body with unlimited power and cosmic energy. It could be your lucky card."

"I'll ask the artist for a copy as my lucky charm," said Laure.

"That might not be such a good idea," replied Corduran with a smirk.

"Why is that?"

"The devil is in the details . . . Especially in these paintings. You see, Lady Frieda Harris belongs to an occult initiatory organization founded by the twisted Aleister Crowley—a good friend of hers. For his disciples, the seven-pointed star is the mark of Babalon, the Scarlet Goddess. A sacred prostitute who represents the unbridled power of female sexuality. This naked woman with blue hair is possessed by Babalon. Beneath its angelic appearance, this card is an invitation to lust."

"That doesn't sound very esoteric," countered Laure.

"Oh, but you're wrong: the esoteric or occult is that which is hidden from most. Once you've been initiated, you no longer see the world the same way—"

Corduran stopped short and his face hardened as Crowley made his way towards them. He bowed to Laure. "I'll take my leave now. I don't think I'd enjoy the company of your . . . friend."

"I didn't know Aleister was the object of such scorn!"

"He is profoundly corrupt, Miss. He perverts everything he touches and embodies the worst of humanity."

Crowley reached them and kissed Laure on the check. "Ah, I see you've met the gallery owner. Has he told you about his racial notions regarding art?"

"Tread carefully, Aleister," warned Corduran.

"Of course," replied the mage. "You see, Laure, our friend here has always had a rather limited notion of what constitutes art. Before the war, he turned away stellar artists like Picasso, Cézanne, Dalí, and Mondrian because he said they were—what was the term you used again?—ah, yes, degenerates. Hitler and his friends are fond of the same vocabulary. Soon enough, those painters became a major hit at Leicester Gallery, just across the street. Poor Corduran here lost a tidy sum."

The gallery owner had gone pale. Laure cleared her throat to diplomatically end the exchange.

"Shall we go, Aleister?" she asked. Then she turned to Corduran. "Thank you for the welcome," she said. "I'll remember that the Star is my lucky card. And I'll try to forget about its more carnal meaning."

Turning his back on Crowley, the gallery owner said goodbye to Laure. The young agent took the mage's arm.

"We don't have time for a scene," she warned. "We're leaving."

"He deserves it though!" raged Crowley. "Corduran and his gang of anti-Semitic friends from Mosley's Blackshirts were all crazy for Hitler before the war. He was smarter than many of them—he switched sides before it was too late. Very clever of him to organize a show on patriotic art."

The two SOE agents walked quickly, as if they might be followed.

"There are opportunistic bastards everywhere—especially in wartime. There are plenty of them in France, too. Get your bag with the films from the cloakroom and let's head to that brothel as quickly as possible. I have a party to get to tonight."

"With other women your age? Can I come?" Aleister asked eagerly.

"Not a chance."

"Fine. I suppose I'll have to settle for my usual depravities at the Hellfire."

15

Back at the orangery, Tristan climbed down the stairs to the cellar. The steps were worn down in the middle. When his foot hit the sand floor, he felt like he'd travelled back in time. The vaulted stone ceiling dated back to the Middle Ages and had been built with great care—the room was neither damp nor draughty—most likely to store a rich merchant's most treasured items. He bent down to examine the foot of a pillar. The corners were decorated with turtle shells sculpted into the stone. It was one of the French capital's many charms: once you got underground, you discovered the real medieval Paris. A vast and largely unknown city beneath the city.

A voice crying out in pain at the far end of the room pulled Tristan from his musings. He looked up to see a naked man hanging from a hook. He'd been savagely beaten. Two candelabras stood on tables on either side of a basin. Tristan strolled over. One of the torturers was washing his hands. The water was blood-red.

"We didn't go easy," said the man, without turning around, "but he didn't reveal much. I don't think he really knows anything. He's just a pathetic little man who thought he could make a little money off his boss."

"He did end up sharing the name of the yid he bought the painting from, but that guy is long gone. We checked. He's probably off counting his money in the Free Zone," said his accomplice, putting his shirt back on and taking care not to dirty his cuffs.

"What's the poor bloke's name?" Tristan asked.

"Bertrand Tustal. We checked with the prefecture: no criminal record and no open cases. Just a caretaker who thought he could play with the big boys. The idiot must have thought he was a master con."

Tristan didn't reply. He'd just realized the two men were French policemen making a little extra on the side by working for the Germans. Discreet, efficient, and perfectly unscrupulous lackeys.

"All right, well, we're out of here. He's all yours now. Go ahead and finish him off."

When he heard them reach the top of the stairs, Tristan began to breathe easier. He hated mercenary collaborators happy to lend their services to anyone for the right price. They reeked of treason—a smell far worse than a ditch full of excrement. He walked over to the dealer. The man was still conscious despite the state he was in. Tristan leaned in to examine him more closely. "Broken brow bone, crushed cheekbone, dislocated jaw . . . Can you still speak?" he asked.

"Yes," mumbled Tustal as bloody saliva streamed from his mouth.

Tristan took out a cigarette, pushed it between the man's lips, and lit it.

"What's the name of the man who sold you this piece of rubbish?"

"Samuel Müller. I already told them," said Tustal.

"Did he have many other paintings?"

"All over the walls. But he wasn't selling them."

"Of course he wasn't," chuckled Tristan as he figured out how the caretaker had been fooled. "Didn't that surprise you?"

"No, why?" asked the man.

"Let me explain. Your collector gave you a fake and used the money you gave him to discreetly move the rest of his collection before disappearing himself. You've been royally outwitted. And then you chose to sell the fake to a Nazi who rather dislikes being deceived."

"Bloody hell, I'm done for!"

"How do you know the collector?"

"He lived on the first floor of my building. I'm the caretaker, so I know him fairly well. One evening, he came to see me. He explained he was Jewish and had to leave town quickly. Then he suggested I sell the painting to the Germans, who would buy anything. It sounded like a great deal—"

"So you thought you'd make some easy money," interrupted Tristan, annoyed. "Got it. But this Müller, are you sure he's Jewish?"

"Well, it did surprise me a bit given that he and his wife went to the Protestant church on the corner of Rue de l'Oratoire every Sunday before they left for the countryside."

"Do you know where they've gone exactly?" asked Tristan, more interested again.

"Madame Müller's father has a farm in Réveillon in the Perche region."

This time, Tristan lit a cigarette for himself. He had an unusual relationship with tobacco: he could go weeks without smoking, but when he needed his neurons firing at their best, there was nothing like the sound of a lighter and the crackle of the burning cigarette.

Tustal kept talking, as though unable to stop. Anxiety had filled his voice, leaving it halting and barely audible. But Tristan wasn't even listening anymore—he was putting together a plan. The situation had turned out in his favour. Apart from the name of the collector, the lackeys hadn't got anything out of their victim. He, on the other hand, had a lead that could bring in a hitherto unhoped for collection of paintings. Rosenberg would be delighted. This Müller, who had chosen to sacrifice his friend the caretaker, thought himself safe at his father-in-law's farm. He was about to get an unwelcome surprise.

Still hanging from his hook, Tustal began to scream. "I'm going to die like a dog in a ditch! The Krauts will kill me! Say something!"

Tristan didn't answer. He was trying to think of a way to save the man without risking his own life.

"They're going to put a bullet in my brain, aren't they? Right here in this cellar. Maybe you're going to do it! Answer me!"

Tristan decided that he might stand a chance of keeping the fool alive if he gave Rosenberg the lead to the collection right away—at least until the Germans found the paintings. After that . . .

"I haven't told you everything. I have more information. I know some resistance fighters. I'm willing to give up their names and addresses—"

Disgusted, Tristan stopped him. "You idiot! Do you really think you can save your own skin by denouncing innocent people?"

"They're not innocent. The church on Rue de l'Oratoire? The pastor there is hiding Jews."

"Jews like your friend Müller? The kind with farms in Normandy?"

"No—real Jews with fake names. Children. They sing in the church choir. They have everyone fooled, but if you dig a little—"

"You rotten piece of shit," interrupted Tristan, trying to contain his urge to hit the man. "You'd betray your own mother if you could!"

"There's an Englishman, too. A pilot. My wife, who cleans the church, heard him there one day. The pastor must be hiding him somewhere in the attic. I think his plane crashed when they bombed Boulogne-Billancourt. Clearly he parachuted to safety—"

Tristan placed his hand firmly over the informant's mouth, cutting him off. "Every time you open your mouth, you send someone to their death. Listen to me now. The Germans already know about the Oratoire network. They've had someone undercover in it for weeks. So, have a good long think: if you tell them about it, do you really believe they'll just let you stroll out of here to blather on to anyone who will listen?"

Tristan let go to see if his bluff had worked.

"I won't say a thing, I swear!"

"I'm not the one you have to convince."

"Whatever you want, just tell me!"

"The name of the pastor."

"Maury. Etienne Maury. Will you convince the Germans to let me go now?"

Tristan walked over to the table and grabbed one of the candelabras. It was made of solid silver—and had probably been stolen by one of Rosenberg's minions. The important thing, though, was that it was heavy enough.

"I don't think so," Tristan replied coldly.

"But I told you everything I know!"

"Exactly. You betrayed your country. What's stopping you from betraying the Germans next? I can't take the risk."

"Please, don't kill me!"

Tristan raised the candelabra.

"Herr Marcas, I see you're interested in silver?" It was Rosenberg's high-pitched voice. Tristan hadn't heard him come down the stairs. "Please, don't stop on my account. Have a good look at it. It's a remarkable piece. Solid silver. A magnificent example of Renaissance decorative art. Our specialists think it was made in northern Italy and brought to France by the Medici family when their daughters married the kings of France."

Tristan took a deep breath. He was not in the mood for lengthy speeches. "Let's talk more about art history later," he said, turning around. "Do you have a team ready to leave immediately?"

Rosenberg hesitated, before replying, "Yes, but where would they go?"

"Normandy. To check in with the local *gendarmes* in a secluded little town called Réveillon. They must have noticed a couple of Parisians—the Müllers that our friend here just told me about—move into a local farm. Probably with a very full lorry."

Intrigued, Rosenberg began to quiver. "And what will have been in the lorry?"

"Dozens of paintings. Originals this time."

"Marcel!" Rosenberg shouted, turning towards the stairs. When the collaborator had made his way downstairs, the Nazi continued. "Take a group of men and drive straight to Réveillon, in Normandy. Look for Jews named Müller. Get them to talk and—"

"They're not Jews," interrupted Tristan.

"No matter," replied Rosenberg. "Bring me their collection. Paintings. But first, take care of this lying cheat," he ordered, pointing at the prisoner.

"But I have more to say," screamed Tustal.

He didn't get a chance. The candelabra Tristan still had in his hand slammed into the back of his neck, breaking it upon impact.

Rosenberg was stupefied. "I wouldn't have thought you capable—" he mumbled.

"I'm full of surprises," said Tristan.

Annoyed by the Frenchman's sangfroid, Rosenberg tensed. "I gave you twenty-four hours to decipher the inscription. There are only twenty left. You'd better get to it."

16

East London

"Get today's paper here! Winston Churchill under fire. Vote of no confidence in the works. Extra, extra! Read all about it!"

Crowley avoided the newsboy standing on a soapbox in front of the flower shop. They'd been walking for over a quarter of an hour and would soon reach the Hellfire Club.

"I hate the press and its reporters," mumbled Aleister. "Especially the tabloids. The news is an evil god, spewing its bile into human minds every day."

"I'm afraid I don't agree. Knowledge is power," said Laure.

"Nonsense! Information is just a new way to enslave humanity. Just like morality, authority, and religion. And let's not forget war."

Laure smiled. She knew from Aleister's SOE file that he had offered to write a practical magic column for *The Times*, as well as instructive articles to boost couples' sex lives, complete with erotic drawings. The editor-in-chief had run him out of his office and informed the authorities.

"Parliament wants the Prime Minister's head!" shouted the boy in his khaki cap as he brandished the paper like Moses coming down the mountain with the Tablets of the Law.

"I thought Churchill was quite popular," said Laure, puzzled. "Britain is full of surprises."

"He *is* popular with the people. This is just political games. Many men are looking to take the old bulldog's place."

The mage watched disdainfully as people jockeyed for position around the newsboy, who had positioned himself in the middle of the pavement. "Watch this, Laure. You'll see just how powerful magic can be. I'm going to invoke the demon Rastruth, master of coincidences."

To the young woman's great surprise, the mage closed his eyes, put down his bag, and raised his arms to the sky. "*Hag meriah belgo andamateh koltar. Krynoria!*" he exclaimed as he waved his arms in the air in the shape of an unknown symbol. "A sign, there will be a sign," he muttered. "Something will happen. Just wait and see."

Well, nothing is happening, thought Laure. Then the newsboy got back to work. "The swastika killer strikes again!" he shouted. "New body found in Shoreditch. Get today's paper here. London lives in terror!"

Crowley burst into laughter and leaned closer to Laure. "The sign!" he bellowed, utterly pleased with himself.

"What sign is that?"

"The boy came out with that headline just before my meeting with Moira. Magic is more powerful than anything. Stronger than life itself." Then he turned towards the few people who'd stopped to stare. "Read my *Book of the Law* instead of wasting your time on such rubbish," he called out to them.

Laure was terribly embarrassed. "Stop making a spectacle of yourself, Aleister!"

Two soldiers noticed the mage and made their way over to him. "Hey mate, what on earth are you doing?"

"I invoked Rastruth, fifth paladin of Lucifer's court. But don't worry, he's only a minor demon. I asked for a sign and received it. But you probably don't understand a word of what I'm saying. Magic can accomplish anything. Anything!"

As Crowley turned to leave, one of the soldiers grabbed his sleeve. "Oh really, Mr. Magician? Could it make us win the war? Is that something you can do?" he joked.

"Of course. As a matter of fact, we're working on it. The only thing left to do is find the last swastika with my colleagues at the SOE and you'll be able to go home to your families. It will only take a few more weeks now," Aleister said matter-of-factly.

"The SOE, you must be joking! That's very kind of you, Mr. . . . ?"

"I'm afraid I can't give you my name. I work for the secret services. You can call me Grand Mage."

The other soldier doubled over and tapped his friend on the shoulder, unable to hide his amusement. "Come on Pat, we don't have all day. Say goodbye to your friend the Grand Nutter."

Crowley raised an eyebrow. He had no intention of letting such an insult go unpunished. He walked over to the man and stared into his eyes. "Look at me!" he ordered.

The warrant officer laughed nervously.

"Look at me!" insisted Aleister, forcing his hypnotic gaze on the man. "Your head hurts, doesn't it? Quite a lot, I imagine."

"Um, no . . . "

"Come now, don't you feel the presence of Pazuzu of Ethiopia, Satan's favourite minion? He is snickering inside your skull. I can see him perfectly. He's digging a tunnel to your soul, which he will devour."

The officer staggered and steadied himself on his friend, then shook his head. "My head, it hurts!" He glued his hands to his temples. "Jesus Christ! It burns! Stop it! Get it out of me!"

The sergeant grabbed Crowley by the collar. "What have you done to him, you bloody madman?"

"I don't like sceptics," Aleister replied coolly. "They've wronged so many wizards."

The officer continued to writhe in pain. "Please, tell him to stop. It's horrible."

"That's enough, Crowley," said Laure firmly.

The suffering WO pushed her out of the way and raised his fist to Aleister's round face. "If you don't stop this, I'll punch your face in. Your own father won't recognize you when I'm done with you."

"My young friend, my bastard father has been dead for years. He's cleaning Beelzebub's toilets now. But if you insist, I will free you. I don't want to deprive His Majesty of a single man."

The officer let go of Crowley's coat. The mage smoothed his clothes before taking the screaming man's head in his hands. "Pazuzu will leave the miserable lump you call a brain to go hump your mother in hell. Now, if you'll excuse me, I have an important meeting with a witch of the nasty sort . . . "

Aleister left the two men standing mouths agape on the pavement and pulled Laure along.

"You're a real piece of work," she said indignantly. "You could have compromised the mission!"

"I had to teach them a lesson. Looks like I haven't lost my touch as a hypnotist. The Hellfire is just down the road, at number six," continued the mage. "Remind me, what are you supposed to do while I'm inside?"

"Wait around and make sure you come out alive. Don't dawdle!" replied Laure.

"That's right, you have your evening out with your friends. If you were to invite me along, I'd certainly be keen to make this quick," ventured Crowley.

"Not a chance. Go on, hurry up."

She watched him walk up to the club, then made her way to a phone box across the street.

The Hellfire Club was rather inconspicuous from the outside. A respectable-looking building with white columns, bay windows, and a varnished black door. A high-end residence like most in the area. Crowley had chosen it for precisely that reason when he'd founded the club years before. He wanted it to blend in, to take any self-righteous neighbours by surprise.

He rang the bell and smiled as he read the rectangular copper plaque on the wall *Pain and Sisters Insurance*. Moira had replaced *Partners* with *Sisters* since Aleister had sold her his shares, for a feminist touch.

A small shutter opened in the top part of the door to reveal a pair of Asian eyes. As the door slowly opened, the sweet smell of incense wafted up to Crowley's nose. A young woman in a red-and-black robe stood in the doorway.

"Mr. Crowley, always a pleasure to see you. Do you have an appointment with my mistress?" she asked.

Aleister recognized Lei Min, the Chinese woman he'd met the night Moira had fooled him into being blackmailed.

"No, but I'm certain she'll want to see me. I have a gift for her. Some enthralling footage of witches and magicians."

17

The National Library, Rue de Richelieu, Paris

The librarians seemed to have enjoyed burying Tristan in volume after volume on epigraphy. Books were piled high all around him, walling him in from the rest of the world. He never would have imagined the topic could be so vast.

Stones had been mankind's very first book pages. Since the dawn of time, men had engraved their names and those of their gods on any rock they could get their hands on. And it turned out epigraphists loved interpreting even the most insignificant inscriptions.

He looked up at the glass dome over the reading room. Indifferent to his plight, the blue sky shone brightly between the metal beams. It had been hours and he'd got nowhere. He was lost in a labyrinth of hypotheses, wandering in a maze of countless possible meanings. The photograph of the stone they'd found in Rue de Varenne sat across from him, propped up against some books. The German technicians had done remarkable work: the black-and-white image they'd produced rendered all of the nuances of the stone's carved face. Tristan could even make out chisel marks around the edges. Gurdjieff must have removed it from a wall to leave a sign for his son.

But Tristan wondered how the Russian could have made off with such a heavy stone unnoticed. One thing was certain: both the father and the son understood its meaning. It had to allude to a place they'd visited together. Maybe a public monument? But he couldn't imagine Gurdjieff stealing a stone from Les Invalides or Versailles. He wouldn't have wanted to attract the authorities' attention.

Tristan looked at the photo again. He was thoroughly intrigued by the inscription. What on earth could ^C^G^1777 stand for?

While consulting the first round of books, he had thought of a funerary inscription. C and G could be the deceased's initials, and 1777 the year of their death. If he was right about that much, the stone alluded to a grave. But during the Enlightenment, people were never buried behind walls. After some more reading, he suspected an architect's signature on a building. Unfortunately, it soon turned out that that custom didn't appear until the 19th century.

"So, have you found what you were looking for?" asked the librarian, dropping off another batch of books. He seemed to be in the mood for a chat, and the reading room was nearly empty. Occupied Paris needed food, not culture.

"Not really," sighed Tristan. "Every hypothesis I come up with collapses when I look into it."

"Do you mind?" The librarian picked up the photograph to get a better look, turning the image this way and that. "Could it be an ex-voto?"

"An ex-what?" said Tristan. He couldn't place the word, but it made him think of incense.

"An ex-voto. They're engraved plaques that people leave in churches to thank God for a miracle. Surviving a severe injury, for example."

Tristan's brain began to churn. If the stone had come from a church, he could exclude any buildings built after 1777, and therefore narrow things down a bit. His eyes darted from one book to another. One of them, he remembered, examined inscriptions found in Parisian churches. Certainly a good place to start.

"Actually, come to think of it, ex-votos always include a message of thanks, and there doesn't seem to be one here, so I doubt it will be one. I'm sorry if I got your hopes up," the librarian said apologetically.

Tristan was hugely disappointed. He glanced at the employee who'd just sent him back to the depths of ignorance. "Well now you've really knocked the wind out of my sails!"

"Maybe you should consult a specialist?" suggested the librarian.

"Do you know one?"

"As it happens, I do. We have our own in-house epigraphist. She's usually transcribing ancient inscriptions, but today I think you'll find her in the medals room. Her name is Juliette Lalande."

"And where is that?"

The librarian gestured for him to follow. "The library is a real maze. I'll take you there myself."

The medals room reminded Tristan of a church. Silence was the rule in the reading room, but here it seemed even quieter. There wasn't a single sound or sign of life amid the huge glass cabinets, which reached the ceiling. The ancient wooden floor didn't even creak. As he walked past one of the cabinets, a huge gold medal stood out. He leaned in to study the inscription: *Ludovico Magno*. Louis XIV. He should have known—only the Sun King would have minted such a trinket to celebrate his own glory.

"Are you looking for someone?" asked a voice.

He turned around to find a young woman with a bun standing in front of him. She was smartly dressed in a tailored grey skirt-suit.

"Yes, I'm looking for Juliette Lalande?"

"You found her. May I ask why you've come to see me?" There was no sign of distrust in her voice, only surprise.

Tristan eyed the desk behind her, which was piled high with books and articles. "I need to ask you a question. I have an inscription I can't place," he said, holding out the photo.

"Where did you find this?" asked Lalande.

"In a Parisian flat I'm inventorying for auction," he lied, having made up his cover ahead of time. Empty flats sat at every corner of the city, and the sale of abandoned furniture and confiscated artwork was many a German's daily bread.

"Do you really think you can sell this piece of stone?" she asked dubiously.

Tristan stayed his course. "It was on display beneath a glass bell, so we assumed it must have some value."

"It doesn't," she replied flatly.

"Does that mean you know where it came from?"

Juliette gestured for him to sit down. "Yes," she said. "From somewhere beneath the city."

Tristan was absorbed in the map of Paris Juliette had requested from the specialist department. He recognized the streets, buildings, and monuments, but couldn't figure out what the dark, often winding marks represented.

"What's this?" he asked, pointing to one of them.

"On 17 December 1774, the residents of Rue d'Enfer in the Saint-Jacques neighbourhood were all scared to death when three hundred meters of their street suddenly collapsed and left behind a huge crater. Not even the bravest of onlookers dared look down to the bottom."

"Given the street name, they must have thought the devil had something to do with it," mused Tristan.

"Perhaps, but it also reminded them of an important fact: the entire city was built over empty space. Quarries had been exploited since Roman times to build every single building in Paris," explained Juliette.

"Does that mean the ground beneath the city resembles a piece of Swiss cheese?"

"Precisely. Look at the map. Every dark mark you see is a former quarry, and that doesn't include the thousands of passages that link them together. It's like an anthill, really."

"In every neighbourhood in Paris?"

"No, most of the excavations took place on the left bank, but there are also quite a few in Montmartre and Belleville. Some of them are dozens of meters deep."

Intrigued, Tristan pointed at a series of pits beneath Montparnasse. "Even there?"

"Yes, but today's residents needn't worry. Any risk of collapse can be ruled out."

"I'm afraid I don't follow . . ."

"As soon as the authorities realized the scope of the problem, they began looking for ways to remedy it. And the simplest solution was to fill in the underground tunnels."

"But what with?" asked Tristan, incredulous.

Juliette crossed her legs and smiled. Tristan noticed her eyes were the same colour as her suit. "A very affordable and readily available material: the bones of the dead!"

"You must be joking."

"I'm not! In 1785, they emptied all cemeteries in Paris—over three hundred of them, most of which dated back to the Middle Ages—and dumped millions of bones into the ground."

"The catacombs," murmured Tristan.

"Exactly. We live on top of the largest cemetery in the world."

Tristan looked down instinctively.

"Don't worry, there weren't any tunnels beneath the National Library. There's no risk this venerable institution will take you down with her."

"I'm afraid I still don't understand how this relates to the inscription engraved on my stone," said Tristan.

Juliette smoothed her skirt, sending the hem down past her knees. "As you can imagine, given the number and size of the tunnels, skeletons—even by the millions—weren't enough to fill them all. So the authorities decided to open a special department—Quarry Inspection—responsible for surveying and protecting Paris's cellar. The department was founded in 1777. Ring any bells?"

Tristan looked down at the photograph despite knowing every scratch by heart.

"An architect known for his remarkable efficiency was made head of the new structure: Charles Guillaumot. Now look at the initials on your stone."

He couldn't believe it. He'd been stuck for hours, and a woman he'd only just met had solved the puzzle as though it were a child's game. He decided to push for more information. "And this Charles Guillaumot spent his time strolling the tunnels beneath the city, carving his initials into the walls?"

"Not him personally, but his employees. Once they'd verified a segment of tunnel or quarry was safe, they carved the initials into a stone to signal their work was done. A bit like medieval masons, who marked every stone they carved with their symbol."

"Can this stone be linked to a specific place, then?"

Juliette removed her hair band, letting her hair tumble down her shoulders. "Unfortunately, no. But since Charles Guillaumot took his post in April 1777, this stone must have been carved between then and the end of the year. You'll need to find out where his teams worked during that period. And you're in luck, we keep the Quarry Inspection's register right here . . . Just ask for it to be brought to you in the reading room."

Tristan jumped up. He was beyond excited. "One last thing: I still don't understand why the initials and the date are separated by triangles?"

"Oh, that? It's a Masonic symbol: Guillaumot was a Freemason. He belonged to the Nine Sisters lodge here in Paris."

"How on earth do you know all this?" balked Tristan.

"Didn't I tell you?" asked Juliette with a smile. "The renowned astronomer Joseph-Jérôme Lefrançois de Lalande is an ancestor of mine. He also happened to be the grand master at Nine Sisters."

18

Hellfire Club, London

Lei Min bowed and led the mage to a sitting room with red-velvet walls.

"You've changed the décor since my last visit," he remarked with a frown. "What happened to my painting of the wrestling Amazons? I can still see their naked bodies glistening in the sun . . ."

"I sold it to an antiques dealer in Kensington," said a voice at the top of the stairs. "It was awfully vulgar."

Crowley looked up to see Moira striding confidently down the stairs. She wore a pair of black trousers and a tailored jacket, her bright-red hair highlighting her pale complexion. Her smile was both charming and cruel—the perfect model for a pre-Raphaelite painting by Dante Gabriel Rossetti. Crowley thought back to the young Irish girl he'd met long ago. She'd been so docile back then. The woman in front of him no longer had anything in common with his former disciple: the student had surpassed the master. Moira had earned her nickname as the Scarlet Fairy.

"I see you're wearing trousers now. How decadent," chuckled Crowley. "How did it go on the Isle of Man?"

"It went well. And I took advantage of the situation to curse a few enemies, including our bloody Prime Minister. But let's get to the point, Aleister. I don't remember summoning you for your monthly report, and I'm in the middle of a meeting. What is it you want?"

"Such poor manners, Moira. I've brought you a gift, as proof of my friendship," he said as he threw his leather bag on the floor.

"What's inside?" she asked. "A newborn for sacrifice? Or better yet, the head of your boss at the SOE?"

"Copies of the footage filmed during Operation Witchfall," replied Crowley. "I thought you might enjoy them."

Moira's features brightened instantly. "Wonderful!" she exclaimed. "To be honest, my Abwehr contact had a hard time believing my account of the ceremony. It'll be a piece of cake to convince him now. As much as I hate to thank you, feel free to have a drink at the bar or enjoy a complimentary session with our latest recruit. She is full of imagination—especially when it comes to punishing men of a certain age."

"I'd rather you gave me some information in return. They've discovered a third body in Shoreditch, just like the one you dumped in Tower Hamlets. The nasty swastika on the victim's forehead bears a striking resemblance to the one you carved into the young woman I supposedly murdered."

"And?"

"Oh, come off it, Moira! I'm no idiot. I have a right to know."

"Since when do I owe you anything, Crowley? Why do you care about these bodies? And what makes you think I'm responsible? This town is full of madmen, murderers, and perverts all too eager to copy my work."

"I care because I don't want any more murders pinned on me!" raged Crowley.

Moira burst into laughter and came dangerously close. "Like all men, you make everything about you."

"Moira, I can't go on like this. Every time there's a new victim I feel like the police are breathing down my neck. Even my SOE colleagues have noticed I'm out of sorts. I won't be worth anything to you if they begin to doubt me. Haven't I proven my devotion by bringing you these reels out of the goodness of my heart?" he pleaded.

The Scarlet Fairy stared at him for a few seconds. "Follow us," she ordered.

Crowley struggled to keep up as Moira and Lei Min took off down a long corridor dotted with doors to what looked like cells.

"Is this still the binding room? Can I watch for a moment?" he asked, having stopped to catch his breath.

"If you like," Moira replied coldly.

Crowley peeked into the room. Several men were tied up inside. One was bound to a Saint Andrew's cross, another to what looked like a pommel horse. A third was chained to the floor and a fourth hung from a ring in the ceiling. A woman in a red-and-black dress and visible corset strode between her clients, eagerly doling out blows and insults.

"I see you're busy!" exclaimed Aleister in surprise.

"I can't wait to give them a proper beating," muttered Moira as she continued down the corridor.

When they reached a half-open door leading to a bar area, they passed a young couple on their way out. The man was very blond and dressed in leather from head to toe, whereas the woman was clad in a straight-cut dress. They glared at Crowley and exchanged knowing glances with Moira before wordlessly disappearing into one of the alcoves.

"Charming couple," said Crowley. "Are they clients or employees?"

"You're very curious, aren't you? A little of both. They enjoy their work. Right now, they're off to brutalize some kinky lord."

They entered the extensive private part of the establishment and, having made their way through a courtyard and several more doors, the unlikely trio got to a spiral staircase. The acrid smell of damp stone tickled Crowley's throat as they descended, and the rusted metal steps became increasingly rickety, leaving the mage wondering whether they would hold his weight.

At last, a final door led them into a freezing room. It was dark, but he could just make out a carcass hanging from a hook.

"I don't understand," said Crowley.

"Then take a closer look," scoffed Moira.

"Do you really think I'll go in there so you can lock me in?"

"Age has made you wary. If I had wanted to get rid of you, I would have done it a long time ago," she said dryly as she turned on the lights.

Aleister was dumbfounded.

It wasn't meat hanging from the ceiling, but a human body—a man in a harness attached to the hook. A swastika had been carved into his forehead.

"Is that enough of an answer for you, my dear Aleister?" continued Moira with a nod to her assistant.

"But . . . Why?" asked Crowley.

"If you want to know more, you'll have to pose for a picture with him."

"So you can blackmail me yet again? No chance."

"What use would that be to me? No, I just need some additional insurance should you ever be tempted to talk to the police. Let us take the picture and you'll get your answers. If not, you'll never know why I've decided to terrorize all of London."

As Laure waited, a hundred meters from Hellfire, she took in the destruction around her—destruction wrought by Göring's bombers. There was nothing but ruins everywhere she looked. The red phone box she stood in seemed to her a symbol of British resistance in the face of this devastation rained down by the enemy. The Frenchwoman lit a cigarette as her eyes wandered over the battered pieces of cement. Blackened steel beams rose from the ground like the claws of a buried monster. She couldn't have asked for a more depressing view—or a more boring mission.

She'd been champing at the bit for six months now, ever since her return from Venice, and was tired of playing private eye. Laure checked her watch and cursed Malorley. She was going to be late, and all because she was waiting around in this no man's land. The surrounding wreckage reminded her of her private life. Every other woman her age had a boyfriend, or at least a few girlfriends to chat with and confide in when they felt down. She had no one. Well, no one she could talk to, since SOE rules prevented her from sharing anything with her roommate or the precious few friends she had to put second.

Laure had made fun of Malorley's lonely flat, but she was in the same boat. All because of these bloody relics. Where was her free will? She felt like a tiny, fragile leaf being tossed around by the autumn wind.

The phone rang, pulling her out of her thoughts. Laure picked up immediately, cheeks flushed with anger.

"Is he still inside?" Malorley asked calmly.

"Yes, and it's been half an hour. He's held up his end of the bargain. Can I go now?"

"Absolutely not. Wait until he comes out," replied Malorley. "We can't be too cautious. Moira O'Connor is unpredictable."

Laure tightened her grasp on the receiver. "Crowley can take care of himself, and you can send a team to take over for me, I'm exhausted. I'm done playing bobby."

"You can't leave until he comes out. Need I remind you that you're on a mission?"

"I'm not staying!" shouted Laure. It was as though all her frustrations had suddenly made their way to the surface. She smacked her palm on the glass. "No more of this!"

"I'll pretend I didn't hear that," Malorley replied impassively.

"You heard me! I'm fed up, do you understand? Fed up with your covens in the countryside, your perverted magicians, your dead bodies at the mortuary, and your bloody magic swastikas. I have no revenge to exact, no oaths to fulfil."

"But, Laure—"

"I know, you don't care! You have no family, no friends, and no wife. And you want me to end up like you!"

There was a long silence on the other end of the line. And then:

"All right, I'll send an agent. Wait until he gets there."

"Good. And I want the same car that brings him to take me to my friends."

19

Boulevard de Port-Royal, Paris

Tristan was sitting on a café terrace across from the entrance to Cochin Hospital. He'd been sipping his beer and people-watching for the past hour. At this time of day, they were few and far between, and none of them lingered, which reassured him.

When he'd finally left the National Library after many more hours with Juliette, he'd taken a winding route, to make sure he wasn't being followed. A car slowed as it passed, then sped off as Tristan looked on. The passenger was a teenager and hence unlikely to be on Rosenberg's payroll.

The face of "Alfred the Terrible", as Tristan had taken to calling him, kept popping into his head. Ever since they'd met, he had been wondering who the official ideologue of the Third Reich really was. Was he trying to win his way back into Hitler's good graces by getting his hands on the jewels of the last tsar, as he claimed, or was he up to something more sinister? Tristan had too many questions and no answers. They were a symptom of a more diffuse anxiety: over the last three years he'd spent pretending to work for the Germans, he kept narrowly avoiding disaster. Yet it drew closer each time. He had the ominous feeling that his luck was running out. He knew luck had little to do with his good fortune so far, but the truth was that he'd only made it out of all his scrapes—from Montségur to Berlin—because he'd been certain that if things got really bad, Erika's love would save him. But now the tide had turned; Erika had become his greatest danger.

To distract himself from his worries, Tristan opened the envelope that had arrived for him from Berlin. It was sealed with wax—proof of how little the Reichsführer trusted Rosenberg. Tristan quickly realized he was holding the report on the study of the *Thule Borealis* he had suggested Himmler have completed. A linguist and a specialist in medieval paper had been chosen to examine the manuscript. His eyes darted across the pages. The linguist hadn't found any semantic indications that part of the text was missing, but the paper expert was certain that one page from the end of the book had been ripped out. An enclosed photograph zoomed in on the area, making it perfectly clear.

So someone has taken the last page, thought Tristan. Someone who understood it was key to finding the last swastika. Someone who might be about to beat him to it.

He got up to dispose of the envelope down a nearby drain. As he did so, he passed the entrance to Cochin Hospital: a huge brick and stone gate built just before the Revolution, which seemed to have been designed with carriages in mind rather than ambulances. *France is all about appearances,* Tristan thought to himself. Take the Maginot Line. Over a hundred kilometers of concrete walls and bunkers topped with cannons designed to keep Hitler from invading the country, but the Führer had simply taken a detour through the Ardennes to reach Paris. Tristan slowed down as he passed the gate to his right, but no one seemed to be paying any attention to arriving visitors. That was France: monumental gates, but no one to guard them.

Once he'd ripped up and thrown away the envelope, he sat down on a bench again. Finding it hard to believe that Rosenberg wasn't having him followed, he wanted to watch a while longer before going in. He wouldn't be surprised to see Marcel's stocky figure appear nearby. As casually as possible, he let his eyes wander over the parked cars and the café terrace. Everything seemed normal. He felt around in his jacket pocket for the picture of the engraved stone he'd finally managed to decipher. All thanks to Juliette.

Gurdjieff's message was now clear: it referred to a particular place in the tunnels beneath Paris—a section Guillaumot's men had verified when he had first been appointed in the spring of

1777. The Quarry Inspection logbook—bone-dry pages that hadn't been opened in centuries—had played a pivotal role in determining precisely which section: the Capucins' network.

Once they had the name, Juliette had tracked down a new, more precise map, drawn up by a certain Eugène de Fourcy in 1855. It indicated the underground networks beneath each of the capital's neighbourhoods. The former quarries appeared in ochre, while the tunnels linking them were red.

An accompanying text explained that the Capucins' quarry was over a kilometer long. Unlike most of the others, it had only a few adjoining tunnels, none of which led to other major quarries. Guillaumot must have chosen it for that reason: if the techniques he was implementing failed, any collapse they provoked would be contained and collateral damage minimized.

Gurdjieff was hiding out there to escape Rosenberg's men, Tristan was certain of it. How the Russians had learned of the tunnels' existence was a mystery to him, but Paris was home to several groups of catacomb explorers who lived to probe the depths below the city. Some of them were on a quest for silence and solitude while others were looking for the ideal venue for a scandalous party. Gurdjieff could belong to either camp—or be a member of one of the secret societies that practised their rituals underground. Rumours told of esoteric ceremonies, magical seances, and even devil worship.

Tristan got to his feet and walked through the hospital gate. All he had to do now was find the entrance to the underground world. As Cochin Hospital had expanded, it had swallowed up neighbouring buildings, and new ones had been added. As a result, the entrance to the quarry had been moved several times. Where was it now, several centuries down the line?

A rather summary sketch by the Quarry Inspection Office had placed it somewhere in the courtyard in front of the Ollier Pavilion located on Rue du Faubourg Saint-Jacques, but there were no further indications. Was it inside or outside today's building? For all he knew, it could be a simple manhole.

A note on one of the more recent maps provided a clue. Just

before the French Revolution broke out in 1789, the Capucines' quarry had been requisitioned for use as an air-raid shelter. Since they were nearly twenty meters below the surface, the capital's former quarries were invulnerable to even the most intense bombings and could accommodate hundreds of people. Tristan concluded that the military must have built a stairwell protected by an armoured door.

He just had to find it.

The hospital felt like a city within the city, made up of eclectic structures from different time periods. Some of them, easily recognizable thanks to their ornate facades, dated back to the Revolution. Several more recent buildings housed laboratories and wards for recovering patients. Tristan walked on, crossing an empty courtyard that smelled of ammonia, occasionally passing a doctor or a distraught woman he assumed to be a widow in mourning. Life and death were indissociable in this place. Moving aside to let a stretcher by, he suddenly realized he hadn't come across a single grey-blue German uniform. At long last, he stepped through a glass door leading to a deserted square with disjointed cobblestones. The entrance to the quarry should be right here, according to the map, Tristan studied the facades one by one. The heavy wooden doors looked like they led to administrative offices or exam rooms. None of them were armoured as indicated on the map.

"I thought you were more perceptive," said a voice.

For the second time that day, Tristan turned around to see Juliette standing in front of him. She had traded her heels for sandals and was wearing a straw hat adorned with a blue-and-white ribbon.

"What are you doing here?" he asked, alarmed. "Did you follow me?"

"No need," she said. "I knew I'd find you here. For a man in charge of inventory, you are incredibly devoted to your work. Do you get this involved with every object you put up for auction?" she asked quizzically.

Tristan realized his cover was blown. There was no point lying anymore.

"Listen, I can't tell you why I actually need to get down there. All I can say is that it is likely to be dangerous and—"

"And I'd better turn around and go home? Too late. Once I'm hooked on a quest, I'm unable to turn my back on it. I want to get to the bottom of it as much as you do—and you know all too well that you wouldn't even be here without my help."

"Juliette," pleaded Tristan, "what I'm about to do could end very badly. Believe me. You really should leave. Some worlds are best left unexplored."

The librarian took off her hat and locked eyes with him. "Let's make a deal," she said. "You take me with you and I—"

"Absolutely not."

"And I'll show you where the door to the Capucins' quarry is," she finished, unperturbed.

Tristan couldn't believe it. He had thought her glued to her books and ancient manuscripts, and here she was, blackmailing him. "How can I be sure you know where it is?" he asked defiantly.

"Our experience so far has shown that I have more of a knack for it than you," she replied, a mischievous smile on her lips.

"You're unbelievable!"

"I'm glad you finally realized that!" she laughed, satisfied with her victory.

Tristan gave in. After all, she could be an asset. "All right, but on one condition," he conceded. "You must turn back when I ask you to."

"I guess I'll leave a trail of crumbs to find my way out, then," she joked.

"You'd better if you don't want to be devoured by the monsters that are likely to be swarming below. But first things first, why don't you show me the door?"

Juliette pointed towards a newer building that had been built against the outer wall. It looked like a warehouse of sorts, its windows covered in dust. "Follow me."

Tristan did as he was told. They crossed the courtyard and

entered the building, which was full of discarded objects. An old cast-iron water-heater lay on the floor amid dozens of bedframes with broken springs and medicine cabinets left ajar.

"Here," she said.

At the corner of the wall that ran along Rue du Faubourg Saint-Jacques stood a black rectangle that resembled the watertight door of a submarine. Juliette walked over and turned a metal bar to unlock it with a loud click. A gust of cool air escaped from the darkness as the door creaked open. Juliette took out a pair of candlesticks from her canvas bag.

"I see you planned ahead," Tristan remarked, holding out a lighter.

Juliette smiled and lit one of the candles. The golden glow on her face made her look like an ancient priestess preparing to worship unknown mysteries. Carefully, to keep the hinges from creaking, Tristan inched the door open.

Juliette stepped inside, the candle in her hand revealing a staircase that led down into the darkness. Then she turned around and bowed. "Welcome to hell!"

20

The Hellfire Club, London

The dead man was swinging back and forth, the butcher's hook creaking ominously against the ceiling fixture. His arms resembled the elegant branches of a weeping willow. Moira gave the corpse a push, like a cat with a toy. She studied the body with a smile on her lips.

"Tom here could have been buried alive in a bombing, hit by a bus, or died of natural causes. A perfectly boring death to end a perfectly boring life. Instead, in just a few days, he'll be famous. Millions of Englishmen and women will know his name, his miserable life story, and how he died. Tom Hackney, Battersea Power Station foreman and father of two," she explained, exalted.

"How come you chose him?" asked Aleister.

"I didn't. I have others to do that for me. But this time, I did tell them I wanted a man. Have you ever noticed that the victims of brutal attacks and murders are almost always women? I decided a Jacqueline the Ripper who goes after men would make more of a splash. The level of fear should be the same for the entire population, don't you think? So, are we taking this picture or not?"

Aleister wanted nothing more than to leave this hellhole, return to the surface, and forget about the Scarlet Fairy. But that would be admitting defeat.

"I accept," he declared.

"Really? Delightful! Come give Tom a hug, then."

Lei Min stepped closer. She was now holding a camera.

"Look as arrogant and deviant as possible next to the good little Englishman," ordered Moira. "This is my own personal insurance, should you ever decide to open that big mouth of yours. Come now, you can do better! Smile! Give him a little kiss."

Crowley put his arm around the dead man's waist as the camera snapped a picture.

"He's freezing," he complained with a frown. "I'll catch pneumonia! All right, now that's done. You've got what you wanted. I'm listening. Why are you killing these people?"

"I told you. It's not me. They kill them and bring them here. I just relay orders and tell them where to dump the bodies for the police to find."

"Who is 'they'?"

The sound of boots and high heels echoed in the stairwell, along with a muffled, rhythmic thudding.

"Well, speak of the devil!" said Moira, turning towards the noise.

A man and a woman appeared at the bottom of the stairs. They were dragging a man with his trousers down around his ankles. The man, who looked to be in his twenties, had a particularly angelic face.

"Aleister, please let me introduce my executioners: Conrad and Susan. They are passionate about their work."

"Who's this bloke?" frowned the woman. "Something about him is a bit off."

"Aleister Crowley, former owner of this establishment, mage in his spare time, and occasional satyr. He's currently one of my employees. Don't mind him. Go about your business."

The couple walked past Moira and laid the second man on the floor. His flabby, white skin spread out over the cold floor.

"Are you going to kill him, too?" asked Crowley.

"Oh no, he's one of my clients. A rather important man. A colonel who coordinates special operations. He's only drugged."

Conrad lifted the dead man off his hook and laid him next to the unconscious military man. Lei Min changed the film in her camera.

"I see," replied Crowley.

"Do you?" asked the Scarlet Fairy with a smirk. "Our German

friends noticed how cooperative you became once I began black-mailing you with the pictures of the dead girl from Tower Hamlets. They were keen to see me do the same thing with my influential clients."

"Clearly, you accepted."

"Without a moment's hesitation. All I need is a steady supply of dead bodies. I simply demanded that someone else handles the murders. I provide the dupe, and my friends here handle the accessories."

"You disgust me, Moira," said Aleister.

"Don't you dare give me a lesson in morality, Crowley. Not you," she replied sharply.

The flash went off again and again in the cold room. The couple strolled over to Moira.

"Just how many do you plan to blackmail?" asked the mage darkly.

"It's less about the number than my clients' strategic positions. I already have a brigadier general and an influential member of the House of Commons in my pocket. Invaluable recruits."

Conrad had lit a cigarette and was watching Crowley in silence as he smoked, as though he was an animal at the zoo. Susan joined him, wrapping her arms around the young man's waist.

"I don't like him, Conrad," she said. "He's ugly."

"And yet he's a very interesting specimen, from a racial point of view," retorted the German. "In the *Untermensch* category, of course."

Aleister glared at them.

"Where did you pick up this charming Nazi couple, Moira?" he asked sarcastically.

"They were sent to me not long ago. He's German, she's English. They met during the Berlin Olympics and got married in Munich in 1939, just before the war broke out. A beautiful love story. Susan has nothing but admiration for the Führer."

"When you spawn," said Aleister disdainfully, "I'll gladly take one of your offspring. I'm always on the lookout for degenerate babies to sacrifice to Satan."

"You reek of betrayal, my portly friend," replied Susan. "You realize that, right, Moira?" she said, turning towards the Scarlet Fairy.

"Would he be of any use to us if he didn't? You're free to go, Aleister."

"Really? You're not going to kill me and hang me up in here for later?"

"What a silly idea. You're more use to me alive than dead. Lei Min will show you out."

"Could I trouble you to call me a taxi?"

"Ask the porter. Now, get out of here before I change my mind," ordered Moira.

Crowley turned and headed up the stairs without further ado.

Once he was gone, Susan turned to Moira. "What should we do with your colonel?"

"Take him back up to the mauve room. He'll sleep for a few hours yet. When he wakes up, we'll show him our artistic portraits."

The German stubbed out his cigarette against the body of the foreman.

"I agree with Susan," he said. "I have zero faith in that fat little man. Are you sure he came alone?"

"What are you getting at?" asked Moira, annoyed to be second-guessed.

"At the Abwehr training centre in Berlin, they teach us to never trust our informants and to always have them followed, to make sure they're not playing us."

"Aleister is too scared to betray me," said Moira as she closed the door to the cold room.

"I'd rather be sure," said the young German.

Without waiting for a reply from the Scarlet Fairy, he shot up the stairs after Crowley.

21

Cochin Hospital, Paris

Tristan was surprised to find the Parisian underground wasn't as cold as he had imagined. When the stairs turned to the right, he noticed a thermometer hanging from the wall. In the trembling candlelight, it read 13 °C.

"The perfect temperature for a wine cellar," announced Juliette. "In fact, in the 19th century, quite a few establishments kept their barrels in the quarries."

After a long series of steps, they reached a second landing. The walls had been covered in cement, and gas masks hung from nails on a wooden panel.

"I doubt these have ever been used," observed Tristan.

"People say the tunnels helped resistance fighters move around without getting caught. Since the Gestapo is after them now, no one dares come down here anymore. But not so long ago, the quarries were still in use."

"They were still extracting stone from down here?" asked Tristan, surprised.

Juliette shook her head. "No, not since the reign of Louis XIV. The Paris Observatory and Val-de-Grâce Church were the last buildings built with stone from down here. But people started coming down here to grow mushrooms and brew beer."

The stairs had just ended across from two tunnels. One continued straight ahead, the other turned to the right. Juliette unfolded a map.

"This is the most recent one I could find. The tunnel to the right leads directly to the air-raid shelter."

Tristan couldn't imagine Gurdjieff hiding somewhere that could be filled with people at the slightest air-raid warning, but he had to be sure.

"You remember your promise, right?" he asked. "Wait for me here."

"What if there's a problem?"

"Go back up to the surface right away. And forget all about me, for your own good."

Tristan made his way down the cement tunnel until he reached a door that resembled the one they had found at the surface. It was slightly ajar. Two tunnels branched out, though according to the map they'd meet up again after some distance. He would have to explore them one after the other. Shielding the candle in case anyone was hiding up ahead, he started to walk into one of them. The compact ground beneath his feet was nearly silent as he walked. According to Juliette, there were neither rooms nor lateral tunnels in this portion of the old quarries. No hiding places. But maybe that was why Gurdjieff had chosen it? Because he thought no one would check.

Every now and then, he stopped to listen in the darkness, but all he heard was the muffled beating of his own heart. He felt increasingly oppressed by his surroundings: the ceiling was low, and the tunnel was growing narrower. At last, he reached a door with a corbelled archway through to yet another tunnel. According to the map, there were stairs at the end that led to the surface. He had to go and see. The Russian could be hiding on the last steps, like a bird on its perch.

Ah, no need, thought Tristan as he stumbled on a pile of rocks. The rest of the tunnel had collapsed, and tonnes of stone were blocking the way. The army must have decided to condemn the old entrance as a security measure. Tristan turned back.

"I see your detour has come to naught?" said Juliette, whose language was delightfully outmoded, probably due to all the time she spent with old books. It only added another layer to her surprising charm.

"I still hope to find what I'm looking for further on."

"I'll be your guide, then," she offered with a smile.

She continued towards a small room where they found a beautifully constructed well. White steps led down to the mirror-like surface of the crystalline water.

"Nothing like the Seine," remarked the librarian. "At this depth, the water is directly supplied by an aquifer. When Guillaumot's workers came down to reinforce an old quarry, the first thing they did was drill a well to make mortar for the supporting walls."

Tristan couldn't resist the urge to dip his hand into the water. It was much cooler than the air around them and looked incredibly pure. Gurdjieff wouldn't die of thirst any time soon down here, that much was sure. If he'd brought some basic provisions, he could survive for weeks.

"Where do we go now?" asked Tristan as he pointed towards the second, narrower tunnel that disappeared into the darkness.

"We'll follow Rue des Capucines until we reach the adjacent street," replied Juliette. When she noticed the look of surprise on Tristan's face, she explained. "To make it easier to get around down here, Guillaumot decided to name the tunnels after the streets above them."

"So, it's identical to the streets on the surface?"

"Precisely. For example, here we're below where Rue des Capucines meets the old Venereal Hospital, according to the sign. I don't need to tell you what sort of diseases they treated there," she added with a mischievous smile.

Juliette led the way, shining the glow of her candle on the walls. Tristan noticed little alcoves on either side. One of them was full of skulls darkened by the passage of time.

"Did you know that the bodies of most of the people who were guillotined during the Revolution were thrown into the catacombs? And to make sure people wouldn't worship them as saints, they made sure to separate the head from the rest of the skeleton. You could be looking at all that's left of Danton or Robespierre," enthused Juliette.

Tristan didn't answer. He'd just caught sight of a long stone wall that seemed to block the end of the tunnel. Juliette glanced at her map.

"That's the supporting wall at the base of Val-de-Grâce Hospital. We'll need to turn right to explore the last part of this section—a real labyrinth! If I needed to hide somewhere, this is definitely where I would come."

"Why do you think I'm looking for someone?" asked Tristan nonchalantly.

Juliette brought the candle towards her face, revealing the colour of her light-grey eyes.

"Because the catacombs have always been fugitives' last resort. Marat hid here, as did members of the Paris Commune years later. When you're running from the law, you leave the surface for the world of darkness," she said ominously.

Tristan was about to reply when a noise made them whirl around.

"Are there rats down here?" asked Tristan.

"No. Unlike in the sewers, there's nothing to eat down here. It was probably just a falling stone. Who else would be down here?"

"You have all the answers, don't you?" said Tristan to change the subject.

"It would seem so, with you."

They'd just turned right. Tristan was listening closely, but there was nothing to hear. He discreetly ran his hand over his belt to feel the grip of his Luger. It was still there.

"And now, we have to choose between two—" Juliette stopped short. The tunnel up ahead came to a dead end. The ceiling had caved in, forming a conical pile of rubble that blocked their path.

"I hope the person you're looking for isn't behind there, because the map says there's no other way out," said Juliette.

Tristan walked over to the pile and began to carefully climb towards the top.

"What are you doing?" Juliette exclaimed. "It's too dangerous. It could give way beneath you!"

"I'm willing to take that risk."

22

Department S, London

"What do you mean, you've not managed to track her down?" exclaimed Malorley.

"I'm back in the phone box on the corner near Hellfire," replied the agent he'd dispatched. "That's where I was when Crowley came out of the club. I've scoured the whole area now, Commander. She's nowhere to be found."

"Find her roommate then. Laure was supposed to meet her and some other friends. Maybe she left without waiting for you. Call me as soon as you have any news!"

Malorley hung up and jumped to his feet. A wave of anxiety crashed into him. It didn't make sense. Laure had asked for an agent to relieve her, and for the car to take her to her night out.

Crowley, who was sitting in an armchair on the other side of the desk, watched the commander pace the room. "She was desperate to get to her friends. You know how she is—impatience incarnate!"

"Maybe, but something about it doesn't feel right. Especially since you told me what Moira O'Connor and her band of killers are up to."

"Do you really think they took her? I don't see how they could have known we were together, unless they followed us there. That said, she might have been standing in that telephone box a little too long to make a credible passer-by."

"That could've been enough to tip off one of Moira's lackeys."

"I suppose you could always send the police to search the

place. The SOE must be entitled to a few favours from Scotland Yard."

"I'd love to, but we'd lose an invaluable asset. German intelligence services will know not to trust the information Moira fed them—and Operation Witchfall will have been in vain if she can't send the footage to Berlin," explained Malorley as he sat down at his desk. The red light signalling an in-house call blinked on his telephone, but he ignored it. "This is all my fault! Laure didn't want to go with you, and I made her. She knew Moira was responsible for the new murders, but I didn't listen!"

"We'll know more in a few hours," Crowley said calmly.

"Several long hours," replied Malorley. "In the meantime, I need you to write down everything Moira told you. If they're blackmailing army officials and politicians, we have to identify them to protect national security. I need to warn MI5 and the Prime Minister. Try to—"

There was a knock at the door.

"Not now!" shouted Malorley.

Although muffled by the closed door, his secretary's high-pitched voice reached them nonetheless.

"Commander, I've been trying to reach you. It's urgent."

"It will have to bloody well wait!"

The door opened and the young woman strode determinedly towards her angry boss.

"Katie, are you deaf? I told you—"

She stood defiantly in front of him. "You would never forgive me if I didn't give you this message," she said solemnly.

Malorley grabbed the piece of paper from her hands. "You'd better hope that—"

He stopped short, hypnotized by what he was reading.

"What's going on?" asked Crowley, who had been getting ready to leave.

Malorley put the piece of paper down on his desk.

"The MI6 intercepted an excerpt from a French SS communication. Himmler has asked his men to keep an eye on Reichsleiter Rosenberg, who is in Paris at the moment—"

"Ah, my dear Alfred, I knew him rather well before the war," interrupted Crowley. "He's fascinated by the occult and is a former member of the Thule Society."

"Not to mention the leading Nazi pillager of the art world," added Malorley.

"But why is the fact that he's in Paris so important to you?" asked the mage.

"It's not that. Himmler alludes to the presence of one of his agents in Rosenberg's inner circle. A man named Tristan Marcas."

"He's alive!" exclaimed Crowley. "That young man must have earned favour with the gods. What wonderful news."

"The moment we learn he's still in the game, Laure disappears. Fate's cruelty will never cease to amaze me. But I've kept you long enough, Crowley. Good night."

23

Cochin Hospital, Paris

When he reached the top of the rubble pile, Tristan scrutinized the blocks of stone. Unlike at the base, the stones here were stacked in an orderly fashion. He moved one, then another, until he felt a gust of cool air. His intuition had been right. Gurdjieff had hoped the rubble would fool anyone who came looking for him. He had climbed to the top himself, cleared a passage, and carefully covered it up behind him.

Tristan turned to Juliette. "I'm just going to explore the rest of the tunnel. I won't be long," he said.

Without waiting for a reply, he jumped through the hole. The slope on the other side was gentler. He quickly found holds for his hands and feet and made his way down to the ground. Now he had to be careful not to scare the Russian. Gurdjieff could be armed, and might react erratically.

Tristan took three steps forward. According to the map, there were only about ten more meters of tunnel ahead. And voices carried further underground.

"Gurdjieff," he said, "I know you're down here. I found the engraved stone hidden beneath the floor in your son's room. The initials and the date led me here."

There was no reaction.

"I also know who you are—a friend of the imperial family. And I even know why the Germans are looking for you."

Silence.

"Listen, to prove you can trust me, I'm going to take ten steps forward and put my gun on the ground, then I'll turn around and walk back here," offered the Frenchman.

Tristan did as he'd promised.

"Don't move," yelled Gurdjieff in a thick Russian accent.

Tristan put his hands in the air.

"Do you have any other weapons?"

"No." Tristan heard the breech of his Luger click as a bullet slid into the barrel.

"Turn around."

Tristan obeyed and found the fugitive standing before him holding a lantern. With his dishevelled grey hair and beard, he bore little resemblance to the elegant tutor who had taught the tsarevich how to ride a bike.

"I'm Tristan," ventured Marcas.

The Russian looked him up and down, a look of terror in his eyes. "Did Rosenberg send you?"

Tristan was surprised. "How did you know?"

"He's been looking for me for years. Sometimes I think he built his entire Nazi career just to find me."

"I don't understand. How long have you known him?"

"We met in 1917, in Moscow."

Tristan suddenly remembered his conversation with the captain on the way to Frankfurt: Rosenberg had studied architecture in Russia just before the Revolution broke out.

"Did you meet at university?"

Gurdjieff laughed. "Rosenberg preferred more intimate, influential circles. Even back then, he was hungry for power," he said, then suddenly brandished the Luger. "Now, tell me what you want."

"Rosenberg knows you have the Romanovs' jewels. He wants them."

"And you believed him?"

"You did sell one of the tsar's treasures to pay for your flat," argued Tristan.

The Russian's face fell, and Tristan took advantage of the situation.

"You have my gun. You can run if you like. But since we found you once . . . "

"Are you threatening me?" asked the Russian, indignantly.

"No, but I do have an offer for you. Your life and freedom for the tsar's jewels. Once Rosenberg has them, he'll leave you in peace."

Gurdjieff's eyes gleamed in the dim light. "You don't understand. Rosenberg doesn't care one bit about the imperial jewels—"

Juliette's scream interrupted the Russian. "Watch out, Tristan. He has a gun!"

The huge figure of Marcel rolled to the bottom of the pile of rubble. He pushed Tristan aside and trained his gun on Gurdjieff. "Put it down, you dirty old Russian, or I'll blow your brains out!" he shouted.

"Hand over the jewels, or else he'll kill you!" shouted Tristan.

Gurdjieff plunged his free hand into his jacket pocket and tossed a bag towards Marcel. A ring escaped and rolled across the floor. In the light of the lantern, Rosenberg's lackey chased after it.

That's when the Russian opened fire.

The collaborator's bloody body slammed into the ground with a thud, but he managed to get off a lucky shot before he passed out. The Russian collapsed in turn.

Tristan snatched the revolver from Marcel's lifeless hand and hurried to Gurdjieff's side. "There's a hospital right above us," he said. "I'll take you there."

"No use," mumbled Gurdjieff.

Tristan ripped off the Russian's jacket. The bullet had entered just above his groin, rupturing the femoral artery. Blood gushed from the wound.

"Rosenberg . . . In Moscow, he was part of . . . occult circles. They thought they were the chosen ones . . . Worshipped the sacred symbol. The spinning star."

"Don't talk, you'll only tire yourself out!" soothed Tristan.

"Everything collapsed because the tsar . . . sent it away. If the swastika had stayed at the Kremlin, the communists could never have . . . seized power."

Tristan froze.

"You mean the sacred swastika?" he asked, incredulous.

"Yes. People said it was in Russia, but I thought it was a legend. Rosenberg . . . he was convinced the rumours were true. Then the Revolution began and . . . the tsar revealed its existence to me. Before sending it . . . to safety."

Tristan was disappointed he had let Rosenberg manipulate him into doing his dirty laundry work for him. And now, because of him, he would soon have two dead bodies on his hands.

"Where is the last swastika?" he asked urgently.

"Safe . . . In England."

I might as well be looking for a needle in a haystack, thought Tristan.

Gurdjieff choked on the stream of blood trickling from his lips. He took Tristan's hand. "In London. Find . . . James Hadler."

When Tristan reappeared at the top of the rubble pile, Juliette was waiting for him, nervously wringing the brim of her hat.

"I heard shouting and gunfire," she said. "And you're covered in blood!"

"You won't hear any more," he reassured her. He needed to make sense of what he'd just learned, but first he had to get the librarian to safety. "Juliette, can you find your way back up on your own?" he asked.

"With my eyes closed, but I can't leave you here!"

"I'm afraid you must," said Tristan, pointing to the rubble. "There are two dead bodies on the other side. One of them is a collaborator. Do you really want to be mixed up with that kind of people?" he asked.

Juliette stopped fiddling with her hat. She realized she had no choice.

"You've been an invaluable help," he said, stroking her cheek. "You saved my life."

"Is there anything else I can do?" she asked.

"Well, there is one more thing. You could go to the Protestant church on the corner of Rue de l'Oratoire and Rue Saint-Honoré."

Juliette looked surprised. "You want me to pray for you?" she asked, perplexed.

"Better than that. You're going to help me out a second time."

"I'm listening."

"Ask to see the pastor. Tell him you have an urgent message to get to England. He'll protest, but ignore him. Tell him you know about the parachutist he's hiding. That should make him get a move on."

"What's the message?"

"Just one sentence. For Commander Malorley: 'The relic is in London.'"

"That's all?"

"Every word counts, believe me."

Juliette put her hat back on. "Consider it done. I suppose I'll never see you again," she added sadly.

Tristan stayed silent.

"What a shame. I'd started to develop a fondness for our adventures . . . and you."

Me too, Tristan wanted to whisper, but held back.

Without another word, Juliette turned and left. He watched her until the glimmer of her candle rounded a corner and disappeared.

Now he was truly alone.

PART THREE

"Today a new faith is awakening: the myth of the blood [...]. Nordic blood is the mystery that has vanquished and replaced the old sacraments."
  Alfred Rosenberg, *The Myth of the Twentieth Century*

"The cemeteries of time are full of the ghosts of people who believed they were immortal."
                Excerpt from the *Thule Borealis Kulten*

24

The Wolf's Lair, Poland

The train sped through the forest towards the Russian border with its lights out. This distant region of Poland was said to be out of reach of British bombers, but the security measures put in place to protect the Reichsführer had been heightened nevertheless. Since Heydrich's assassination in Prague by a British-trained local commando unit, the head of the SS seemed to be everywhere. Now, whenever he travelled, several itineraries were communicated to the authorities, only one of which would be chosen at the last minute. To leave nothing to chance, a specially created Gestapo unit was spreading rumours about his presence in various places across the country. His office even announced visits only to cancel them at the eleventh hour. After Hitler, the Reichsführer was the most protected man in Germany.

Himmler had just finished reading Tristan's report. He had a lead on the location of the last swastika. Better yet, he'd thwarted Rosenberg's ambitions. The Reichsführer had eliminated all other competitors in the race to the final relic.

And he would find and use it.

Himmler lifted the blinds and glanced out of the window. Despite the growing darkness, he could still make out the tops of the trees, which stood out against a cloudy sky. *The forest alone can guide you to the truth*, he thought. *It's the only place you can really commune with the forces of nature—the forces that mould superior men once they've vanquished their own fears. That's why Germanic tribes lived in the woods and refused to build cities like the Greeks. Civilization saps man's vitality.*

He flipped open his notebook. This was an idea he couldn't afford to forget. He would add mandatory survival training in the forest to the SS military training programme—with no food, water, or weapons. To guide Europe, the new elite would first need to get in touch with its roots. Only then could it grow into a mighty tree with branches growing as high as the sky.

"I'm sorry to interrupt, Reichsführer," said an officer who had appeared in the doorway. The train slowed. "We've arrived at the Wolf's Lair."

Hitler's Bunker, Zone 1

The Wolf's Lair had begun to be built in the autumn of 1940 as an operational command post for the future invasion of the USSR. Located in a seemingly endless forest in Poland, the concrete fortress included tunnels, a train station, a landing strip, and a few log cabins with thatch roofs for local colour. While most of the Nazi officials hated the place and considered it ugly and depressing, Hitler felt at home at the Lair, and visited whenever his presence at the Chancellery or the Berghof wasn't required. He didn't mind the grey walls or the constant glare of artificial light. In fact, his appreciation of the austerity had grown with every year the war raged on. His quarters were in the heart of Zone 1, the most guarded part of the site that also accommodated his general staff. Göring had done his best to make himself at home in the stark space and had covered the floor with Persian rugs to accompany his masterpieces on the wall. Even so, the head of the Luftwaffe hated his lodgings just as much as the meeting room where Hitler now awaited him.

"*Mein Führer*," exclaimed Göring as he came in, "why spend the summer here in this mosquito-infested Polish forest? Let me take you back to Berlin. You'll see, a week back in the capital, and you'll be a new man!"

Hitler stared at him as though he were a child. "You seem to have forgotten, Hermann, that we are waging a war against the forces of evil: the Russians, British, and Americans."

"I certainly haven't, *Führer*, but we have already triumphed over Poland, destroyed France, swept through the Balkans, and brought England to her knees. Even with help from the Yankees, a handful of degenerate Slavs won't stand in our way!" Göring countered, pounding his chest for emphasis. Each impact made his countless medals jump off his pristine white uniform.

"It may be true that we have celebrated many great victories, Hermann," hissed Goebbels. "But that was when we could still count on an air force worthy of the name."

Göring spun around in irritation. He hadn't heard the Dwarf arrive. "My dear Joseph," exclaimed the master of the Luftwaffe, "how delightful to see you! But you've come without Magda. When will we have the pleasure of seeing her star in one of your delightful propaganda films? Her blonde beauty is so very Aryan! I've never understood why you waste the leading roles on second-rate Czech actresses."

Goebbels stood upright. He had made his way to the top of the Nazi hierarchy through sheer willpower and eloquence, and had no intention of letting this go.

"Speaking of the ladies, how is Emmy, Hermann? I hope your charming second wife will last longer than the first! What was her name again? So sad she didn't survive your way of life."

"I forbid you!" shouted Göring.

Hitler watched on impassively. The more his advisors quarrelled, the less they opposed his decisions.

"Gentlemen," the Führer interrupted finally, "I didn't bring you here to the *Wolfsschanze* to talk about your wives. The topic at hand is our military situation. Himmler will be here any moment."

"Ah, good old Heinrich," chuckled Göring. "What do you suppose he'll tell us this time? Maybe he's found Thor's Hammer!"

"Or the Holy Grail," chimed in Goebbels. "Last time he was certain he'd found it in a Catalonian monastery."

When it came to mocking Himmler, the Ogre and the Dwarf always joined forces.

"Maybe he'll suggest sending a new expedition to Tibet to learn levitation!" Göring continued enthusiastically.

"Or to the Canary Islands, to commune telepathically with the survivors of Atlantis!"

There was a shy knock, and Hitler signalled his men to open the armoured door. Himmler stepped in and clicked his heels. He was surprised to see Göring and Goebbels beaming at him.

"Hello, Heinrich," said Hitler. "Please sit down. Now, gentlemen, let's take a closer look at our position on the eastern front." The Führer put on his glasses and walked over to a map of the USSR. It was cut in half by a black line.

"Our troops are currently holding a line from Leningrad to Sebastopol, from the Gulf of Finland to the North Sea," explained Hitler.

Göring joined Hitler and studied the line, which covered thousands of kilometers and was made up of four million men. Its weaknesses were obvious. It was too long to defend and too far from Germany to supply easily. A strategic folly and logistical nightmare. Hitler picked up a ruler with his left hand and pointed to the south-eastern corner of the map.

"In late June we launched a new offensive in a bid to reach the Caucasus. The Russian lines have collapsed, and the Volga is now only about a hundred kilometers away. We'll have reached the Turkish border within weeks," continued the Führer.

Goebbels stared at the map, hypnotized. What fascinated him was not the victorious advance of the German army, but the immense territory that was left to conquer. The river that was the Reich's army seemed to be dwindling to trickling streams that would eventually dry up and disappear, subsumed by Russia.

"This attack has two goals," explained Hitler. "To panic the Soviets and force them to thin their main line near Moscow, where they've gathered their best troops—and to gain access to the oil fields in the Caucasus, to ensure a steady supply for our tanks."

"Stalin should have a bag at the ready!" exclaimed Goebbels. "He'll be enjoying the charms of a German prison cell before long."

Himmler kept quiet, letting his nemesis proffer the flattery. The Reichsführer was no sycophant.

"What about you, Heinrich," asked Hitler. "What do you think?"

"We've been fighting a war from the Atlantic to the Ural Mountains and from Scandinavia to Africa since last year. In addition to England, we're also opposing the two most powerful countries in the world—the United States and the Soviet Union—which have near unlimited resources and manufacturing capabilities," Himmler replied solemnly.

"You're quite the pessimist, my friend," smirked Goebbels. "Our flag now flies from Kiev to Tripoli!"

"I'm afraid I can only agree, Heinrich," said Göring. "Why are you always so glum?"

Himmler turned towards the Führer, whose features had become impenetrable. Over the last few months, he'd begun to seethe at the slightest contradiction, but his faith in Himmler was unshakeable.

"Our soldiers might be brave and the entire country mobilized, but the supply line can't keep up. We don't have the planes to compete with the British and American squadrons, and we're losing our submarines because their technology is obsolete. Our tanks will be next. I think of our army as a tired, old tiger. If we pounce to catch yet another prey, we'll fall—and never get back up."

Himmler drew a file from his inside pocket.

"Here are all the studies and statistics, *mein Führer*," he continued. "The originals—not the doctored versions you usually receive. All of them reach the same conclusion: our victories are the trees that hide the forest. Without a miracle, we will not be able to hold our position for more than three years. And doing so would cost us millions of lives."

"What do you propose?" exclaimed Goebbels.

"A miracle."

The men were silent for a while, and the only sound in the room was the buzzing of the aeration system.

"You must be joking, Heinrich," Goebbels finally said. "You can't possibly think you can save Germany with a swastika forged before the dawn of time just because you read about it in a dusty old book!"

Hitler said nothing. He'd folded his arms across his chest.

"And you want to go looking for it in London, at the heart of England—our worst enemy!" added Göring.

"We found the first swastika in Tibet in 1939," Himmler resumed unperturbed. "Two years later, we found the second in southern France. Both are safe at Wewelsburg Castle. But the third slipped through our fingers in Venice, and our military position has stagnated ever since."

"This is taking things too far!" shouted the head of the Luftwaffe. "You've lost your mind!"

Goebbels had halted his attacks. He was thinking. Though he openly mocked Himmler's esoteric beliefs, he also knew what a strong empire the man had built in just a few years. What if the Reichsführer was on to something? "Heinrich," he said. "You've always conducted your little quest on your own. And you were right to do so since I doubt anyone would have believed you. Why are you telling us all this now?"

"Trust me, I would have been delighted to continue on my own. But I need your help. The SS can't get a man into England, provide a cover, and protect him with a network on its own. Only one of our services has the means to do that: the Abwehr," said Himmler.

The faces in the room fell. Himmler, Goebbels, and Göring were all incredibly wary of the military intelligence service—it was the only organization the Nazi party had never managed to infiltrate. Handing over such an important mission meant taking a risk with unpredictable consequences.

All eyes were on the Führer, who was staring at the map again.

Finally, he looked up. "We've conquered Germany in the name of the swastika. It will help us conquer the world now," he declared, gesturing towards Himmler. "Reichsführer, retrieve the last swastika from London. Whatever the cost."

25

Laure opened her eyes to nothing but darkness and silence. She kept blinking—in vain. Her right cheek seemed to be resting on a cold, smooth surface, but that was the only sensation she could register. The rest of her body didn't seem to exist anymore. What on earth had happened?

Slowly, the cogs in her brain began to turn again.

The telephone box. Images wriggled through her consciousness like worms struggling to escape their holes. Malorley's call. The car that was supposed to pick her up and that couldn't have been far.

The image of a young blond man with emerald-green eyes suddenly came back to her. He had walked up to her with a broad smile on his face. When she'd asked if Malorley had sent him, he'd nodded. And then, everything had happened very quickly and ended with the searing pain of a needle in her left arm.

She had been tricked and kidnapped. Like a novice.

A wave of panic washed over her. Yet she kept still on the floor, as she had during the most challenging moments of her training, when they'd knocked her out, tied her up, and interrogated her for hours.

Laure tuned into her breathing, as instructed. It might not help her escape, but it channelled her fear—and she needed to regain control of her body. The substance she had been injected with had paralyzed her.

Little by little, a strange odour made its way to her nostrils. A blend of damp, wet dog, and rancid butter. The curious combination grew stronger and more unbearable with every breath. The smell was surprisingly familiar, but still she couldn't put her finger on it.

Laure tried to focus on the positive—the fourth technique taught to SOE agents, should they ever be captured. She was still alive, and the agent Malorley had sent to replace her would report her disappearance. They would be looking for her.

But another feeling was stronger. Anger. Her kidnapper had ruined her first night out in months. It was a ridiculous thought, but her anger was blissfully real.

The clang of metal pulled her from her thoughts. Footsteps made the floor vibrate. A halo of light appeared that could've been centimeters or kilometers away. Suddenly something hard was slipped under her cheek to prop up her head. Whatever it was, was swathed in the smell of old leather and urine.

"I'm so glad you're awake. Truly. Are you afraid?" asked a surprisingly gentle male voice.

The sound was so sweet, she almost expected him to declare his love for her.

"I'd be scared if I were you. Lying on the floor in the dark in a strange place, and at the mercy of a stranger."

Laure tried to reply, but no sound escaped her mouth. She struggled to move her lips, which felt dry and limp—about as useful as a spent match.

"You can't talk," continued the voice. "The substance I injected you with paralyzes the limbs, but it can also affect the vocal cords. I'm not great at administering the product. My apologies." The tip of the shoe pulled out from under her cheek, sending Laure's head crashing into the floor.

The man knelt by her side. She could smell his cheap cologne and feel his fingers at the corner of her lips. He slid them down to her chin, then stopped at the top of her throat. "I'm pinching you as hard as I can," he said, "but I'm sure you don't feel a thing. I could send a knitting needle through your eye to your brain, and it would only tickle."

She felt his hand lift her chin, then drop her head onto the floor once more. Again and again. Her cheekbone slammed into the stone each time, but she felt no pain. Her abductor was playing with her head as though it was a basketball. Laure's head thudded a final time against the floor.

"We'll have to wait for the sedative to wear off so you can talk," the man sighed lazily. "Such a waste of time." His footsteps faded into the distance. A moving shadow blocked out the dim light.

"Maybe you'd like to see a bit better," said the man. "How rude of me."

Laure heard a crackling sound far overhead. Blinding white light erupted all around her. She closed her eyes to escape the biting glare.

"Feel free to get to know your cellmate," said the voice. "Though I'm afraid he's not a big talker."

Laure waited a few seconds, then opened her eyes. It took her a few seconds to adjust to the dazzling light.

A man was staring at her, eyes open wide. He was lying on the ground, like Laure, his face only centimeters from hers—close enough to kiss. His lips were purple and his skin grey and puffy. His forehead bore a strange symbol. A swastika.

Laure suddenly recognized the smell she'd noticed earlier—the sickening scent from the mortuary. She suppressed the urge to vomit.

Her attacker's voice spoke again, though he was now too far away for her to see. "My name is Conrad, by the way. I'll be back in a few hours with my wife, Susan. I'm sure the two of you will get on splendidly."

26

Near the Pantheon, Paris

Back in his office, Rosenberg was examining the jewellery Tristan had retrieved from the Parisian underworld. Having carefully separated the rings from the necklaces, he was now studying a tiara that sparkled in the light.

"It's a shame we'll need to remove the stones from the settings and melt down the metal. But these pieces are too well-known to be sold as they are."

Tristan sat quietly in his chair. He knew Rosenberg was right. This was undoubtedly the surest way to transport and sell the family heirlooms for a fortune. He tapped his finger on the table, making a pair of earrings jump. "I asked your men to secure the perimeter of Cochin Hospital," Tristan said. "Officially to track resistance fighters—unofficially to dispose of Marcel's and Gurdjieff's bodies."

"I'll miss Marcel," replied Rosenberg, looking truly saddened. "He's irreplaceable when it comes to getting reluctant collectors to talk. Which reminds me—will you send a report to the Reichsführer?"

Tristan had already sent the report, which Himmler had probably already read, but he decided not to share this detail. "Of course, sir."

"I would appreciate it if you could omit the discovery of the imperial jewels. I'd like to be the one to present the Führer with this treasure."

Tristan nodded. He knew that Hitler would never see a single piece from the collection. As for Himmler, he already had a gun trained on Rosenberg. "Certainly," he said. "I imagine you'll take advantage of your next trip to Berlin to hand over the prize, before taking up your new position as Minister of the Eastern Territories?"

"Precisely. As for you," Rosenberg said, handing over a telegram, "you're expected at the Lutetia Hotel in one hour. The order has come directly from the Reichsführer's office."

Tristan got up. He was eager to escape the company of the corrupt ideologist.

"Before you go," continued Rosenberg, "did Gurdjieff say anything to you?"

"He didn't have time," replied Tristan, already halfway out of the door.

Lutetia Hotel, Boulevard Raspail, Paris

The foyer of the Lutetia was full of German officers. High-ranking Wehrmacht officials rubbed elbows with members of the Luftwaffe and the Kriegsmarine. It looked like the luxury hotel was hosting a plenary meeting of the Reich's general staff. The SS, however, was nowhere to be seen. Tristan knew the appearance was deceptive: they rarely mingled with the regular army, but their spies where everywhere. The Frenchman slalomed between a colonel with a monocle and a general in riding boots to reach the reception desk.

"Tristan Marcas," he said. "I'm expected."

The concierge glared at him, assuming he was a collaborator, then consulted the register. "Room 66 on the second floor. Please take the stairs to the right."

Tristan wound his way through the crowd of uniforms over to the stairs, and climbed slowly. Having fooled Rosenberg and warned Malorley, his position was relatively strong. But he had better not rest on his laurels. Experience had taught him to be wary of his employers. Spies—and even more so, double agents—were the first to be sacrificed. That's why he always kept certain information to himself, as he had the name of James Hadler, the London contact Gurdjieff had mentioned. It was his secret weapon—one that could keep him alive.

A group of officers accompanied by a gaudily made-up woman laughed as they strolled down the stairs. Tristan was forced to lean back against the railing to let them pass. This humiliation, however small, rankled his ego. Since he'd been back in Paris, the presence of the enemy had been harder to bear. He couldn't wait to get out of the sullied French capital.

The door to room 66 was slightly ajar. Tristan knocked, then stepped inside. Half-empty lunch plates sat on a pink marble table. He noticed there was only one place setting. Next, he made his way towards the bedroom. The bed was made, and a single open suitcase lay atop it. Tristan leaned over to get a better look at the contents.

"Are you going through my lingerie?"

Erika stepped out of the bathroom in a terry towelling robe. With her bare feet and wet hair, she looked nothing like the skinny, tormented woman he'd last seen. A sudden wave of desire rushed over him.

"Turn around, so I can get dressed," she ordered.

Tristan did as he'd been told, and found himself facing a sculpted 19th-century fireplace. It depicted a biblical scene: The Parable of the Sower. He would have preferred a mirror.

"I arrived this morning, straight from Berlin," announced Erika. "I have research to do in France. As you know, the Ahnenerbe's mission has been reviewed."

"So I've heard," replied Tristan.

"The Reichsführer has made identifying Jews his priority."

"More like an obsession, don't you think?"

Erika ignored him. "Certain Ahnenerbe researchers see it as an opportunity to boost their careers. Do you remember Bruno Beger?"

"The blond Hercules who went to Tibet?"

"That's the one. He now wants to apply the anthropological studies he conducted in Lhasa to Jews. He says he needs to measure skulls to do so—and guinea pigs without any cumbersome flesh attached."

Tristan almost whirled around. "You aren't going to help him, are you?" he said, disgusted.

"No, but I'm going to buy some time by giving him a mission here in France. A preparatory study. See, he's not the first to come up with the idea of measuring skulls to outline racial criteria. One of your countrymen beat him to it."

This time, he couldn't help but turn around. Erika was buttoning the top of her blouse. Her straight grey skirt was already in place. "You must be kidding!" he exclaimed, incredulous.

"Not at all. You must have heard of him: Vacher de Lapouge. A brilliant 19th-century academic. As a militant atheist, he was opposed to religion in all its forms—and a determined socialist. He was convinced that mankind's happiness depended on rigorous natural selection. And to determine who was worthy of the opportunity to forge the new human race, he developed a passion for measuring skulls."

"Don't tell me his studies were successful."

"Incredibly! He determined a rule he deemed universal: intellectuals' craniums are significantly larger than those of other individuals. An average seven centimeters longer and four centimeters wider, to be precise."

Tristan brought his hands to his head in disbelief, as if to check the size of his own skull.

"And what's more—the difference is hereditary. According to de Lapouge, it's measurable from the age of one," continued Erika as she slipped on a black jacket with pearl buttons. "So, I'm going to suggest Beger study and verify Lapouge's work. That should keep him from going anywhere near living subjects for a while."

"You've changed," Tristan remarked.

"No, it's not me. It's the world we live in: it's become incredibly dangerous. Your own lover might even be involved in an attempt on your life."

"Erika, let's not go back down that road!" Tristan exclaimed indignantly.

Studying her reflection in the mirror, Erika pulled her long blonde plait over her right shoulder.

"I remember everything," she declared solemnly. "Absolutely everything. So now you have to choose: either I hand you over to Himmler, or you work for me."

Tristan glanced towards the door, looking for an escape route.

"You were working with Di Stella who shot me. There's no point lying. And don't even think about throwing me out of the window to fix your little problem. I've taken every precaution."

"What do you want?"

Erika leaned in and brushed her lips against Tristan's. "You'll find out shortly, my love. In the meantime, you're expected in the foyer."

"What do you mean? Who's expecting me?" asked Tristan, stunned.

"Reinhard Gehlen. A charming man, you'll see."

The Lutetia had several small sitting rooms that had welcomed young couples before the war. Now they hosted secret conversations between German officials. When he stepped inside, Tristan was surprised to find a frail-looking man in a wrinkled and poorly tailored suit. He had dark circles under his eyes and thinning hair.

"Reinhard Gehlen, of the Abwehr," he said bluntly, as Tristan sat down in front of him.

Tristan didn't bother to introduce himself. Gehlen undoubtedly already knew everything about him.

"The Reichsführer has asked us to send you to England. Which means you'll need an undetectable cover and an introduction to the network we have there."

Tristan stifled a relieved sigh. He would soon be able to put some distance between himself and Erika.

"We know nothing at all about your mission. We're simply in charge of logistics," explained Gehlen.

"My life is still in your hands."

"And mine in the Reichsführer's, if you fail."

The quest for the final swastika had clearly become a priority for the Reich. Tristan realized Himmler must be under intense pressure.

"You mentioned a cover?" said Tristan.

"We have several covers waiting in every enemy country. We prepare and maintain them, sometimes for years. You'll get the best we have, of course."

Tristan sat back in his armchair. "So tell me about my new life," he asked casually.

"In May, a man by the name of Alvin Pepperbrock died in London. An Englishman with no family and an uneventful life story. He owned a small two-storey building in Bloomsbury, where he lived alone."

"How did you find him?"

"He was an art lover and especially enamoured of German expressionism. Often purchased his paintings from a Dutch gallery owner who fled the invasion of Holland."

"A gallery owner who works for you?"

"One who left his mother in Rotterdam. An old woman with diabetes who needs a steady supply of insulin. He pointed us in the right direction," continued Gehlen. "When Pepperbrock died, his solicitor began the search for heirs. He found them in Canada. Alvin had a sister, Clara, who'd moved to Ottawa. She had a son, named Adam."

"An only child, I suppose?" asked Tristan.

"You learn quickly. In March 1940, Clara and her husband died in a car accident near Sherbrooke in Quebec."

"So when his uncle died, Adam became his sole heir?"

"Precisely. Adam is twenty-six years old with brown hair like yours and he's about the same height. And most importantly, since his father is French Canadian, his French is much better than his English. Since the month of May, he's been the proud owner of the building in Bloomsbury."

"And where is Adam now?" enquired Tristan.

"On a boat heading for London. Well, at least someone

bearing his name, his papers, and all his correspondence with the solicitor is."

"And the real Adam?"

"Dead and buried in a beautiful park near Ottawa. May he rest in peace."

27

Churchill had never come to Buckingham Palace in the middle of the night before. He'd attended plenty of state dinners, but they rarely ended after eleven o'clock.

He could have done without this unexpected summons from the King. Only a few days earlier, he'd come out victorious in a vote of no confidence at the House of Commons, where a coalition of jealous MPs had demanded his resignation following Britain's catastrophic defeats in North Africa. They'd dared to defy *him*, the most popular Prime Minister in the country's history! Nevertheless, the political attack had come at the worst possible moment, just as he was starting to organize his trip to Moscow to seal a historic alliance with Stalin.

When it rains it pours, he thought, as he joined the King for a stroll around the enormous palace gardens. Churchill would have enjoyed the visit were he not utterly exhausted.

"Don't let the opposition in the House of Commons get to you, Winston," the King said gently.

"I envy Hitler, Mussolini, and Stalin," replied the Prime Minister. "Dictators don't have to worry about others criticizing their every move. An unwelcome comment is enough to send someone to the firing squad. But not to worry—at least this vote of no confidence has forced my enemies out into the open. I don't want to brag, but I'm an excellent shot. I'll take them out one by one!"

"You're a clever man, Winston. And brave. Sometimes I feel like you are now the true sovereign of our nation, and that I am your shadow."

"Never, your Majesty! You and the royal family are the embodiment of unity in our country and throughout the Commonwealth. I don't dare imagine where we would be if Edward had retained the throne. We would have been Hitler's allies in his bid to destroy humanity.

'Anyway, I've prepared an outline of my upcoming discussions with Stalin. Uncle Joe wants us to open a western front to get Hitler to pull back in Russia. The general staff and I, as well as the Americans, are all opposed to the idea. I plan to—"

The King shook his head. "We'll get back to that later. I have every confidence in you to conduct the negotiations with Russia. I'd rather hear how things are going in the search for the fourth swastika."

Churchill looked at the sovereign in astonishment, then rubbed his face in his hands. "Your Majesty, with all due respect, I think we have other priorities, and I have little time. That last sitting in parliament was exhausting, and I am desperate to get to bed."

"I understand, Winston, I understand. But, you see, I have good reason to believe that the search for the final relic is just as important to the outcome of the war."

"Why is that, your Majesty?"

"I'm afraid I cannot tell you. Maybe someday."

"You don't trust me."

"That's not it. Let's just say that some secrets must be kept. They open the doors to dark realms where reason sometimes fails. And I don't want to upset you."

Churchill's face went livid from a combination of anger and fatigue. "I apologize, your Majesty, but I've had enough of these ridiculous mysteries. I'm running a war with millions of your subjects' lives on the line and managing an empire stretched across five continents. I'm about to meet with the second most terrible monster humanity has ever known, and you want to talk about superstitions and magical trinkets? It seems you will succeed where the vote of no confidence failed. I'll hand in my resignation tonight. Find a Prime Minister you can trust. Good night, your Majesty."

The blood drained from George VI's face. He'd never seen Churchill in such a state. All of his frustrations and anger had just exploded like an earthquake bomb.

"Wait, Winston," pleaded the King. "Please don't give up now."

"Other men, just as competent as I am, will pick up where I left off."

"Your resignation would be a disaster for the free world. No one would understand, in the wake of your victory at parliament. I refuse to bear the responsibility for that."

The two men stood in silence for a moment. For some, hesitation was a weapon; for others, it could be deadly. The King knew he had to make a decision—right now. He placed his hand on Churchill's shoulder.

"Swear to me on what you love most in this world that you will never share what I'm about to tell you with a single soul, including your wife and children."

"I swear it."

"Even if you write your memoirs one day?"

"I give you my word."

"In that case, come with me."

Ten minutes later, the two men were comfortably seated in the King's private library. Churchill remained ensconced in an armchair, cigar in hand, as George VI got up to open a wall safe above a secretary desk.

"If I were a thief, your Majesty, I would make quick work of your safe. It doesn't seem particularly robust."

"Come now, Winston. You should know that English burglars are all monarchists."

The sovereign pulled a grey envelope from the safe, out of which he drew a yellowed letter. He wordlessly handed it to Churchill, alongside a magnifying glass with an ivory handle.

Winston stooped over the document. "The 19th of February, 1918. This coat of arms, the red griffin with a sword and shield, is the Romanovs'," he said, eyebrows raised with interest. "The letter is in English and signed by Nicholas and addressed to his 'dear cousin'. No need to be Sherlock Holmes to figure out it was sent to your father King George V from the last Tsar of All Russia."

"The tsar abdicated nearly a year before that date. He and his family were being held captive in Tobolsk, Siberia. But please, read on."

"Hmm. Nicholas asks his cousin to grant him asylum because he fears for his life and those of his family. I already knew about this," said the Prime Minister as he placed the letter down on the table. "A tragedy. Your father should have accepted. The tsar could have operated from London."

"Like your de Gaulle with the French?"

"Quite right. Even though that blasted general behaves more like a king than a president these days."

"My father knew that Nicholas was too unpopular in his country. It would only have prolonged the suffering of his defenders. He also feared the communists might spread their beliefs in Great Britain to get revenge. This is why he refused. But when he learned a few months later that the imperial family had been slaughtered in Yekaterinburg, he was devastated. He regretted his decision for the rest of his life."

"Your Majesty, this letter is a moving historical document, but I don't see what it has to do with the legend of the relics."

"You read it too quickly. Turn it over."

Churchill picked up the piece of paper and looked at the back to find a text in much smaller writing. To his great surprise, a swastika had been drawn at the end of the message.

"Are you quite certain this letter was written by the tsar? Because I can't believe it."

28

"You must believe it, Winston. As you can see, Nicholas II offered my father part of the Russian government's gold reserves—three tonnes protected by a loyal garrison in Vladivostok—and a sacred relic that could 'change the course of history'."

"I would imagine your father was more interested in the gold than the relic," replied Churchill.

"Well, you would be wrong. He had known of the relic's existence for years!" exclaimed King George. He walked over to a mahogany curio cabinet containing daggers set with precious gemstones, gold chalices, silver crosses, and Japanese and African masks, among other things. "I consider this to be my own personal museum," he continued, removing a large gold egg with blue enamel stripes from a shelf and taking it back to Churchill's armchair. "I won't insult you by telling you what this is."

The Prime Minister gingerly took the egg. "A Fabergé. It's magnificent. This is the first time I've ever held one."

"Nicholas gave it to my father in 1913, on an evening when they had retired to this very room. The same night the tsar brought up the relic. I was hiding behind a decorative screen near the window, to eavesdrop on their conversation."

"Princes are no different from other children," chuckled Churchill.

"Nicholas explained that the Fabergé egg was nothing compared to an extraordinary talisman his dynasty had possessed for the past three centuries. A relic more precious than his entire collection of eggs and more powerful than the mightiest English battleship. According to him, this talisman was the source of the Romanovs' power and protected Russia and its allies."

"And we're talking about one of the four swastikas?"

"Indeed. I remember that my father erupted into laughter. He was a practical man with a big personality. A bit like you."

"I'll take that as a compliment," said Churchill as he exhaled a column of smoke towards the ceiling.

The King placed the egg safely back on its cabinet shelf and went on. "Nicholas didn't back down, though. Instead, he told him the surprising story of his dynasty's beginnings. In the early 17th century, Russia was faced with hard times. Poverty, famine, and chaos ravaged the country. The Poles, Estonians, and tribes to the east raided constantly, murdering anyone who got in their way. There was no tsar, and the empire was governed, for better or worse, by a council of nobles and clergymen. They needed an emblematic figure to give the people hope and unite the country."

"History always repeats itself. When times are hard, the people need a saviour—a king, a Führer, a tsar . . . "

"Or a Prime Minister," said the King with a smile. "In any case, a name came to the fore. A teenager who lived in a monastery near on the banks of the Kostroma River. A noble related to the former reigning dynasty. There were other candidates, but God chose the young Mikhail Romanov, who was crowned tsar in 1613."

"With all due respect, your Majesty, I do know a little about the history of Russia," Churchill smiled.

"You're too impatient, Winston. What I'm about to reveal can't be found in any history book. Nicholas told my father a secret that had been passed down from generation to generation in the Romanov family. Before he became tsar, the young Mikhail had been helping the monks clean the monastery. One day, the abbot tasked him with moving bodies from tombs in the crypt, in preparation for some renovations. Upon opening one of the tombs, Mikhail found a secret passage that led to another room underground, which must have dated back to pagan times."

Winston put down his cigar and rubbed his temples. He hoped the King was nearly finished. "This sounds like a Quatermain mystery!" he exclaimed.

"It does indeed," agreed George. "Mikhail found an altar bearing a strange cross—a cross we would now call a swastika. When he spoke to the abbot about it, he was told he could keep it. The very same day he found it, the council in Moscow, three hundred kilometers away, named him Tsar of All Russia."

"A coincidence. Life is full of them," countered Churchill.

"I still haven't finished, Winston. Mikhail continued to support the monastery during his reign. Indeed, he and his successors made it one of the most important spiritual centres in Russia. He left the swastika at the monastery and warned his descendants never to remove it. As long as it was safe there, the Romanov dynasty would rule Russia. A curse would befall whosoever chose not to heed this rule. For centuries, the tsars respected Mikhail's wishes."

"All but the last tsar, Nicholas II, I suppose?"

"Precisely. Russia wasn't prepared for the Great War. Riots spurred by the revolutionaries sprang up all over the country. Out of fear, Nicholas had the relic removed from the monastery. A month later, he was forced to abdicate. The curse of the Kostroma monastery had struck. Now you understand why my father knew exactly what relic the tsar was alluding to when he received this letter."

"I have to admit this is a fascinating story, your Majesty. But that's no reason to take it seriously."

"I told you that my father was a man of reason. But the murder of his cousin by the Reds shook him to the core. His personality changed. He hoped to make amends for his failure to save the tsar by helping his aunt, the Dowager Empress, escape to England, but nothing could ease his guilt. In 1936, on his death bed, my father made my brother and me promise to find the relic, whatever the costs, to re-establish balance in the world. He made us swear on the Bible! Edward assumed it was nothing more than a dying man's ramblings, but I knew better. My promise haunts me still.

After he died, I conducted discreet research on the legends that surrounded the relics of power. Not long ago, I learned that there were others. If you'll remember, one of your SOE officers spoke in front of the Gordon Circle about the Nazis' interest in the occult. He also mentioned the legend of the swastikas."

Churchill nodded. "Now I understand why you insisted I authorize the operation at Montségur monastery, in France."

"It was a shock to learn there were other relics out there. And when your man brought the first relic back to England, I couldn't wait to send it to our American friends. I didn't want it to fall into the Nazis' hands if they ever successfully invaded our island. Speaking of which, do you know exactly where it is now?"

"Last I heard," Churchill replied wearily, "it was being studied in a laboratory somewhere near Boston. The Americans are real pragmatists. If this . . . object has the powers you claim it does, they might find a way to use it, thanks to their scientific advances."

"I don't doubt it," said the King. "That being said, the relic may also bolster their power—just like the swastika from Tibet strengthened the Germans. This is why we must get our hands on the last talisman—to ensure the United Kingdom has a place at the table after the war."

"Your Majesty, I'm afraid you've still not won me over. But if you were indeed correct, these relics would be cursed objects. They've brought nothing but misfortune, suffering and chaos to the world."

"The relics of chaos," mumbled George VI.

The clock struck one. The King stood up briskly. "I've taken up too much of your time, Winston. I won't keep you any longer. I know I haven't convinced you, but I do hope I've answered your questions."

"It's honourable of you to keep the promise you made to your father. God chose wisely when he placed you on the throne over your brother. As soon as I hear from Commander Malorley, I'll let you know."

The King accompanied the Prime Minister to the door and shook his hand at length. His expression was grave. Churchill bowed and turned to leave. He'd just left the library when the sovereign's voice rang out.

"Wait, Winston. One last thing about the Romanov curse." The King hastily joined him in the corridor. "Since you know your Russian history," he continued, "you must remember the name of the place where Nicholas II and his family were murdered."

"Yekaterinburg," replied the Prime Minister. "In the home of a merchant. Ipatiev House. It was in all the papers at the time."

"Ipatiev, that's right," the King said solemnly. "Did you know that the monastery in Kostroma was also called Ipatiev?"

Churchill didn't know what to say.

King George went on: "Coincidences are often telling signs on the map of destiny. Those who understand them are more likely to head in the right direction. You must find the last relic, Winston, at any price. And you must find it before the Nazis do. The fate of the world is in your hands."

"And if I fail? I haven't had any news from the SOE. No new leads."

"Then may God have pity on our souls."

29

Lutetia Hotel, Paris

Tristan had stayed at the Lutetia to work on his cover, with Gehlen's help. In his discreet room, far from the constant comings and goings of German officers, he felt like he was back at university. Except that his teacher was a master spy rather than a learned professor.

Until he left for England, he had to be on his toes. After years in Himmler's service, this would be his one and only chance to escape to the free world. For the moment though, he was holed up here with Gehlen, who had built his entire career on his ability to sniff out a lie. What did Tristan really know about him? What if this whole thing was just a charade to bring years of deceit and manipulation to a swift end? Tristan had no intention of offering himself up as a trophy, so he was keeping a low profile.

He was particularly wary of Gehlen because he was so different from other German officers. They were typically known for their stiff, disdainful demeanour, but Gehlen displayed a remarkable ability to adapt. He was the kind of man who wore his heart on his sleeve, which put people at ease—like a dog who holds out a friendly paw and then bites.

To prepare the Frenchman for his mission in London, Gehlen wanted to focus on a single subject: survival in hostile territory. Much to Tristan's surprise, he didn't recommend keeping the mind on high alert at all times, on the lookout for the slightest danger. Instead, he told him to be as transparent as possible. Tristan wondered if Gehlen was speaking from experience. Since things had turned sour on the eastern front, Germany's intelligence services had been under suspicion. The Nazis accused them of underestimating the Russians' military capabilities. Some, like Goebbels, even accused them of treason. A purge couldn't be far off. Tristan was certain Gehlen would make it out alive. He was too clever to fall with the others.

The Frenchman was surprised, however, to learn about the extent of the German intelligence network in Britain. The Abwehr agent was detailing an elaborate organization the British apparently knew nothing about.

At some point, Tristan got up. He'd pretended to be impressed with Gehlen's revelations, but in truth, the German hadn't given much away—he certainly hadn't given Tristan any concrete information he could use as leverage with the British. Now that he would be heading to London to find the last swastika, he couldn't help but wonder how the British would react once he'd found it. He trusted Malorley, but not Malorley's superiors at the SOE. Wouldn't it be in their best interest to bury the dangerous object and Tristan along with it? As long as there was a sacred relic to be found, he was useful. But after that, he wasn't so sure. Unless he had something to bargain with . . .

Tristan turned towards Gehlen. "Why don't you tell me more about the parts of the network that are involved with business and politics?"

The German checked his watch. "As much as I'd love to, I promised to finish up here soon. Besides, don't you have a meeting with the head of the Ahnenerbe? I wouldn't want to disappoint one of the Reichsführer's most beloved servants."

As he walked down the corridor, Tristan kept coming back to the word "beloved". Was Gehlen alluding to a relationship between Erika and Himmler? Though Goebbels' affairs were the most talked-about, there were also rumours that Himmler had had a liaison with his secretary. Some people even whispered that the child she'd recently given birth to was by an unknown father. Had the Reichsführer become a Don Juan? Was Erika one of his conquests? Tristan knew he couldn't let himself be thrown off guard by these questions—but his efforts to repress the jealousy burning inside him were futile.

Erika's room was one of the most luxurious suites at the Lutetia. From the sitting room, which looked out over two streets, Tristan could see both the Saint-Germain-des-Prés steeple and the entrance to the Bon Marché department store. He was surprised. The Erika he'd known in France and Crete couldn't have cared less about comfort and had openly disdained luxury. That no longer seemed to be the case. With its enormous bed and profusion of sculpted mirrors, the room looked better suited to a famous actress. Erika stepped out of the bathroom in a cloud of hot air. She strolled over to her bed, lighting a cigarette on the way. She was beautiful and she knew it. Maybe she had too much of a hold on him.

"How was your meeting with Gehlen?" she asked.

"I didn't know you smoked," replied Tristan, changing the subject.

"Now that I know my life can be brought to an abrupt end at any moment, I no longer refuse myself certain pleasures. Now, tell me about Gehlen."

"Why are you so interested in him?"

"I'm interested in the Abwehr. The Ahnenerbe will be conducting more and more scientific studies, and I need a solid research base in other countries. I've told Gehlen that we should have a scientific espionage department within the Abwehr."

"Do you really think other countries are wasting their time measuring skulls to find out who is Jewish?" balked Tristan.

Erika exhaled a column of smoke towards the ceiling. "At Himmler's request, we're also focusing on medical research."

"Don't tell me you're going to play Frankenstein," scoffed Tristan. "Building the *Ubermensch* from scraps?"

Erika ignored him. "Tell me about the quest."

"I'm leaving for London. My new lead points in that direction."

"Right. The tsar's relic supposedly left Russia just before the Bolsheviks seized power. And was taken to England."

"I see you've read the report I sent to Himmler."

"Quite right. Don't forget: you are still a member of the Ahnenerbe and under my orders."

Erika shifted in her bathrobe, exposing more of her legs. Tristan wondered if her injury had changed her personality. "Before you sent me to meet with Gehlen, you accused me of being in cahoots with your attacker, and threatened to tell Himmler. What are you playing at?"

"I hope you realize you're not even defending yourself anymore. You haven't even tried to protest your innocence."

"There's nothing I can do about your visions. Why don't you go rat me out to the Reichsführer, if you're so sure of yourself? Come on, go ahead!"

Erika lit another cigarette. "Did you know that moments before death, the brain records everything it perceives down to the slightest detail?"

"But you're not dead . . . "

"And yet, I remember precisely who was with me on Lido beach. The pictures I could draw from my memory would be as reliable as photographs. I could compare them with King George VI's roster of spies . . ."

"You're losing your mind!"

"Maybe I should talk to Gehlen about it. Do you think he'd still let you go to London?"

Tristan leapt forward, but Erika held up a hand to stop him. "I wouldn't do that if I were you. This isn't a forgotten castle in Pomerania—it's a hotel full of German soldiers. And if I scream, you'll find yourself in the hands of the Gestapo. Is that what you want?"

"That's enough, Erika!"

Amused by her lover's anger, von Essling stretched across the bed like a cat in a ray of sunlight. "Do you think I don't know that if you find the last relic, you'll give it to your English friends? There's just one thing you've forgotten: as soon as they get their hands on it, you'll become an inconvenient accessory to an embarrassing quest."

Tristan burst into laughter. Though Erika's observation aligned perfectly with his own doubts.

"Where would you say I have a better chance of ending up with a bullet in my brain—in England or in your charming country?"

"I'd say your chances are about the same if I talk," she replied coldly.

Tristan rested his elbows on the windowsill. He was certain Erika was bluffing, but there was something about her accusatory attitude he couldn't put his finger on. And then there was something else that worried him: Erika kept mentioning the Abwehr officer. Had she already spoken to him?

"Even if you share your hallucinations with Gehlen, it won't be up to him if I go or not. Himmler wants to get his hands on the relic, no matter what."

"You're right. I'd need time to convince Himmler. But it will be much easier to persuade the English. I know so much about you, my love. And I can share it with them directly."

"Thanks to your new friend Gehlen? And what would you give them? You're making this up, Erika."

"What makes you think I'd tell them the truth? Do I look like a child? No, I'd tell them that you helped Di Stella scare the English commando unit away in Venice. That we'd planned it that way. My survival is proof enough."

Tristan watched her without speaking. It was as though she were playing a role. She wasn't playing it very well—the Erika he knew would never behave like that—but while her cynical attitude was off, her words struck a chord.

Erika blew smoke in his face, rousing him from his thoughts. "Of course, I wouldn't omit the fact that you didn't throw the relic into the lagoon. The Abwehr has a gift for fabricating evidence, and Gehlen can leak it to the right people in Britain. Once you arrive in London, you could be a dead man walking, my friend." Erika undid the belt of her robe. "And we wouldn't want that would we? So I'd suggest you bring the relic back to Germany once you've found it, and then I'll be happy to forget about certain events." She pulled him close. "Should you decide otherwise, this will be the very last time you make love."

30

London

Laure blinked. The light was blinding as she emerged from her chemically induced sleep, but she'd regained consciousness more quickly this time. She was seated on a chair bolted to the ground, wrists fastened to the armrests, feet tied to a stool out in front of her. Laure realized they had readied her for torture.

She tried to wriggle free, but every movement heightened the searing pain in her wrists. They'd used wire to bind her. She gave up and took in her surroundings. Her kidnapper had moved her. This room was windowless, and she could guess it was underground. The flaky, grey walls reeked of damp, reminding her of the cellar of the castle in which she'd grown up. A startlingly bright lightbulb hung from the low ceiling. Laure had a closer look around her. No dead bodies this time. The only pieces of furniture were the table across from her and a few empty crates stacked up in a corner.

She suddenly felt incredibly thirsty. She licked her lips to wet them, but her mouth and throat were so dry they felt like sandpaper. Laure had no idea how much time had passed since she'd been kidnapped. The drug could have knocked her out for days or weeks. Strangely, she was less anxious now than she had been the first time she'd woken. And she was still hopeful. She was still alive, which meant her attacker needed something from her or he'd have killed her straight away. Besides, Malorley would have sounded the alarm.

Laure heard a muffled sound on the other side of the door. She listened intently. Whispering. The lock creaked and the handle moved. Instinctively, Laure sat up straight. The feeling of the wire cutting into her skin nearly knocked the wind out of her. Fear washed over her once more. The SOE's calming techniques suddenly seemed useless.

Conrad appeared in the doorway, accompanied by a woman. *His wife*, Laure thought. Just like Conrad, she was young—about her own age. She seemed sporty, with a distinctly more masculine face than his.

Conrad smiled as he strolled over. "How is our little spy doing? I do hope you're enjoying your new accommodations."

"Let me go right this instant!" shouted Laure.

The woman sat down on the edge of the table and studied her in disgust. "I told you, Conrad. Frenchwomen are such a pain."

"Not all of them. I knew a girl from Lyon before the war. She was exquisite. I've always liked France," countered the German.

"So much so that you invaded it," Laure pitched in sarcastically.

The German ignored her. He reached out to stroke her cheek. "So, tell us. What were you doing in that telephone box?" he asked.

"Planting artichokes," said Laure defiantly. "What do people usually do in phone booths? Let me see—make calls, maybe?"

The couple exchanged a glance. "You're really being too kind to this girl," said Susan.

Conrad looked confused. "Artichokes? I'm sorry, humour sometimes escapes me in foreign languages, though God knows I love a good joke."

"Like all Germans! That's why your Führer stole Chaplin's moustache. He's a real funny bloke."

Conrad smiled. "I got that one! The French are so clever. I love your language and colourful expressions. I've noticed though that you're not very clean."

Laure swallowed hard. He was trying to provoke her, it was obvious. He took her hand and inspected it. His fingers were rough.

"Let's see," he said, leaning closer. "Just as I suspected. Lots of dirt under your nails. Probably full of bacteria. A teacher taught me to recognize inferior races by checking for dirty nails."

"What are you? Some sort of Nazi manicurist?" Laure taunted.

"Very funny," replied Conrad, without a smile. "Susan, my love, would you please clean up our friend?"

The Englishwoman nodded and came to sit next to Laure. Her heady perfume barrelled into Laure's nostrils. Susan placed a small, pink, leather toiletries bag embroidered with delicate flowers on the table, then took out a silver nail file.

The German held down Laure's hand and pulled up her little finger as Susan blew some imaginary dust off the file. Laure felt her heart begin to race.

"Don't worry," said the Englishwoman. "I really was a manicurist before the war." Susan began carefully filing Laure's nail.

The Frenchwoman held her breath, hypnotized by her abductor's precise movements. Satisfied, Susan blew the filings from the edge of the nail, all while staring into Laure's eyes. "You have lovely hands," she said. "It's such a shame . . ."

"Why a shame?" Laure asked naively.

"To have to ruin them," replied Susan as she pushed the pointy tip of the file under the freshly manicured nail. Laure arched her back and cried out in pain. The German pushed her back down into her chair as his wife continued to push the file deeper. Blood flowed from her little finger, dripping down onto the floor.

"Please!" shouted Laure. "I haven't done anything wrong!"

"Of course not," replied Conrad. "I just want to know what you were doing outside the Hellfire Club. That's not a suitable place for a lovely young Frenchwoman."

Susan pulled the file out from under the nail of the little finger, then shoved it into her middle finger as Laure screamed again. Conrad gestured to his wife, and the file stopped a few centimeters short of the nail bed.

"Speaking of colourful expressions: I've always loved that English phrase, 'A little bird told me'," said Conrad. He held his hand up to his ear and moved it like a beak, nodding as though he were on the phone. "*Ach*, yes, I understand. My little bird just told me you're hiding something, young lady. And *my* little bird is rarely wrong. So, we're listening. Why were you spying on us? We know you were there with that chubby little Crowley."

Laure's brain was spinning. She knew she wouldn't last long under torture. Her instructors at the SOE had warned her—she might be able to buy a little time, but hardly more than a few hours. A person's ability to resist pain depended on several factors, but courage, no matter how strong, was not one of them. Incredibly brave agents had fallen to pieces in the hands of the Gestapo, while other, more middling spies had resisted until the bitter end.

"I . . . I was waiting for a friend, who—"

The file slid deeper under her nail and into the dermis.

"While we're at it, I might as well tend to your thumb as well. It does look rather dirty," said Susan, who kept smiling as she tormented her victim. "For years I cared for the nails of clients who treated me like shit. Back then, I could only dream of shoving my file deep into their warped flesh—today however . . ."

Laure's screams echoed off the walls of the cellar. Conrad leaned down and whispered in her ear as he stroked her hair. "You think that Nazis are sadist monsters, but you're wrong. I don't take any pleasure in making you suffer. I'm not in the SS. I have a mission to accomplish, and the ends justify the means. Talk, and we'll let you live."

Susan shook her head. "You're wasting your time, Conrad. Can't you see she's a stubborn one?"

Laure was shaking from head to toe. She knew she would break soon. She didn't dare look at her fingers.

"Let's move on to a new instrument," continued the Englishwoman as she put down the bloody file and picked up a pair of silver nail scissors. "In my profession, it's important to have reliable tools. This little instrument has cut thousands of nails but is as sharp as ever. Made in England, of course."

She ran the scissors along Laure's cheek and drew the open blades to her lower eyelid. "Have you seen *Port of Shadows*?" Susan asked, pressing the sharp tip into Laure's translucent skin. "It's a French film from before the Great War starring Jean Gabin and Michèle Morgan—two remarkably Aryan-looking actors, I might add."

Laure choked back tears. "Yes, except those two Aryans left for the United States because they didn't want to collaborate with the Germans. Unlike you," she levelled.

"That's beside the point. I loved the scene where Gabin said to Michèle, 'You've got lovely eyes, you know,' as he pulled her close. It gave me goose bumps. But, you see, if I gouge your eye out right now, no man will ever want to hold you close again. And if I get to the second one, too, you'll spend the rest of your life in the dark," Susan explained coldly, waving the scissors in Laure's face. "I could also cut off the end of your cute little nose or give you a wider smile . . ."

Laure's heart was about to burst out of her chest. Fear had pervaded every cell in her body.

Suddenly, the cellar door flew open and a burly man with a shaved head stepped inside. He merely glanced at Laure before placing his hand on Conrad's shoulder. "I need your help, it's urgent."

"We were just about to get her to talk," complained the German.

"That can wait. You've been assigned to a more important mission."

"Looks like we'll have to take a rain check," sighed Susan as she disappointedly gathered her tools. "But not to worry, we won't be long."

31

Bloomsbury, London

London looked nothing like the images Tristan had seen in Nazi propaganda, which depicted the British capital as destroyed and full of starving survivors fighting for scraps of food. Uniformed soldiers and hurrying civilians filled the bustling pavements, in stark contrast to occupied Paris.

Tristan was walking along the edge of a park at a much slower pace. The trees lining the fence cast a sliver of shade onto the pavement. Despite the heat he'd kept on his jacket and hat, which made him look like a pompous provincial on his first visit to the big city.

Young couples had taken up position on the lawn, while children played among the bushes under the watchful eye of a policeman. Tristan felt a pang of emotion. It had been so long since he'd been in a city where people were free and happy to be alive! From devastated Barcelona to Nazi-filled Berlin, he'd forgotten what life could be like in a democracy.

And yet, a quick scan of the newspapers had informed him of the difficulties facing this last European bastion of freedom. Behind her carefree appearance, London was on the verge of boiling over. Political crises and social issues were rampant. And then there were the murder victims with swastikas carved into their foreheads. That surely wouldn't make things easier: the authorities would be on the lookout for Nazi spies.

At the top of Russell Square, he turned right onto Bedford Way. Faded brick university buildings formed a compact grey block that contrasted with the park's summery colours. It was one of the landmarks he had memorized to help him reach Gordon Square, where his new life was waiting.

With the help of old photos and Abwehr specialists, he'd committed a map of the centre of London to memory. He'd need to turn left at the end of the street, then take the first right and continue on to number 26—his uncle's house. Gehlen himself had helped Tristan adopt his new identity, teaching him everything about the life of the young Quebecer who had died so Tristan could carry out his mission. Since he'd only lived to the age of twenty-six, his biography was rather thin. Once Tristan had memorized the various schools he had attended, learned about his artistic studies, his passion for canoeing, and his love of Canadian whisky, he and Gehlen had been forced to make up the rest to create a credible identity that would hold up during interrogation.

Tristan caught sight of Gordon Square, the small park across from his new house. He took off his hat and jacket as he studied the façade he'd only ever glimpsed in photographs. It was a three-storey building with a tidy gate. Each floor featured three windows set into the brick wall. The front door was black.

"Adam?" asked a stranger standing by the gate. With his plaid morning coat and swollen, red face, the man looked like he'd stepped straight out of a Dickens novel. "I'm Mr. Boswell. The solicitor. Welcome to Bloomsbury!"

Tristan returned the greeting.

"You've had quite a journey," continued the solicitor. "Did you know your uncle?"

"I'm afraid I never met him," replied Tristan. "And my mother rarely spoke of him."

"Yes, they were close at first but, over time, their relationship grew more distant. In any case, the law is clear: you are the sole heir. And since the old chap was rather thrifty, he's left you a tidy sum in the bank. You'll have enough to pay the inheritance tax and then some. Do you plan to settle here in England?"

"I do. My mother might not have said much about her brother, but she was always going on about her country. I'm keen to learn more about my roots."

"A fine objective," nodded Mr. Boswell. "Well then, let me show you around."

The solicitor skipped the kitchen to the left, and led Tristan straight to the lounge, which had two windows that overlooked the street. This detail made Tristan uncomfortable. He'd have to make sure no one could see in. Good that the large glass door leading to the garden provided a second source of light.

"As you can see," explained Boswell, pointing to a deep leather armchair and a porcelain tea set, "your uncle was as English as they come. Except when it came to his taste in artwork, that is."

Tristan looked up to find a collection of expressionist paintings on the walls. They reminded Tristan of Klimt and Schiele's works.

"I don't understand what he saw in them," sighed the solicitor.

Tristan didn't bother telling him the paintings would be worth a small fortune in the near future—that was information Adam wouldn't have known.

They made their way upstairs, which comprised two large bedrooms. Tristan decided not to ask which one his uncle had died in. He was pleasantly surprised to discover a library on the top floor. He wouldn't have to black out the downstairs windows after all—he could work here instead.

The rows of books had another surprise in store. "Almost all of these are about the English aristocracy!" he said.

Boswell shrugged. "Ah well, it was your uncle's favourite pastime. He discovered a loose tie to King George I after exploring your family tree, and this started his fascination with the aristocracy. Towards the end of his life, it bordered on obsession: it was the only thing he talked about."

Tristan listened carefully. He'd add this to his cover biography. It was something Gehlen had taught him: always have a family anecdote on hand. They buy time and help you evade difficult questions under interrogation.

"Right then. I think we've covered everything," said the solicitor.

"Thank you very much. Let me see you out," replied Tristan.

"Wonderful. I've left the keys on the table. Once you're settled, please come down to my office. I have some papers for you to sign."

As they passed the kitchen, Tristan noticed a dark wooden board nailed to the floor. "Was my uncle doing some renovation work?"

Boswell smiled. "Yes, he had the trapdoor to the cellar boarded up. He hated draughts and kept complaining about the cold air invading the kitchen. Another strange obsession of an old bachelor . . ."

Tristan decided he would reopen it shortly. A cellar—particularly a deep, quiet one—could come in handy.

Once he'd thanked the solicitor and seen him on his way, Tristan went to the kitchen to make some tea. Taking a steaming cup with him to the library, he then made a teetering tower of the books that interested him, before opening the first one on the pile.

He was determined to find James Hadler.

Tristan had been pondering the name for quite some time already. What links could possibly exist between a relic that once belonged to the Tsar of All Russia and this rather quotidian English name? Was he the man who had organized the transfer of the swastika to London? Or the one entrusted with its safety? What ties linked him to the imperial family? Tristan concluded that James Hadler couldn't have been completely unknown to Nicholas II— there had to be a connection. Especially given that Nicholas had always maintained close ties with the British aristocracy—after all, his wife was Queen Victoria's granddaughter. He was hell-bent on finding some mention of James Hadler in these registers.

And yet, even after skimming the very last specialist book in his uncle's collection, he hadn't found a single trace of the man. James Hadler was neither a baron, nor a member of the House of Lords—not even a forgotten provincial noble. The only other possibility was that he was a member of the Establishment. James Hadler could be a high-ranking government official, a diplomat, a banker, a businessman . . . there were so many options. So many that there was only one book that could get him further: *Who's Who*.

The directory had been a bestseller from its first edition onwards, and even nearly a hundred years later, its annual update was eagerly awaited by red-top readers and aspirants alike. Lucky for Tristan, his new uncle's library contained several editions. Tristan settled on the 1920 volume, which was the closest he could get to the date of the Russian Revolution.

It didn't take long for him to find his prize. Not only did James Hadler exist—his biography was also utterly enlightening. With an Oxford degree in the bag, Hadler had joined the Foreign Office and worked his way through several departments before his first posting to an embassy. Starting out in Madrid, he had moved on to Rome, then to Vienna. Tristan immediately noticed that the young diplomat had occupied posts in the most prestigious capitals, each move bringing him closer to the beginnings of the Great War. What talents could James Hadler have had for him to be wherever history was unfolding? The last line of his biography was particularly striking. In 1917, Hadler had been sent to Moscow.

Tristan could feel the excitement in him growing, much like the feeling he got when he discovered a new painting. He was back in the game. The quest was calling to him yet again. Conveniently, the entry even provided Hadler's address: 15 Holland Road, Kensington. Tristan shot down the stairs, grabbed the keys off the table, returned to the map of London in his head, and began heading east.

As he arrived outside Hadler's house, Tristan realized his cover would be of little use. If Hadler had somehow helped import or protect the swastika, he would be wary, and Tristan had no intention of attracting attention. With its pristine white columns on the porch, the house confirmed its owner's social standing. The curtains of the two windows that looked out onto the street were closed, as were those on the upper floors. He wondered if its owners had fled the stifling heat for a second home in the countryside. A short fence closed off the narrow alley between the house and its neighbour. Tristan climbed right over it, as though he'd forgotten his keys. At the far end, he found a small garden bordered by tall hedges. Tristan leaned into the foliage to inspect the windows on the back side of Hadler's house. The curtains were all closed here, too. One of the windows on the ground floor wasn't too high up and a wisteria was growing up a stake just beneath it. He unearthed the thin metal rod and slipped it between the window and the frame to unfasten the hook inside. In a matter of minutes, he stood in the kitchen.

Tristan realized right away that no one had been in the house for quite some time. A thin layer of dust covered all the furniture. He made his way into the lounge, where he found a wall of photographs showing James Hadler at different stages in his life. Tristan recognized one, which he knew had been taken in Buen Retiro Park in Madrid. Another featured a famous brewery in Vienna. Mr. Hadler looked at home wherever he went. Was this his secret talent? How unfortunate that there weren't any pictures from Russia. Tristan removed two frames from the wall and swapped their places. If Hadler was the kind of man he suspected, he would notice as soon as he came home. It would unsettle him and force him to react. And that was exactly what Tristan wanted. He needed his prey on the move so he could follow and analyse it.

The bedrooms on the first floor provided no clues, except for the absence of women's clothing in the cupboards. Hadler was either a bachelor, a divorcee or a widower. Tristan stepped into the office. The desk drawers were all unlocked. Most of them contained nothing but administrative documents, invoices, and collections of letters carefully classified by sender. Tristan jotted down each of the names, to look them up in his uncle's *Who's Who* and get a better idea of the milieu James Hadler frequented.

He skimmed a few letters from each file, but quickly realized nothing would come of it. Most of them were banal exchanges with distant family members. As he continued his search, Tristan couldn't help but wonder if Gurdjieff had led him astray by offering up a random name just before he died in the catacombs.

Suddenly, he heard the front door open. Voices became loud downstairs. Tristan slipped into the corridor. He could make out a woman's voice now. Silently, he made his way down a few steps to hear what she was saying. There seemed to be several people in the house, but the woman's voice was leading the conversation.

"As I explained, the kitchen overlooks the garden. It gets wonderful light. I'll open the curtains, which have clearly been drawn for some time. Ever since the former owner's death, in fact . . ."

And just like that, it all made sense. The layer of dust on the furniture, the perfectly made beds in the rooms upstairs—James Hadler wouldn't be coming back. Tristan's only lead had just gone up in flames. He returned to the office and opened the window. It was too high to jump. He would have to wait for the visitors to enter one of the bedrooms to slip out and get to the front door.

"You'd want to redo the lounge, of course," continued the estate agent.

To make sure he had left no stone unturned, Tristan inspected the office one last time. He leafed through a few volumes on Russia from the bookcase, but found neither notes nor pieces of paper between the pages. The rest of the collection was devoted to economics and horse-riding. That left only the display case. The first shelf featured figurines of *Don Quixote* characters. The second a collection of ceramic pipes, probably brought back from Austria. The third was home to several gaudy Russian nesting dolls. He opened the babushkas one by one, layer by layer. Nothing.

Something was off. How could a diplomat who'd attended Oxbridge have such poor taste?

The woman's voice was drawing closer. "I'll take you up to see the bedrooms now," she said.

Tristan turned his attention to the pipes, hastily turning each of them over. Nothing. He was running out of time. He had to get out. The figurines.

"Here's the first bedroom. Don't be bothered by the wall-paper..."

Don Quixote, on a perpetual quest for the ideal. Why not? Tristan moved the figurine aside to find an object no larger than a pack of cigarettes. A thin stone rectangle crowned with a cone. He quickly shoved it into his pocket.

"Now the master bedroom. You'll see, the bathroom is superb!"

The Frenchman tiptoed down the stairs, then made a mad dash for the front door. Squinting in the sunlight, he turned left, then right, then right again. The map of London in his head was coming in handy. He'd be home soon.

Once back in Bloomsbury, Tristan felt a wave of relief wash over him. This mission was making him feel more tense than ever before. He was caught between two dangers: having narrowly escaped Erika's public accusations, he was now within Malorley's reach. But in all honesty, he feared them both equally. That was why he hadn't gone into detail when informing the SOE officer of his presence in London. For the Germans, Tristan could turn into a traitor at any moment. All the while, he could easily become the man who knew too much for the English. He was caught between a rock and a hard place.

At last, he reached Gordon Square. The reassuring façade of number 26 wasn't far now. He'd almost made it to the gate, when a car door slammed.

"Hello, Frenchy!" called a voice.

A young couple stood smirking at Tristan.

"Gehlen sent us. He wanted to make sure you wouldn't forget about him."

"Who are you?" he asked.

"We're your guardian angels," said the woman with a mischievous smile.

32

A fire engine's siren blared amid a concerto of honking in the busy street below. Having spent a sleepless night at his desk, Malorley leaned out of the window to see if a fire was raging nearby, but he saw no flames. Since the beginning of the war, he had come to love the discordant symphony of London traffic. It reassured him that life was carrying on, with all its troubles big and small.

Crowley watched as Malorley returned to his desk. The mage had stopped by to see if there was any news—and he wasn't fooled by his boss's apparent calm. Laure had been missing for almost a week, and no one had heard from her.

"I know she's still alive," said Aleister. "I consulted my tarot cards. The Star—Laure's card—appeared twice. Once with the Tower and once with the Chariot. But she's in grave danger."

"You don't say," Malorley replied coldly. "Any chance your cards could tell us something useful too? Where she is, for example?"

"You're constipated," affirmed Crowley. "It's terrible for your health."

"What a strange thing to say, Doctor Crowley. As far as I'm aware, I don't have any digestive problems."

"I mean you're mentally constipated. You bottle up your anxiety, hoping it will preserve your judgement, but that's a mistake. Anxiety burrows into your consciousness like a worm into an apple."

"I see you're a psychologist now as well," Malorley replied, dubious.

"Let's just say I learned a lot on the topic from Professor Freud in Vienna. We've read each other's books. In fact, I suspect he plagiarized my theories on the importance of sexuality. But that's a story for another day. To sum things up: you're worried sick about Laure."

"I worry about every agent under my authority."

"But you care more deeply about that charming little Frenchwoman."

This time, Crowley had gone too far. Malorley had had enough of the plump, perverted know-it-all. "You're nothing but a worthless degenerate! Don't you dare make insinuations about me!"

Despite this personal attack, Crowley kept quiet. He knew how to kowtow when necessary. It was the secret to his survival. "I'm sorry, sir, I misspoke. What I meant was that Laure is like a daughter to you. And since you are the one who asked her to accompany me to the club, you feel all the more guilty."

"I don't want to hear another word of your quackery! None of this gets us any closer to finding Laure!"

"Send a team to the Hellfire. I know the place like the back of my hand. I can—"

"No! If I turn up at Moira's place, I'll blow Laure's cover. And if the Germans find out, she'll be out of the game. The people at the top wouldn't understand why I sacrificed this operation to save the life of a single agent."

"Then Laure will die," Crowley observed solemnly.

There was a long silence.

"There may be another option," mumbled Malorley. "We could use a pretext to draw the evil witch out of the club and force her hand. We could turn her without alerting the Germans."

"She would never accept," affirmed Aleister. "She hates England. She'd rather sell her soul to the devil—already has, in fact—than work with you."

"I'd do anything to save Laure."

The red light on Malorley's telephone was blinking. The commander pressed the speaker button, letting his secretary's airy voice fill the room.

"Commander, you have an urgent call from SOE headquarters," she said.

"Have they found Laure? Alive?" he exclaimed.

"No, it's about one of your other agents."

"Put it through."

There was nothing but static for a few seconds, followed by the usual clicks from the Walthamstow telephone exchange, which handled all communications between intelligence services.

"Commander Malorley, this is Commander Draymore of Department F. We've received a message from one of your men. Code name 007."

Malorley jumped to his feet. Crowley hurried to his side to listen in. "What? Could you repeat that number?"

"007. He went through our contacts in Paris. Your agent says he'll be undercover in London to continue the quest. There are no further details."

"Nothing at all?"

"Nothing. I'll have to let you go; I'm in the middle of a briefing."

Malorley hung up as Crowley looked on, eyes wide.

"This means Tristan Marcas is . . . here. In London. On the hunt for the fourth relic. We have to find him. Whatever the cost."

London

The portly grey rat held perfectly still. Laure would have thought him dead, were it not for his ridged tail, which wagged ever so slightly on the table. His tiny black eyes stared at her, never blinking. Laure had never been this close to a rat before. She could see the different shades in his coat, the rolls of fat around his neck, and the wet fur on his hind legs. He and the millions of his kind could be found in droves beneath London since the beginning of the war. Unlike the capital's human population, they didn't seem to suffer from malnutrition due to rationing.

The rodent had climbed up the textured table legs to sit across

from her, as though he'd been summoned to carry on the interrogation her abductors had begun. Upon spotting him in the
doorway, Laure had instinctively tensed. The rat had sniffed around
every corner of the cellar before finally noticing her presence. At
last, he had inched closer. Her screams had kept him away for a
time, but he had eventually worked up the courage to climb onto
the table.

Once her disgust had lessened, Laure got used to the creature
and came to think of him as a companion in her misfortune. She
kept an eye on him, though, and thanked God her kidnappers had
left the light on. But the bulb that hung from the ceiling kept
crackling, as if ready to give up the ghost at any moment.

"You won't hurt me, will you, Tommy?" Laure asked the rat.
"We make a good team, you and me. I could train you to perform
circus numbers to distract that pair of psychos and get out of
here."

She would have laughed if her hand didn't hurt so bad. The
tips of three of her fingers were already swollen and covered in
pus and drying blood. She didn't dare move them, for fear of
heightening the already unbearable pain.

The rat moved a few steps closer and held out its snout, as
though it understood what she was saying.

"Between us, Tommy, I'm not sure how much longer I'll last."
She no longer had any illusions about what awaited her when her
torturers returned. The idea of Susan chopping her to bits with
her scissors left Laure in a cold sweat. "We both know how this
will end."

Her kidnappers hadn't bothered to hide their faces, which meant
they had no intention of letting her live. Making her wait for the
next torture session was probably just a part of their interrogation
strategy. Laure stared attentively at the rat, as if trying to forget
her suffering.

"Do you think there's a God up there somewhere who will
reward me for my commitment to the cause? Finding those bloody
swastikas, that has to count for something."

The rodent looked down, seemingly unconvinced.

"You're right," continued Laure. "God has never given a shit about us. Sometimes I even think he's secretly helping Hitler. Maybe he's selected a new chosen people and thinks the Nazis and their bloody thousand-year Reich are delightful. He's probably reserved heaven for the goddamn Aryans."

Thinking of heaven brought her father to mind. He had shared the Cathars' beliefs, and Laure wondered if he'd been right. The heretics had been certain that the world was run by a cruel, sadistic god, who had enjoyed tormenting his flock since the dawn of time with wars, disease, famine, rape, and a host of barbaric and terribly effective tortures. The real God, on the other hand, welcomed the deserving to a better world once their time on earth was done.

But Laure wasn't Cathar, nor even Christian. For her, neither heaven nor hell existed. There was nothing but oblivion and eternal nothingness.

"You see, Tommy, I never would have imagined I'd spend my final moments speaking with a sewer rat. Never thought I'd die here. Alone, without anyone to mourn my passing. At the ripe old age of twenty-five." Dark thoughts swirled around her head. She would never meet the man she was meant to be with. She would never have children. Her future held nothing but suffering and death. Laure felt tears well up in her eyes.

She ran her tongue over her last molar on the upper left-hand side of her mouth. The bump was still there. It would take two minutes at most to leave this world once the cyanide capsule was broken. That's what her SOE instructors had taught her. It wouldn't break on the first bite, though. They couldn't have agents accidentally killing themselves during dinner. It would take several very hard impacts. Then the cyanide would flow into her throat and do its work.

Suddenly, the light blew out and darkness filled the room.

"Tommy, don't you go climbing on me in the dark, all right?" She took a deep breath. She'd made up her mind.

When her kidnappers returned, she'd sit up tall and defy them until the end. She wouldn't give them a single piece of information. She'd rather die.

33

Bloomsbury, London

The couple had invited themselves into the house. Tristan wondered how this arrogant Anglo-German couple had ever been recruited by the Abwehr.

"We've been instructed to help you with your mission," explained the young woman, whose short hair framed a freckled face.

"What are your names?" asked Tristan.

"I'm Susan," she replied, "and the tall, handsome man rummaging through your kitchen is Conrad."

"What do you know about my mission?" he asked.

Susan put her feet up on the coffee table. "That you're looking for an object coveted by Berlin's finest. We're here to make sure you don't do anything stupid."

It occurred to Tristan that they might be on drugs. Rumours circulating in Germany suggested that the Nazis had been giving pilots and elite soldiers drug cocktails to inhibit fear. The Ahnenerbe had even helped with some of the research. The herbs used by medieval witches had attracted much attention.

"I'm not sure I understand," replied Tristan.

"It's very simple," Conrad said with a sigh as he sat down next to his wife. "You get on with your mission, we watch you. Gehlen doesn't trust you, and rightly so, of course. You're French. An *Untermensch.*"

"Subhuman," translated Susan.

"Oh, I understood him," Tristan replied coldly. "But I think the term is better applied to the two of you."

Conrad jumped to his feet. "Don't get smart with us, pal. A single word or doubt and—"

"And you'll die first," concluded Tristan.

"That's enough," Susan intervened. "Focus on the mission. As for you, Frenchy, just know we'll stick to you like your shadow— there's no shaking us," she threatened as they made their way towards the door.

As he passed the table where Tristan had emptied his pockets, Conrad stopped short. "I see you're not only French, but also a thief!" he said, holding up the object Tristan had brought back from Hadler's house. "Why do you have a *Schlüssel der Engel*?"

"An angel's key," Susan translated promptly. "It's a religious object. You can trust Conrad on the topic—he was about to begin seminary school when he met me."

"What is it, exactly?" asked Tristan.

"A key that opens a shrine. More precisely, the glass tombs that contain saintly relics. Sometimes just a few bones, other times full bodies," explained Conrad as he pointed to one of the rect-angular sides of the stone, which was dotted with a series of indentations. "These are carefully placed to align with the lock. When correctly positioned, you simply turn the key and the tomb opens. Where did you find it?" he enquired.

"With the keys to the house," replied Tristan.

The German shrugged, no longer interested. He and Susan continued towards the door. "We have to go. Susan has a manicure to finish," he said with a smile.

When they stepped outside, Susan turned around. "Don't forget—we're watching you."

Strangely, the threat posed by the deranged couple wasn't what preoccupied Tristan. He was more concerned with their behaviour. They seemed to think they were invincible, but given their lack of discretion, British intelligence probably already had them under surveillance as part of its efforts to dismantle the Abwehr network. And if that was the case, Tristan, aka Adam, would be found out much sooner than he would have liked. He wouldn't be able to stay in the Gordon Square house much longer; he'd have to find a new safehouse. But first, he needed to learn more about the key. Could Hadler have hidden the last swastika inside a reliquary? Tristan remembered learning about them at art school in Paris. They often looked like tiny glass houses covered in ornate decorations and precious stones. The relics housed within had belonged to medieval churches and monasteries, and used to draw pilgrims from all over Europe.

Tristan made his way upstairs to the library, where he pulled out a series of art history books. To no avail: he found no mention of shrines or reliquaries in any of the churches in the United Kingdom. All of a sudden, it came to him why: the British had converted to Protestantism, which rejected the worship of saints. As a result, shrines had been shattered and reliquaries melted down. He was at a dead end yet again.

This quest had often left him uncertain who he was working for and why. He wasn't even sure who he loved anymore. His meeting with Erika had been destabilizing. It was as though there were two different women inside her. One of them had a place in his heart; the other was cold, determined, and devoted exclusively to her country and mission. And he wasn't sure which one was the real Erika. Tristan had thought he'd be able to manipulate others' feelings and come out unscathed, but it seemed he had been wrong.

The quest took up so much space in his life that he sometimes felt like one of the Knights of the Round Table, scouring Arthur's kingdom for the Grail, which was always just out of reach. But he wasn't as pure of heart as the knights of yore. And the people giving him his orders paled in comparison to the pious King of Camelot. He trusted Malorley more or less, but not the men above him in the hierarchy. What would they do if they found the last relic? Would they choose to use him to get their hands on the swastika, blowing his German cover, or would they decide to send him back to Germany? Which was more useful to them: a relic that may have magical powers or a spy at the top of the SS?

Neither situation would turn out well for Tristan. If he found the last swastika and handed it over to the British, he would be of no more use to them. If he returned to Germany, the Nazis' growing paranoia meant he would be found out sooner or later. There was only one scenario with a favourable outcome for him: he had to find the swastika on his own and disappear. The war wouldn't last forever, and once peace had returned, he could negotiate a new life for himself.

He walked over to the shelves and picked up an atlas. Where would he go? He imagined a small city hidden away behind ancient ramparts, where he would listen to the church bells while hiding from the sun beneath impressive stone archways. He imagined a life with Erika. The Erika he had once known.

His musings kindled memories of Castelló D'Empúries, a town in the Catalonian countryside where he had lived after the fall of Barcelona. A town where he'd assumed the identity of a dead man—Juan Labio—and become the curator of a local museum. And where he'd also met Lucia.

Thinking of their time in the museum together, he realized how silly he'd been to place the reliquary in a church or monastery. If such an object had survived the tests of time, it would be in a museum . . .

The first reliquary Tristan discovered was in a book on London's best-known museums and was Thomas Becket's casket, held by the Victoria and Albert Museum. The archbishop had been assassinated at the order of Henry II in the middle of mass in 1170, and Rome had made him a saint three years later. The museum wasn't far from Hadler's home. If the swastika was hidden there, its last protector had kept it close. But Tristan refused to jump to any conclusions. An important question remained unanswered: how had Hadler stored the swastika inside such a precious and heavily protected object?

The second reliquary he came across was at the British Museum. It harboured one of the holy thorns from the Crown of Thorns Christ wore on the cross. Louis IX of France had built the Sainte-Chapelle in Paris to house the crown in its entirety, but over the centuries, subsequent kings had gifted individual thorns to prestigious noblemen. They were often diplomatic presents designed to strengthen political ties. The reliquary held by the British Museum had been fashioned in the1390s for the Duc de Berry, one of the most influential men of his time. It then made its way into the hands of the Holy Roman Emperor Charles V, before becoming a part of the Imperial Hapsburg collection in Vienna, and finally being purchased by Anselm von Rothschild in the 1870s. His son, Baron Ferdinand de Rothschild, left it to the museum in 1899. Tristan's head was spinning. The reliquary had been passed among the most illustrious families in Europe for centuries.

The perfect place to hide the swastika—except that there were no ties to Hadler. He'd served as a diplomat in Vienna, where the reliquary had spent quite some time, but the dates didn't line up at all. Tristan had the frustrating impression that the answer was just out of reach. He returned to the shelf on which he'd found the volume on the British Museum. He returned to the shelf and spotted several exhibition catalogues. One of them, devoted to medieval art, featured a two-page article on the Holy Thorn Reliquary. Tristan read it carefully and discovered that the piece had been restored in 1919. A number of benefactors were recognized in the article. Tristan hastily scanned the alphabetical list. James Hadler's name was among the Hs.

At long last, the fog seemed to be clearing. Everything lined up: the key to the reliquary, the reliquary in the British Museum, and Hadler's donation, which would have granted him direct access. There was light at the end of the tunnel, Tristan was certain of that. He knew where to find the last swastika. The quest, which had taken him all over the continent, was nearing its end.

Now all he had to do was break into the British Museum.

34

The Kremlin, Moscow

The rhythmic pounding of boots on pavement echoed in the antechamber to Stalin's office. The two guards outside his door—a Red Army captain and a sergeant—stared coldly at the NKVD officer heading their way. The vast room was richly decorated in marble and gilding, but Evgueni Berin no longer noticed the Kremlin's splendour. He had walked the same route once a week for years. The NKVD headquarters at Lubyanka were only a stone's throw from the tsar's Moscow residence.

The captain saluted. "Hello, Colonel Berin. I'll let him know you're here."

Once the captain had disappeared behind the heavy oak door, Evgueni dropped his bag onto the long, brown leather couch nearby. He stayed on his feet to better contemplate the extravagant painting on the wall—a recent addition, it would seem. It featured a knight in shining armour on his trusty black steed, brandishing a glowing sword. Beneath his boots, men in white capes, whose black crosses were covered in blood, begged the victor for mercy.

Evgueni needed no explanation. Every Russian knew of the heroic exploits of Alexander Nevsky, the Prince of Novgorod, who had defeated the German Teutonic Knights during their invasion of Russia in the 13th century. Before the war, Stalin had ordered production of a film celebrating the exploits of the legendary hero, to appropriate his glory for himself.

Evgueni smiled as he stepped closer to study the noble's face. "Unbelievable," he murmured. "Shameless sycophants!"

Indeed, with his thick, slicked back, grey hair the brave Russian warrior bore a striking resemblance to Stalin himself. Thankfully, the artist hadn't gone so far as to saddle the hero with Stalin's anachronistic moustache.

Evgueni lit a cigarette as he continued to ponder the ostentatious but poorly executed painting. It was probably the work of one of the propaganda painters who swarmed around the Politburo eager for work. Evgueni knew that the country's leader was acutely aware of the way people worshipped him. Stalin may well have possessed one of the most calculating and cynical minds Evgueni had ever encountered; he was more superstitious than a Georgian peasant. He had probably appealed to the spirit of the Orthodox saint to ward off the bad luck that plagued the motherland.

Berin exhaled a column of smoke in the Prince's direction. After thirty-five years of revolution, he had reached the conclusion that the people would always revere tyrants and autocrats. Whether their blood was blue or red mattered little. One tsar had replaced another on the Russian throne. The people feared Stalin, but also saw him as their brave defender in the face of the German invasion.

Stalin knew all this and used it to his favour. On the twentieth anniversary of the October Revolution, he had delivered a moving homage to the former tsars.

Evgueni turned his nose up at the painting. It would take more than a work of art to defeat the Teuton hordes this time. The latest report he'd received on the country's military situation was extremely worrying.

Though Moscow had escaped Hitler's reach, the situation remained critical. The key city of Rostov-on-Don had just fallen. When the news had spread, panic had taken hold in every corner of the Soviet Union. The German offensive line slashed through the motherland's tormented face like a huge scar. One that stretched four thousand kilometers and changed ever so slightly after every bloody offensive and counteroffensive. To the north, Leningrad had been under siege for nearly a year. The residents who hadn't been evacuated had as much chance of dying of hunger as they did from the bombs that rained down on the city night and day. The former Saint Petersburg continued to resist the panzers, but no one knew for how much longer. Towards the middle of the line, the Nazis held fast to their positions, like hunting birds grasping their prey. Stalingrad, which sat in a bend of the Volga, was the invaders' new target. If the city fell, the Germans would quickly make their way to the Caucasus, where they would seize the oil fields of the Caspian Sea. That would be the end of the Soviet Union—there would be no need to take Moscow.

The door opened without a sound.

"Please come in," said the captain.

"An associate of mine should arrive in a few minutes. Please have him wait here," said Berin.

"Is he on the protocol list?" asked the suspicious officer.

"No, but I'm certain comrade Stalin will want to meet him."

Evgueni stubbed out his cigarette in a vase, picked up his bag, and entered the Red Tsar's sanctuary. Warm light filled the large room, and the wainscoting featured the same varnished oak as the door. It was divided into two separate spaces: on one side, there was a large desk crowned with Lenin's death mask protected by a large glass dome; on the other, a long rectangular meeting table. There were four portraits on the walls. Marx and Lenin, of course, but also Kutuzov and Suvorov—imperial generals who had earned names for themselves fighting Napoleon.

Stalin was looking out of an open bay window that overlooked all of Moscow.

"Ah, Evgueni, you're just in time for the show!" he exclaimed without turning around. "Come over here."

Evgueni did as he was been told.

"Listen to the song of the Night Witches!" the Soviet leader exclaimed ecstatically.

Evgueni could hear a muffled roar rising from the north. Suddenly, a flock of silver birds sailed overhead. The fuselages of the Polikarpov Po-2 biplanes glimmered in the sunlight as they skimmed the tops of the buildings, so close that Berin could make out the pilots' profiles. The bombers flew in elegant formations through the sky over the capital, then disappeared to the west.

"What remarkable pilots, Joseph. Why do you call them witches?"

"They're all women, my dear Evgueni," replied Stalin as he closed the windows. "The 588th Night Bomber Regiment. They wanted to pay tribute. Their raids are so efficient that our enemies nicknamed them the Night Witches—they strike when the sun goes down. Yet more proof of socialism's progressive nature. Our English and American friends would never let women pilot their planes."

There was a knock at the door. Stalin barked for whoever it was to come in. A captain walked over with a file and placed it on the desk. The Soviet leader's features darkened.

"More papers to sign," he complained. "So much of my time is wasted on paperwork."

Evgueni glanced at the file and saw that there was only one document to be signed. Stalin quickly skimmed it, took the pen the officer held out, and scribbled his name at the bottom of the page.

"Order 270. No more backing away!" Stalin said proudly.

"What do you mean?" asked Berin as the captain closed the door behind him.

"I needed to make a show of authority after the fall of Rostov. Discipline is fading in the ranks of the Red Army. So I issued a series of orders to bolster our troops. From now on, special squadrons will stand behind the lines and shoot anyone who tries to retreat without an order to do so. The Germans invented the technique, which has proved to be remarkably effective."

Evgueni studied his leader, wondering just how far he would go. There may have been a few desertions, but overall, the Russian soldiers had fought like lions. It seemed a bit excessive to be executing them on the spot. Nevertheless, he admired the man's iron will.

"So, Evgueni," said Stalin as he took Berin by the shoulder, "do you have any good news for me before that capitalist bastard Churchill shows up?"

"Yes. I've brought you a report from my analysts. The English Prime Minister is expected to be in good spirits. He seems impressed by the courage of the Red Army in the face of our enemies."

"And what about me? Is he as enthusiastic about me?"

"He respects you, comrade. You're a desirable ally. I'm certain he'll shower you in praise."

Stalin burst into laughter. "You're lying, Evgueni! Like a dishonest fabric peddler at the Tbilisi market! Churchill has always seen me as a tyrant and a butcher. I must fit in somewhere between the devil and Hitler in his pantheon. But history has brought us together, and now I'm his best ally. The scoundrel will have to shake my hand and toast the birthplace of international socialism," barked Stalin with a laugh. He paused to smooth his moustache, clearly enjoying the imaginary scene. "But jokes aside," he said in a deeper voice, "what have your agents in London and Washington reported? I really only need to know one thing: will they open a second front, as Churchill promised?"

Evgueni coughed, then answered. "Yes. They're preparing for a massive invasion. Operation Torch. The general chiefs of staff of the two countries met, and one of our informants—a union representative at a shipyard in New Jersey—has recorded a massive rise in orders for landing crafts."

Stalin beamed. "At long last! They're going to land on the French coast. Do you know if it will be Normandy or somewhere else?"

Evgueni had been putting off finishing his report, but he no longer had a choice. He had to deliver the crucial piece of information, though he feared it would kindle a devastating rage. "It won't be in France at all. They've chosen North Africa. Morocco, then Algeria and Tunisia, to surround Rommel and the Afrika Korps."

Stalin's smile vanished. Evgueni tensed, waiting for the explosion—but it never came. Stalin squinted and fiddled with his moustache. "Those idiots!" he mumbled under his breath. "Cowards. We have to fix this."

A wave of relief washed over Berin. Even faced with enormous disappointment, Stalin remained rational.

"According to my sources," Evgueni replied, "the Americans backed the idea of invading Normandy, but Churchill torpedoed the project, claiming they weren't ready."

Stalin slammed his fist into the desk, and Lenin's face wobbled beneath its glass dome. "That dirty, old, English toad! He still resents me for signing the Pact of Non-Aggression with Hitler in 1939. As if I had any choice in the matter . . . What do you think I should do, my friend?"

"You're right, comrade, he can't get over our former alliance with the Nazis. And you can't blame him: he was left to face the Germans alone after they defeated France. And it's true that his army lacks the proper training to invade Normandy. In the long run, another defeat in France would be even more catastrophic for us."

Stalin paced the room in front of the window, fists clenched behind his back. "This Operation Torch isn't enough! I must demand compensations."

Berin held out a new document. "I agree," he replied. "I took the liberty of drafting a list of demands you could make of Churchill."

Stalin took the piece of paper and quickly read through it. The colour was returning to his cheeks. "Cannons, lorries, weapons, planes, food . . . How do you think I should react when the wily old fox tries to negotiate? After all, I'm not supposed to know about this planned invasion."

Evgueni kept quiet. The last time Stalin had asked a general what he should do, the man had found himself in front of a firing squad two days later. Like all paranoiacs, the leader of the Soviet Union was wary of everyone around him—especially those who could see themselves in his place. "There is but one Stalin," Berin replied prudently. "Only you know what is best."

Stalin's lips curled into a weak smile. "Your reply lacks sincerity, but it is proof of your wisdom. That's why you've spent so many years by my side. How long have you worked for me now?"

Evgueni felt the hairs on the back of his neck rise. He had survived all of the regime's purges, even the one that had decimated the NKVD in 1938. Fourteen thousand political police officers had been executed along with their leader, who was replaced by the worst kind of monster. And yet Evgueni had survived. Nevertheless, he knew the tide could turn as quickly as a harvest ruined by a summer storm.

"Nearly twenty years," he replied.

"And you're still just as loyal. But I suppose that's to be expected of the man who witnessed Nicholas II's assassination. I would have loved to have been there for that pivotal moment in the Revolution."

Evgueni's expression was impassive. "You know how I feel about that night, Joseph," he said solemnly.

Stalin laughed and put his arm around the police officer's shoulders. "Yes, yes. The massacre of women, children, and servants. Oh, Evgueni! You're such a sentimental man, and you don't even know it. If you didn't do such remarkable work at the NKVD, I'd have you transferred to the Bolshoi to look after the ballerinas!"

Berin placed another document on the table. "Speaking of Nicholas, there is one more thing you could ask Churchill to give you. Read this."

Stalin skimmed the document, then handed it back to Evgueni. For once, he seemed truly surprised. "They've got a lead on the tsar's relic? Where did you get this information?"

"As you know, our network of spies in Germany is powerful. I always have someone undercover in the SS."

Stalin watched as the sun began to disappear to the west. "The Romanovs' relic in England? After all these years of searching . . .you never gave up."

"You know how important this is to me, Joseph. It could make all the difference. Will you mention it to the Prime Minister?"

Stalin raised his right eyebrow in doubt. "I don't think it's a good idea, Evgueni. Why should we take this relic seriously?"

"May I introduce you to someone who can tell you more about its powers? He's waiting just outside."

Before Stalin could reply, an officer stepped inside, clicked his heels and spoke. "Today's military operations report, comrade. I'm afraid it's not good news."

35

The British Museum, Great Russell Street, London

Tristan had planned for every possibility but one—the bomb that had fallen on the British Museum on May 10, 1941, demolishing an entire wing and setting much of the rest of the institution on fire. At least, there hadn't been any victims—the museum had been closed to the public ever since 1939. Civil Defence volunteers stood guard in front of the gaping holes in the structure, while a volunteer cleaning crew relayed rubble out of the building. Tristan was surprised to see that they were still clearing the site more than a year after the bombing, but then he remembered that every neighbourhood in London had been hit by German bombs—there were worksites all over the city. Suddenly, Tristan's confidence began to crack. What if the Holy Thorn reliquary had been destroyed and the last swastika lost forever?

He was furious. His entire life had just gone up in a cloud of smoke. He'd spent years on this quest, only to fail so close to his goal. He stood in a daze across from the sign, as though he were reading his own tombstone.

One of the volunteers nearby cried out to him. "Hey, sir, if you're here for the reopening, you'll have to wait until the war's over!"

"Is the damage very bad?" asked Tristan.

"The buildings were hit in six different places, and the fires spread far beyond there, so you can imagine! Thank goodness the curators had evacuated the museum before Adolf hurled his bombs at us!"

"Do you mean they moved the artwork?"

"Everything they could, yes. But given that there were seven million objects inside, hard to know exactly what was saved and what's still here."

Tristan's mood suddenly rebounded. The first thing was to find out if the reliquary was still in the museum. He consulted the visitors' map of the museum in his hand. The medieval gallery, named after King Edward VII, was on the ground floor of the south-west wing. Tristan got his bearings with respect to the main entrance. In just a few steps, he reached the building he was looking for. It seemed to have escaped the bombs. The corridor that linked it to the entrance hall though was a pile of rubble. He moved closer, but members of the Civil Defence Service firmly asked him to step back. There were quite a few of them in this area, and they seemed rather nervous. The government had to be concerned about thefts. Tristan stepped aside and stood across from one of the holes in the wall where cleaning crew volunteers emerged from the building carrying heavy pails of dirt and rubble, which they emptied into a dumper truck parked in the street.

A manager blew his whistle twice, and the volunteers left their posts, many of them lighting cigarettes. Clearly, the teams worked in shifts. Tristan followed one of the groups to a pub. He glanced discreetly through the window and smiled. He wouldn't even have to ask any questions—he could simply listen. The best way to get information was to be wherever people talked freely. Pride and vanity would do most of the work for him. The tactic was simple: find the man or woman who had an irresistible need to be listened to. And he usually had his pick. Tristan made his way towards a table where one of the volunteers, pint in hand, was sharing his opinion with anyone who would listen.

"I'm telling you. We're nowhere near finished. We've been clearing away rubble for weeks, but why?"

Tristan immediately identified the man as a pessimist who was dying to convince his listeners of his point of view.

"Have you seen the number of charred books we've cleared? The number of display cases that have been reduced to nothing but ashes? Every day they say they evacuated the museum, that they stored the most precious objects in a safe place, but I have my doubts. In fact, I don't think those lazy curators did a damn thing!"

"Don't be so dramatic. You know full well that the museum is more or less intact—except for the library and the coins and medals building, that is!"

Unable to bear being contradicted, the pessimist leapt to his feet. His red face betrayed his drinking habits, which visibly failed to take the edge off his dark ideas.

"Tell me then, why are there so many areas we're not allowed to see? Why are there so many Civil Defence volunteers guarding the entrance? I think they're hiding something."

Tristan had heard enough. Some of the collections were still in the museum, and to find out if the reliquary was among them, he'd have to get into the guarded galleries. Tristan left the pub, picked up a cone of fish and chips, and sat down on a bench across from the museum. The building was guarded, but no one seemed to be paying any attention to the volunteers' comings and goings. Managers signalled the beginning and end of shifts, but they never counted the number of people working. Most volunteers wore blue overalls covered in pale dust that even lightened their hair. He jumped up. It wouldn't take him long to find a second-hand clothes store. A pound of flour mixed with a bit of dirt and he'd fit right in.

It was five o'clock and crowds of office workers had begun to flood the streets, followed by groups of soldiers from every corner of the British Empire: Indians in turbans, Australians with thick accents, Canadians built like lumberjacks. Tristan felt like he was in the Tower of Babel given all the different languages he could hear. The diversity was a welcome surprise: no one gave him and his dusty work clothes a second glance.

When he arrived near the museum, he looked at his watch. He now knew that the next shift was set to begin in three minutes, so he made his way towards the pub to wait for the group of volunteers. As they stepped outside, an older worker's battered military jacket caught Tristan's eye. It bore the Polish flag—the man was probably a refugee. Knowing that there was a long flight of stairs up to the museum entrance, Tristan fell in next to him. Exhausted as he was, the Pole would probably struggle up them, and Tristan would be only too happy to help. A perfect cover in case anyone was checking identities.

But no one asked any questions as he made his way into the museum's former lobby. Tristan was concerned about the loose security. It was either an oversight so glaring that nobody had noticed it, or a sign that there was nothing valuable in the part of the museum the volunteers had access to. The south-west wing, however, which was heavily guarded by the Civil Defence Service, probably still housed works of art—and that was where the Holy Thorn reliquary would have been before the bombing.

Beneath the partially shattered glass dome, the teams were dispatched to complete specific tasks. Outside, Tristan had only seen the volunteers responsible for clearing rubble, but inside, there were also restoration teams repairing the building. Damaged walls were being built up, and welders climbed up massive scaffoldings to repair the metal beams of the dome.

"You lot, go upstairs," ordered a manager. "We have to finish clearing the ethnography gallery. The roofers will be here next week."

Tristan's team ambled up the stairs. An indescribable smell stung his throat. When he coughed, his neighbour turned towards him in sympathy. "Did you know this used to be the library? When the bombs hit, two hundred and fifty thousand books went up in flames. The walls are covered with tiny bits of ash and the air is absolutely awful."

Tristan looked up in surprise. "And that?" he said, pointing to the barricaded doors at the far end of the room.

"It's to keep people out. Everything on the other side has collapsed. You can't reach the medieval gallery anymore. Too dangerous."

Tristan pretended to find this piece of information perfectly insignificant. They'd just reached the first floor and were walking past a series of empty rooms. Shards of glass covered the floor. The works of art must have been evacuated in haste. At a convenient moment he slipped off to explore the deserted rooms. A painting of Isis over one of the doors told him he was in a gallery that had once housed the Egyptian collection, though there wasn't a single mummy or hieroglyph left.

"Hey, you're not allowed in here! Get back to your group."

Tristan was about to step back out into the corridor when he noticed what looked like a bathtub hidden away at the far end of the last room. He rejoined his group only to sneak away again a few minutes later. Once up close to the intriguing object, he realized his mistake. It was a tall stone basin, whose sides were covered in hieroglyphs: a sarcophagus. The stone coffins contained wooden caskets the Egyptians used to paint with portraits of the deceased. Tristan moved closer still. It must have been too heavy to evacuate. The stone lid was partially open. He pushed it until he could slip one hand in, then two. The stone inside was freezing.

Tristan shivered with joy.

He had found the perfect hiding spot.

36

Two hours! Stalin and Evgueni had sat through two hours of
updates from the front, which had grown progressively worse as
the meeting dragged on, leaving the Red Tsar in a particularly
surly mood. Night had fallen quite some time ago. Sitting across
from Stalin, Evgueni was unable to decode his expression. The
NKVD officer was afraid to break the silence. He knew Stalin
despised last-minute visitors. Plagued by thoughts about potential
insurgent groups, Stalin tended his paranoia with as much care as
a dedicated gardener his roses.

"Evgueni," barked Stalin, "I don't remember seeing your guest's
name on the schedule for this evening."

"I took the liberty of asking him to come and shed new light
on the nature of the relics," Evgueni replied calmly.

Stalin popped his knuckles. "I read your report from last month
about Hitler and Churchill both sending commando units to try
to find it. And about the failed mission in Venice," Stalin replied
sternly. "Where exactly is this coming from?"

"As explained, I have access to an informant I had infiltrate
the SS. He managed to earn a place near Himmler."

"Ah, Evgueni, the relic is your obsession! You've been going on
about it ever since that glorious night at Ipatiev House in which
that despot Nikolai got his due. Let's not forget that I have always
sanctioned your quest, asking only that you continue to perform
your duties at the NKVD."

"And I have never faltered."

"I know. That's why you're here with me instead of rotting in your family plot at the Novosibirsk cemetery," Stalin replied with a laugh.

"Joseph," pleaded Evgueni, "I've survived every purge for the past two decades. I'm beginning to think that we may be friends."

"It's strange," replied the dictator as he got to his feet, "you must be one of the only people in my entourage who doesn't fear me. Your superior, Beria, goes to pieces like a pope facing a peasant woman's ripe ass whenever I so much as raise an eyebrow."

"My loyalty is unfailing. And I trust your judgement."

"You're clever, Evgueni, but don't think your flattery will fool me. To get back to your relics, you know that I hate mysticism of any kind. My time at the seminary cured me of all my silly beliefs. I now worship only Saint Marx, electricity, and the T-34 tank. That's *my* holy trinity," Stalin affirmed.

Evgueni kept quiet. The dictator was lying. Evgueni had known for some time that Stalin relied on the services of a personal fortune teller and a medium. Since the German invasion, whenever he became too filled with doubt or despair, he invited them to his dacha just outside Moscow to help him with decision making. The medium joined Evgueni after every meeting to secretly relay the details in a safehouse far from the NKVD offices.

The most recent debriefing had been particularly useful. Stalin had summoned the medium to enquire about the history of the former tsar's relic and the possibility of finding it. The medium had gone into a deep trance and had been extremely persuasive when he emerged. Evgueni had taught him well.

Stalin lit a pipe. A Dunhill—his only weakness when it came to the temptations of capitalism. "The fact that Himmler and Churchill are after the relics is no reason for me to start believing this fairy tale," he said disdainfully.

"If you really felt that way, you would have thrown the report straight in the bin," Evgueni replied with a smile. "You are known for your insatiable curiosity. And I know you too well. You think there might be some truth to it and that it would be a shame to miss out on it. That's why you should listen to the man waiting outside. His name is Dimitri Radenko, Professor Radenko. Does his name ring any bells?"

Stalin's gaze fixed on Lenin's death mask, as if probing his mentor for cues. Evgueni knew that the Red Tsar would find the answer. His memory was so remarkable that just the week before, he'd humiliated a judge in court by reciting a list of the last forty people found guilty for counter-revolutionary acts during the 1937 purges.

"Hmm," mumbled the dictator. "Your man. Doesn't he have a beautiful wife? A charming, blonde actress who starred in *Alexander Nevsky*?" Evgueni smiled as Stalin continued. "But I doubt he's brought his wife with him tonight. Radenko works for you at the NKVD. He runs the poisons department I believe?"

"I prefer to call it Department 31," replied Berin. "Professor Radenko is working on a new modern chemical and bacteriological arsenal for our military. Along the way, he has also found several drugs that have proven extremely useful for eliminating our enemies."

"Beria tells me he also conducts research in the field of telepathy and a few other rather unorthodox areas—from a Marxist perspective, I hope."

"Quite to the contrary, Joseph! It's all science—extrasensory perception, to be exact—and the results are quite promising. Professor Radenko is a true materialist who believes magic and the supernatural are phenomena that science must study to properly explain."

Stalin crossed his arms over his chest and leaned back against the wall near the window. "Two years ago, comrade Beria suggested we should hire telepaths to probe Hitler's mind. I laughed in his face that day . . . What does Radenko have to do with your relics?"

"I think he'd do a much better job of explaining that."

Stalin nodded. Evgueni got up to open the door to the ante-chamber and ushered in a short, wrinkled man in a worn three-piece suit. He hesitantly stepped into the office. Professor Radenko peered at Stalin through a pair of unbecoming wood-rimmed glasses. Evgueni had always wondered how he had ended up with such a beautiful wife.

The scientist bowed to Stalin.

"The NKVD's head poisoner!" exclaimed the dictator, a dubious look on his face. "What an honour! My ears are all yours. I hear you have some crucial information to share."

"I'll need at least an hour to explain it all. I—"

"I'll stop you there," said Stalin, interrupting Radenko. "You've just wasted several precious seconds." He poured some vodka into a small amber-coloured glass. "Drink some of this exquisite Zbyrova to get you going. Bottoms up, comrade!"

Evgueni offered the professor a soothing smile. Radenko downed the liquid, then stood up straight.

"It all began in May 1923. The NKVD had sent an exploratory mission to Tibet to seal an alliance with the local authorities. The idea was to establish a bridgehead there and use it to spread our revolutionary ideas throughout the British Empire. They came to me because I had been to Tibet a year earlier with a painter and explorer friend. But the mission was a failure. The lamas threw everyone in prison. They believed we were of the devil—well, of *one* of their devils, since their pantheon is full of demons."

"Oh yes, I remember that," replied Stalin. "The man who suggested the ridiculous expedition was executed for incompetence."

"I was detained for nearly a year," continued Radenko, without any visible reaction to the dictator's interruption. "They treated me rather well and once they realized I wasn't a threat, I could come and go as I pleased. Before long, I had access to their libraries. Over the course of several months, a translator among the monks helped me learn about their civilization and customs—particularly through their sacred books."

Stalin sighed ostentatiously. "This story is boring, comrade. I'd rather listen to your wife recite Mayakovsky poems."

"You must be patient, Joseph," said Evgueni. "Let him finish."

The professor took out a roll of parchment paper and opened

it on the table. A text in thin, tightly knit characters filled columns separated by illustrations of dragons and monsters.

"This is a manuscript I brought back," explained Radenko. "It tells of the existence of a mythical city settled thousands of years ago in the Himalayas and known as Shambhala. The people who built it are said to have come from a civilization that had survived a global cataclysm. A disaster caused by careless use of a mysterious and terrifying power: Kundali."

"Excellent," said Stalin with a laugh. "I could use a weapon like that to destroy Hitler. I don't suppose you brought any Kundali back with you, did you comrade?"

"No. It's . . ." mumbled the frightened scientist.

"Continue, Radenko," said Evgueni reassuringly. "Our great leader is joking."

"They say Kundali is the prodigious energy present in all things on earth—minerals, plants, animals. Kundali is the original fountain of Kundalini, the energy yogis believe flows up and down our spines. It is the source of both life and destruction. And according to this manuscript, the Shambhala survivors forged four swastika-shaped relics to divide and contain this universal energy."

Stalin leaned over the scroll and placed his index finger on a drawing of an emerald giant with four faces, four arms, and ruby eyes. His limbs had been severed at the wrist, and flaming swastikas sat where hands should have been.

"What is this?" balked Stalin. "An ancient Nazi bastard?"

"This figure represents the god king Kundali, the master of the cosmic life force, power and immortality. See the four swastikas severed from the god's arms? They symbolize the dispersion of the relics. My translator explained that the legend claims one of them was hidden in a cave in Tibet, but that no one knows where the other three were sent. During the rest of my time in prison there, I learned the art of Tibetan poisons and remedies, which I have used to serve the revolution thanks to comrade Evgueni."

"And how did the two of you meet?"

"I met Professor Radenko in Moscow, where he was giving a talk about Tibet," explained Evgueni. "When he detailed this legend

of the relics, I immediately connected it to the tsar's swastika. I
went on to hire Professor Radenko to head up our chemical and
bacteriological programmes. When he can find the time, he also
gathers useful information on the existence of the relics."

Stalin's eyes narrowed. "You've never mentioned this research
to me, Evgueni . . . But to get back to the issue at hand, how did
Hitler and Churchill find out about them?"

"We don't know," replied Evgueni. "We do know, however, that
the Nazis found the relic in Tibet during the SS expedition there
in 1938. And that the British sent commando units to southern
France and to Venice for two more."

Stalin's eyes darted over to Lenin's mask once again. "That's
all very interesting," he said as he turned back to the professor,
"but you still haven't given me anything concrete on the power
these knick-knacks might have. Right now, you sound more like a
babushka who's listened to too many Middle Eastern fairy tales
than a man of science."

Radenko's face went red as he placed his palms on the table.
"There is nothing magical about these relics," he replied. "I am
utterly convinced—and I'm not alone in this—that aeons ago, an
incredibly evolved society laid the base for all this. A civilization
that mastered advanced technologies not through sorcery or magic
but through science. Neither social classes nor money had their
place within this society, since each individual worked to benefit
the community as a whole. There was no war, no murder, no theft.
A supreme guide, whose authority was eagerly accepted by all,
tended to the fate and happiness of his people."

Stalin's face lit up. "It sounds like you're describing our beautiful communist society, comrade! And I would have succeeded in
implementing it if the war hadn't gotten in my way."

Evgueni glanced at the dictator in surprise. He had just told a
brazen lie—but that was when Stalin was most convincing.

The professor puffed up his chest. "Yes, comrade, a Marxist-
Leninist society that existed tens of thousands of years ago.
Before Rome, Egypt and even Sumer! That's why it's important
to find the vestiges of this civilization—to show the world that

revolutionary socialism is part of history's natural course. And even more importantly, if we could get our hands on one of the relics and study its technology, we would be several steps ahead of everyone else. And that would be sure to please the people—and their Supreme Guide."

Stalin put down his pipe and slowly applauded, then looked deep into the professor's eyes. "You've won me over, Radenko. But I want to be sure of your sincerity. You see, the vodka I served you contained one of your poisons, supplied by comrade Beria. But you are in luck: I have the antidote here. Have you told me the whole truth?"

All colour left the professor's face as he stared at his glass. Evgueni stepped forward, but Stalin stopped him with a wave of his hand.

"You should be grateful, Evgueni, that I didn't serve you the same potion. I don't appreciate it when you keep things from me."

"I knew you would be sceptical and didn't want to waste your time," objected Evgueni.

"I alone will be the judge of that. So, professor?"

"I swear it's the whole truth! On the lives of my wife and my two sons," exclaimed Radenko in a panic.

Stalin watched the professor unravel as the fear set in. "I beg of you . . ." he pleaded.

"Joseph! He's always been loyal to you!" shouted Evgueni.

The Red Tsar finally looked away from the professor. "Ramp up your research on the tsar's swastika. I'll look into it myself as well . . ." he said, matter-of-factly. Then he grabbed the bottle of vodka by the neck and took a swig. "So delicious!" Stalin exclaimed, bursting into laughter when he saw the look of confusion and relief on the professor's face. "Maybe I'll pull the same prank on Churchill."

37

British Museum, Great Russell Street, London

From his hiding place inside the sarcophagus, Tristan listened to the noises around him. He suspected it was dark outside by now. At night, museums—like most places—led secret lives created by the imagination. He couldn't help but wonder who had been laid to rest in that same tomb thousands of years earlier. He imagined the careful strokes of the craftsman who had engraved the hieroglyphs on the outside, and the embalmers who had prepared the body before placing it in its stone coffin for all of eternity—or so they assumed. Since the sarcophagus was rather narrow, Tristan had folded his arms over his chest like the ancient Egyptian mummy that must once have lain in his place.

What would happen if an overzealous guard decided to check out the tomb? He'd most likely faint or run away screaming. Although so far, surprisingly, Tristan had not actually heard any guards making their rounds. The museum appeared to be deserted. Administration must not have thought anyone would try to lock themselves in a museum—or maybe the decision maker had laughed heartily when someone had suggested the possibility. The answer to most problems lay in what other people took for granted.

And yet, the hardest part of his mission was still to come. The area of the museum he needed to access—the medieval gallery— was inaccessible since the corridor linking it to the main building had collapsed. Even if he managed to get through the door, he would have to make his way through the rubble, with what was left of the roof threatening to cave in at any moment. He wasn't even sure that the floor would be in any shape to support his weight. As far as he knew, the building had been damaged right down to the basement.

He slowed his breathing again, to listen closely. The old wooden floor would likely creak if a guard walked by. But he heard nothing at all—it was dead silent around him.

He would have to decide when to leave his hiding place. Had he given it enough time to detect any guards? What if they began their rounds later in the night? Or what if there was a guard who simply sat in one place? What if . . . Tristan was used to this never-ending list of questions without answers. It was fear. He might be a mere few meters from the last swastika and would have to stop psyching himself up to avoid making fatal mistakes.

He couldn't bear to stay put any longer, so he slowly slid a hand outside and moved the lid. He got to his feet, stretched and took a deep breath, before silently making his way towards the windows that overlooked the street. The guards were still there but wouldn't pose a problem: they didn't seem interested in what went on inside the museum. Some were playing cards while others were resting. Tristan felt elated, like a teenager who had successfully slipped out at night. The feeling was invigorating and restored the mental agility he felt he had lost in Venice. He was alone, free to do whatever he liked inside one of the biggest museums in the world. He almost gave in to the urge to dance. His doubts had disappeared: the game was about to begin.

He made his way through each room of the Ancient Egyptian galleries until he reached the stairs. The faded wooden floor seemed to absorb his footsteps. There still wasn't a single sound, except for the wind outside, which swayed the temporary lights hanging from the façade. Their dim glow provided enough light for Tristan to move safely and discreetly. He'd reached the landing now. The stairs led down to the lobby. If there was only one guard, that's where he would be. Tristan knelt down next to the railing and inched his way down the steps one by one. When the lobby came into view, he paused. The middle of the stairs was covered with a red carpet held to the edge of each step with a long metal rod. He scooted over a few centimeters and unscrewed the decorative head from one end of a rod. The lobby, which had once housed the library, was now a construction site full of piles of metal beams, bags of cement, and wheelbarrows of sand among other things. Tristan aimed the finial for a can of paint. The small piece of metal struck a beam, ricocheted against some scaffolding, and bounced across the floor. Tristan waited.

When no one came to check out the noise, Tristan knew for certain he was alone. He raced down to the lobby, picked up a crowbar and a sledgehammer and hurried towards the boarded-up doors that led to the medieval gallery. The boards had been nailed in hastily and were easy to remove with the crowbar. A final impact from the sledgehammer made quick work of the door itself. Tristan found himself looking at an indescribable maze of dangers including collapsed beams and gaping holes in the floor. He finally realized why there were no guards—there was no way across. Even if he made his way carefully through the debris, he would eventually come across an unstable wall of rubble or a hole in the floor too big to jump over. It seemed he would have to choose between being swallowed up by the darkness or crushed out of existence.

And yet, the medieval gallery was only a few dozen meters away. He could make out the entrance in the darkness, but a huge crater gaped right in front of it. As his eyes adjusted to the gloom, Tristan could make out more details. The collapsed beams supported one another like the jumbled masts of a sailboat ravaged by a storm. They all seemed to touch, but near the top, like a canopy of trees. If he could climb to the top of one of them, he might be able to move across to the next.

Hurrying back to the lobby, he searched in vain for metal cleats. Some rope and two sharp axes would have to do.

On his return to the medieval gallery, a sudden flash of light sent him scurrying into the shadow of some scaffolding. He brandished an axe and waited. The light was coming from the entrance to the museum. The yellow circle moved rhythmically on the floor. Tristan realized someone was walking with a lantern in hand. Strangely, he couldn't hear any footsteps. Suddenly, the light disappeared. Tristan stuck his head out and looked towards the entrance. The heavy glass door was still closed. When he turned back around, the light appeared again, a few meters away, but dimmer this time, as though it was shining through a piece of fabric. Tristan stepped back into his hiding place. If someone came through the lobby, they might not see him beneath the scaffolding.

All of a sudden, a window to his left lit up. The only one that wasn't protected by blinds.

Tristan was furious he hadn't noticed it before! There had to be a patrol on the other side of the glass, inspecting the inside of the museum through the window. The light disappeared, then came back to its place on the floor each time the guards passed a window. Tristan gathered the ropes and axes, crossed the former library, and headed back to the collapsed corridor he had to navigate. A ceiling beam rose up before him. He tried to catch the rope on it, but there was nothing to hold it in place. He wouldn't be able to lasso his way across the debris. The darkness made it more difficult, but he finally located a beam that was thicker than the others lying across the top of a pile of rubble. He walked over to its base and decided it was wide enough to walk up, one foot after the other. However, there was nowhere to hold on. Tristan slammed the first axe into the wood as high as he could, then leaned on the handle to drive the second one into the beam even higher.

A few minutes later, he reached the top and jumped onto the pile of rubble. He was standing on an island in the middle of a sea of mutilated walls. Luckily, the outside wall was still standing, protecting him from view.

The entrance to the gallery was now several meters below him. The door, too, had been damaged by the explosion and hung open over the void. One hinge held it fastened to the wall. If he wanted to get into the gallery, he had but one choice: he'd have to use it like a trampoline. He dropped the rope and axes and took a run up. The door began to give way as soon as his feet hit the wood. Tristan pushed his back up against the wall, clinging to the door-frame, using his elbows to keep from falling. Despite all the cuts on his arms, he managed to hoist his upper body to safety, but his legs still dangled over the abyss. He was breathless and bleeding, but at least he was alive. Slowly, he crawled to the middle of the floor and got up.

The medieval gallery was intact. None of the display cases had been emptied. He took the angel's key out of his pocket and hurried left towards the Waddesdon room.

The reliquary was there.

Tristan had only ever seen black-and-white photographs of the piece and was caught off guard by its beauty. All around the alcove that housed the Holy Thorn, a rich collection of characters covered in gold and precious stones struggled through the trials of the Final Judgement. Tristan shivered. He had to find the lock that fit James Hadler's key. He carefully studied each scene, then finally found two sculpted doors on the back of the reliquary that seemed to close a second alcove. There was a keyhole to the left. He inserted the key, but it wouldn't turn. He had to find the right alignment for the indentations engraved into the side. When he heard a sliding sound, he realized he'd succeeded.

After a moment's hesitation, he reached into the alcove.

His fingers instantly recognized the unique shape of a swastika.

He removed it carefully. It was smaller than the ones from Tibet and Montségur, but Tristan knew its size had nothing to do with its power. He slipped the relic into his shirt pocket.

He suddenly felt dizzy. How many people had worshipped it? How many men had hoped to get their hands on it? And now it was against his skin. The last swastika, the one that could change everything.

The dizziness intensified abruptly. Everything went dark around him. A wave of intense heat seemed to emanate from his chest and radiate through the rest of his body, like the roots of a plant reaching through rich soil. The energy—he could think of no other word to describe it—was travelling through his blood and muscles. Tristan staggered and grabbed onto the reliquary to keep from falling. His vision blurred, and his mind was in torment as rays of light ripped his consciousness to pieces. He could feel himself growing smaller. His body was no longer his. He stumbled, unable to endure the pain.

"No, not now . . ."

His legs failed him. He was no longer in the museum. Images raced past.

A cliff battered by the wind. A black horizon in an electric-blue sky. The muffled sounds of the waves in the distance. It all seemed so real. He turned his head. All around him were stone slabs standing on end, sharp and hostile like an army of rocky barbarians. He made his way forwards like a sleepwalker on deserted land.

It was a waking dream.

Suddenly, a tall, dark statue came into his field of vision.

A woman. A stone woman. She was holding an open chest.

Tristan stepped closer to get a better look at her face. It seemed peculiarly familiar. His heart jumped into his throat. Erika. She seemed to call out to him for help, a look of terror on her silent face.

A moment later, the statue's arms shattered and the chest fell to the ground, revealing the swastika. The wind picked up. Tristan could barely stand. The stone idol fell backwards. He wanted to keep it from tumbling into the abyss, but in vain. Everything went black. Tristan passed out as Erika fell from the top of the cliff.

38

The Secret Garden, London

Although Moira hated the British, she did appreciate a few of the things they had to offer. First and foremost: scones and Cornish clotted cream—and the sharp bitterness of Assam black tea from north-west India. When Crowley had asked for an urgent meeting at the Secret Garden, a small teahouse near her home that was open late, the Scarlet Fairy had readily agreed. She expected new documents. Crowley was too afraid to return to the brothel, but claimed he was under surveillance by British intelligence.

When Moira stepped into the teahouse, she spotted Crowley at once. He had picked a table in the back, near the till. The Secret Garden featured a soothing décor of slightly faded lavender walls dotted with stylized paintings of tea flowers and of course the inevitable portrait of King George VI. Next to the till stood a small display case stuffed with fresh pastries. Moira was pleased to see there were still plenty of scones. The teahouse was nearly deserted, except for a couple engaged in a deep discussion, their eyes locked. Moira placed her order at the counter and sat down across from Crowley.

"Aleister, I hope you've got new documents for me and that they're worth dragging me out like this," she said.

"Oh, yes. I hope you noticed I chose this place because I know you like it. As for me, I've always hated that revolting oriental infusion. It yellows the teeth and does nothing for the complexion."

Moira smiled and studied the menu on the table. "I don't have much time, so let's get on with it. You said you thought you'd been followed after your last visit to the Hellfire Club?"

"Yes. Before I went in, I saw one of my young colleagues from the SOE," whispered Crowley. "I'm certain it was no accident she was there."

Moira put down the menu and gestured to the waitress at the counter. "I'm aware—we spotted her as well. In fact, she's with our German friends as we speak."

Crowley remained impassive as the employee placed a pink porcelain teapot on the table. He waited for her to leave, then leaned closer to Moira. "It would be a shame if anything were to happen to her," he said.

"Why is that, Aleister? Have you gone soft?" Moira picked up the teapot and poured herself a cup of the amber liquid.

"Hardly," he replied, "but the SOE wouldn't take lightly to the torture of one of its agents. Their *esprit de corps* is rather strong."

Moira sipped her tea contentedly, keeping her eyes focused on the mage. "It's delicious," she said, "though it's not the variety I'm accustomed to. It's slightly spicier. Listen, Aleister, my main concern is keeping myself out of it. What did you tell Malorley?"

"That I'd been to the Hellfire to pocket the last sum owed to me for my shares."

"Did he believe you?" asked Moira, who was beginning to feel lethargic. She put her cup down on the saucer and massaged her temples.

"What's wrong Moira? Don't you feel well?"

"It's too hot," she said as she undid the top button on her blouse. "I—"

Moira felt two hands land on her shoulders. She turned to see a stranger leaning over her. She wanted to stand, but her strength had abandoned her. Her eyes were searching for Crowley—in vain. The muscles in her neck seemed to have turned to stone.

"You bastard," she managed to mumble. "You drugged me."

"I'm merely returning the favour. After all you put me through last year at the Hellfire Club to blackmail me . . . Don't worry, the people at the SOE assured me that this drug paralyzes the muscles but leaves the mind functioning normally. That will be perfect for our romantic little jaunt," said Crowley.

"Jaunt?"

"Commander Malorley is very eager to meet you."

Moira felt her mouth go numb. As they lifted her up and carried her to a car parked behind the teahouse, she had the terrible sensation of being in a coffin. A coffin made of her own flesh. They laid her on the back seat of the Ford, and Aleister got in next to her. Then they sped away into the traffic.

"I know you can hear me, my dear," Aleister said softly. "How does it feel to lose control of your body? Uncomfortable, isn't it? I could do as I like with you. Right now, I'm stroking your thigh with my hand, but you can't feel a thing. I could move it up higher and you wouldn't even know. You're like a paraplegic forgotten in some hospital."

Moira listened to the sound of traffic outside and studied the sky, which she occasionally glimpsed between the tops of buildings. As they continued their journey, trees appeared. She silently invoked the goddesses of the night, begging them for help. The incantations went round and round her head, to no avail. She was alone. Her magic was of no help.

Nearly an hour had passed when the car finally stopped in front of a hunting lodge surrounded by a dense wood. The numbness in Moira's body had started to fade. Two men seized her arms and legs and let her fall onto the ground like a bag of dirty laundry. When her elbows struck the gravel in the drive, pain radiated through her arms.

"Must you really be so rough, you bastards?"

She couldn't believe she had just spoken. Her mouth still felt like papier mâché. Her kidnappers impassively lifted her again to carry her into the house. Crowley walked by her side, his lascivious eyes glued to her body.

The men took her upstairs to a room with blackened

wainscoting. The walls were covered in hunting trophies—there were heads of stags, boars and pheasants everywhere she looked. Hundreds of them. It seemed every hunter in the country had chosen this place to display their trophies. They sat her down in a chair, her hands and feet handcuffed.

Across from her, a man was tied to the radiator. His head hung to his chest and blood had stained his shirt.

"Ah, our favourite witch," exclaimed a voice. "You're early. I'm not quite finished with this interrogation, but ladies first, as they say. I'm Commander Malorley. I hope the drug has begun to wear off. Can you speak?"

"Indeed. You have no right nor reason to kidnap me!" protested Moira.

"In times of war, secret services like mine have every right. Could you please look at the wall to your left?"

Moira turned her head to find large photographs of the mutilated body of the young woman she'd left in Tower Hamlets.

"Do you recognize her?" asked Malorley. "You murdered her last year to blackmail Aleister. He's willing to testify against you. And when we leak your name to the press, they'll give you the headlines for sure. *Hellfire Madam plays Jack the Ripper . . .* "

Moira didn't seem concerned. Her confidence had returned. She spat on the floor to get the bad taste out of her mouth and mark her disgust. "I won't be the only one with my picture in the papers! I could also leak the names of many loyal customers: members of parliament, police officers, respected doctors, diplomats, pastors, journalists and maybe even a member of the royal family. Every month I make a list of my customers' names and their . . . practices in a little notebook. Since I always think ahead, I also have photographs taken of them during their sessions. They're my life insurance."

"You're a clever woman," conceded Malorley.

"Those close to me have strict instructions to send the pictures to the press if I disappear. Even with the threat of censure, the papers will be delighted to publish them, dragging the pinnacles of British society through the mud."

"I don't give a shit about your pictures. All I want to know is what you've done with the agent who was on duty outside your brothel during Aleister's last visit. Either you tell me, or I get rid of you immediately."

Moira shrugged. "You wouldn't dare. You're too much of a gentleman. Think of the pictures of my customers, I—"

Malorley's palm suddenly struck her cheek. Moira's head swung to the right.

"I'll ask just one more time. Where is my agent, Miss O'Connor? I couldn't care less about your customers since I'm not one of them."

"You bloody English bastard! You're bluffing!"

Malorley walked over to the man tied to the radiator and lifted his head. The left side of his face was one big bruise. Dried blood was caked at the corners of his mouth. Malorley stepped behind him and placed his hands on the man's shoulders. "This is Graham Slenders," he explained. "Owner of Slenders Transport, a small company established in Devonshire since 1935. Last month, a violent storm blew through the region and one of Slenders' lorries ended up in a pond. When emergency services pulled it out of the water, they found three crates of dynamite hidden beneath its legal cargo of cod. Our friends at MI6 were alerted. I'll spare you the rest of the details, but they led us to Graham here, and to his house, where we found a fine German-made radio." Malorley pulled Slenders' head back by the hair. "After a friendly interrogation, he admitted to working for the Abwehr. You know, the same German agents you give information to."

Moira remained impassive, as though nothing could touch her.

Malorley leaned in, placing his face right next to hers. "Graham betrayed his country, just like you."

"My country is Ireland! Which you occupy and whose people you brutalize!"

Malorley gestured to one of his men, who stepped behind Slenders. "Let's end this, Tom."

The SOE agent slowly took a small bit of rope from his pocket and wrapped it around the spy's neck.

Slenders' eyes filled with fear as he mumbled, "No, please, I told you everything, I—"

He didn't have time to finish he sentence.

His face turned purple, his eyes went wide, and his tongue hung out of his mouth. His body made one last attempt at escape, then went limp on the floor.

Malorley's men untied the corpse and dragged it by the feet towards the door. The commander waited for them to leave the room, then turned back to the Irishwoman, whose face was now livid.

"If I were a gentleman, the SOE wouldn't have hired me," Malorley said coldly. He leaned in: "So, if you won't answer my questions, you'll receive the same treatment as poor Mr. Slenders, including the torture you sadly missed. And a few days from now, when they find your swollen corpse floating in the Thames, I'll savour the articles on your customers' perverse passions alongside a fine cognac."

"You'd better collaborate, Moira. If you don't, your adventures will end here—and it won't be pretty," urged Crowley.

The Scarlet Fairy was no longer quite so brazen. There was real fear in her eyes. "You'll let me go if I tell you where she is? We'll be even?"

"Not even close. From now on, you'll work for me as a double agent. We'll use you to communicate with your pals at the Abwehr."

Moira hesitated. She was racking her brains for a solution. Knowing she had to buy herself more time, she finally nodded. "The girl's not at the Hellfire Club. She was taken to Southgate, a building at the far end of Salvation Road. A warehouse for a meat wholesaler. That's all I know."

Malorley signalled his agents.

"We're headed there now. Don't let her out of your sight."

"Can I have some water?" pleaded Moira.

"Of course, we're not the Gestapo," replied Malorley.

"You English are such bloody hypocrites," she said with a smirk. "You use the same methods. If you ever change sides, I'll write you a letter of recommendation for the SS!"

Malorley ignored her and left the room with Crowley. They walked down a corridor to the far end of the hunting lodge.

"She's not exactly wrong," argued the mage. "I never would have thought you capable of murdering a man in cold blood."

A guard opened the door ahead of them, which led to a large room. Three men were sitting around a table playing cards. Crowley stopped short. One of the men was none other than the spy who had just been strangled. His executioner was sitting across from him, looking rather glum.

"Three aces! Hand it over, boys," exclaimed the miraculous survivor as he scooped up the pile of coins.

The men stood up when they saw Malorley.

"Please, stay seated. You all right, Malcolm?" asked the commander.

"Fine, sir, though Fitzpatrick did pull a little too hard. I really thought he might not stop in time."

"I should have kept going, by God! I really should have. Then you wouldn't be taking me for all I'm worth at poker. But I'll win it back, I—"

"I'm afraid you won't have time. You're coming with us to Southgate. We must move quickly."

Just as they were leaving, the telephone rang.

"They've found Tristan," exclaimed Malorley's secretary over the receiver. "He's in central London."

"If you know exactly where, spit it out!" ordered the commander.

The secretary paused for a minute, still surprised by what she was about to say. "At the British Museum."

Malorley looked out of the window in shock. "But the museum has been closed for ages and badly damaged by the bombings! It must be a mistake."

His secretary insisted. "The surveillance team is certain: they saw Tristan Marcas enter the museum this afternoon with volunteers in charge of clearing rubble, and no one ever saw him come out."

"How did they identify him?"

"I don't know, Commander. What are your orders?"

Malorley placed his palm over the receiver and turned towards Crowley. "Aleister, go to Southgate without me. Do your best to bring Laure back alive."

As the mage rushed out, Malorley put the phone back to his ear. "Heighten surveillance at the museum. I'm on my way."

39

The British Museum, Great Russell Street, London

Tristan felt like Lazarus when he awoke from the darkness. He touched his shirt. The relic was still in its place. He stood up slowly, happy to have escaped this terrifying nightmare. He had no idea how long he'd been unconscious—he hadn't experienced anything like that with the other relics. Maybe each of them possessed different powers? He slipped his latest discovery into his trouser pocket and started to walk. The relic was *his* talisman—the key to a better world where neither Himmler nor Malorley existed. He felt a heady wave of euphoria wash over him, as though the power of the relic was flowing through him. He'd have to calm down before the first shift of volunteers entered the museum. There was no margin for error now. The journey back over the abyss seemed much less laborious than on the way there. Back in the first gallery, he pushed the lid of the sarcophagus back into its original position, slightly ajar. It was unlikely anyone would notice such a detail, but Tristan needed to control every aspect of what came next.

He left the Egyptian gallery and hurried down the stairs to inspect the worksite with its scaffolding, materials, and tools, looking for any clue that could give him away. He had a strange feeling of being both hunter and prey. Within minutes, he had nailed the boards at the door to the medieval gallery back in place. No one would notice a thing. With James Hadler dead, no one knew that the British Museum had ever housed the final relic, and no one would know Tristan had taken it.

Now he needed to figure out his escape. He would either join a team clearing rubble and disappear during the first break, or take advantage of the general toing and froing to vanish right away.

Before he could make up his mind, the main door creaked as it turned on its hinges. The workday was beginning.

Great Russell Street

Malorley had been waiting for hours. He'd joined the surveillance team on the second floor of a house with a bay window that looked out over the entrance to the museum. The owner—an elderly woman with a Welsh accent—had been terrified to see SOE men turn up in the middle of the night. Out of fear, she'd handed over her lounge without any questions.

"No one has come out yet," said one of the men.

Malorley didn't reply. He was trying to knit together the few pieces of information he had. In a nearby pub, the owner of a second-hand clothing store had bragged about having traded brand-new clothes for a battered pair of overalls. "What can I say, the French are crazy!" he had added. No one would have paid him any attention—London was full of French refugees—were it not for a police officer sitting nearby. He remembered seeing the wanted notice Malorley's men had sent to every police station in London. The overalls in mind, SOE agents narrowed it down to the restoration work at the British Museum and began to watch the neighbourhood. Their hunch had paid off: they'd identified Tristan among a group of volunteers enjoying a smoke outside the museum. But at the end of the day, no one saw the Frenchman come out.

"Are you absolutely certain he's still inside?" Malorley asked for the tenth time.

"Yes, sir. And there's no other way out. The perimeter is guarded by Civil Defence."

Malorley rubbed his temples. He was trying to wrap his head around the obvious: if Tristan had spent the night, it was because he had found the last swastika and was securing it. A masterful feat. Except that he hadn't informed the SOE. Malorley supposed he knew he was being watched by German spies and had to work alone. Unless . . . Unless he'd decided to strike out on his own.

"Commander, what are your orders if the suspect comes out?"

"Intercept him."

"Gently, or . . . ?"

Malorley's features hardened. "Alive. I want him alive."

The British Museum

Tristan joined the incoming team as they walked past the Egyptian galleries. No one noticed him. When they reached the area they were scheduled to work in, a supervisor handed him a wheelbarrow and a spade, and he got to work scooping charred books off the floor. A service stairwell had been covered with rickety boards to roll the wheelbarrows down to the ground floor. No one liked making the run, especially since there had been several accidents. Tristan offered. On his way down with the first wheelbarrow, he timed it. Three minutes to the lobby, two to walk through, two more to reach the dumpster just outside the doors. Seven minutes total, plus the slightly longer return journey. He would have fifteen minutes before anyone noticed he was missing. More than enough to disappear. Now, all he had to do was choose the best time for his escape. And undergo a transformation. A Pole in rags was shovelling ashes not far from him. Like many of the immigrants on the team, he had only volunteered because he needed the three meagre meals the job provided. Tristan asked for a cigarette. The Pole shrugged, so Tristan suggested exchanging clothes for four cigarettes. The Pole didn't hesitate for long. When Tristan began heading down with his second load, dressed like a pauper, he was unrecognizable.

Great Russell Street

No one had come out of the museum. Malorley checked his watch. The first team had been inside for an hour. If Tristan had found the swastika, he had to be eager to leave as soon as possible. So, why hadn't he? He couldn't have been caught, or the police would have alerted the SOE.

Malorley turned to one of his agents. "When do the workers take their break?" he asked.

"Every two hours. The men leave to smoke or get a pint."

"How many come out at a time?"

"About forty."

The commander frowned. Too many to watch all of them. They'd have to innovate.

"Mike, gather a bunch of newsboys. Show them a picture of Marcas and pay them to run up to the workers whenever they come out of the museum."

"What if one of the kids recognizes him?"

"Tell them to pretend to slip and grab hold of his legs and cry out. That should give us enough time to get there."

The British Museum

The pile of sand was dwindling. Two workers were shovelling it into the spinning cement mixer. A few more spadefuls and it would be ready. Another volunteer poured in a bucket of water to humidify the mixture. As he stepped back, he ran into a man in rags who was struggling with a wheelbarrow full of ashes.

"Watch where you're going, Polak!" he roared, as though to a dog.

His colleagues burst into laughter.

"Look at those clothes! A proper beggar!"

"If they fight like they dress, it's no wonder Hitler rolled over them!"

Tristan carried on, his head bowed. The Germans weren't the

only racists here. These idiots should be ashamed—the Poles had fought valiantly against the Germans. In vain. And they were one of the most heavily represented nationalities among resistance fighters. Yet Tristan couldn't help but smile: his disguise was working. He'd now finally reached the entrance. The door was open.

He put down the wheelbarrow and scanned the square in front of the museum. It was deserted except for one Civil Defence volunteer, who was smoking a cigarette. Three steps carried him through the doorway, five took him outside, seven and he'd be free. The temptation was too great. He made a break for it.

Great Russell Street

"Mike's found a bunch of newsboys. They're on their way back," announced one of the agents.

Malorley picked up the binoculars but noticed something other than a gang of children waving newspapers around. "Someone has just left the museum," he said.

All the agents rushed to the windows.

One of them immediately burst into laughter. "You mean that scarecrow?"

"Look at his rags!"

"What *I* see," shouted Malorley, "is someone escaping right under our noses!"

The SOE men hurried out of the building and into the street. Malorley trained his binoculars on the entrance to the museum. The suspect had already made it down the stairs and was turning left towards Bloomsbury. The commander swore under his breath. His agents would never catch up in time. Malorley decided to head out himself. If it was Tristan, he'd quickly make his way towards the adjacent streets and disappear. The neighbourhood between Great Russell Street and Bloomsbury Way was a maze of courtyards, passages, and buildings in ruins due to the bombings. Tristan would easily be able to find an empty cellar to hole up in. No one would ever find him. Malorley picked a street and started to weave his way through the crowd. If his instinct was right, he just might run into him.

Streatham Street

Tristan slowed his pace. There was no point in drawing attention to himself. He would casually walk over to Hadler's house, then wait outside and watch the entrance. The pavements were full of beggars from all over Europe, so it was unlikely anyone would notice him. If the house wasn't being watched, he'd go back inside to gather a few valuable objects to sell on the black market. With the money, he'd—

"Tristan!"

He stopped in his tracks. Only one man in London knew his name. He turned around to see Malorley leaning against a nearby house wall to catch his breath.

"Tristan, I know you have the swastika. Don't blow this operation now. Tell me what you want."

Tristan didn't move or speak.

"Believe me, you have my word, this is your last mission. Give me the relic and you can do whatever you like afterwards."

Tristan thought back to his last meeting with Erika. What if she and Gehlen really had been spreading lies to turn the British against him? If they had convinced Malorley that he hadn't thrown the swastika into the lagoon in Venice but given it to the Nazis instead, no one could save him now.

"I've always had your back, Tristan," continued the commander. "Think of your father—"

Before he could finish, a lorry pulled up and screeched to a halt, blocking the alleyway. Conrad was the first to get out, followed by Susan and two other Abwehr agents.

The German drew a Browning and took aim at Malorley a dozen meters away from him. The first bullet threw the Englishman back against the nearest house wall; the second sent him to the ground.

"Get a move on, Marcas!" shouted Conrad.

Tristan stood transfixed over Malorley's limp body. He couldn't let him die here like a dog. Horrified, he ignored the order and knelt down next to the commander.

"What the hell are you doing?" shouted the German angrily, as the SOE agents materialized across the street, guns in hand, and fired in the direction of the lorry. Conrad spun around to retaliate. "Susan!" he yelled. "Get the relic. We'll cover you."

Having got down on her hands and knees to avoid the rain of bullets, she crawled towards Tristan, who was holding Malorley's hand. The commander was now lying in a pool of his own blood.

"Leave the swastika here, please. I beg of you," Malorley mumbled.

"I promise," replied Tristan. "I'll get you out of here."

"No, it's over for me. I'll be seeing your father soon. I'm glad I got to see you again. You did some great work," he struggled to say between shallow breaths. His eyes went wide. "Look out, behind you," he managed to shout.

Tristan turned around to find Susan standing over him, the barrel of her gun pointing right at his head.

"So you know each other," she said coldly as she placed the pistol on his temple. "You're a bloody traitor. And I can't stand—"

Before she could finish, the roar of a volley fired by the SOE agents sent her staggering like a drunk dancer. Then she slumped to the ground right next to Tristan.

"No, Susan!" shouted Conrad as he turned around.

The grenade rolling towards the SOE agents went unnoticed for several precious seconds. When they finally noticed its distinctive shape, it was too late to take cover—they were hit hard by the explosion.

Conrad seized the opportunity to hasten to his unconscious wife. Tristan groped for the gun she had dropped, but a German got there first. Another Nazi helped the Frenchman to his feet. There was nothing Tristan could do. He was trapped.

"Let's get out of here," shouted Conrad. "This place will be swarming with Brits soon."

He hugged Susan close. "Hold on, my love. I'll save you!"

The Ford's engine roared to life in the deserted street. Just seconds later, the lorry disappeared, along with Tristan and the final relic. Malorley's lifeless body had been left on the pavement.

40

London

The cellar was pitch black except for a tiny sliver of light. The rat had taken advantage of the darkness to settle on Laure's right thigh. She could feel the warmth radiating from the rodent's stomach through her trousers. The idea was repugnant, but also strangely soothing.

Suddenly, she heard footsteps in the corridor. Her heart began to race as she sat up straight. Her kidnappers were back. She ran her tongue over her molar. It was time to end this.

"Goodbye, Tommy," she whispered. "Take good care of yourself."

Laure took a deep breath. Her last taste of oxygen. They'd told her the cyanide would stop her heart almost immediately once absorbed. It would all be over soon.

The door creaked loudly as it swung open. Light streamed into the room.

Laure averted her eyes. They couldn't be the last thing she'd see on this earth. "Fuck off, you bloody Nazis!" she shouted as she bit down hard.

But no matter how hard she clenched her jaw, the capsule wouldn't break.

She was about to try again when a shadow fell on her. Blinded by the light of a torch, Laure couldn't make out the people across from her.

"Laure, it's all right! We're here."

She recognized the voice but wondered if she was dreaming. She blinked and squinted. "You . . ."

"You're safe now!"

"Aleister . . . What?"

The beam of light moved and the mage's plump face came into view above her. She felt hands cut the wires that tied her to the chair. The rat had scurried away.

"Malorley was very persuasive with Moira. She finally told us where to find you," explained Crowley. "Oh, you poor thing," he whispered when he noticed her hand. "The wounds are already infected. We'll take you to the hospital."

"There's a . . . couple," mumbled Laure. "A young German and an Englishwoman. My kidnappers. Did you get them?"

Crowley shook his head. "We found two men in the warehouse and took care of them. You're alive, Laure. That's all that matters."

She wanted to hug him. "I've never been so happy to see you, Aleister."

"Remember that when I ask you to sleep with me," he said glibly.

She managed a smile as two agents helped her to her feet. "Where's the commander?" she asked.

"He's looking for Tristan. Your friend is in London."

Laure perked up. "I would so like to see him again... I can't believe I almost cracked my cyanide capsule."

"It wasn't your time," said Crowley prophetically. "I knew it. The tarot Star watches over you."

"Either that, or His Majesty's poisons aren't of the finest quality . . ."

As she started towards the door, she suddenly felt tiny grains on her tongue, followed by the flavour of sweet almond.

She panicked. "Oh God, no!"

"What?"

She could barely speak and her eyes were full of terror. "The capsule. It broke. I—"

"Spit it out now!" shouted Crowley as he pushed her face towards the floor.

Laure felt like she was spinning. Everything was going hazy.

"Hold on! You must vomit it up. Let me help you," urged

Crowley as he leaned over as if to deliver mouth-to-mouth. Instead, he spat onto her tongue.

One of the agents recoiled in disgust. "What the hell are you doing?!" he shouted.

"Do you have a better idea?" asked Crowley, indignant. "If she doesn't vomit this instant, she'll die!"

Laure felt her stomach churn. Her eyes opened wide as she expelled a stream of brown bile.

"That's not enough," said Crowley as he put his hand in her mouth, probing for her uvula.

Laure vomited again and again, covering the ground. Everything was spinning. She felt as though her body had turned to mush and was coming out through her mouth.

"Whatever you do, Laure, don't go to sleep!"

She reached out for Aleister as she collapsed onto the floor.

"Not such . . . bad quality . . . after—"

Her eyes closed and her muscles all went limp as she passed out.

Infirmary, Department S

The doctor leaned over to examine the naked body on the cot. He placed his stethoscope on her chest and held his breath. A nurse was dabbing Laure's forehead.

"Her heart is still beating," concluded the doctor as he stood, "but it's weak." He pulled the sheet back up to her shoulders.

"You said the same thing ten minutes ago!" raged Crowley.

"Well, there's no reason to expect spontaneous improvement. It all depends on her body's ability to fight the amount of poison she ingested."

"In short, you have no idea."

The doctor shrugged. "You should be thrilled she's alive at all! An antidote is being prepared as we speak. After that, only time will tell."

"Do you really think I'm going to let you run this show? I'll be taking care of her from now on!" exclaimed Aleister.

"And how exactly do you plan to treat her?" the doctor asked sarcastically.

Crowley grabbed both nurse and doctor by the wrists, ushering them out of the door. "It's very simple," he replied. "I'm going to bring her back to life."

Alone in the room with Laure, he removed the sheet that covered her body and folded it into a triangle, placing one of the points at her groin. Then he took off his jacket, rolled up his sleeves, and placed his hands on her temples.

"I beseech you, oh lord from below, do not feast upon the soul of this mortal. Do not draw this unfortunate girl into the darkness, lord of the abyss! Do not grant her the privilege of knowing your glory!" Crowley felt a vein begin to pulse beneath his fingers. "Oh Belial, do not plunge your greedy claws into this defenceless flesh. Oh, Zebub, do not possess her soul. Do not drag her down into the darkest night!"

The door opened and the doctor stepped back inside, a phial in hand. He stopped short, a look of shock on his face. "What on earth are you doing?" he asked. "Are you conjuring demons?"

"Demons, ha! Lowly servants. Who do you take me for? Such philistines! When *I* call out to the devil, we speak face to face!"

The doctor refused to gratify Crowley with a reply. He walked over to Laure, uncorked the phial, and poured its contents into her mouth. "This will certainly help more than your nonsense!"

"You imbecile!" shouted Aleister. "If she wakes up, it's because I have a direct line to Lucifer!"

"You're mad! I'll report you. People like you don't belong here. You'd be better off in an asylum."

At the sound of the last word, Crowley jumped back as though he'd been doused with holy water. He couldn't stand it when people took him for a madman. He pointed his left index and little finger at the doctor. "May Satan dry out your body and putrefy your soul—"

The sound of a violent cough kept him from finishing his

curse. Laure had just opened her eyes. She looked at Crowley in confusion.

"What are you doing, Aleister?" she asked.

"Nothing, nothing at all. How do you feel?"

"Like I no longer have a body. Like it's all wobbly . . ." she tried to explain, taking the mage's hand. "Where's Malorley?"

The look on Crowley's face told her she'd asked the wrong question.

"I'm sorry, Laure," he said. "He was on a mission to exfiltrate Tristan and things went pear-shaped. He was shot several times. That's all I know."

For a moment, Laure was speechless. "And Tristan?" she finally managed.

"The Germans took him. He's disappeared again."

PART FOUR

"And out of the shadows, the older gods had returned to man:
the gods forgotten since Hyperborea, since Mu and Poseidonis,
bearing other names but the same attributes.
And the elder demons had also returned,
battening on the fumes of evil sacrifice,
and fostering again the primordial sorceries."
    A Vintage from Atlantis, Clark Ashton Smith

"Men believe in destiny; the gods believe in themselves."
    Excerpt from the *Thule Borealis Kulten*

41

Luftwaffe command post, Gouvieux Airfield, France

A wild and unpredictable summer wind was toying with the Focke-Wulf FW 58, but its pilot remained unperturbed as he headed for the glowing beacons of the landing strip a few hundred meters below.

"Hold on tight, it's going to be a rough landing!" he shouted to the two passengers.

Tristan grabbed hold of one of the leather handles dangling from the ceiling and Conrad tightened his grip on the armrests of his seat. A red light flashed overhead, casting an ominous glow throughout the cabin of the twin-engine.

Tristan tried to determine where they were landing—in vain. Aside from the lights of the landing strip, there was nothing but darkness around them.

This was in keeping with his current state of mind. He had failed. Miserably.

And now, he'd be joining the ranks of evil yet again, to deliver his precious prize to the victors.

It had been so close. He could have got rid of the Germans and kept the relic for himself, scoring a spectacular victory and regaining his freedom. But fate had decided otherwise. Just as in Venice. Except that this time, the Nazis had won. Worse still, Malorley had been shot down right in front of him.

Malorley. His father's friend. His own protector. The man who had got him messed up in this maddening quest in the first place.

The tragic scene near the museum was on constant replay in his mind. Tristan didn't even get a chance to speak properly to his mentor. He felt a pang of regret for not having trusted his boss when he needed him the most. The worst moment had been in the car that had carried him and the Abwehr agents to safety outside London. Before dropping off Susan at the hospital, her husband had gone into the details of kidnapping and torturing a French SOE agent. Tristan was certain it was Laure.

She had also fallen victim to the horrors of this war.

He had hoped to find an opportunity to escape during the long drive to the temporary airport in Kent, but clearly his luck had run out.

The plane was about to make its final descent. Ever since he'd stepped into the cabin, Tristan had been praying for the aircraft to crash and for the cursed relic to disappear in the explosion. Or for them to be shot down by RAF pilots over the Channel. But it seemed destiny had decided to favour the Nazis—the Focke-Wulf seemed immune even to the strong winds.

"Don't look so glum," laughed Conrad, who was sitting across from Tristan. "The FW 58 will shelter you even through the strongest storms. *Deutsche Qualität!*"

"I hope you're right," lied Tristan, who could feel his stomach roiling from the turbulence.

The plane finally landed with a jerk, bouncing three times before coming to a stop at the end of the strip and turning towards a series of illuminated hangars.

Tristan looked out the window in surprise. This wasn't a simple airfield. Hundreds of fighter planes were lined up as if preparing for a parade. There were Heinkel 177 bombers with portly snouts, heavy latest-generation Messerschmitt Me 410 hornet fighters, and even Junkers Ju 390 cargo planes. An entire fleet deployed before Tristan's eyes. He couldn't help but wonder if the Germans were planning a new attack on Great Britain.

"Where are we?" he asked, intrigued.

"At a Luftwaffe operational command post," the pilot shouted over the deafening sound of the engines. "Looks like you've earned a welcome committee!"

The plane stopped outside a three-storey concrete bunker

crowned with a radar antenna and German flags rippling in the wind. Tristan noticed a group of armed soldiers patrolling in front of an anti-aircraft squadron. Nearby, two officers in dress uniform stood to attention next to a shiny, black sedan.

"Charming," mumbled Tristan as he unbuckled his seatbelt and picked up the briefcase containing the swastika. Now that the engines had finally stopped, the only noise he could hear was the wind battering the flanks of the aircraft.

"I'd like to know why this object is so very important to our leaders," said Conrad sharply. "I'd like to know what Susan risked her life for."

"Maybe your Führer thinks art can change the world more effectively than cannons."

"I'm in no mood for your French humour!" shouted the German.

"Sorry, it's all I have left," Tristan replied flatly.

The door of the Focke-Wulf opened, and Tristan jumped onto the tarmac, followed by Conrad. One of the officers rushed over to meet them. Tristan would have liked to know who'd sent them. Himmler, Rosenberg, or the Abwehr? He had a hard time keeping track of the different Nazi factions.

The commander's SS uniform provided an answer.

"We're delighted to welcome you, Herr Marcas. Do you have the package?"

"Yes. Who should I give it to?"

The officer held out his hand. "I'll take it, thank you. A plane bound for Berlin is waiting for me at the other end of the runway."

"What about me?" asked Tristan, still holding on to the case.

"Your mission stops here. The Reichsführer is pleased. As a reward, he thought you deserved some rest in Paris."

Tristan had no desire to be stuck with Erika and Gehlen back at the Lutetia. "Commander, I've taken great risks to obtain this relic. I'd like to deliver it to the Reichsführer myself."

The officer continued to smile, but his gaze hardened. He placed a gloved hand on Tristan's hand. "Herr Marcas, if you hope to continue working for us, you'd better learn not to question orders. The case, please."

Reluctantly, Tristan did as he'd been told. Any hope of changing the situation had just evaporated. The officer inspected the contents of the small leather briefcase, then closed it again, visibly satisfied.

"That's settled," he said. "My man here will take you to your new quarters. He's French, like you. Enjoy yourself—you've earned it."

"Unfortunately," Conrad butted in, "*I* don't have time to enjoy myself. I have to get back to London right away."

The SS officer shot the spy a disdainful glance, as though he'd only just noticed he was there. "Not my problem," he said. "You can complain about that to your Abwehr superiors." He turned on his heels and disappeared behind a hangar.

"Bloody SS bastards," raged Conrad. "They always get the goods. I should've punched his face in. And yours, too, while I'm at it!"

Tristan stepped aside. "Knowing full well the punishment for insulting an SS superior is death, I suppose?" he said with a smirk.

Conrad finally kept quiet.

"Why not go back to torturing poor, defenceless girls then. I've got better things to do."

Ten minutes later, Tristan was comfortably seated in the back of a powerful Citroën as it drove through the dark. The Frenchman sat next to him was gnawing on a toothpick. Short with olive skin and black hair, he was a far cry from the Aryan ideal, despite his SS uniform.

"Jean Vinas," he said. "*Enchanté.* I hear you're Himmler's favourite."

"Tristan Marcas."

"So, you've just arrived from London? Lucky you. They say it's nice there. Fancy a drink? It's cognac, the good stuff," announced Vinas as he took a flask out of his pocket and held it out to Tristan. "What'd you do in London? Did you off a bunch of Brits? Or Gaullists?"

"I'm good, thank you. I visited the British Museum and brought back a . . . work of art."

"What are you then? A painter?"

"More like an expert in paintings and sculptures."

"But that's exactly what we need! With all this junk we take from the Jews, we need specialists to spot the good stuff. There's plenty of dough to be made. You seem like a clever bloke. We make a funny pair though: a criminal and an intellectual, both working for Hitler."

Tristan was intrigued. "What is it that do you do for the Führer?" he asked. "It's rare to see a Frenchman in a German uniform."

"That's just for show, when the commander needs me at the airfield. I'm a member of the French Gestapo. The Nazis hired me and a bunch of my friends to sort out our beautiful country. However we deem fit. Haven't you ever heard of Henri Lafont and Detective Bonny?"

"Never heard of the French Gestapo. But I've spent a lot of time abroad these past few years."

"You'll learn quickly. Before the war, Monsieur Lafont spent more time in jail than outside of it. Same as me. When the Nazis turned up, they asked him to put together a team to beat up resistance fighters and Jews. Someone had to get their hands dirty, but they didn't want to involve official services. See what I mean?"

"I think so."

"So Lafont recruited a couple of us, including a cop, Pierre Bonny. A real piece of work. Worse than many of us others, really. As for me, Lafont sprang me out of Cherche-Midi prison. I've been helping him out ever since."

Tristan couldn't believe his ears. Despite all the time he'd spent around the SS, they still found new ways to disgust him. Vinas pulled a small piece of green card from his jacket pocket. It bore his photograph alongside some SS insignia.

"You see this card? It's magic. A *Soldbuch*, delivered by the SD on Avenue Foch. With this, you're the king of the world. It opens every door. People practically piss themselves when I pull it out."

"Really?"

"Including the cops. Last year, we robbed the Crédit Commercial bank on Rue des Victoires. Three million! The first heist under the Occupation. You heard right! And you know what? When the coppers caught up to us, we simply waved our *Soldbücher* in their faces, and they ran off like scared little girls."

"Congratulations," offered Tristan.

The saloon car had left the woods and was now gliding through a series of deserted villages. The jet-black sky was turning lighter shades of grey as the dawn neared. Vinas swallowed another swig of cognac before putting away his flask.

"It'll be another hour or so. We've taken some nice digs from the Jews in the 16th arrondissement. We have about a dozen places, but that's where you'll be staying. I'll give you the keys and drop you at one of the flats. A driver will come pick you up tonight. You'll get to enjoy a real Parisian party!"

"But I'm exhausted. And not really in the mood for a party," objected Tristan.

"Don't be ridiculous! You can rest all day! You won't regret it, believe me. The party is at the Carlingue."

"The what?"

"Oh, right. I forgot you just turned up. That's what we call Lafont's place—the headquarters of the French Gestapo on Rue Lauriston! Once a month he hosts a party and invites everybody who is anybody. You're lucky to be on the guest list!" exclaimed Vinas, slapping Tristan on the thigh. "Isn't life grand?"

"Any better and I couldn't bear it," Tristan muttered wearily.

42

The venerable Hildebrand Rarity bookshop was located on Morpeth Terrace—a small street next to Westminster Cathedral. Laure had never set foot in this affluent neighbourhood before but got her bearings quickly. She'd become a proper Londoner in no time.

As she neared the shop, the monumental brick and stone façade caught her eye. If she'd had the time, Laure would have liked to light a candle for Malorley in the cathedral. Her boss was in critical condition at Chelsea Military Hospital. Laure knew she was lucky to have survived the cyanide and escaped her torturers with nothing but three maimed fingernails.

The bookstore itself looked as dusty and faded as the collections on display in the window. She read the note Malorley's secretary had given her one last time. *Hildebrand Rarity, 7 Morpeth Terrace.* She was at the right address. It was a strange place for an SOE summons.

A bell rang as Laure pushed through the door. The shop looked deserted.

"Hello? Is anyone here?" she asked loudly.

A noise came from behind a row of shelves, and a burly man in a grey shirt emerged. He crossed his arms over his big chest to let her know she could go no further. "We're closed for inventory," he grumbled. "Come back next month."

"That's a shame," she replied. "A friend told me you had an original edition of *Risico* by Kristatos."

"The illustrated edition?"

"Yes. The one by Yaroslav Horak."

She'd learned the phrases by heart but had no idea what she was talking about. Or if the work and author even existed. The bookseller stepped aside, as if under a spell.

"Follow the corridor next to the till. My colleagues in the back will tell you where to go next."

Laure did as she was told and walked into a small waiting room guarded by two men sitting on rusty chairs. Both were wearing machine guns across their chests. She flashed her SOE ID at them.

"I was told to be here at nine o'clock," she said.

"I have to search you," said one of them while the other checked a handwritten list for her name.

"Follow me," ordered the agent once he'd checked all her pockets. He opened a metal door and started down a brightly lit corridor.

"Where are we?" asked Laure.

"I'm not authorized to share that information," he replied dryly.

They arrived outside a large glass room. Inside the fishbowl, twenty men and women in uniform hurried to and fro. Bulletin boards were covered in maps and telephones sat on most of the tables. It looked like military headquarters. Laure followed the guard along one side of the room when she realized it was beginning to fill with white smoke. Huge columns snaked down from the ceiling as a strident alarm rang out. Laure stopped. The people inside calmly made their way to the cupboards to put on their masks, then formed a single-file queue and left the room in a surprisingly organized fashion. In less than a minute, the group had disappeared at the far end of the corridor.

"What's going on?" she asked.

"A gas attack exercise. This room is used as a training centre for the teams working at headquarters," explained the guard as he showed her into a tiny windowless room sparsely furnished with a metal table and two chairs placed across from one another. A man in his forties was sitting on one of the chairs studying a file on his lap. His hat obscured the right side of his face.

"Hello, Laure," he said without looking up. "Please sit down."

She'd never seen this man at the SOE. But then there were always so many people around that that didn't mean much.

"Where are we?" she asked again once she was seated.

"At Orchid Centre," he replied, still reading the file. "The enemy knows the location of our headquarters on Baker Street, and we prefer optimal discretion."

"And who are you?"

"No one. You can call me Major," he replied, finally looking up. His eyes looked faded and were set deep into their orbits. There was something sad about them. The man was sitting with his left side towards Laure. From the little she could see, it looked like the right side of his face had collapsed. Now she understood why he was wearing a hat inside.

"I've read your file carefully," he said. "We have something in common."

"What's that?" asked Laure.

The man lifted his hat to reveal the right side of his face, tapping a finger on his ravaged cheek. "We both took a bite out of the poison apple."

"I don't understand."

"The cyanide capsule. I used mine when I was arrested by the Gestapo in Reims. The Germans made me throw it up, but the poison had plenty of time to damage the mucous membranes and muscles of my cheek. But I shouldn't complain—I'm still alive. French resistance fighters helped me escape."

Laure didn't know what to say. She couldn't help but stare at the melted half of his face.

"Fate has been kinder to you," he continued, placing the file on the table. "You escaped your kidnappers and the poison left you relatively unscathed. Luck plays a major role in any spy's life. And I like to have lucky agents around."

"I'm sorry, but I don't understand why I'm here," objected Laure. "I work for Department S, run by Commander Malorley."

The man shook his head. "After the fiasco at the British Museum, Department S was mothballed. Its mission is over, and your superior is in no condition to return to work. You've been reassigned to Section F of the SOE, which oversees operations in your country. I'm here to evaluate you. We desperately need more female field agents."

"Can I see Commander Malorley?" asked Laure.

"I'm afraid that's impossible."

"And my colleague, Aleister Crowley?"

"Ah, the mage," he said with a smirk. "We've sent him to rest in the countryside at a specialized institution. Psychiatrists there will know best how to handle him. I do wonder why Malorley recruited him. He clearly has a personality disorder. Maybe a few sessions of electroshock therapy will restore his reason."

"That man saved my life! Have some compassion!"

"Compassion is a luxury we can't afford in our profession."

"So I've seen," she replied angrily, brandishing her bandaged hand. "Speaking of which, I don't believe you ever even asked me how I feel about your offer. Did it occur to you that my 'manicure' session might have cured me of any desire to play spies?"

The man glanced impassively at her hand. "The medical report indicates you will regain full function of your fingers in a few months."

"I'm talking about my head. I thought I was going to die in that dungeon! I don't want to risk having to go through that again."

"So saving your country no longer interests you? That was the main reason you signed up in the first place. You were sent to Venice and—"

"It's all been such a joke!" she exclaimed, cutting him off. "I wasted my time following ridiculous leads!"

The man shook his head and stood up, the file beneath his arm. "Take some time to think about it," he said. "In the meantime, you'll be transferred to the administrative department at Baker Street. One of the employees is pregnant. You'll make a fine replacement."

Laure laughed, waving her hand again once more. "Wow, a

job as a secretary. What a promotion. I'll be a real whiz on the typewriter."

"You won't have to type anything at all. It's the logistics and operations department for Europe. You'll help plan missions. And maybe you'll change your mind after a while."

"I seriously doubt it."

The man shrugged. "Then we'll win the war without your help."

43

The Carlingue, Paris

A company of waiters in livery danced their way through the crowd of prestigious guests spread through the gilded lounge. There were Frenchmen in dinner jackets, Germans in dress uniforms, and women in evening gowns. As usual, Mr. Lafont had gathered all of collaborationist Paris. It was a savvy blend of ambitious civil servants, Germanophile journalists, businessmen who profited from the black market, high-ranking Wehrmacht and SS officers, budding actresses, high-end call girls and demi-mondaines. A perfectly orchestrated "champagne and sausages" party, as less enthusiastic Parisians called them.

Sitting atop a stage decorated with generous bouquets of scarlet roses and white lilies, a chamber orchestra played the popular melodies regularly broadcast on the German-run Radio Paris.

Tristan grabbed a champagne coupe in passing. He was observing his surroundings with a strange combination of fascination and revulsion. Never would he have imagined such luxurious parties could be happening while the rest of France was stuck with rationing.

Two women resplendent in lamé dresses sauntered past him. The brunette gazed alluringly at Tristan, her lips curled into a mischievous smile. She whispered in her friend's ear, then returned to the dancefloor.

Tristan directed his attention to the sumptuous buffet, which included seafood platters with oysters on the half shell and piles of thick slices of roast beef and game. Ravenous, he hurried over.

As soon as Vinas had dropped him off at a luxurious flat on Avenue Mozart, he'd fallen into bed immediately and slept until the early evening. He'd woken up with just enough time to shower and ponder his situation. Since no one was watching the building, he assumed he was free to come and go as he pleased. A little after seven o'clock, a driver had rung the bell to deliver a dinner jacket in his size and take him to the party at the Carlingue.

Tristan had decided to accept the invitation. The idea of setting foot in the French Gestapo headquarters disgusted him, but it could be a little experiment the SS had set up to test his loyalty. In any case, he was stuck there until he heard from his masters in Berlin. At the moment, they no longer required his services— the quest was over. They could have him assassinated at any moment.

Erika's face popped into his exhausted mind. Through Gehlen, she probably already knew where he was, but hadn't contacted him yet. Now that he was back with the SS, she had once again turned into the ultimate threat. She could turn him in at any time, out of self-interest or jealousy. But something told him she still loved him.

His mind was racing again, on the verge of paranoia.

For a moment, he thought about contacting the Oratoire Network to get a message to London. But to say what? That the relic had been sent to Berlin? That he had failed them once and for all?

Tristan felt about as useful as a sewing machine at the butcher's.

The orchestra began a slow but upbeat musette number that clashed with the ostentatious décor and crystal chandeliers. But Tristan was too busy polishing off a delicious piece of veal roast to be concerned with the music.

"So, how is Himmler's pet? Don't spend the whole evening alone, my friend!"

Tristan turned around to see Jean Vinas standing next to a young blonde woman who was at least a head taller than him.

"Sweetheart, let me introduce my friend Tristan. He doesn't look like much, but he's a pro when it comes to paintings and statues."

"He's cute," purred the girl. "I could introduce him to some of my single friends—"

"And he knows people in Berlin. He works directly for the SS boss, Himmler."

"Let's not exaggerate," objected Tristan.

Suddenly, the music stopped. A portly man had climbed onto the stage and glued his sweaty face to the silver microphone. All eyes turned towards him.

"That's Mr. Lafont," whispered Vinas. "The big boss! Look at all these losers. They're eating it up from the palm of his hand, when just two years ago, he was banging his bowl against the bars of his cell in the Cherche-Midi prison."

The head of the French Gestapo raised his arms and smiled broadly. "My friends, your attention please. I'd like to begin by thanking the Reich's ambassador, His Excellency Otto Abetz, who has graced us with the honour of his presence tonight."

A blond man with a rectangular face bowed to thunderous applause.

"I also wanted to share my joy," continued Lafont, "at seeing France follow in Germany's footsteps. As you know, in June, Maréchal Pétain passed a magnificent law that made it mandatory for all Jews to wear their foul symbol—the yellow star—on their clothing. At long last! If any of you would like to wear one on your dinner jacket, I can get you a discount. I own shares in the company that makes them. We'll hand out samples as you leave tonight!"

He stopped for a few seconds to size up the audience, then chuckled, pleased with himself. "No, I'm only joking," he continued.

Laughter burst out in every corner of the room—lavish praise for their host's sense of humour.

"I also wanted to celebrate a date we will cherish for years to come," he explained. "July 16th. The day of the Vel d'Hiv Roundup. Let us thank the head of the police who is here with us tonight, Mr. René Bousquet! Some of you may not know that he is the one who so flawlessly executed the operation two weeks ago."

All eyes turned to a thin, dark-haired man in a perfectly tailored uniform, who raised his coupe to the crowd.

"We often tout the merits of German organization, and we're right to do so," continued Lafont, "but this time we can be proud of our own national expertise. Mr. Bousquet informed me that more than 13,000 Jewish men, women and children were rounded up in just two days. At that rate, the Yid threat to France will be taken care of by the end of the year. And all thanks to five hundred French policemen and gendarmes. Let us applaud their courage and abnegation!"

"Where did you send the Jews?" asked an old man with a bushy moustache. "Not back to Jerusalem, I gather?"

"They've all been sent by train to concentration camps in Poland, where they'll discover the virtues of hard work and fresh air. You'll take good care of them, won't you, Colonel Knochen?"

An SS colonel with an angelic face—the head of German police services in Paris—smiled warmly. "I promise we will. They've already been reunited with their like from Holland and Belgium. And, contrary to what some of you may believe, we National Socialists can also be delicate and poetic. We've called this European roundup Operation Spring Breeze. Let's hope it keeps blowing, bowling over all of the Great Reich's enemies."

Sustained applause saluted the colonel's tirade. Tristan felt the hairs on the back of his neck stand on end. In Berlin and Wewelsburg, he'd eavesdropped on many conversations about the camps in the east. It was no mystery what awaited Jewish people there.

Tristan was disgusted to be there listening to these abominations. It was time for him to leave this gathering of demons in human clothing. Sharing the air with them was torture.

As Henri Lafont rejoined the crowd, the orchestra began a languorous interpretation of "Lili Marlene", sending couples to the dancefloor.

Tristan made his way through the throng of guests towards the exit. On his way, he walked past the head of police responsible for the Vel' d'Hiv Roundup. He was engaged in an animated conversation with a sturdy man whose austere features were accompanied by an unattractive moustache.

"My dear Darnand, I must insist. The keystone to the Nazi cathedral is the SS. Without Himmler and his troops, the monument would collapse, and Hitler would fall from his throne. The Reichsführer oversees all of the police and intelligence services and part of the army with his Waffen divisions. The SS is a state within the state and the spearhead for the regime's racial policies. Himmler is more than a leader—he's a mystic and a technocrat. A unique man. His industrial management of the Jewish problem is clear proof of that. It all ties back to him: the camps, deportations, racial laws in occupied countries, dispossessions . . ."

"You're forgetting the Führer's charisma," objected Darnand. "He leads the people."

"Yes, but if Himmler didn't enforce order, it would be chaos. I work with the SS nearly every day, and I can tell you they consider themselves the new German elite."

"Maybe, but they're not invincible. You saw what happened after Heydrich's assassination in Prague. The Germans were very nearly overwhelmed. Their efficiency has limits. If anyone ever got to Himmler, I'm not sure the SS would survive. The Wehrmacht generals would make quick work of them."

"It's true that his death could put the breaks on Operation Spring Breeze," agreed Bousquet. "So, let's drink to his health. I, for one, would like to rid France of the Jewish hordes once and for all!"

Tristan had heard enough. The expression "industrial management of the Jewish problem" had made his stomach turn. Anti-semitism ravaged the mind of everyone it infected. And Tristan had spent enough time with the Reichsführer to measure the scope of his power.

The keystone to the Nazi cathedral—Bousquet's choice of words couldn't have been more fitting. The expression turned round and round in his head.

He bumped into Vinas and his companion on his way to the exit.

"Did you enjoy the boss's speech?" he asked.

"About as much as a deportee enjoys the fine air in Poland. There are rumours of mass murders of Jews in the eastern camps," replied Tristan.

Vinas shrugged. "It's true they've taken things a bit too far, especially with the women and children, but hey, you can't go soft in this profession! Come on, egghead, enjoy the party. Look, it seems you've caught the eye of Princess Euphrosyne."

On the other side of the buffet, the attractive brunette in the lamé dress stared longingly at Tristan.

"Is she a real aristocrat or is that just a nickname?"

"Some say she's a real blue-blood, others assert she's just like you and me. We hired a posh group of marquesses, princesses and baronesses with limited cashflow. They open the doors to high society for us and pull up their skirts in service to the Great Reich. We call them the Gestapo Countesses. Come, I'll introduce you."

"No thanks. I'm going back to the flat. I want to be well rested in case Himmler calls me back to Germany tomorrow," replied Tristan.

"Your friend's no fun at all," complained the blonde as she pulled Vinas by the sleeve. "Let's dance."

Tristan suddenly thought he could hear muffled groans coming from behind the fireplace. "That's strange," he said. "It sounds like there are noises coming from the wall."

Vinas sighed and pushed the blonde towards the dancefloor. "Mimi, go ask the lobster from the buffet to dance. I have to take care of something."

He hurried over to Henri Lafont and whispered in his ear. The head of the Gestapo's features expressed annoyance and he gestured to the conductor. The slow rendition of "Lili Marlene" was replaced with a fortissimo Viennese waltz.

The Gestapo lackey made his way back to Tristan and led him out of the lounge. "Before you go though," he explained excitedly, "Let me give you the backstage tour. First, I'll open the doors to heaven for you—and then, the doors to hell."

44

Conrad strode up the street, staring at the ground and periodically walking in circles as if looking for a lost piece of paper or a key. After a while, he stopped, bent down to the pavement and picked something up. Only his hand was empty. The night provided some cover, but he needed to rule out being followed. Conrad leaned back against a house wall, lit a cigarette and inspected every window within sight. Malorley's men could be hidden anywhere and descend upon him like a flock of vultures. When he was confident he was alone, he rang the bell of number 62, whose copper sign indicated a doctor's surgery. An older, balding man opened the door with a suspicious look on his face, but let the German spy in right away.

"Hello, Conrad. Your wife is resting upstairs. I'm glad you're here. She's been desperate to see you," explained the doctor.

The two men climbed the rickety stairs to the second floor. This wasn't Conrad's first time in the building. The doctor, who had been a Nazi supporter for a long time, was a member of the Abwehr network, and his surgery had housed many agents over the years. But this time, the doctor had gotten his hands dirty trying to save Susan.

"How is she?" asked Conrad.

"Not great, I'm afraid. I've given her a lot of morphine because she's in so much pain. And for good reason—she has several very serious wounds. I managed to extract three bullets, but one is too close to her heart. She needs to be operated on properly. But," he said, stopping to place his hand on the young man's shoulder, "you know the rules in such cases."

"No need to remind me. Our agents cannot be treated by the enemy. I've applied that rule too many times to count. Aren't there any other options? Couldn't I take her back to France on the same plane that brought me here?"

The doctor shook his head. "She wouldn't survive the journey. I'm sorry. I know how much you love her."

"I don't think you do, doc . . ."

Conrad walked into the attic bedroom. The heady smell of disinfectant filled the dark room. At the foot of the bed, there was a bucket full of used compresses and soaked bandages. His heart raced as he sat down next to his wife.

Susan seemed to have shrunk. Her face was almost white, and her eyes half closed. Conrad took her ice-cold hand.

For the first time in years, the Abwehr agent almost fell to pieces. He had never regretted killing enemies of the Reich, but couldn't bear the idea of death taking his wife. He wanted to scream out in rage. He felt powerless and angry. The evil relic had trampled their life and plans.

Susan lightly squeezed his hand. "Conrad, my love, is that you?"

"I'll leave you two alone," muttered the doctor from the doorway. "Call me if you need anything."

Conrad ran his hand over Susan's feverish forehead. "I won't leave you again. Everything will be okay. Thanks to you, we've succeeded in our mission."

Susan suddenly grew agitated, as though she'd just received some bad news. She lifted her head and opened her eyes wide, tightening her grip on her husband. "No . . . They beat us to it."

"Who?"

She could barely breathe. It took all the strength she could muster to speak. "Tristan fooled us. The Englishman . . . in the street. They knew each other."

Conrad couldn't believe his ears. They'd been tricked and now his wife was going to die.

"Warn Berlin. Quickly. He's a traitor."

45

Tristan and Vinas made their way down a corridor to a partially open bedroom door.

"The blue room," said the collaborator. "Welcome to heaven. Take a good look, my friend!"

Tristan stuck his head inside and was shocked to see a group of naked men and women writhing harmoniously on the four-poster bed. A large-breasted woman wearing an SS cap sprayed champagne over the two men beneath her on the Persian rug. She caught Tristan's eye, beckoning him to join in. Tristan hastily retreated to find Vinas's lips curled into a lewd smile.

"If you want, you can bring the countess back here with you to join the fray. She loves it."

"No, thank you," replied Tristan. "But now I understand where the screams were coming from."

Vinas shook his head. "Afraid not. Not the same type of scream. Follow me."

They made their way down the stairs to the basement and found themselves in front of a massive metal door. It stood wide open.

"Mammoth forgot to close it again," complained Vinas. "You'd think he'd remember to shut the door to hell . . ."

A strident scream rang out. The collaborator led Tristan into an oblong basement whose grey walls were covered in damp. A bathtub sat alone in the middle of the room. At the far end, three men stood around a prisoner tied to what looked like an easel. Pieces of flesh pulled away from his bloody face. One of the torturers was swinging a large spatula covered in razor blades in front of the victim. Sobs attracted Tristan's attention to the other side of the room, where two women lay on the floor.

"Abel," shouted Vinas, "how many times do we have to tell you to shut the damn door? The boss is having a party upstairs!"

The man with the spatula—a giant with rough features—turned around. "Sorry. The Yid won't give up the names of his gallery owner friends. It looks like we'll have to tend to Mummy and their lovely daughter."

"I swear I don't know anything. Please," begged the tortured man.

Tristan glanced anxiously at the two women. "You're not going to torture *them* are you?"

Vinas shrugged. "That depends. Most of the time, the men crack before we have to really get our hands dirty, but not always."

"But what if he's telling the truth and really doesn't know anything?"

"Then they're out of luck . . . I never mess with women, but Abel the Mammoth enjoys his work. It's a technique perfected by our German friends at the Gestapo. Nothing works better to get resistance fighters and Jews to talk. Between us, they say your pal Himmler is the one who came up with it."

"He's not my pal," growled Tristan, who was beginning to feel that all the horrors he was seeing were tied to the Reichsführer.

The bloodied Jew mumbled and cried, begging for mercy.

"What will happen to them?" asked Tristan, his heart in his mouth.

"If the Yid cooperates, we'll turn him to use as an informant and his wife and daughter can go home. We can use them as leverage as long as they're alive. If he refuses, we'll rape them both in front of him and dump all their bodies in the Seine."

Tristan refused to look away. He stared at the victim and the terrified women.

A flame sparked in his mind, setting his anger ablaze. All of a sudden, his doubts and despair disappeared. There was nothing he could do to save these poor people, but he knew how to put a stop to the source of this evil. It was so obvious. He should have opened his eyes long ago. All he had to do was wait for destiny to put him back into play.

"I've seen enough," he said flatly. "Very educational."

He turned and left the cellar as if on autopilot, followed by Vinas. He walked back past the blue room where the orgy was taking place and couldn't help but notice that heaven was located just above hell. Clenching his fists, he picked up the pace and made for the exit. As he passed the entrance to the lounge area, an SS captain cut him off.

"You have an urgent call from Berlin, Monsieur Marcas. From the Reichsführer's office. You can take it in Mr. Lafont's secretary's office. I'll escort you."

Tristan felt a curious tingling in his face and hands. Fate was at it yet again.

"Blimey, a call from Himmler himself!" marvelled Vinas. "Tell him about me, will you? No better Aryan out there!"

"Of course," lied Tristan. He followed the SS man to the office and closed the door behind him.

He recognized the female voice immediately.

"Congratulations on finding the relic," exclaimed Erika von Essling. "It's just arrived at the Ahnenerbe. In fact, I'm looking at it right now. This swastika seems to emit its own unique energy. It's strange. I nearly blacked out when I first held it. This is a great day for the Reich."

"I'm happy for you," replied Tristan. "But I'm not in a great mood tonight. I've just left a basement where they were torturing an innocent man in front of his wife and daughter."

"I'm sorry to hear that," Erika replied coldly. "I also wanted to share some good news."

"I'm dying to hear it."

"A ceremony will be held to celebrate the arrival of the fourth relic," explained the archaeologist. "I've asked the Reichsführer to put you on the guest list. It's the least we can do since you're the reason we have the swastika. He'll also award you the 1st Class

Iron Cross. It'll make a nice addition to the 2nd Class award you already have."

The line went quiet.

The Frenchman felt his heart leap up into his throat. He would be near the relic again. But that wasn't even the most important part. The party, with its drunken attendees, debauchery, and torture had finally shown him the light.

"I'd love to come. I'm eager to see you again," he finally replied. "Where are you?"

"On a Danish island in the Baltic. Bornholm. The Ahnenerbe has opened a satellite there. I'll have a plane sent for you. I also just wanted to say . . . I miss you."

"I miss you, too, Erika. I'm—"

She'd hung up before he could finish. Tristan's mind was spinning as he left the office. The game was back on, but this time he knew how it would end. And he would be calling the shots.

In the corridor, on the way back to the salon, he ran into Vinas, who was in deep conversation with Henri Lafont. The collaborator introduced Lafont, who held out his hand to Tristan. He took it as though it were a venomous snake.

"So, I hear you were on with Himmler himself!" exclaimed Lafont.

Tristan thought of evading the question but quickly changed his mind. "Indeed. He's going to award me the 1st Class Iron Cross in a few days' time."

Lafont whistled, clearly impressed. "You are very influential, Monsieur Marcas. I'd fancy an Iron Cross myself. Even a 2nd Class would do."

Tristan smiled. "I might be able to help you out," he offered.

"Anything you want, just tell me. Women, money . . . Even my favourite mistress!"

"No, nothing like that. Just let the people you're holding in the basement go. And promise to forget about them."

Lafont frowned and turned towards Vinas. "What did we bring them in for?"

"Not much. They're Jews. Mammoth is convinced the man

knows some gallery owners who are hiding paintings, but he doesn't have much to go on."

Lafont glanced suspiciously at Tristan. "Why do you want them freed? Don't tell me it's out of the goodness of your heart. I don't see how Himmler's protégé could have a soft spot for Yids."

"I knew him before the war," lied Tristan. "He got me out of a tight spot with the police. Kept me out of prison."

Lafont's face lit up. "Ah, the ties that bind! That I understand! Are you sure you can get your boss to give me the Iron Cross?"

"It would be an insult to your intelligence to promise such a thing, but I can make sure your request lands on the top of the pile," affirmed Tristan.

"Sold!" exclaimed Lafont. "Vinas, let them go right away. And present my apologies. Give them a little something to help them forget about all this," he ordered. "Well, I'm off to join my lady friends in the blue room."

The head of the French Gestapo was so pleased with the bargain he'd struck that he nearly skipped down the corridor.

"Do you want to be driven back to the flat?" Vinas enquired.

"No, a little fresh air will do me good."

"See you tomorrow then?"

"We'll see. Good night."

Tristan waved to Vinas and left the building. Only one thing was on his mind now: successfully conducting his new priority mission. But to do that, he needed to get word to London. He picked up the pace and prayed that the Oratoire Network was still operational.

A cool wind swept over his face. His thoughts had never been sharper and clearer. In fact, it didn't even matter if London couldn't put together an operation in time. He knew what counted now—and it wasn't the relic. Fate had grabbed him by the collar of his turncoat for one single reason.

He had to decapitate the monster that was the SS, which was spreading its reign of terror throughout Europe. He should have done it long ago. The two collaborators' conversation he'd overheard earlier had been a sign.

He had to take out Himmler.

In Venice, he'd had the chance to kill Hitler. But at the last minute, obsessed by the quest, he'd chosen to take the relic instead.

That had been a mistake. A terrible mistake.

And he wouldn't make it again.

Himmler would pay for Hitler. He would pay for all their crimes.

The countdown was on. Seven days until Bornholm. He would do it just as the Reichsführer was awarding him his medal. He would pull out his Luger and shoot him point blank, emptying his clip into his face.

It would be his final blow.

A blow that just might change the outcome of the war. Certainly more than any relic ever could.

46

The Kuntsevo Dacha, suburbs of Moscow

It was pitch-black outside, but the forest surrounding the imposing dacha was lit up like a Christmas tree thanks to the searchlights that lit the security perimeter. Not even a squirrel could have snuck into Stalin's luxurious country retreat. The dictator had chosen the venue for the state dinner with Churchill, who had arrived three days earlier with his diplomatic suite and the American ambassador.

Evgueni used the tip of his boot to crush a small toad whose croaking had been annoying him for nearly fifteen minutes. In addition to the usual three hundred NKVD guards, he had ordered two armoured units and three infantry units to take up positions in concentric circles around the dacha, covering the surrounding area ten kilometers out. That added up to nearly a thousand men. There were also several strategically placed anti-aircraft guns among them.

It was highly unlikely the Germans would choose this moment for an attack, but Evgueni—having been entrusted with protecting the place—would take no risks with his life and career. Tensions were running high enough as it was.

He knew the future would be decided tonight between the leader of the USSR and Churchill. The delegations had been trying to reach an agreement for days, but Britain's refusal to open a second front in France had enraged Stalin. Tonight was the last night before the British returned home, and both parties were aware of the terrible consequences a failed alliance would bring. Evgueni had insisted that Stalin add the relic to his list of material demands.

Had he been a believer, he would have prayed to God for a happy ending. Instead, he invoked Lenin.

Satisfied with his inspection of the area north of the dacha, Evgueni strode through the exuberant gardens and greenhouse, which led to the main entrance. Stalin fancied himself green-fingered, and the glasshouse was one of his favourite places. He spent hours tending to his plants, and the three full-time gardeners spared no effort to please him. Their zeal was the product of their high salaries—three times those of the guards—and of their fear of being shipped off to Siberia should aphids overrun the roses or fungus attack the watermelons, which were their leader's new passion. Stalin had planted the two full rows of melons himself and loved serving them at official dinners.

As he reached the main door, Evgueni nodded to the guards on duty and stepped inside, glancing at the clock on the wall. Ten past eleven. Knowing Stalin as he did, Evgueni was certain the main course had yet to be served, but the alcohol had been flowing freely for hours. Getting his adversaries drunk was one of the dictator's most efficient strategies. He preferred to dine first and negotiate after, relying on his ability to hold his liquor—unlike most of his guests.

But this time, Stalin had met his match. The British Prime Minister had survived three such meals accompanied by copious amounts of alcohol without so much as a hiccup.

Evgueni discreetly cracked open the door to the dining room. The twelve members of the British and Russian delegations stood around the long state table covered in an immaculate white tablecloth and decorated with bouquets of scarlet roses, brandishing their chiselled glasses towards Churchill and Stalin at the head of the table.

"I salute the courage of the Russian people and the determination of their leader, Marshal Stalin!" shouted the Englishman. "May our two countries find a way to trust one another and work together to end this war!" Churchill swallowed his glass of Caucasus wine in a single gulp, all the while keeping an eye on his Russian host. The Red Tsar drank in turn.

"A new day is dawning for humanity," affirmed Stalin as he placed his glass down on the table. "I hope that very soon, we will be toasting in Berlin, in the Chancellery dining room. Over Hitler's corpse if possible!"

Laughter filled the room. This was the eighth toast since the beginning of the dinner, and the roasted suckling pigs were only now reaching their plates. The American ambassador Averell Harriman, handpicked by Roosevelt, was conversing with Foreign Affairs Minister Molotov—the very same man who had signed the Pact of Non-Aggression with the Germans three years earlier.

The Russian and German leaders sat down, followed by the rest of the guests, and tucked eagerly into their plates amid a friendly din. Evgueni closed the door. He smiled, thinking to himself that the real main dish—the negotiations—would be served later, in the adjoining room.

An hour later, the two heads of state and their interpreters were alone in a room with purposefully understated décor. Evgueni had positioned himself on the other side of the door, where he could hear every word of their conversation.

The light that fell from the ceiling exaggerated both men's features. Stalin in particular looked completely different. His jovial nature had disappeared, leaving behind an icy mask. He didn't look like he'd had a single drop of alcohol.

"Prime Minister, you're leaving tomorrow, and we have yet to reach an agreement. I admit I'm disappointed. My cabinet has provided a list of my demands."

Churchill nearly choked on his own saliva. "You cannot ask for all that. Not even the Americans provided that much for Britain! You'll need to lower your expectations. They're beyond the realm of possibility."

Stalin's features darkened further. "As we sit here talking, my people are being butchered by the Nazis. Your refusal to open a second front in France has created a river of blood—Russian blood on your hands."

Churchill jumped to his feet. "A man responsible for the deaths of millions before the war, with your bloody purges and organized famines, is in a poor position to be giving ethics lessons. You even made a pact with Hitler, which condemned Poland and led to the defeat in France! So, don't you get on your high horse with me."

The interpreters exchanged terrified glances. A heavy silence filled the room. Stalin was livid with rage.

Churchill sat back down, picked up a bottle of whisky, and served his counterpart a generous glass. "Now that we've got that off our chests, let's drink. I'm not here to ask for your hand in marriage. We're just joining forces for a little while to reach Berlin and send Hitler back to hell," he said, raising his glass. "Think about it! We'll land in North Africa and chase the Afrika Korps back up to Italy. That clown Mussolini won't be able to stop us, so Hitler will have to pull divisions from the Russian front to save him. But if you won't get on board, let's finish this bottle and you can continue the war alone!"

Stalin drank slowly, savouring the amber liquid. "You know that Stalin means steel in Russian," he began, "but I think you are made of the same stuff. I am man enough to recognize my equal."

"Thank you for the compliment," replied Churchill, "but I've always been partial to my real name. Unlike you, Ioseb Jughashvili."

It was nearly two o'clock in the morning by the time they'd come to an agreement. Churchill, who wanted nothing more than to climb into bed, was at the door when Stalin spoke again. "I have one final request," he said.

"Another one! Will it never end? If you want the King of England to sing the 'Internationale' on the balcony of Buckingham Palace, I'm afraid you're out of luck!" exclaimed Churchill.

"My request has more to do with a tsar than a king. My intelligence services tell me a precious object that once belonged to Nicholas II is now located in your country. In the name of Russian heritage, I would like it back."

Churchill frowned. This was the one demand he had not expected. "Oh really," he lied. "I haven't heard anything . . ."

"Of course you have, Winston. It's a small relic, shaped like a swastika. Are you certain that doesn't ring any bells? It belonged to the Romanovs and was sent to England during the Revolution. A swastika forged before the dawn of time. The subject of a strange legend. Are you quite sure you don't know what I'm talking about?"

"Believe me, Joseph, I don't have time for legends at the moment."

The Red Tsar laughed. "You lied better earlier, but no matter. I'm well informed. I know that your SOE agents got their hands on it. So, in the interest of our newfound alliance, I must insist you return it to us."

Churchill kept quiet. This relic had once again found its way into his life—and how? Through Stalin, no less! The Russian seemed to know all about its powers. How could a communist—the worst kind of materialist—believe in such nonsense? "I'll reach out to my intelligence services and make your request a priority when I get back to London," offered the Prime Minister.

"Doublespeak won't serve you here, Winston. I want the relic. Now."

Churchill thought he could almost see Roosevelt's angry face behind Stalin, urging him to give the Russian what he must. The problem was that he had nothing left to give. "All right, Joseph. I'll be honest with you. Your information is accurate but incomplete. The swastika was hidden at the British Museum, but Abwehr agents stole it and fled to Germany."

"I'm not sure I believe you. What about the one you found in the south of France? Where is that now?"

"I really don't know. I swear it."

Stalin could tell that the Englishman was in an awkward position and that he was lying outright. Evgueni had briefed him on Hitler's and Churchill's bids for the objects. The Russian smoothed his moustache as Churchill wiped his forehead. The NKVD colonel might be right after all—the relics had to be powerful to put the bulldog in such a state.

He would give Evgueni carte blanche.

Abwehr Communications Hub, Berlin, Germany

The warrant officer in charge of communications from agents in England stormed into his superior's office.

"Woah, Hermann, have you just seen Hindenburg's ghost?" joked the officer in charge.

"You have to read this message. It's urgent. From Conrad, one of our agents in London."

"Urgent . . . Did Churchill catch a venereal disease in Moscow? Let's see . . ." said the officer as he put on his glasses. He paled when he saw Himmler's name and immediately picked up the phone.

"Get me Admiral Canaris, please. It's urgent. Code Orange."

A few seconds later, a hoarse voice clearly used to giving orders sounded on the line. "What do you want, Colonel?"

"One of our agents in London has just informed us that a Frenchman working for the SS is a double agent. His name is Tristan Marcas and he was taken to Paris from England last Thursday to deliver an archaeological object stolen in England to the Reichsführer."

"An archaeological object? For a chicken farmer?" Admiral Canaris asked dubiously. "Send the information to the RSHA counter-intelligence service. And next time, if you want to keep your rank, don't bother me with such nonsense."

The admiral hung up.

"So?" asked the warrant officer.

"I have to call the bloody SS. And I'm not looking forward to it."

47

The S 22 speedboat was quickly approaching its destination. The silver sea-spray glittered in the bright sunlight. Tristan held tight to the railing on the rear deck, taking deep breaths of the salty air in a bid to cleanse himself of the filth he'd inhaled in Paris.

Bornholm was growing by the second, floating at the border between the cobalt sky and the dark Baltic Sea. Tristan's stomach roiled as he lit his first cigarette. The crossing from the German port of Kolberg had been short: less than two hours. He'd never been on such a fast boat before. The captain seemed determined to beat his own personal best—much like the Luftwaffe pilot who had flown him from Le Bourget to the Kolberg airfield in northern Germany.

Speed was one of the rare qualities Tristan recognized in the Germans. Just like the rest of Europe, they had conquered France at the speed of light. Tristan might have spent considerable time with the Nazis, but he still wasn't sure if their velocity could be put down to the militarization of German society, or if Hitler had somehow kindled his people's innate gift for it.

He picked up a pair of binoculars and aimed them at the coastline. Much to his surprise, Bornholm looked more like a Mediterranean island than the wild Viking sanctuary he had imagined. Exuberant vegetation crowned a line of hills in various shades of green dotted with a smattering of red roofs.

Bornholm. He'd never heard of the Scandinavian island until just a few days ago, but fate had spoken. This was where his quest—begun years ago and thousands of kilometers away with the pillaging of a Catalonian monastery—would end. His memories surfaced like images in a kaleidoscope. The bloody confrontation in a Spanish bullfighting ring, the excavations at the Cathar castle . . . and meeting Erika, who still held a piece of his heart. They had formed an unlikely alliance in the race for the swastikas: she chased them for the Third Reich, while he was working for the Allies.

And now the final act would take place on this northern isle. The trail had come to an end.

As had his existence, most likely.

A whistle interrupted his thoughts. The crew busied themselves on the foredeck as Rønne harbour appeared in front of them.

Tristan went below deck to retrieve his bag. He pulled out an SS cap bearing the skull symbol and slipped his Luger into his belt. A broken mirror hanging next to Himmler's official portrait seemed to portend the future of the SS: it would soon be shattered.

Once he'd climbed back up with his bag, he noticed two sailors who were obviously avoiding him. Just like the captain, who had barely spoken to him during the crossing. Himmler's men didn't seem to be very popular with the Kriegsmarine.

The S 22 slipped past a destroyer anchored about five hundred meters from the entrance to the harbour, then came up alongside a concrete jetty lined with battered tyres. The whistle sounded again from the bridge, and the crew jumped over the starboard side to attach the lines to the metal cleats on the pier, then lowered the gangway. The captain looked on coldly as Tristan staggered off the boat.

Warm air, heavy with the acrid smell of fuel oil, filled his nostrils. Tristan made his way along the pier towards the inner harbour, where three more towering warships were docked. He couldn't help but wonder what sort of strategic advantage had attracted so many military resources to this tiny island. On the other side of the harbour, a dozen fishing boats were better suited to the postcard-ready image of the town. Red and yellow fishermen's huts and charming houses whose balconies overflowed with flowers completed the picture.

Tristan crossed paths with a group of SS soldiers gathered near the water. In fact, every corner of Europe, from north to south, seemed to be full of soldiers—as though the Germans had been procreating, at record speed ever since their 1918 defeat, to create a generation of soldiers at the ready for the Führer.

Upon reaching the control post, Tristan caught sight of a blonde woman standing next to a convertible ATV. His heart skipped a beat. Erika had kept her promise. She'd come to collect him. The soldiers looked on as he ducked under the barrier. He tried to hug her, but she stiffened and barked "*Heil Hitler*", raising her arm in salute. It took him a few minutes to remember he was wearing an SS uniform. And Himmler's men were not the type to make public displays of affection. He reluctantly returned her salute. They had no sooner climbed into the VW 82 Kübelwagen than Erika sped off. She still hadn't said another word. She weaved along the coastal road, honking and shifting gears in silence. Tristan held tight to the door handle.

"I expected a . . . warmer welcome," he said finally.

"We'll have to wait until we're alone. I saw at least two men from the Gestapo at the control post. Did you have a good trip?"

"It was a little rough. I would make a terrible sailor. Where are we going?"

"To the Ahnenerbe excavation site in the northern part of the island. That's where the ceremony for the relic will take place."

"Why here? What makes this island so special in Himmler's eyes?"

"You'll find out when we get there."

The road moved inland. Tristan watched as Erika drove on, her hair blowing in the wind. There was something different about her. She seemed to be avoiding meeting his eyes. And she was distant. Cold, even. Alarm bells went off in Tristan's head. What if the whole Iron Cross business had been a trap? But then, why would they bother to bring him to this remote island to get rid of him?

The car slowed as it made its way through the small village of Nyker, which was rather nondescript except for its whitewashed fortified church, which featured unusually rounded architecture. Tristan had never seen anything like it. "Strange design for a church," he said, intrigued.

"It was built in the 12th century. There are three others like it on the island," Erika replied in a neutral tone. "They were built to survive invasions."

"Has the Ahnenerbe studied them?"

"Oh, no. Himmler considers them to be Christian stains on the island. Last year, he wanted to burn them to the ground, but the local Ahnenerbe representative managed to dissuade him. Legend tells us that the Templar Knights built them. Their round architecture is surprisingly similar to the circular churches built in many of the order's commanderies in Europe."

"Fascinating. I didn't realize they had made their way so far north," observed Tristan.

The car accelerated again as they left the village.

"Unfortunately," continued Erika, "we have nothing to prove that theory. The Templars might have never set foot here. From a historical perspective, the only interesting thing about the island is that it is the birthplace of the Burgundians—the barbarian tribes that invaded your country and founded Burgundy."

The Kübelwagen suddenly slowed as they rounded a sharp turn, then stopped in front of a brand-new Panzer IV parked in the middle of the road. Its cannon was aimed directly at them.

Bendlerblock, Berlin

The Abwehr colonel dialled the number of a colleague at RSHA counterintelligence. The SS, who valued loyalty and efficiency above all else, were about to learn an important lesson. The line rang for nearly a minute. A woman answered.

"SD Ausland," she said. "How can I help you?"

The colonel presented his credentials, then got to the point. "I'm calling on behalf of Admiral Canaris to warn you that a double agent has infiltrated the SS. A Frenchman named Tristan

Marcas. He's just returned from London to France, where he landed at Gouvieux airfield and was met by the SS on arrival. The Abwehr has plenty of proof and witnesses, should you require them."

"We will handle the situation immediately," she replied coldly. "Transfer all information you have. I'll contact the officer in charge of operations in France."

48

Nyker control post, Bornholm

Three soldiers in SS uniforms emerged from a small log cabin by the side of the road and surrounded the Kübelwagen. A man in a black raincoat followed them and made his way towards Erika's door. She handed him their papers, which he studied with a smile.

"Ah, Director von Essling, it's always a pleasure to see you. Who is your guest?"

"It's reassuring to have the Gestapo on the island, Untersturmführer Kanner," Erika replied warmly. "I just collected Tristan Marcas here from the harbour. He's a personal guest of the Reichsführer, who will be awarding him a 1st Class Iron Cross."

"A Frenchman. Unusual," Kanner mumbled with a suspicious glance at Tristan. "He must have rendered Germany a great service to be decorated by Himmler himself. You don't mind if I make a call to verify his name on the visitors' list, do you?"

"Of course not," replied Erika. "It's your job."

The officer returned to the cabin with Tristan's papers.

"I see you all trust one another blindly," he joked.

"Himmler's imminent arrival has unsettled them. Since Heydrich was assassinated in Prague, they have ramped up security measures around high-ranking Reich officials."

Kanner returned five minutes later, handed Tristan his papers, and gestured to the tank to move out of the way. He exchanged a few more words with Erika, an affable smile on his face, as they waited for the barrier to be raised, then waved them on.

"Do you know each other?" Tristan asked once the car was under way again.

"This isn't the first time I've driven this way. And I'm a woman . . ."

He reached for Erika's thigh and moved closer to her. He wanted to take advantage of his final hours. "Yes, that's hard to miss," he replied. "Speaking of which, is there somewhere we could stop along the way?"

He felt the car speed up.

"I don't think that would be a good idea. Our relationship could get us in trouble."

"That's never stopped you before," he said disappointedly.

"Times change."

Tristan scooted back to the centre of his seat, feeling the sting of rejection. "Is that your way of telling me you and I—"

She turned towards him, a sad but determined look on her face. "No. It's more complicated than that. Even just between us. In Paris, you were almost hostile."

"So were you . . ."

"Listen, I've been under constant pressure for weeks and don't have time to think about us right now. We'll see once the ceremony is over, all right?"

"Sure," Tristan replied impassively. He knew it would be his last evening on earth.

The car made its way through a few golden wheat fields that rippled in the wind. In the pristine blue sky overhead, a flock of seagulls was heading east. Once more, Tristan was struck by the beauty of the island.

"Why is Himmler so interested in Bornholm?" he enquired.

"He considers it to be a sacred place," replied Erika. "First because Christianity struggled to gain a foothold here until the 10th century, but also because of its pagan ruins. You'll see for yourself in a moment. This is Midgard—the land of the men and women from the North. Himmler believes the legend that claims it was one of the birthplaces of the lost Hyperborean civilization. Over fifty thousand years ago, before the pole shift, Scandinavia was a lush, warm Eden. The Baltic was no more than a lake and Bornholm was attached to mainland Denmark. They say it was one of the most renowned and powerful sites of the mythical continent that left us the *Thule Borealis Kulten* and the four swastikas."

"Have you found any archaeological proof?"

"The Ahnenerbe set up a permanent camp here right after we invaded Denmark. We've excavated much of the island, looking for anything that might confirm this hypothesis. In vain. Until recently."

She turned left at a junction, onto a dirt road dotted with potholes that led through a dense wood of oak trees and ferns. It grew darker and darker as they made their way deeper into the forest. Only the tiniest slivers of light shone through gaps in the canopy. The cool air smelled of damp earth and peat. Tristan had a strange feeling. It was oppressive. Irrational. He couldn't explain it, but a quiet yet hostile atmosphere seemed to reign over this part of the island.

Erika glanced his way. "When I was little, my mother used to tell me that forests are like spells—they can be good or evil. They are home to both fairies and witches."

"A wise woman. This feels more like the latter kind," he replied as he looked around warily.

"I feel at home here, in the silent kingdom of the ancient Norse gods, Æsir and Vanir, and the sanctuary of the little people of the forest. I feel calm, far from the tumult of mankind and their violent ambitions."

"Do you really believe in all that?"

She offered him a radiant smile for the first time since he'd arrived. "Of course not. I love fairy tales. But I'm a woman of science. You know what a staunch materialist I am. Though Himmler doesn't . . . When I see some of the research projects he has the Ahnenerbe working on, I can't help but be shocked at the insult to reason."

"Do you hide things from me too?"

"You'll never know . . . But let's get back to our legends. Pay attention, we're entering the land of the talking stones."

Behind the trees on either side of the road, grey stones of various sizes had been placed at regular intervals. Some of them were triangular and narrowed at the top; others were rectangles. They could have been the teeth of a buried monster.

"These stones," continued Erika, "are all engraved with runes. There are hundreds of them, maybe more, on the island. They say the oldest sanctuaries were here in this wood. When the first Ahnenerbe team arrived in 1938, they thought the stones were thousands of years old and that they were proof the Hyperboreans existed. Unfortunately, they were proved wrong. They only date back to somewhere between the 9th and 12th centuries. No further."

She turned right onto an even bumpier path. The light began to return as the trees grew sparse and before long, the car emerged from the wood across a grassy heath. Tristan could see the sea again. To their left, atop an emerald-green headland, stood an imposing fortress in ruins. Its grey stone and red brick ramparts took on an orange hue in the light of the setting sun.

"Another castle," remarked Tristan. "Given Himmler's passion for old stones, I imagine the ceremony will take place there?"

"Certainly not. He hates that castle, which was built in the name of Christ. Hammershus was constructed by the Swedish diocese to symbolize the Church's domination of the island. A very poor choice indeed for an SS ritual," she corrected.

The Kübelwagen swiftly made its way down to the beach alongside the granite cliffs.

"We're here," announced Erika. "You'll get your answers. This is one of the best kept secrets of the Third Reich."

The car came around a sharp turn and made its way out onto the wide beach of polished white pebbles trapped between the granite walls and sparkling surf. Tristan's eyes opened wide. He couldn't believe what he was seeing.

"Incredible!" he exclaimed.

Erika cut the Kübelwagen's engine.

"Welcome to Valhalla 66, the legendary door to the kingdom of the gods."

SD Ausland, RSHA, Prinz Albrecht Palace, Berlin

The SS captain in charge of France cursed his telephone. The line to Paris kept cutting out, and his mission was an absolute priority. The Abwehr had just warned them that a double agent had infiltrated the SS. He had to avoid a scandal by handling the problem before the Reichsführer found out.

It had been easy to pick up Tristan Marcas's trail in Paris. Everything at the SS was centralized, and he had quickly been put in touch with the head of the French Gestapo—a lowly but well-informed criminal. His voice came through over the static.

"I'm having a hard time hearing you, Mr. Lafont," said the captain. "Could you say that again please?"

"I said that Marcas left for Germany. A flight to Kolberg, I think."

"Did he say why?"

"He's to be decorated by Himmler himself. A 1st Class Iron Cross. Speaking of which, I've also done quite a lot for Germany and I—"

Before Lafont could finish, the captain had gone pale and hung up. He rushed out of his office along a dark corridor and stormed into his boss's office without knocking. "Colonel! We have a big problem!"

49

Bornholm

The granite cliffs towered over them like an insurmountable wall. One face, which looked out over a particularly wide stretch of white pebble beach, featured the mouth of a huge cave at least five storeys tall that was lit from the inside. Monumental construction trucks were busy working just outside. But the strangest part of the scene was the presence of two huge radar antennae—Tristan had never seen anything like them—mounted on a track that disappeared inside the cave. The surrounding beach had been secured with barbed wire and two watchtowers. Overhead, anti-aircraft guns sat at the top of the cliffs along with a line of long-range searchlights. Access by sea was also cut off: a few hundred meters off the coast, behind a tiny island that looked like a bear sculpted into the rock, Tristan could make out the shadow of a cruiser.

"You call this an excavation site?" he asked incredulously as he followed Erika. "It looks more like a military camp equipped to fend off attacks. What exactly are you looking for with those radars in this monstrous cave?"

"I told you Ahnenerbe researchers had been excavating on the island. Just under a year ago, while studying the engraved stones at the top of the cliffs, one of them fell into a crevice. The rescue team unearthed a man-made tunnel that ran some distance beneath the rock. Inside, they found runes that had been carved centuries before the engravings they'd found on the surface. As they continued exploring, they found a host of tunnels that extend far below sea level. A real maze."

"Submarine galleries," mumbled Tristan. "I didn't think the Vikings were capable of such technical feats."

"They weren't. The Vikings had nothing to do with it. The tunnels must have been dug over ten thousand years ago. At least. They date back to a civilization unknown to modern archaeologists. A civilization much older than the one that set out the dolmens we saw earlier. And that's not all. Follow me."

They walked past a security post, but this time the guards didn't stop Erika.

"We're not sure why the tunnels go so deep. At first, we thought they might lead to mines, but there are no metals or precious gemstones on this island."

"I imagine you've sent men to explore them?"

"Yes, but we can't get to all of them. There are hundreds! Many of them were blocked off at some point by falling rocks. Others lead to larger galleries, which lead on to more tunnels. In the past six months alone, we've lost three men in the labyrinth."

"In that case, it would be best to focus on one area and map it out to understand what it was used for."

"That's exactly what we've done. The Reichsführer asked us to make the larger parts of the network a priority. Do you see the ship near the island over there? It's anchored just above one of the galleries that winds beneath the sea. The problem is that parts of the tunnels have collapsed, so we have to send in excavation teams to move the rubble out of the way."

Tristan watched the trucks moving back and forth between the mouth of the cave and a pile of debris. "Why did you dig such a huge opening in the cliff face?" he asked.

"To house the dig's logistics base and the construction trucks. Autumn and winter are particularly harsh here. It can also accommodate Loki's Horns if we're under attack."

"I'm sorry, what?"

"This is one of the Third Reich's most recent operations. Loki's Horns are experimental long-distance radar antennae that could secure airspace for thousands of kilometers in every direction."

"Why bring them here, to the dig site?"

"Marshal Göring has lent them to Himmler for testing. And to explore one of the Reichsführer's favourite theories: that we are, in fact, inside the earth looking up at an outer membrane. These antennae will send signals towards the stratosphere to study their reverberations. The experiment is scheduled to take place this autumn."

Tristan looked confused. "Don't tell me you believe in any of that nonsense?"

"Of course not, but what makes the Reichsführer happy makes me happy."

"All right. But I still don't understand why you've organized the ceremony here. It can't be just because of the tunnels."

"We found something new last week. Something that left us all speechless. Follow me."

They reached the man-made mouth to the cave. It was so wide that three trains could run through it side by side. Strands of lightbulbs strung up along the walls cast a yellowish glow. Tristan felt like he was in an anthill as the workers scurried to and fro and the excavators pulled massive clumps of dirt and stone from the hillside. Three tunnels disappeared into the cliffs.

They stepped over the radar rails and finally reached a wooden hut built against the cave wall. A man sat hunched over a table covered in lamps and tools. He was inspecting a map held down by large stones.

"Hans, this is our guest, Tristan," explained Erika.

The man looked up. Pale eyes looked out from a pale face covered in a busy beard. He was so thin he floated in his canvas pants and military jacket. He took out a handkerchief to wipe his sweaty forehead.

"Tristan, this is Professor Hans Bolgar," said Erika. "He's in charge of excavations. He also participated in the Schaeffer expedition to Tibet in 1938. The expedition that recovered the first swastika."

Bolgar shook Tristan's hand fiercely. "Delighted to meet you, Herr Marcas. I've heard much about you and how you helped Erika in the quest for the other relics. I think you'll be impressed by our discovery. Come! It's just over here."

They walked along the cave wall, then into a wide chasm they had secured with thick timber support poles.

"Look! Isn't it magnificent?"

Tristan was dumbfounded.

The rays of the setting sun lit up a statue that stood over ten meters tall. The bust of a man whose face expressed intense suffering. He seemed to have been closed into the wall at the waist. His arms reached out and his hands formed a basin.

"That's impossible," mumbled Tristan. "It's just like the one at Montségur."

"And the one in Tibet," added Bolgar.

"It must have held one of the relics! The one I found in London?"

Erika nodded. "Professor, will you explain, please?"

"On your way here, you drove past Hammershus Castle. As you know, the island had just converted to Christianity when it was built. And the Church had made a habit of building monuments on top of former pagan sanctuaries to affirm its domination. When we discovered this underground network, I decided to go to Rønne to consult the island's archives. I found a 17th-century book on Hammershus written by a local historian. According to one of the chronicles cited in his work, a Swedish Cistercian monk who visited the castle found a pagan statue holding a unique cross. He saw it as a sign from God and went on to preach conversion in faraway lands. After many years of travel, he spent the rest of his life in Russia, where he converted to Eastern Orthodoxy."

Erika stroked the statue's cheek. "Yes," she said, taking over. "And he died in Russia's most famous monastery: Ipatiev."

Tristan felt a shiver run up his spine. "The very same place Mikhail Romanov lived when he founded the Romanov dynasty four centuries later!"

"But the relic never belonged to the Russians," intervened the professor. "So we're only taking back what's rightfully ours."

"You'll have to refresh my memory," Tristan said harshly. "I thought you were German, not Swedish or Danish. So your claim is no stronger than the Russians'."

The bearded researcher glared at Tristan. "We share the same Norse blood. Unlike you, Frenchman."

"Oh right, like the Tibetan monks who had the first relic. I see the resemblance . . ."

A growl interrupted their heated exchange as a bulldozer pulled up next to them, followed by a group of soldiers with their sleeves rolled up.

"Be very careful!" shouted Bolgar. "If you break it, you'll be sent to the eastern front tomorrow morning!"

The bulldozer stopped in front of the statue, which the soldiers were carefully wrapping in blankets.

Tristan and Erika made their way back to the mouth of the cave, leaving Bolgar to oversee the removal.

"Where are they taking it?" asked Tristan.

"To a headland at the top of the cliffs for tonight's ceremony. Himmler plans to return the relic to its rightful place. He thinks the ritual may boost its powers. Afterwards, he'll have the statue and the swastika taken to Wewelsburg, to the crypt where the other relics are kept."

"That's insane!" exclaimed Tristan.

"Not for people who believe in this sort of thing. And the Reichsführer is definitely one of them."

A muffled buzzing ripped through the dusk sky.

"Speak of the devil," joked Erika as the Heinkel came into view. "The Reichsführer's personal plane. Right on time. He has the swastika with him. According to his schedule, he will be stopping in town before making his way here. Which leaves us with two hours to kill . . ."

There was a mischievous glint in Erika's eyes.

SD Ausland, RSHA, Prinz Albrecht Palace, Berlin

Sitting in his vast and luxurious office, the head of SD Ausland had been holding the line for Himmler's secretary for the past ten minutes. He stubbed out another cigarette he'd barely touched.

He hated bureaucrats. If it were up to him, he'd send them all to work in concentration camps. The SS and the Reich would be better for it.

"Hello, Standartenführer Schellenberg," a voice finally said. "How can I help you?"

"I need you to put me through to the Reichsführer immediately. It's of the utmost importance."

"I'm afraid that's impossible. He is on a personal trip. The details are confidential."

"Not for me. I know that he's in Denmark, on the island of Bornholm."

The secretary on the other end of the line paused. How could Schellenberg at counterintelligence have got his hands on such information? Regardless, Himmler had specifically asked not to be disturbed under any circumstances.

"I'm sorry," she finally said. "I have strict orders directly from the Reichsführer—"

"I don't give a shit about your orders! A double agent is on the island and is scheduled to be decorated by Himmler himself in just a few hours. I suspect he will make an attempt on the Reichsführer's life. If that happens, I doubt anyone will be very pleased with you."

"Of course, right away, sir. I'll contact our men on site immediately."

50

Bornholm

It was a beautiful summer night. The stars shone brightly, and the Milky Way was clearly visible. The two lovers lay in each other's arms on the soft grass behind the castle ruins.

"I missed you so much," whispered Erika.

"Me too," replied Tristan with a gentle kiss. "This is much better than in Paris."

"Isn't it funny how the relics brought us together? Without them, our lives would never have crossed paths."

"Yes, but the quest is over now," he replied, trying to hide his anxiety.

"But another is just beginning!" she exclaimed. "We don't know anything about the mysterious civilization that created the swastikas. Maybe somewhere below this island we'll find artefacts or books. Or even a lost city!"

"Like Troy."

"Yes—the dream that made me want to become an archae-ologist."

"You're living it now," he replied warmly, hugging her close. "If only this bloody war would end . . ."

Erika let herself enjoy his embrace for several minutes, then took his face in her hands. "It's time to go," she said.

Tristan reluctantly got to his feet. "I suppose it is . . ."

"You don't seem very enthusiastic about it," she remarked.

He took out his gun and checked the clip to make sure it was full. "Of course I am. Let's go, we don't want to miss the ceremony."

"You have nothing to fear here," she said. "Your Luger won't be of any use."

"You never know. I'll keep it in case a group of Danish resistance fighters decides to crash the party."

"Are you sure you're okay?" she asked as she kissed him tenderly on the lips. "It won't last long. I've asked for some time off . . . with you. I found a lovely cabin in the southern part of the island, right on the beach, overlooking the turquoise water. No soldiers, no police officers, no uniforms."

Tristan felt his chest tighten as he took Erika in his arms. Her words cut through his armour. His determination was crumbling with each passing second. He could still choose. After all, what did the outcome of the war matter to him? He'd done enough. He could decide not to assassinate Himmler. Someone else could take care of it. The last relic may be lost, but there were other ways to continue to fight. Together, the United States, Britain and Russia had millions of men who could end Hitler's reign.

Erika's warm body, her kisses—that was life.

"I'll quit," she said. "I want to live with you in Germany. I . . . I love you," she whispered as she kissed him passionately.

Tristan wavered.

Suddenly beams of light shot up from behind the cliffs like silver columns to the sky.

"We better hurry, the ritual is about to begin!" exclaimed Erika, a look of fascination on her face.

"We could stay here to watch from afar," suggested Tristan.

"Out of the question! It will be spectacular. I wouldn't miss it for anything in the world. I've always loved these ceremonies."

"They do know how to put on a show," Tristan said wearily.

The spell was broken. His lover seemed to be bewitched. Like her fellow countrymen—millions of Ulysses enthralled by the song of a siren with a stiff moustache and swastika armband. Tristan stepped back. It was time to add a discordant note to this evil symphony.

Rønne

Chaos reigned in the Gestapo offices, which had been set up in a small hotel the Germans had requisitioned in the centre of town. In the courtyard, which they used as a car park, a group of soldiers jumped into a lorry. Upstairs, an officer was shouting into the phone.

"What do you mean you can't reach Valhalla 66?"

"We received orders to cut all communications. From the Reichsführer himself. He didn't want to be disturbed during his visit."

"I'm sending a detachment as we speak. And get me Kanner!"

Nyker security post

Kanner sat smoking a cigarette on top of the Panzer parked on the side of the road. He felt he would die of boredom on this forgotten island. Nothing ever happened here. It had been six months since he'd requested a transfer to Copenhagen or Norway, where there was plenty of work to be done tracking resistance fighters. Here on this island paradise though, he was withering like a sunflower deprived of sunlight.

"Sir, there's an urgent call from Rønne!" shouted a soldier as he emerged from the cabin.

Kanner flicked his cigarette butt to the ground, jumped off the tank, and stepped inside to take the call. His superior's voice made the receiver tremble.

"Kanner? Did you see a Frenchman in SS uniform come through there?"

"Yes, with Director von Essling. About two hours ago."

"He's an assassin on Britain's payroll, come to murder the Reichsführer. I've sent a detachment, but you're closer. Get there as fast as you can."

"A bit of action at last!" exclaimed Kanner as he hung up.

Valhalla 66

The ancient statue towered over the audience at the top of the cliffs, its back to the sea. Behind it, the anti-aircraft searchlights shot up towards the sky. A row of smaller lights set up along the edge of the cliffs cast an eerie glow over the headland.

The enigmatic idol sat at the top of a staircase that had been carved into the rock. The stairs zigzagged between two rows of raised stones that seemed to be bowing to a god. A cool wind had picked up, bringing the black banners bearing the silver SS symbol to life.

Suddenly, drum rolls rang out all around them. It felt as though the ground itself were vibrating to the beat of a huge buried heart.

"They've placed speakers behind the dolmens," Erika explained as she leaned towards her lover.

They were standing at the bottom of the staircase, near a raised stone, just behind a small group of SS officers and Ahnenerbe archaeologists, who were seated on benches that had been set up for the occasion.

In his black dress uniform, Himmler climbed the stairs slowly, followed at a respectful distance by a young lieutenant holding a silver box. The drum roll accelerated as they neared the top.

The statue seemed to be contemplating them, its arms held out to receive the offering.

Himmler bowed to the idol, then opened the box. He took out the relic and placed it on the stone hands. The drums suddenly stopped. The headland fell silent. Then the voice of the Reichsführer rang out. "Here, in this place, I proclaim the return of the sacred relic to its true owners. In the land of Hyperborea, birthplace of the Aryan race. May the relic grant us total victory over our enemies!"

He knelt before the statue and bowed his head again. The drum roll started once more, louder this time.

"Magnificent," mumbled Erika, as though hypnotized. "As beautiful as a performance of *Parsifal* in Bayreuth! A true *Gesamtkunstwerk*—a total work of art!"

Tristan glanced discreetly at Erika, whose eyes shone as though she was possessed. His feelings for her evaporated into the night air. He would never see the little house on the beach.

"You Germans do have a gift for showmanship, I'll give you that," said Tristan.

But another show, another total work of art, was on his mind now. A show in which blood and suffering featured prominently. The tortured Jew with the ravaged face and the two starving, terrorized women. The cellar and the mansion from hell. The Lauriston mansion. That was what the Nazis were really about. They could put on neat uniforms and shiny boots and pretend they were the superior race. They could put on open-air parodies of Wagner operas. But really, they were just thugs with oversized egos. Cruel, greedy ruffians in boots and helmets.

As Tristan watched Himmler kneel, it occurred to him that given the extent of his megalomania, the Reichsführer must be disappointed by the size of the audience. Especially since he was the star for once, with no Führer to overshadow him.

"Total artwork," Erika said again. "When you truly understand what that means, you understand everything."

"I can't leave without contributing my own touch," Tristan said enigmatically.

The drum roll quietened as Himmler bowed a final time and started back down the steps. The lieutenant stayed next to the statue to put the relic back in its box.

Tristan tightened his grip on the butt of the Luger. He could shoot from this distance, but he would likely miss his target.

"You're so lucky that Himmler himself is going to award you the Iron Cross in this sacred place," Erika said as she took his arm, but Tristan was too focused on his ultimate goal to listen.

They made their way towards the benches, where Tristan was to receive the decoration.

Only a few more seconds.

Evil incarnate was walking towards them, his arrogant, entitled face puffed up with pride.

Tristan would wipe that smile off his face. He would empty

half his clip and then put a bullet in his own brain. The end.

Himmler was no more than thirty meters away now.

Tristan stood still. He had to wait for the monster to get closer. Tristan slowly pulled the Luger from its case. He held his breath to boost his confidence. His index finger stroked the trigger.

It was time.

Suddenly, Erika whispered in his ear. "Don't do that or I'll have to kill you."

He felt something hard and cold against his back.

"I'm holding my own loaded Luger. Don't do it. It would ruin everything."

Tristan tensed.

Shouts rang out below. A detachment of SS soldiers was running towards them at top speed. Tristan recognized Kanner from the control post. When he reached one of the officers on site, the detective pointed at Tristan. "*Verräter! Verräter!*"

Erika wavered.

The shouting drew nearer. Kanner and the officer rushed to protect Himmler, who was holding Tristan's Iron Cross, while soldiers ran towards Erika and Tristan. He felt the gun move away from his back. That's when he bent sideways and struck Erika's hand, sending her Luger to the ground.

"Tristan! Stop!" she pleaded, clinging to him.

"Let me go!" he shouted. "I—"

Before he could finish, a series of simultaneous explosions rang out, along with volleys of machine-gun fire. A cloud of orange smoke covered the headland. Men in black uniforms emerged from the darkness, shooting German soldiers on sight.

Once the initial shock wore off, Himmler collected himself as his men made a human wall around him.

Tristan took cover behind a raised stone, bullets whizzing past him on either side.

He saw two men in black take down Himmler's young lieutenant. He fell into the grass, the box still in hand. A piercing siren rang out through the night air as another explosion boomed at the base below.

Erika tried to stand, but she was pinned down by gunfire.

Chaos reigned. A commando unit seemed to be attacking the place. Tristan had to get to them if he hoped to make it out alive. He watched as Himmler fled. He'd failed yet again.

"Tristan?" asked a voice behind him.

He turned around to find himself face to face with a member of the unknown commando unit. Tristan couldn't place the man's accent. He was covered in sweat and his cheeks were blacked out with shoe polish.

"Yes?"

"Come, we don't have much time. I'm under orders to bring you with us."

The man held out his hand to help him to his feet.

Erika was in tears, her back against the stone. "Go, Tristan. Quickly. The SS will kill you if you don't."

Tristan bent down to help her up. "Come with us," he said.

"I can't."

He grabbed her wrist. "Come with me! I can't leave—"

A blow to the back of his neck knocked him out. The last thing he saw was the desperate expression on Erika's face.

51

The Baltic Sea

A searing pain at the nape of his neck woke him. It felt as though someone had driven a hot poker between his vertebrae. Everything around him was blurry. He was lying in a tiny windowless room. Another man stretched out on a cot next to him was reading a book, seemingly unperturbed by Tristan's presence. Tristan stood up, but his vision still hadn't returned to normal. He felt a muffled purr vibrating beneath his feet.

"Don't get up too fast. Take a deep breath and you'll feel better," said the man in a thick Russian accent.

Tristan sat down on his cot and massaged his eyes. It felt like his head was about to explode. "Who . . . who are you?" he asked.

"I'm Colonel Evgueni Berin of the NKVD. We're currently somewhere beneath the Baltic Sea. Welcome aboard the Stalinets-class S-13 submarine, the pride of the Soviet navy."

Tristan's vision was growing less cloudy. "I was on Bornholm. I was about to shoot Himmler . . . What happened?"

"We put together a commando operation to retrieve the relic and you with it. We are allies after all."

"Why on earth would the Soviet Union put together a risky offensive hundreds of kilometers from its borders to get its hands on an archaeological relic?" Tristan exclaimed incredulously.

Evgueni smiled. "It is our property," he affirmed. "Though it's true the concept of ownership no longer holds much water in my country. I'm certain you already know that the relic once belonged to Nicholas II. So, it's only logical for it to return to the USSR. The submarine will drop us off near Kronstadt. From there, we'll take the swastika to Moscow. Comrade Stalin wants to see it with his own eyes."

"We?" Tristan said dubiously.

"Yes. You're a guest of the Soviet Union."

An alarm sounded in their cabin. The colonel stood up. "I need to get to the command post."

"Of course. I'll use the time to stretch my legs."

"I'm afraid you're confined to your quarters during the crossing. We'll bring you your meals. If you're lucky, we'll reach land in two days. That is, unless we're sunk by German patrols or naval mines, of course."

"You say we're allies, but you're treating me like a prisoner."

"The Soviet navy is very protective of its technology. They're afraid you might look a little too closely."

"I couldn't care less about your submarine, comrade! How did you even know the relic was in Bornholm?"

As he opened the door, Evgueni pulled an envelope from his jacket and held it out to Tristan. "Here," he said. "You'll understand once you've read it. The person who wrote it asked us to get you out."

He closed the door and bolted it behind himself.

Then he unfolded the letter.

Tristan, my love,

If you're reading these words, then you're safe and sound. Thank goodness. I wrote this letter the morning you arrived on the island. I already knew how things would end.

I've been working for the Russians for several years now. Yes, that's right. And believe me, I wish I could be a fly on the wall to see your face right now! To cut a long story short, we're on the same side. That's why I didn't turn you in when I remembered what happened in Venice last year. But I'm sure you're wondering why a German aristocrat would decide to work for a communist regime.

I'll tell you a story. My story. Which I keep hidden deep down.

*Before the war, I loved a man. My first. He was my archae-
ology professor, and much older than I was. He was also a socialist
activist who published tracts condemning the Nazis. I didn't share
his ideas, but I was terribly smitten. One morning, he was arrested
as he left the flat we secretly shared. A group of SA soldiers had
been waiting for him. I saw it all from the window, where I stood
terrified. They beat him, stripped him naked, and hooked him
up to a lorry by his feet so they could drag him through the
neighbourhood. When they were done, their leader leaned him up
against the door to the building and shot him in the head. I
sobbed hysterically, too petrified to go down and see his body.
One of his friends found me and took me in. He was a communist who worked for the NKVD. He told me that if I ever wanted
to get my revenge on the Nazis, he could help me. I returned to
my parents' estate to rest and recover, but spent weeks struggling
with horrifying nightmares. My father—that bastard—even
punished me when he found out I'd had a socialist lover. Little
by little, my pain morphed into anger. A cold, implacable anger.
I hated the men who had murdered my first love and the despic-
able regime that had given them power. I went back to university
and earned my degrees with flying colours. And I spent a lot of
time with my communist friend. I wanted to do my part. He
knew that, thanks to my parents, I was familiar with the upper
echelons of German society, including Marshal Göring, who was
a family friend. I played my role as good Nazi aristocrat, attending
dinners and parties, and I passed on anything useful I learned.*

*Then, when I joined the Ahnenerbe, I began working for Colonel
Evgueni Berin. He was also passionate about the quest for the
swastikas. I shared everything about the hunt for the relics with
him.*

*After Venice, I wanted to tell you the truth so many times, but
wasn't brave enough. I think it was the right decision—it would
have made our missions harder. I do regret threatening you in
Paris, though. It was all a show. You must have hated me for it.
But you had to come back with the relic, so the Russians could
get their hands on it. Please forgive me for manipulating you.*

I know I mentioned an isolated cabin on the island where we could enjoy our love far from the rest of the world. Please don't judge me for that. I still want to think it will become true one day.

The colonel assured me that once you reach Moscow, you'll be sent back to London via Iran and Egypt. He promised, and I believe him to be a man of his word. I hope I'm right.

Now the Russians also have a swastika.

Look on the bright side: you won't have to keep playing both sides. You won't have to pretend among the monsters anymore. My future is different. I'm going to try to retrieve the relics from Wewelsburg, but to succeed I'll have to delve even deeper into the horrors of the SS. I recently learned that high-ranking SS officials organized a meeting in Wannsee, near Berlin, to discuss their plans to exterminate the Jews of Europe. And the Ahnenerbe will become a pseudoscientific cog in their monstrous machine. They're already conducting inhumane medical experiments in the camps. Tell your superiors in Britain what's coming. They must be stopped. At all costs.

But I want to end on a positive note.

I told you before that I loved a man in my youth.

Now I love another.

You.

But if I'm honest with myself, I know there are few chances our paths will ever cross again. In this war, our lives are no more than leaves carried off in a storm. I won't be angry if you love another. I only want you to be happy and to remember the German woman who refused to march in step with the rest.

With all my love,

Erika

Tristan dropped the paper onto his lap. Tears rimmed his reddened eyes.

52

Highgate Cemetery, London

Laure was sitting on a tiny bench across from Malorley's grave. The August sun warmed her cheeks. She couldn't help but think that it was a beautiful day to be buried, despite the absurdity.

She looked down once again at the newspaper on her lap, unfolded to the obituaries page. The commander had earned little more than a few lines, with a photograph that hardly did him justice. The brief article announced he had died of an unexpected heart attack.

Heart attack did have a better ring to it than murder. Most importantly, it attracted less attention. The SOE knew who had killed Malorley. Conrad had bragged about it to Moira O'Connor, who had immediately shared the information with her new contact: the man with the mutilated face who had replaced the commander. Even worse, though, was the news that the Abwehr agent had blown Tristan's cover with the SS. He was as good as dead.

Laure stared at Malorley's photograph. Not only had he been murdered, but the perpetrator would go unpunished. In the interest of state security, it was better to keep Conrad under surveillance and maintain Moira's cover, to continue tricking the Nazis.

The good guys were in the grave—or as good as—and the bad guys were running the streets. That's where the government's negotiations with morality had landed them. But Laure was no longer willing to swallow the pill, however patriotic it may be. She had resigned the day before, at SOE headquarters.

She put the newspaper in her bag and stood up to say her final goodbyes. She had brought a single red rose with her. The discreet funeral had just ended. The commander didn't have any family except for an older sister, who was about as warm and friendly as the raven that had followed the procession. Most of the attendees worked at the SOE. They stood alongside a handful of his Masonic brothers and a representative sent by the Prime Minister. Laure had been surprised to run into Captain Ian Fleming, who had run the commando operation in Venice. After a chat about their adventures, she had accepted the charming intelligence officer's invitation to dinner that very night.

Life was too short. Especially in times of war.

Laure crossed the path towards Malorley's headstone, which shone brightly in the sun. A gardener was tending to the neighbouring grave, hunched over his rake like an old man. He groaned as he worked. She stepped around him to place her flower on the tombstone.

The gardener spoke in a high-pitched voice. "Not so clever, are we, Miss? You should have bought a potted plant. They last much longer and require less work."

Laure couldn't believe anyone could be so rude as to chide her while she stood beside Malorley's freshly dug grave. In a fit of rage, she turned towards him. "I may not be clever, but you're downright rude! Do you really think—"

She stopped mid sentence as the gardener dropped his rake. It was Aleister Crowley. He offered her his weird smile as he glanced around them suspiciously.

"I'm sorry, my dear, but I couldn't officially attend the funeral."

"I thought you had been institutionalized!" replied Laure as the surprise began to wear off.

"I was, but the intelligence community was unaware that the head doctor at the asylum was a loyal customer at the Hellfire Club back when I ran it. Thanks to him, I've been given a clean bill of mental health. The best in the country, in fact!"

"What will you do now?"

"They'll keep watching me for a while, but I've found new

protectors who appreciate my talents for all they're worth. The story of the relics has kindled quite a bit of enthusiasm in certain circles. But it's all very hush-hush, of course."

Laure glanced towards Malorley's grave again. "The swastikas . . . Poor Malorley. Maybe it's better he's no longer with us. Knowing that the Germans got their hands on the one from London would have destroyed him. So much effort for nothing."

"He never would listen to me. If he had just accepted a tarot reading . . ."

"Aleister," Laure admonished.

The mage clasped his hands together to ask for forgiveness. "Let's talk about you, dear. Still working for the SOE?"

"No, I quit yesterday. A friend of Malorley's got me an interview for a new job. An hour from now, in fact. If that doesn't work out, I'll become a florist or maybe a madam . . . Who knows."

"I'd hire you on the spot to open a brothel worth calling it that! Together, we'd be a sensation!"

Laure burst into laughter for the first time since she'd recovered from her "manicure".

"Do you ever think of Tristan?" asked the mage.

Laure kissed Aleister's plump cheek. "Every day, but I still remember a rule Malorley taught me when he hired me," she whispered.

"What's that?" asked Crowley.

"Don't ever get attached to another agent. Tristan Marcas has disappeared. For once and for all. But maybe *our* paths will cross again, Mr. Wizard."

"They will, Laure. It's in the cards. And don't forget *your* card. I've brought the original sketch of the Star for you. May it bring you luck, my pretty spy."

He slipped a rolled-up piece of paper into her hand, smiled a final time, and disappeared into the bushes.

An hour later, she was sitting in a comfortable office on the third floor of a discreet building on Duke Street. The headquarters of the *Bureau Central de Renseignements et d'Action*—Free France's intelligence and operations agency in London. A French general and colonel were sitting across from her.

"I've studied your file, sent over by the SOE, Mademoiselle. It is remarkable," said the man who introduced himself as Colonel Passy. "Truly remarkable. We are in sore need of female agents of your calibre."

"Thank you, but I'm not going to lie. I'm still quite shaken up by my kidnapping. I'm not certain I'm ready to go back out into the field immediately."

The general lit a cigarette and stared at her without a word. Laure couldn't help but feel impressed by the tall man and the authority he exuded.

"You could begin in the counterintelligence department," continued the colonel. "You would be on the lookout for enemy agents trying to infiltrate our network. The Germans occasionally give it a go. You already have some experience in the field. What do you think, General?"

Charles de Gaulle stood up, taking his time to reach his full height. "That seems appropriate. Just so you know, Mademoiselle, I knew Commander Malorley. And I know about the legend of the sacred relics and Hitler . . . France's fate would have been very different, had we been in possession of one of them when things started to get serious."

He offered an enigmatic smile as Passy looked on in confusion. "What relics?" asked the colonel.

"Forget about it, Colonel. Laure and I know what we're talking about." Then he turned towards Laure. "You'll need to come up with an alias. Everyone here has one. Like Passy here. Whatever pops into your head will do. Unless it's already used by another agent. When we win this war—and we will—I want our heroes to be able to keep their aliases as part of their real names. So we never forget these dark times."

Laure thought for a few seconds. Then her eyes lit up. "I've got it," she said. "You can call me Marcas."

Epilogue

Nikolskaya Tower, The Kremlin, Moscow

Evgueni watched with satisfaction as the workers set up the huge winch next to Nikolskaya Tower, which stood tall at the entrance to the Kremlin. Since the revolution, each of the five tallest towers had been crowned with a scarlet star weighing a tonne and a half—symbols of the revolution's triumph. Evgueni had convinced Stalin to hide the swastika inside one of them. The relic's power would protect Moscow and the USSR.

The Kremlin would be the Ipatiev Monastery for the communist era, providing the new dynasty of red tsars the country needed. Stalin had enthusiastically approved of the idea.

The colonel checked his watch. It was nearly three o'clock and Stalin still hadn't made an appearance. He had promised to attend the placing of the relic in the star, which was now lying on the ground. A team of craftsmen had created a glass cube to seal it inside.

"Evgueni! I'm sorry I'm late. Nothing but bad news coming in from the front," explained Stalin as he looked out over Red Square and made his way towards Evgueni.

"Everything's ready, comrade!" Evgueni exclaimed happily.

"I'm afraid we can't go through with this," said the dictator. "The Germans have launched yet another attack in the south. They're very close to breaking through to the Caucasus oil fields. If we lose them . . ."

"Yes, comrade. But what does that have to do with the relic?"

"Stalingrad is in their path. You know that if the Nazis take the city, they'll have control of the Volga and will be able to cut off the supplies the Americans send us. And then they'll head straight for the Caucasus. That will be the end of the Soviet Union. From a strategic point of view, Stalingrad is now more important than Moscow! Do you see what I mean?"

"I'm afraid I don't, comrade . . ."

"I've decided to send reinforcements to strengthen our lines at the southern front, but I've also decided to send your relic to Stalingrad! If it really has the power you believe it does, it will protect the city from the invaders. However, if Hitler's minions take Stalingrad, then we'll know it was all just superstition. You see, I'm both openminded and pragmatic."

Evgueni was shocked. This decision seemed to come out of nowhere. Stalin clapped him on the shoulder. "And I'm handing this mission over to you personally."

Evgueni felt the hairs on his neck stand on end. His master was sending him on a one-way trip to hell. "What do you mean, Joseph?" he asked worriedly.

"Go to Stalingrad with the relic and don't come back unless we triumph over the Germans. Then we'll know if you were right or not," said Stalin matter-of-factly.

"You know what that means. Life expectancy there is a fraction—"

"Indeed. But you'll be a great hero of the Soviet Union if you succeed."

"Have I done something to displease you, Joseph?"

Stalin lit his pipe, his eyes like ice. "If I were displeased, you would be dead and buried by now. But I did recently learn that you often meet with my medium after he leaves my dacha."

Evgueni wanted to protest, but he knew it was a lost cause.

Stalin stared straight at him. "But let's forget that . . . Take the French spy who was undercover in the SS with you. The British don't know he's here. He has no place in Moscow."

"I gave him my word that we'd send him home."

"Perhaps, but I didn't. And I am your commander in chief. Before you leave, make sure to give your superior at the NKVD the name of the agent you have implanted close to Himmler. The information could come in useful."

Stalin's grip on Evgueni's shoulder grew more insistent. "Good luck in Stalingrad, my friend. I hope you have a lucky star."

Los Alamos, New Mexico, United States of America

A hot wind swept across the cracked dirt that reached as far as the eye could see. The temperature was nearing 43°C. Even the few cacti that dotted the landscape seemed desperate to escape the stifling heat. The soldiers stayed in the shade as much as they could to avoid passing out. The unbearable temperatures had slowed the set-up of the secret base, which had been dubbed Site Y. Luckily, the construction teams, which could only work at night, had already installed air-conditioning in the research labs. Inside one of them, a sprawling single-storey building with pale stucco walls, three men gathered in a windowless office, enjoying the cool air blowing down from the ceiling.

Secretary of War Henry L. Stimson dropped two aspirin tablets into his glass of water. He hadn't been able to shake his headache during his trip across the country from Washington, D.C. To make matters worse, he'd had nothing but bad news since his arrival. He fiddled with his white moustache. The President wouldn't be happy. Not at all. The two scientists sitting across from him in white lab coats looked disappointed.

"If I've understood correctly, you're saying that the project is at a standstill, and you haven't even started?"

"Yes. We're unable to stabilize the fissile material. We've tried and tried, but—"

The Secretary cut them off to spare himself the scientific explanation. "I understand. What I want to know is what you need to fix this."

"Time, sir. Quite a lot of time . . ."

"The President doesn't *have* time. As you may have noticed, we're at war."

One of the scientists shot his colleague an urgent glance, then spoke. "Well, there might be a way—"

"I'm listening," said the Secretary gravely.

"Last week, a physicist friend at MIT called me to discuss an object the government had sent him to analyse. It came from England. During his study of the object, he discovered a uranium isotope inside with unique properties. He'd never seen anything like it. He asked me what I thought."

"Yes," added the other scientist. "We could hardly believe what he was telling us. It's possible, of course, that MIT made a mistake in their calculations, but it's still worth trying. Do you think you could get us that object? He told us it's held in a top-secret army warehouse."

"I'll have it sent to you right away. Project Manhattan must move forward, whatever the cost, Professor Oppenheimer," replied Stimson. "Do you have a reference number for it?"

The two physicists seemed troubled.

"It's just that—" began one.

"You'll think we're making fun," finished Oppenheimer.

"Good God, men, you're working on the biggest scientific military operation in the history of the United States. You're developing the atomic bomb. Speak!"

"Our colleague at MIT told us it was an archaeological object. Some sort of relic."

The Secretary of War stared at them, clearly puzzled. "And you say it has unprecedented physical properties?" he asked, incredulous.

"Yes, but that's not all," said Oppenheimer, clearing his throat. "It's a swastika."